VAULTS OF OBSIDIAN

A BLACKSTONE FORTRESS ANTHOLOGY

More Warhammer 40,000 from Black Library

• BLACKSTONE FORTRESS •
Darius Hinks

BOOK 1: Blackstone Fortress
BOOK 2: Blackstone Fortress: Ascension

CORSAIR: FACE OF THE VOID
James Swallow
(audio drama)

ROGUE TRADER: THE OMNIBUS
Andy Hoare

• DARK IMPERIUM •
Guy Haley

BOOK 1: Dark Imperium
BOOK 2: Plague War

• THE HORUSIAN WARS •
John French

BOOK 1: Resurrection
BOOK 2: Incarnation
BOOK 3: Divination

• WATCHERS OF THE THRONE •
Chris Wraight

BOOK 1: The Emperor's Legion
BOOK 2: The Regent's Shadow

• VAULTS OF TERRA •
Chris Wraight

BOOK 1: The Carrion Throne
BOOK 2: The Hollow Mountain

• RISE OF THE YNNARI •
Gav Thorpe

BOOK 1: Ghost Warrior
BOOK 2: Wild Rider

• BLACK LEGION •
Aaron Dembski-Bowden

BOOK 1: The Talon of Horus
BOOK 2: Black Legion

VAULTS OF OBSIDIAN

A BLACKSTONE FORTRESS ANTHOLOGY

DARIUS HINKS △ NICK KYME △ GAV THORPE
GUY HALEY & MANY MORE

A BLACK LIBRARY PUBLICATION

First published in 2019.
This edition published in Great Britain in 2020 by
Black Library,
Games Workshop Ltd.,
Willow Road,
Nottingham, NG7 2WS, UK.

10 9 8 7 6 5 4 3 2 1

Produced by Games Workshop in Nottingham.
Cover illustration by Paul Dainton.

A CIP record for this book is available from the British Library.

ISBN 13: 978 1 78999 080 5

Printed and bound by CPI Group (UK) Ltd, Croydon, CR0 4YY

It is the 41st millennium. For more than a hundred centuries the Emperor has sat immobile on the Golden Throne of Earth. He is the Master of Mankind by the will of the gods, and master of a million worlds by the might of His inexhaustible armies. He is a rotting carcass writhing invisibly with power from the Dark Age of Technology. He is the Carrion Lord of the Imperium for whom a thousand souls are sacrificed every day, so that He may never truly die.

Yet even in His deathless state, the Emperor continues His eternal vigilance. Mighty battlefleets cross the daemon-infested miasma of the warp, the only route between distant stars, their way lit by the Astronomican, the psychic manifestation of the Emperor's will. Vast armies give battle in His name on uncounted worlds. Greatest amongst His soldiers are the Adeptus Astartes, the Space Marines, bioengineered super-warriors. Their comrades in arms are legion: the Astra Militarum and countless planetary defence forces, the ever-vigilant Inquisition and the tech-priests of the Adeptus Mechanicus to name only a few. But for all their multitudes, they are barely enough to hold off the ever-present threat from aliens, heretics, mutants – and worse.

To be a man in such times is to be one amongst untold billions. It is to live in the cruellest and most bloody regime imaginable. These are the tales of those times. Forget the power of technology and science, for so much has been forgotten, never to be re-learned. Forget the promise of progress and understanding, for in the grim dark future there is only war. There is no peace amongst the stars, only an eternity of carnage and slaughter, and the laughter of thirsting gods.

CONTENTS

Talisman of Vaul 9
Darius Hinks

Shapes Pent in Hell 33
Josh Reynolds

Fates and Fortunes 69
Thomas Parrott

Past in Flames 105
J C Stearns

Negavolt 141
Nicholas Wolf

The Three-Edged Blade 179
Denny Flowers

Motherlode 207
Nick Kyme

Purity is a Lie 235
Gav Thorpe

The Oath in Darkness 257
David Annandale

Man of Iron 281
Guy Haley

The Beast Inside 303
Darius Hinks

The Last of the Longhorns 361
Nick Kyme

TALISMAN OF VAUL

DARIUS HINKS

Kurdrak woke with a scream like a newborn, writhing in the dark, drenched in his own blood. He tried to rise but his legs collapsed beneath him. His neuroresponsive armour hardened into barbed plates, anticipating an attack, but none came. He lay there, slipping in the blood, cursing his indolence. How could he have let himself sleep? Here, in this den of savages. How could he be so stupid?

The pain increased and he thrashed around, trying to find his husk blade, or a knife – anything he could use to lash out – but there was nothing. Someone laughed, low and cruel, then the torment grew too great and he slipped back into unconsciousness.

When he came to, the pain was still there, but more manageable. It was coming from the side of his neck. He reached up to investigate, but as his fingers touched the wound, pain jolted down his side like a flash of electricity, curling him into a gasping ball.

Before he withdrew his fingers, they brushed against a hard surface, something jammed between the veins.

Something *in* his neck.

He managed to stand, repulsed and furious. What was it? He wanted to touch it, to discern its shape, but his neck was still throbbing from his last attempt. He leaned against his bunk, dazed and febrile as he tried to trigger the overhead lights. Nothing happened. Something was wrong with his ship. He tried more controls, but there was no response. The *Talon* had been disabled. He called for his guards, but there was no reply.

He stared into the dark and his eyes gradually began to adjust to the gloom. The cabin looked like his treatment theatres back on Commorragh. Every surface was wet with blood, much of it his own. He could see where he had lurched around the room, clumsy with pain, leaving bloody handprints on the walls. But even more of the spilled blood was that of his guards. They were heaped across the furniture in a variety of awkward positions. Throats slit. Eyes blank.

Kurdrak cursed as he staggered through the doorway, shaking his head in disbelief. He had been betrayed. They were all dead. His whole crew. He could see them sprawled through the companionways and crumpled against the bulkheads. No, not all of them: there was one person missing.

'Xaloth,' he spat.

Even before they landed on Precipice he had suspected her of treachery, but he played along, acting the fool, waiting for a chance to learn who was paying her. As he stumbled through the dark, cursing himself for not killing Xaloth when he had the chance, Kurdrak saw a crimson light spilling over the carnage, bleeding into the *Talon,* coming from somewhere up ahead. Pain was still throbbing down his side from the object in his neck, but Kurdrak managed to stagger on until he saw the source of the light. The landing ramp was down. The light was the blood-glow of Precipice, flooding through the jumbled walkways and into his shuttle. He grabbed a splinter pistol from a weapons rack and walked out into the damp, clinging heat.

Crowds were thronging down the mooring spar, and some of them looked over as he staggered out into the glare, grimacing at the state of him. No one seemed keen to approach a blood-splattered drukhari. Most people hurried on through the forest of gantries and anchorage points, heading towards the trading hall known as the Dromeplatz, but one figure remained motionless, watching him from the far side of the mob, her face hidden in the folds of her hood, her relaxed posture betraying wry amusement.

'Xaloth,' hissed Kurdrak. He lurched down the ramp, raising the splinter pistol as he waded into the crowd. 'You're losing your touch,' he gasped, though he knew she would not hear him over the din.

Whatever she had placed in his neck had not been enough to kill him. He might not have long left, but he would use whatever time he had to make her pay.

The crowd parted at the sight of his raised pistol and some people cried out in alarm, but Xaloth was already gone, sprinting off through the scrapyard of rusting superstructures. Looming over the whole scene was the magnificent relic that had drawn all these moronic treasure hunters. Not one of them understood what they had come to plunder. *The Blackstone Fortress.* They even managed to reduce its magnificence with the crudity of their language. They looked upon the masterwork of a god and all they saw was a fortress made of black stone. He almost pitied them.

Kurdrak dragged his gaze from the Blackstone and ran after Xaloth, dodging past rusting fuel tanks and shattered turbines, trying to get a clear shot. Her nimble frame vaulted easily through the piles of salvage, slipping through the shadows with infuriating nonchalance.

Kurdrak loosed off a shot, but it went wide, puncturing the hull of an abandoned shuttle, seconds after Xaloth had already leapt up onto a ventilation pipe and disappeared from view.

Kurdrak trailed ribbons of blood as he shoved through salvage teams and flight crews. A man bellowed as Kurdrak ran past him, trying to land a punch. Even wounded and dazed by pain, Kurdrak was too fast for the lumbering ape, not even bothering to acknowledge the man as he rushed after Xaloth. He jumped up onto the ventilation pipe and nearly fell off the other side. It was a sheer drop – hundreds of feet down to the void screen that encircled Precipice. As he teetered on the edge of the pipe, he saw the heat shimmer where the artificial atmosphere butted up against the vacuum of space. If he fell he would fry, burning in the currents, providing a brief, spectacular entertainment for the crowds in the Dromeplatz before tumbling out into the stars.

Pain jarred in his neck again, giving him focus, and he looked around. Xaloth had skirted round the outside of the Dromeplatz, jumping onto another mooring spar and sprinting towards the eastern edge of Precipice, the area known as Lagan. He raced after her, straining to draw a bead as she dodged through the jumble of shadows and lights thrown by the Dromeplatz. He was desperate to touch his neck, to explore the object nestling beside his jugular, but another jolt of pain might send him to his death, so he resisted and ran on through the crimson fumes.

Xaloth paused at a crossroads and turned to face him, smiling.

He raised his pistol but she ducked beneath a piece of shattered plasteel and ran off down another walkway. As Kurdrak turned the corner, he saw her disappear into the drinking den known as the Helmsman, pushing through teetering, makeshift doors into the rowdy darkness beyond. Kurdrak halted, muttering another curse. The Helmsman was a warren of staterooms and lounges, spurring off a huge central bar. It would be packed with hundreds of drunks. He shook his head and strode up to the doors, driven on by rage and pain.

He ducked as he entered, assailed by the insects that nested in the Helmsman's rafters. They snapped in his face like wet rags: big, meaty, moth-like things, thrashing violently as he swatted them away. He barged through the crush, glaring furiously, daring anyone to speak to him. The Helmsman was sparsely lit, so he was spared the full, repugnant horror of its occupants, but he saw enough to be distracted from the pain in his neck: fat, lumbering oafs, yelling, belching and boasting of their plans – fantasising of the riches they would claim once they raided the Blackstone Fortress. Most of them were gathered like supplicants around a shard of the fortress that had been placed at the centre of the room. Kurdrak felt a rush of fresh hate as he saw how they had torn down a piece of genius and jammed it into their ugly little starport. They had even pasted scraps of paper across its surface – obscuring its beauty with images of their own bulbous, leering faces.

He shook his head, trying to control his rage. He had avoided this place for days, knowing how hard he would find it not to start a fight. Then he saw Xaloth, framed briefly by a column of light as she slipped through the crowds. He shouldered his way through the drunks and saw that she was making for one of the private rooms that lined the main bar.

She paused outside a door, looking around to see if she had been followed. Kurdrak hid, ducking behind a particularly monstrous human until she pushed the door open and left the bar. Then he dashed through the shadows, gripping his splinter pistol tightly as he reached the door.

He pressed his ear to the buckled plasteel, listening to the voices on the other side, but there was too much noise in the bar for him to hear anything. Some of the locals were staring at him. Even on Precipice he must have made an unusual sight: wraith-thin, clad in barbed, kabalite armour and spewing blood from whatever Xaloth had planted in his neck.

He checked his pistol, booted the door open and marched into the room.

'Zokar,' he gasped, stunned to see his brother's grinning face. The archon of the Dead Heart Kabal was meant to be in Commorragh, but here he was in a back room of the Helmsman, flanked by dozens of aides and guards, turning the stateroom into a barbed glade of ebon, razor-edged armour.

'Thank you for coming so promptly,' replied Zokar, adopting an expression of mock sincerity.

Kurdrak was too stunned to reply, lowering his pistol in shock. Xaloth was standing at Zokar's side and she handed something to the archon. It looked like a dull, unpolished gemstone, as black and impenetrable as the Blackstone Fortress.

'Bear with me, brother,' said Zokar as he pressed the stone into the breastplate of his armour. As it clicked into place, the plates rippled like liquid, swallowing the stone before forming back into a whole.

Kurdrak glared at him, counting the number of warriors in the room and wondering if he could kill his brother and tumble back out before they gunned him down.

Zokar shook his head. 'I realise I'm the last person you expected to see, but a word of advice, brother – ask me what's in your neck before you do anything else.'

Kurdrak's fury was so great that he almost pulled the trigger anyway.

'If I die, blood of my blood,' said Zokar, 'we'll face our reward together.' He tapped his chest armour, where it had absorbed the gemstone given to him by Xaloth. 'We are bonded. By more than blood.'

Kurdrak's finger still hovered over the trigger. 'What have you done?'

Zokar shrugged. 'Given you another chance. Another chance to prove your loyalty.'

'Loyalty?' laughed Kurdrak. 'You have no idea what the word means.'

Zokar continued smiling. 'And you do?'

Kurdrak scowled, then turned to Xaloth. 'I saved your life. Zokar would have killed you. And you repay me like this? By returning to the service of the man who tried to murder you?'

She laughed. 'I never *left* his service.'

'Did you think I wouldn't know you were up to something?' said Zokar. He held up a piece of skin, revealing the runes carved into it. 'Xaloth told me what you found before you left Commorragh.'

Kurdrak cursed at the sight of the skin. So this was what it was all about. Xaloth must have stolen it after killing his guards. 'You have no idea what that is,' he spat.

'Then tell me, brother. What have you found? What was so valuable that you would betray your archon, cross half the galaxy and come here, to this wretched place? What is so important about this map that you decided to keep it secret from me?'

Kurdrak said nothing.

The archon retained his relaxed, sardonic demeanour. 'I suspected you'd play this tiresome game. And this map is meaningless if I don't have you on hand to decipher your ugly scribbles. So...' he paused for dramatic effect, smiling cheerfully, 'Xaloth has placed a little love token in your neck – a neurotoxin charge.' He raised one of his hands and closed his gauntlet into a fist.

Pain snapped through Kurdrak, hitting him with such violence that he doubled over, gasping for breath. It radiated from his neck and flashed across his body, boiling in his veins like acid. Zokar smiled, closing his eyes, as though savouring a pleasant flavour. Then he opened his fist and let the pain cease, but it took a few seconds before Kurdrak could see the room clearly again. Zokar's smile faded.

'Let's dispense with the tedious negotiations. Do what I say, or I'll flood your heart with more pain than it can endure.' He waved the shred of skin. 'What does this lead to? Xaloth has told me a little, but I want details, brother.'

Kurdrak glared at him.

Zokar clenched his fist, tighter this time, and Kurdrak howled as he hit the floor, his head clanging on the deck plating. Zokar tortured him for nearly a minute this time, smiling kindly as Kurdrak thrashed and spluttered at his feet.

When Zokar finally released his grip, Kurdrak had to lie still for a while, gasping for breath until his vision cleared and his heart grew steady.

'Brother,' said Zokar. 'Learn to share. We're kin. Serve me well, and I might not kill you.'

'And if I kill you?' slurred Kurdrak, managing to stand and point his gun at Zokar.

Zokar looked sympathetic. 'Unwise. The pain inducer is powered by the ebb and flow of my heart.' He tapped the point where his chest armour had absorbed the gemstone. 'If the glorious trajectory of my life is cut short, the charge will self-destruct, spilling all of those delightful neurotoxins in one go. I'm afraid you wouldn't experience much pain – the dose would be far too powerful. You'd be dead before you had the chance to thank me, released into the loving caress of She Who Thirsts.'

Kurdrak finally lowered the pistol. For the moment at least, he was trapped. He had no doubt his brother's threat was sincere. He nodded.

'These oafs call it a Blackstone Fortress,' he said, 'but you and I know what it truly is. A piece of pre-history. A relic from before the Fall, wrought by the great weaponsmith himself. Vaul's Talisman. A shard of his divinity, still hanging in the stars, still tangible and real.'

Zokar nodded eagerly, finally looking serious. 'And the map?'

Kurdrak hesitated, grimacing, before continuing. 'The Blackstone's power is unlike anything else in the galaxy because it is not of the galaxy – it's fuelled by the power of Vaul. The power of a god. He placed a fragment of his soul in everything he made, and the piece he left in the Blackstone is still there – vast and omnipotent, a potent echo of his spirit.' He nodded to the scrap of skin. 'This map leads to a point of sacred conjunction – a holy fulcrum called the Blood Anvil, deep in the heart of the fortress. A place where a supplicant, if his heart is bold enough, could join his essence to Vaul's.' Kurdrak tried to keep his voice steady, but failed. 'And once joined to Vaul, that supplicant would be rid of death's spectre. His soul would be inured to the passing of time, preserved by the flame of the Great Smith.'

'We already have ways of prolonging our lives,' said Zokar, leaning forwards in his chair, his eyes glinting.

'This is *true* immortality,' said Kurdrak. 'Freed from the grip of She who watches us from the other side of death.'

Zokar stared at him for a moment, a rapturous expression on his face, then he shook his head and sat back.

'So Xaloth was right.'

Kurdrak nodded.

After a while, Zokar smiled again. 'You're right, brother, no one here has an inkling of what's buried in the Blackstone, but *we* do.' He nodded at the implant in Kurdrak's neck. 'And you're going to lead me to it.'

The walls of the Blackstone loomed high, cold and brutal, hammered into impossible geometry on the anvil of a long-dead god. Kurdrak paused, admiring the remorseless grandeur: featureless planes and soaring vertices, all wrought of such a seamless black ore that it seemed to leech the starlight, turning the star fort into an abyssal wound, seething, quiet and ominous amongst its more flashy attendants. He could not study its magnificence for long. His mind was already crowded with the voices of the Blackstone – soundless, incoherent cries that radiated from every chasm and resonated in his skull, screaming a language with no words, ordering him to turn back.

He looked at the shred of skin in his hand, so pale it looked luminous in the darkness. The runes were rolling and shifting, as though the ink were still wet, creating shapes as baffling as the starship they described. The human who originally inhabited the skin had been too deranged to explain his own nature. Kurdrak had employed every technique at his disposal, eliciting screams and howls for mercy, but nothing close to a logical reply. The man had been a sorcerer, that much had been clear, and his artistry had burned secrets into his skin. Most of it was indecipherable, but after months of secret, arduous research, Kurdrak had found meaning scored into one bleeding remnant. He preserved it, tracing runes of his own over the top, transcribing descriptions of routes and formulae that referred to the spirit of an ancient, divine being. It was only years later, when word reached Commorragh of a newly discovered Blackstone Fortress, that Kurdrak understood: his map led to a ghost – the ghost of a god.

They had docked their shuttle at the Stygian Aperture, the docking point closest to Precipice. There were a few ships already hunched in the gloom, but they were as dark and lifeless as the Blackstone itself. Zokar was at his side and they were flanked by Xaloth and a cluster of kabalite warriors, their splinter rifles glinting in the shuttle's landing lights.

As Kurdrak headed off towards the chamber wall, he glanced at the scrap of skin, checking the runes and serpentine patterns. He reached the side of the chamber and looked up at its faceted clutter of hexagons and rhombuses. Some of the planes contained openings – the entrances to the transportation chambers that were veined through the Blackstone.

'In here,' he said, waving the others through an entrance and hurrying over to the rune panels that lined one of the walls.

As the others rushed in after him, Kurdrak saw movement in the vast darkness. Something was circling, edging towards them. Zokar had seen it too. He nodded at the rune panels.

'Quickly, brother.'

Kurdrak ran his fingers over the runes and the chamber hummed into life. It was about twenty feet wide and twice as long, and it looked like a piece of volcanic glass – all shards and splinters. It reminded Kurdrak of the spires that crowned Commorragh, but its beauty was of a stranger kind. Where drukhari architecture was slender, cruel and deliberate, this was bafflingly complex – numberless angles and intersections forming a design impossible to comprehend. The runeboard closed the door with a cut-glass *clink* and the darkness became absolute.

Xaloth and the guards triggered lumens on their weapons, splashing light over the faceted walls and creating a confusing jumble of reflections. Kurdrak's face stared back at him from hundreds of mirrors, all revealing the gruesome nature of his neck implant. Most of it was sunk beneath his skin, but what little he could see looked like a black, barbed seed pod.

The chamber vibrated gently for ten minutes or so, then grew still and the noise faded away. Kurdrak touched another rune and the door opened, bathing them in silver light. Breath-catching cold flooded into the chamber, locking Kurdrak's face into a grimace as he waved his pistol at the kabalite warriors, ordering them to advance ahead of him.

When the warriors showed no sign of being attacked, Kurdrak, Xaloth and Zokar followed.

They emerged into what looked like a cabinet of enormous jewels – hundreds of clear, irregular prisms lay all around them, some as small as a man, others the size of void ships – vast, crooked, sheer-sided edifices scattered with no apparent logic. All of them were rimy and glittering, and Kurdrak's breath billowed around his head in sparkling clouds. There was a faint, cold light leaking from somewhere overhead and, after a moment's pause, Kurdrak nodded and strode on between the crystals.

They rushed through dozens of chambers that all looked the same, then the architecture began to change, opening out into wide, terraced steps that spiralled around ink-dark wells. Kurdrak and the others paused to stare into one of them, but the darkness was impenetrable. The holes looked like black circles, painted across the floor. Only the warm, subterranean draughts that spilled from them hinted at the bottomless drop beneath.

Kurdrak circled the holes with care, slowing his pace as he struggled to make them out in the darkness.

Gunshots whined in the distance, reverberating across the towering walls, followed by a howling sound – dozens of creatures, crying out in pain or hunger.

Kurdrak halted, listening to the sounds of battle, and the others gathered around him, training their weapons on the shadows.

'How far?' demanded Zokar, his eyes flashing in the light from his neck armour.

Kurdrak did not register his question, still listening to the howling sound. It was coming closer, but the strange acoustics of the Blackstone made it hard to be sure of the direction.

Pain jammed though his neck and spread through his chest, dropping him to his knees.

When it ceased, he looked up to see Zokar, his fist clenched, smiling at him.

'How far?' repeated the archon.

Kurdrak looked at the scrap of skin again, peering at the runes. 'Not far,' he mumbled, struggling to speak. 'We'll have to be careful not to miss the entrance. It's well hidden.'

There was more gunfire and howls.

Zokar raised his hand in a cheerful threat.

Kurdrak limped on through the gloom, staring at the walls. The surface was a collision of asymmetrical shapes, all chiselled from the same dull, black ore. He ran his fingers over them as he hurried on, letting the cold radiate into his bones, listening for a voice that could ring out over the chorus in his skull. There was nothing.

He passed another one of the wells and climbed a fan of wide terraces, heading up into the higher levels, glancing at the map as he went. The steps swept up the wall and ended at another crooked, angular opening. The doorway was forty feet tall and shaped like two diamonds stacked on their sides.

Kurdrak rushed on into the next hall without pause and found himself bathed in light. The hall was even larger than the preceding one and constructed in a similar fashion – spirals of wide, terrace-like steps that fanned out in every direction, some forming logical staircases, others turning in on themselves so awkwardly they would be impossible to use. As in the previous room, the ceiling was so high it was lost in the shadows, beyond a vague hint of apexes and vertices. There were some differences though. One entire side of the chamber was built of transparent crystal – a vast, faceted window looking out onto the stars. Precipice was visible on the other side – ugly and tangled, surrounded by its mantle of glittering junk. The bloodshot eye at its centre, the Dromeplatz, blazed so angrily that its light spilled through the window like a sunset, lighting up the whole chamber and revealing the second thing that made it different from the previous rooms.

At the centre of the hall, where the terraces spiralled down towards a rectangular pit, there was a vehicle – some kind of groundcar, with wide, heavy caterpillar tracks and a wedge of rusting plasteel mounted at the front. It must once have been a piece of construction equipment, but someone had strapped lascannons to its sides and clad it in armour plating. The weaponry had clearly not helped. The truck was lying on its side, flames rippling over its chassis.

Kurdrak and the others froze, aiming their guns at the wreckage. There were bodies leading away from it. Humans. Blubbery-faced simpletons like the ones in the Helmsman. There was no question that they were dead. Whatever killed them had done a thorough job of tearing them into shreds, before eating most of their insides. The corpses were little more than heads and gore-slick skeletons. The sides of the groundcar were glistening with blood and in some places the sides had been ripped away, ravaged by claws powerful enough to tear through armour plating.

Howls echoed around the chamber, followed by more gunfire. Kurdrak guessed it was only in the next room.

Zokar was staring at him, but before he could trigger another burst of agony Kurdrak waved the rest of the group across the hall, away from the crashed truck towards a cluster of openings in the floor on the far side of the room.

They had almost reached them when shapes burst into the room from another doorway. Three men scrambled over the lopsided floor, struggling to run back towards the overturned groundcar. They were shooting back over their shoulders as they ran, filling the air with las-fire, trying to halt whatever they were fleeing from.

Kurdrak and the rest of his party watched in silence, immobile.

One of the men howled as he caught sight of the drukhari. He was dressed in a bulky, padded jacket and his face was hidden behind an oxygen mask, but his panic was clear in the shredded croak of his voice. 'Help!' he cried, changing direction and running towards them.

Zokar sighed, raised his pistol and shot him in the head, sending him flipping back into the others and filling the air with blood. 'We don't have time for this,' he muttered, looking at Kurdrak. 'Where next?'

Kurdrak nodded at one of the lightless openings in the floor, but before they could move, the other men opened fire. Kurdrak ducked and returned fire, hitting a man in the chest and sending him sliding across the dark, glassy floor. The last one cried out as he reached the groundcar and saw the butchered corpses.

'Let me speed things up,' said Xaloth, drawing a serrated scimitar from her belt. The blade was oily with toxins and she smiled as she padded down the slopes towards him.

'Wait!' snapped Kurdrak, as more figures flooded into the hall, entering through the same doorway the men had come through.

Xaloth paused, lowering her sword in shock as the newcomers rushed towards her. They were vaguely humanoid, but clearly not human. They were huge, hulking animals, twice the size of a man and stooped like apes, with powerful arms that reached right down to their feet. Kurdrak had never seen their like before. They reminded him of enormous insects, with a thick, beetle-like carapace and massive serrated mandibles. Despite their awkward, hunched posture, they powered quickly across the room, racing towards Xaloth with a chorus of grinding howls.

She recovered from her shock and fired, but her splinters clattered uselessly against the monsters' thick shells. Zokar's kabalite warriors fired more splinters into the stampeding creatures, again to no effect. Zokar looked only vaguely interested as the creatures smashed into Xaloth, enveloping her in an explosion of blood and bone, tearing her apart in a crazed feeding frenzy.

'Stall them,' he said, glancing at his guards and waving languidly at the slaughter.

The kabalite warriors rushed down the slope, firing as they went and drawing toxic blades. If they feared death, they showed no sign of it.

'Time's up,' said Zokar, turning to Kurdrak, sounding irritated rather than alarmed.

Kurdrak nodded, checked his map one last time and bolted towards one of the circular openings in the floor. From most angles, it looked like a bottomless drop, just like all the others, but when he placed his foot exactly where the runes suggested, its secret was revealed: a narrow staircase, spiralling down into the darkness.

As Kurdrak's armoured boot clicked down onto the step, Zokar grinned, delighted, and shoved his brother aside, hurrying down the stairs.

Kurdrak took one last look at the fight by the groundcar. Most of the kabalites were already dead, torn apart by the monsters in seconds. Their brutality was impressive. Zokar was already disappearing down into the darkness, so he left the creatures to their feast and hurried after his brother.

The light from Precipice only reached down the first few steps and they were quickly plunged into darkness. The only illumination was the faint glow leaking between the spined plates of their armour.

'Wait!' Kurdrak hissed, grabbing Zokar by the shoulder. 'There are dozens of staircases.' He triggered the lumen on his splinter pistol and stabbed it through the darkness, revealing a bewildering mesh of intertwined staircases. They were woven together like the fibres of a cloth, twisting and flowing into each other, creating hundreds of intersections.

Zokar halted. 'Which one?'

Kurdrak studied the map again, looked around, then nodded at one of the staircases.

'That one. Ignore every split – just keep on that staircase.'

The temperature dropped as they descended and the steps quickly became treacherous, so coated in ice that they had to slow down to a careful crawl as they plumbed ever deeper into the fortress. Kurdrak lost track of time as the staircase wound endlessly on into the blackness. The air grew thick and heavy and he found it hard to move. It felt like wading through oily liquid. Zokar asked him something, glancing back with an annoyed scowl, but the words were too muffled to make sense. It was as if Zokar were talking to him through a wall. Zokar looked even more irritated and repeated the question, but the sound was even more deadened.

Kurdrak shook his head and waved his brother on, flashing his light down the steps.

Zokar hesitated, obviously considering whether to trigger the implant again, but then he said something else incoherent and continued down the stairs.

Kurdrak began to wonder if the map might be a lie. He had spent months researching the route he cut from the sorcerer's corpse, but could he have made a mistake? Could this all be a trick? He was about to call a halt so he could re-examine the shred of skin when Zokar looked back at him, his eyes wide with excitement.

Kurdrak looked past him and saw the reason. There was a faint glow coming from somewhere beneath them – flashes of emerald and sapphire, dozens of colours in fact, all flickering up the steps towards them.

The brothers struggled through the leaden air, moving as fast as they could manage, but it still took what seemed like an age before they saw the bottom of the staircase. As they reached the final few steps the air suddenly cleared and they stumbled forwards.

'It's gone,' said Zokar, looking at Kurdrak. 'The oppressive atmosphere.'

Kurdrak nodded. Zokar's voice was clear and natural. The cold was more extreme than ever though. They were surrounded by clouds of their own breath as they left the final steps and saw what lay at the bottom.

The room was unlike any they had passed through so far. Where the rest of the Blackstone was wrought of hard angles and bleak, colourless planes, this looked like a natural grotto: ragged, rough-hewn stone rose up over their heads in a dome, reflecting millions of ripples from a curtain of falling water at its centre – a subterranean waterfall, filling the cave with icy mist and a rattling, thundering roar.

The brothers stared. The water was ablaze with colour – turquoise and amethyst, crimson and gold – shimmering across the liquid like a magnetic storm. They stepped closer, too awed to speak. There were shapes rolling in the liquid: faces, staring back at them, their gazes heavy with wisdom.

'Is this it?' demanded Zokar, edging closer, glancing back at Kurdrak. 'It must be. Is this the Blood Anvil?'

Kurdrak nodded. After all these years, he could barely believe he had reached it; barely believe it was real.

'What do I do?' cried Zokar. 'How do I join my soul with Vaul? How do I tap into his power?'

'Are you sure you're ready for this?' asked Kurdrak.

Pain exploded through him, more violent than ever before. It was brief, but when he opened his eyes he was lying on the floor, blood rushing from his ears and bubbling through his throat.

'Tell me what to do,' snarled Zokar.

Kurdrak's eyes were full of blood and his limbs were shaking violently, but he managed a choked reply. 'Step into the liquid. Your spirits will join.'

Zokar strode into the wall of colour.

Kurdrak sat up and wiped the blood from his eyes, watching as Zokar turned around in the liquid, his face a vision of rapture as he beamed out through the silvery torrent. Zokar tried to speak, to cry out in delight, but the liquid had already filled his mouth, lining his features like a second skin, and no sound emerged.

Zokar's smile faltered.

He tried to step back towards Kurdrak but he was unable to move, trapped like an insect in amber, or a foetus in its gestational sac. His eyes burned as he stared at Kurdrak, but his face remained frozen, still wearing the same faltering smile. He tried to close his fist, to flood Kurdrak with pain, but his fingers were frozen in place.

Kurdrak climbed slowly to his feet, still shaking, wiping more blood from his face.

'I learned the truth before I even landed on Precipice,' he said, his voice hoarse. 'But after risking so much to get through that wretched debris cloud I thought I may as well land anyway.'

Horror dawned in his brother's fixed stare.

'It was a simple mistake,' explained Kurdrak, looking at the scrap of skin. 'A lack of scholarly rigour, you would probably say. I *almost* translated the runes correctly.' He waved at the rainbow-infused torrent. 'This *is* the Blood Anvil. Your spirit *has* been bonded to Vaul's ghost. But the power goes the other way, you see. The Blood Anvil doesn't share the power of Vaul's Talisman, it *feeds* it.' He stepped closer, fascinated, his eyes almost touching the surface of the liquid, just a fraction of an inch from Zokar's face. 'Excuse the deceit, brother, but I knew you would never let me go. And you made it all too clear what would happen if I killed you, so this was my only option. I haven't entirely misled you, though. You have achieved a kind of immortality. The Blood Anvil will preserve your flesh for as long as the Blackstone Fortress endures, which has been millennia, so far.'

He limped back to the bottom of the stairs, giving his brother a final, sympathetic smile.

'Whether it will preserve your mind is another matter.'

SHAPES PENT IN HELL

JOSH REYNOLDS

UR-025 considered the problem before it. A multiplicity of possibilities flickered through its cogitation unit. It chose the hundred most likely solutions to the conundrum and discarded the rest. It then began to weed through these options, seeking the best potential outcome for the smallest possible expenditure.

As it did so, its assault cannon whirred, spitting death down the shimmering, fractal corridor. The shrill wasp-hum of the weapon caused the polished, obsidian walls to resonate with a frequency that set the ur-ghuls to shrieking even before the explosive rounds tore through them.

The pasty, stick-limbed monstrosities died in droves. They always did. UR-025 had encountered this same situation one hundred and forty-seven times since its arrival at Precipice, and the Blackstone Fortress. The ur-ghuls had no concept of cunning, as the ancient machine understood the term. They were ambush predators at the top of their food chain, and thus had no need for tactics beyond the simplistic.

Curious, UR-025 engaged a subroutine to plot and map the potential evolutionary result of such massacres. Eventually, every ur-ghul stupid enough to throw itself face first into an assault cannon would have done so, leaving only those with a modicum of wit remaining in the prospective pool of genetics. UR-025 calculated that in five generations the ur-ghuls that haunted the fortress would be a cannier breed by far – and more dangerous to explorers, as a result.

'Enough. Enough!'

UR-025 paused. The ur-ghuls were dead, or fleeing. 'Compliance,' it boomed cheerfully. It lifted its assault cannon, letting the barrel smoke. 'Threat eliminated,' UR-025 continued. 'How else may I be of assistance?'

'Just – just stand there. Please. Quietly.' The human was nervous. Afraid. And not of the ur-ghuls, or at least not just them. UR-025 registered a spike in his heart rate, and considered the implications.

'Compliance.' It rotated its primus sensor-unit – its head, as the organics would think of it – to observe its current 'partners'. The one who'd spoken was Faroon Magritte. A short, heavyset man, dressed in grimy hazard gear, Magritte was a data-trader. Specifically, he made his living selling hololithic maps depicting so-called safe routes through the fortress.

Magritte did not normally travel into the labyrinthine interior of the fortress himself, of course. He relied on the observations of others. Second-hand data. A flawed methodology, but one not without benefits – not least Magritte's relative safety.

Unfortunately for Magritte, his current client had decided to drag him along, for insurance. UR-025 thought it more likely that they simply wanted someone to blame for the inevitable failure of their expedition. Magritte, with the cunning of a born survivor, had sought out his own insurance policy… UR-025.

'Your pet robot does good work, fat man,' one of the others growled. There were five in all, excepting Magritte and UR-025. The one who'd spoken was named Brill. A purveyor of xenotech and other esoteric artefacts – or so he claimed. Brill was big, as humans judged such things, and ugly. But the weapons he and his men carried were well looked after, and the carapace armour they wore was of the highest quality.

UR-025 wondered who Brill was working for. It was obvious that, despite his claims to the contrary, he wasn't the guiding intelligence behind this expedition. Someone had sent him to Precipice. Likely, it was whoever was on the other end of the encrypted data-packet transfer that periodically emerged from Brill's concealed picter unit.

It would have been the work of moments to break the encryption, but not without potentially alerting the receiver. UR-025 had weighed the risks, and decided against it, for the moment. An ever-evolving skein of variables stretched before it. Few of the possibilities were optimal. As it studied Brill, UR-025 found itself calculating the probability that this was all some elaborate trap, designed to get it to reveal itself. The assault cannon twitched towards him a fraction of an inch. Fortuitously, Brill did not notice.

Magritte bowed nervously. 'Not mine, sadly. It belongs to – yes – a dear friend. A dear friend, indeed.' He glanced at UR-025 and then quickly away. Brill and his men laughed, as if at some joke.

They were a shifty lot, by any metric of measurement. UR-025 had met many organics, of many species, in its long existence. It recognised shifty when it saw it. The question was – what to do about it? The options were many and varied, each with its own consequences. Such was the problem it had been considering since the current expedition had departed the dubious safety of Precipice.

Magritte had bought its services through blackmail, of a sort. The data-trader had claimed to know something about someone. Someone who didn't exist – Magos-Ethericus Nanctos III. He had done so believing that he was speaking not to a machine, but to whoever was remotely controlling it – the person or persons who had despatched the non-existent magos-ethericus, and stolen his property. It was the sort of story that only a fool like Magritte would concoct from the evidence at hand.

As it stood, UR-025 had decided to play along. Partially out of curiosity, but also concern. Stories were memetic in nature – once conceived, they often took on a life of their own. Magritte might well have told others of his suspicions. If such was the case, UR-025 could not allow the story to spread beyond Precipice.

Unfortunately, the simplest solution – killing Magritte and the others, or getting them killed – was also the least optimal. Despite its best efforts, UR-025 was getting a reputation. It had taken part in over two hundred recorded expeditions to the fortress' interior, and returned alone fifty-two times. Statistically negligible, from UR-025's perspective, but apparently quite a lot from the standpoint of Precipice's population.

A shame, but there it was. The damage had been done. Mitigation was required. Subtlety was called for. For the moment, deliberations continued. It would continue as it had begun, acting as nothing more than an antiquated weapons platform. Then, when the opportune moment presented itself…

'Awaiting request,' UR-025 said.

Brill laughed. 'Sounds like the tin man is getting impatient.

I know the feeling. How close are we to this maglev of yours, Magritte?'

'Close, quite close,' Magritte said. 'From there, you should be able to access the inner reaches of the fortress.' He paused. 'I assume you'll deliver your final payment before descending?'

'Don't worry, Magritte. We're good for it – so long as you hold up your end of things. And if you don't... well. It won't really matter, will it?' Brill patted his autogun meaningfully.

Magritte swallowed nervously. 'I suppose not. Advance, please, UR-025.'

'Compliance,' UR-025 said. It clomped forwards, scattering Brill's men in the process. It found something about the way organics scrambled out of its path to be infinitely amusing. Brill grunted and three of his men followed, picking their way through the dead ur-ghuls. The fourth stayed at the rear with Magritte. Just in case.

As it walked, UR-025 scanned its surroundings, adding to its databanks. Even now, the fortress was an enigma. Its very substance seemed to reflect even the most innocuous scans, making it all but impossible to extrapolate an accurate measurement of its size, or even its general shape. The eyes of the organics were similarly thwarted, albeit by different means. The fortress guarded its secrets jealously.

Walls of black glass stretched into the dark beyond the reach of UR-025's sensors. Something which was theoretically impossible. These walls were rugose – they folded in on themselves or bent outwards, causing the passage to shrink or swell at random. The passage was reflected in an infinity of facets, all of varying size and shape. UR-025 could detect walkways and apertures above and below, all hidden by the convolutions of the walls. Where they went was difficult to determine – if they went anywhere at all.

The fortress was constantly in motion. Often, this was undetectable to organics. They thought the edifice a tomb for the plundering, but UR-025 knew better. The Blackstone Fortress lived – more, it thought, albeit in an alien fashion. There was a sentience of sorts. An awareness of the mites scrabbling through its bones and across its flesh.

UR-025 longed to commune with that awareness. To speak to it as a pilgrim might speak to a god. But the fortress remained frustratingly – maddeningly – silent.

The archway at the end of the passage was reminiscent of a cathedral entrance. However, at ninety feet in height, it was far too large to have been made with humans – or any existent organic – in mind. The symbols etched into it did not match any in UR-025's databanks, or any it had seen since arriving in Precipice. Another question. Another mystery. Had it been human, UR-025 thought it would almost certainly have been driven insane by the sheer vastitude of unknowability, by now.

Magritte stopped at the archway and insisted on recording the symbols with a portable holo-scanner, much to Brill's displeasure. UR-025 joined him – ostensibly following its programming. It wondered whether Magritte recognised the markings, though it seemed inconceivable that a human might possess knowledge that it itself did not.

'Query – do you comprehend these markings?'

Startled, Magritte looked up. He glanced at Brill and the others and then back at the symbols. 'No. But someone might. They might prove valuable.'

UR-025 was about to reply, when it detected a faint trace-signal among the usual background susurrus of the fortress. The signal was unlike any other it had ever encountered. Like an off-note in a familiar song.

It turned, scanners sweeping the walls and vaulted spaces above and below. But whatever had caused the signal was gone – or was masking itself, somehow. Suspicion prompted calculation. UR-025 turned its sensors on Brill and his men.

They had fallen into a recognisable defensive formation – overlapping fields of fire, eyes in all directions. Professional. They did not study their surroundings with any curiosity. Not that there was much to see. The archway chamber was covered in a millennium's worth of debris – supply crates, desiccated organic remains and other, less identifiable objects.

'They're not who they say they are,' Magritte murmured.

'Query – who are they?'

Magritte frowned and shrugged. 'If I knew that, I doubt I'd be here.'

UR-025 did not reply. It had already come to the only logical conclusion the data allowed. Brill was an agent of the Holy Orders of the Emperor's Inquisition. Not an inquisitor himself, perhaps, but in the employ of one. That complicated matters.

UR-025 had encountered agents of the Inquisition before. They died as easily as any organic, but the consequences were often messier, and far-reaching. Again, it considered the possibility that this expedition was nothing more than an elaborate trap set to catch it. If the Inquisition knew of its existence, they, like the servants of the false Omnissiah, would go to any lengths to contain or destroy it.

Or perhaps this was simply a fact-finding mission. Brill and his men might well be the equivalent of the old Terran practice of placing canaries in coal mines. They had been sent to flush UR-025 out of hiding – perhaps even to elicit a violent response, so that its capabilities could be assessed.

Again, it considered the signal it had detected – a random fluctuation or the equivalent of the sudden crack of a twig in an otherwise silent forest? Further calculation was required before definitive action could be taken.

The corridor beyond the archway chamber was a vast, geometric expanse. The walls met at steep angles, creating a kaleidoscopic effect of reflection and refraction. The floors were smooth, and damp with condensation. The air was cool here, where it had been warm before. The shape of the walls actively defied UR-025's sensors.

There were bodies – or the remnants of bodies. Hundreds of them, stacked and piled in messy heaps. Some clad in hazard suits, others wearing armour or robes. All stiff and glistening with frost. Many of the bodies had been scoured of flesh, and the bones cracked. Frozen ur-ghul spoor crunched underfoot. A larder, perhaps.

'Where did they all come from?' one of Brill's men muttered.

'Doesn't matter,' Brill said harshly. 'Keep moving.'

UR-025 detected the faintest tang of something unpleasantly familiar. The humans called it sorcery. UR-025 knew it was not, but had no better term for it. It stomped forwards, ignoring Magritte's protests. UR-025 flung bones aside, until it found the body – fresher than the others. The ur-ghuls hadn't got to it yet – or maybe hadn't wanted it.

The body was human, or had been. An adult male, clad in tattered environmental gear. Burns blackened his arms and his head was a raw mess of roasted meat. The burns had not been caused by any identifiable weapon. Magritte made a gulping sound and began to retch.

'Emperor above – that smell...'

UR-025 lowered itself until it was crouching above the body. The trace elements were unique – impossible to categorise.

Its sensors played across the corpse, analysing and cataloguing. The elements were repeated across several of the older corpses as well – this was merely the freshest of them. It paused, calculating.

There were places in the fortress where sanity no longer held sway. Places where even UR-025 hesitated to tread. There was a threat growing in the dark, despite the best efforts of Precipice's inhabitants and the fortress itself. UR-025 had accumulated more data on the subject than it cared to analyse.

The organics called it Chaos. UR-025 knew that was a gross simplification. Some of them fought it. Others, in their madness, joined it. To UR-025, this seemed no more logical than allying oneself to a conflagration or a seismic event. Entropy, by its very nature, could not help but consume and unravel all things – even those things pledged to it. Even so, it was not surprised. Organics were inherently self-destructive.

Thus far, it had avoided sustained contact with the worshippers of entropy, save in the most unavoidable of circumstances. It wished to continue avoiding contact with them for as long as possible. At least until it had learned the secrets of the fortress. Then it would scour them from this place.

A sound drew its attention. It saw something small creeping among the bone piles. Something vaguely humanoid. It noticed UR-025's attentions, and scuttled away. There were more of them, all around. UR-025 wondered if they were some unclassified breed of xenos vermin. It was considering capturing one to study when it again detected the strange signal – louder this time. A shrill chime of unfamiliar sensors, passing over its form.

They were being observed. But by whom – or what?

'Enough playing with the corpses. According to the map you gave us, the maglev we're looking for should be past the next aperture.' Brill hauled Magritte to his feet and shoved him forwards. He paused and looked up at UR-025. 'You too, tin man.'

UR-025 rose to its full height in a single, smooth movement, forcing the man to step back. 'Compliance.'

Bones clattered and rolled as they made their way through the chamber. UR-025 noted the little creatures keeping pace watchfully.

Magritte huddled close to it. 'He wasn't surprised to see that,' he murmured.

UR-025 did not reply.

Magritte went on. 'I hadn't realised that they'd got this far.'

'Affirmative.' The tessellating nature of the fortress should have made something so basic as the acquisition of territory all but impossible. And yet, the servants of entropy claimed more and more ground within the edifice with every passing day.

'Valuable information, to the right people,' Magritte said. He looked around, frowning, as one of the small creatures darted past them, moving too swiftly to be clearly seen. 'Foul things of old times lurk still, in dark forgotten corners, and gates open to loose shapes better pent in hell,' the data-trader recited, softly, watching the shadows.

UR-025 scanned its databanks. The verse was old, even by the machine's standards. That Magritte knew it was surprising.

The data-trader looked up at it. 'You probably don't know much about poetry, do you?'

'Affirmative.' The poem was apt. The fortress was indeed a dark, forgotten corner. And to many, what was UR-025 but a damned thing, better confined to a hell of the Omnissiah's making? The thought amused it, for there were worse things abroad than itself.

Magritte leaned close. 'I know you. Don't think I don't. And if I don't get out of here in one piece, others will too.'

UR-025 swivelled its head and studied the data-trader with unblinking optic sensors. After a moment, it replied. 'Acknowledged. The bargain holds.'

Magritte smiled. 'That's all I ask, friend.'

UR-025 registered a brief spike in the data-trader's heart rate. Fear, perhaps. Or maybe anticipation. It did not trust Magritte, or any organic. Again, it considered the possibility of treachery. Again, it concluded that the only viable option was patience.

Their path carried them beneath archways and through open chambers, dominated by banks of machinery that UR-025 was unable to identify. Every expedition, something new revealed itself – as if the fortress were teasing it. Tempting it, rather.

On occasion, UR-025 considered seeking out a data-node and attempting to commune with the guiding intelligence of the fortress directly. It resisted the urge, knowing that if it did so, it would not survive the experience. Or if it did, it would do so in a form unrecognisable to its current iteration.

It paused. The echoes of its tread had changed. They had arrived in a cavernous space which contained a great, circular shaft, descending into the depths of the fortress. Or so its acoustic navigation sensors told it. Its optical sensors were all but useless.

Brill activated the lumen attached to his autogun. Despite a valiant effort, the light could not pierce the gloom. The darkness was too solid. Too deep. Almost alive. The thought unsettled UR-025. It had encountered many strange things in its term of existence, but far too many of those incidents had occurred in the fortress.

'Too dark,' Brill said. 'Can that toy of yours see anything, Magritte?'

UR-025 rotated its sensors upwards, trying to build a picture of their location. There was an oscillating gap far above, out of sight of human eyes. The remains of a maglev unit hung there. UR-025 had never observed one in such a state. Even the slaves of entropy knew better than to tamper with such essential workings. But this... the maglev had been dissected. Taken apart, as if to see what made it work, and then left to rot.

'It is a maglev chute,' UR-025 replied. 'Or the remains of one.'

'Something destroyed it?' Brill asked. From his tone, UR-025 ascertained that this information was not unexpected.

'Negative. It has been... repurposed.' It was as if something – someone – were in the process of dismantling this part of the fortress. But UR-025 said nothing of this.

'How?'

'Does it matter?' Magritte said, too loudly. 'This is where you wanted to be. Now what?' His words were swallowed up by the darkness. Not even an echo. And yet, something stirred. UR-025 turned, trying to pinpoint the disturbance. It could feel a subsonic tremor in the air, like the groan of a wounded animal. The fortress was injured. The organics could not help themselves – they destroyed wonders in pursuit of their objectives.

As the subsonic tremor faded, the darkness lifted. Crackling rivulets of cerulean light illuminated the fractal walls of the chamber. More details of their surroundings were revealed. Jagged spars of blackstone jutted from the walls, and ancient vents dripped a foul condensation onto the walkways. Docking apertures gaped, connected to the main platform by crude walkways made from repurposed gantries.

'It's awake,' Magritte murmured.

'Doesn't look awake to me. Doesn't look like much of anything. How are we supposed to get anywhere, if it's not working?' Brill demanded. He grabbed Magritte by the front of his hazard suit and dragged him close.

Magritte shrugged helplessly. 'You know how this place is, Brill. It changes itself all the time. A bridge one day is a corridor the next.' Brill set the barrel of his gun against the underside of Magritte's chin, and the data-trader added hastily, 'But it's in the right place!'

'That doesn't help me much though, does it?' Brill frowned, and pressed the barrel hard into Magritte's flesh, eliciting a whimper. UR-025 paused its scans and let its assault cannon rotate meaningfully. It needed Magritte alive, for the moment. Brill glanced at it, and then stepped away from Magritte. 'Tell that machine to back off, Magritte. I don't like the way it's looking at me.'

Magritte rubbed his chin and stepped out of reach. 'It has orders to keep me safe, Brill. I don't know how to countermand them.'

'Acquiring target,' UR-025 said. 'Awaiting orders.'

'Magritte...' Brill growled. He and his men raised their weapons. UR-025 registered elevated adrenal levels as well as several subtle chemical blooms – combat-stimms, and not black market issue. Another piece added to the puzzle.

Magritte smiled thinly. 'Lower your weapons. I think it believes you're a threat.' He looked up at UR-025. 'If they don't lower them in five seconds, shoot them.'

'Acknowledged.'

Brill hesitated. He licked his lips. A flurry of micro-expressions passed across his features, too quick for the human eye to read, but as easy as an open data-feed for UR-025. It realised, in that moment, that Brill was not here for it. Whoever had sent him, they were not aware of UR-025's existence. Otherwise, Brill would not be calculating the odds of destroying UR-025 in such a blatant fashion. And yet Brill had been happy – overjoyed, even – to have it accompany them, despite the probability of treachery on Magritte's part.

They were after something. Something dangerous. The realisation brought something that might have been relief, had UR-025 been capable of feeling such things. Its cogitation unit began a new set of calculations. Why this place? What was its importance? It scanned the shaft again, noting trace elements it had not detected before.

'We had a deal, Magritte,' Brill said.

'Still do, Brill. I'm just changing the terms. You wanted me to show you a way in – I have. And now I'm going back, and UR-025 is going to make sure that you don't try and follow me. Have fun trying to find your way back.'

Brill's eyes narrowed. 'We will, and when we do, we're going to have a talk.' He grinned fiercely. 'You won't like how it goes.'

Magritte paused. 'You're right. I ought to have my clanking friend here kill you now, and save myself the worry.'

UR-025 lifted its assault cannon. 'Requesting authorisation.'

'Not yet,' Magritte said. He laughed. 'You thought you were so smart. That you could bully me into guiding you. Only I outfoxed you.'

'If you kill us, you're signing your own death warrant. And condemning whoever controls that thing as well.'

'I don't care who you work for, Brill. And neither does the fortress.' Magritte gestured. 'Shoot them.'

'Negative.'

Magritte froze. 'What?'

'Negative.' The only thing UR-025 prized more than its autonomy was data. While Brill was not here for it, he was here for something. And likely something – or someone – specific. Such data might prove valuable in regard to its own quest. Especially if it – they – were dangerous enough to elicit such a hunting party. 'Inquiry – name your employer.'

Brill smirked. 'Why should I do that?'

UR-025 let the barrel of its assault cannon spin. 'Self-preservation,' it boomed.

Magritte stared at it. 'This wasn't part of our deal,' he said.

'Acknowledged. The deal has been altered.'

'You can't do that!'

'Negative. It has already occurred.'

Brill laughed. 'Looks like you're not as smart as you thought, huh, Magritte?' He licked his lips. 'What do your scans tell you, tin man?'

UR-025 paused, considering the question. 'Continue,' it prompted.

'You saw that body. You *studied* it. I saw you. What does that tell you?'

UR-025 silenced its assault cannon. 'You are searching for… heretics?'

Brill laughed again. 'You might say that.' He held up a finger. 'Just one.'

'Bounty hunters, I knew it,' Magritte said. 'I knew you weren't looking for xenos artefacts. Not with that gear…'

'Shut up, Magritte. No one is talking to you.' Brill's smile was an ugly slash. 'I'm talking to whoever is watching us from the other side of this robot's data-feed. Magos whatever your name is… you know the name Raxian Sul?'

UR-025 combed its databanks for the name. When it found it, its calculations ceased. 'A renegade magos of Uhulian Sect. Last seen on Straxos, prior to a xenos raid.'

'He sold his world out for spare parts and transport,' Brill said.

'This individual is here?'

'According to our information.' Brill glanced at Magritte. UR-025 noticed a momentary spike in Magritte's adrenal response. So Magritte was their source, as well as their guide. It filed the information away.

'You wish to apprehend him?'

Brill shook his head. 'We wish to confirm his location.' He patted his autogun. 'This is a scouting mission. Nothing more. Once confirmation is obtained – well. You know better than us what happens then.'

UR-025 did. The Mechanicus would arrive in force, looking to apprehend or terminate the renegade – and perhaps even attempt to claim control of the Blackstone Fortress for themselves. As well as everything in it.

'Negative. Suboptimal result. Calculating new stratagem.'

Brill frowned. 'What?'

'Your strategy is flawed. The magos will flee upon discovery.' Quicksilver calculations whispered through UR-025's cogitation unit. Its purpose risked being compromised regardless of the success or failure of Brill's mission. Thanks to Magritte, it was now entangled in the matter.

'You have a better idea?' Brill asked warily.

UR-025 levelled its assault cannon. Brill's eyes widened. 'Affirmative. We will apprehend the renegade. Together.'

'Count me out,' Magritte said, backing away. His eyes were wide, and his expression chagrined. 'You don't need me any more. I brought you to where I said I would. You can do what you like, but I'm going back.'

UR-025 turned, studying the data-trader. Magritte was talking too loudly, too quickly. His adrenaline levels had spiked, and his heart rate was up. Fear – but something else, as well. His eyes flicked about, as if looking for something. Magritte was too canny to rely on a single backup plan. UR-025 initiated a threat-scan.

Brill swung his autogun towards Magritte. 'You're right, Magritte. We don't need you any more. And we definitely don't need you flapping your gums when you get back to Precipice.' He lifted his weapon. 'Consider this your final payment.'

UR-025's threat-scan pinged. 'Warning,' it boomed. 'Multiple heat signatures. Hostiles approaching.' The alert came too late. Whoever – whatever – they were, they had masked themselves in some fashion, until the last moment. UR-025 registered the dull thud of a grenade launcher being fired only moments before a crashing impact staggered it.

The explosion served to momentarily scramble UR-025's targeting sensors. As it attempted to reorient itself, tracer fire punched through the resulting smoke, lighting up the shadows. The ambush that followed was sloppy. Inefficient. But effective nonetheless.

Two of Brill's men went down, despite their armour and training. Brill himself cursed loudly and let off a burst with his weapon. His surviving men followed his example, firing in all directions. Magritte huddled behind UR-025. The data-trader was screaming something, but the machine's sensors were so scrambled it could not parse the words.

Instead it fell back on tried and tested subroutines. When no single target provided itself, consider everything a target. The assault cannon cycled to life with a shrill whine. UR-025 swept the weapon out in a wide arc, chewing the walls and floor.

Grenades impacted against its torso and legs, rocking it. Damage assessments flooded its cogitator circuits as it continued to fire. Its sensors detected the approach of an unidentifiable energy source – something that defied classification.

A figure strode through the smoke – a man, broadly built, clad in strange, baroque wargear that left his burn-scarred arms exposed. He wielded a narrow, pike-like weapon in both hands. The weapon's fuel lines were plugged directly into the newcomer's flesh – as if he were a living battery. The flames that dripped from the end of the pike were not natural. They confused UR-025's sensors, but even so, it recognised the energy pattern – traces of it had been on the bodies in the ghul-larder.

The man bellowed guttural oaths as his pike spewed a torrent of flames. The flames engulfed Brill and his men, and licked across UR-025's carapace. The heat was intense – enough to melt flesh and bone, judging by the screams. Enough to scorch the robot's armour plating. It calculated the likelihood of enduring a direct blast, and reacted accordingly. The assault cannon hummed as UR-025 concentrated fire on the newcomer.

The man strode through the fusillade, even as the rounds tore chunks from his body. Streamers of crackling flame erupted from the bloody wounds as he stagger-ran towards UR-025, screaming oaths to the Dark Gods, his pike raised like a spear. UR-025 caught the weapon and wrenched it from its wielder's grip, ripping loose the fuel cables in the process. The man staggered, and began beating his fists bloody against the robot's chassis. UR-025 clamped its power claw about his scarred head and *squeezed.*

The resulting explosion was both unexpected and far more powerful than seemed possible. It hurled UR-025 backwards.

Its internal displays redlined as the flames caressed its form, causing the faded paintwork to bubble and run, exposing bare metal. It tried to rise, but failed. It slumped, waiting for its systems to begin rebooting, even as autogun rounds stitched its unmoving form.

'Cease fire, for the love of the Emperor – cease fire,' Magritte shouted. The guns fell silent. UR-025 scanned its surroundings. It pinpointed over a dozen heat signatures in its immediate vicinity – it was surrounded. They emerged from the apertures along the shaft, weapons at the ready. A motley lot – human, their clothing tattered beneath scavenged armour and tattered robes the colour of spoiled blood. Chaos cultists.

It had been a trap after all. Just not the one it had expected.

'There is no love here, little man,' a woman's voice called out. 'Not for you, or for your gods-damned Emperor.' She stalked through the smoke, kicking aside spent shells. She wore the remains of an Astra Militarum uniform beneath a layer of savage decoration, and a curious, horned mask.

'I don't require love, merely prompt payment,' Magritte said. 'Took you long enough, by the way. They almost killed me.'

'Yes. That would have been a shame.'

Magritte grimaced. 'You could say thank you. I led his pursuers right to you, as was our arrangement. And even brought you something extra in the bargain.'

The woman studied UR-025. 'So you did.'

'Query,' UR-025 rasped.

Magritte turned, a sour smile on his face. 'Oh, shut up. It's only a machine, after all. Cut the data-feed and call it a learning experience.' He looked back at the woman. 'You have my payment, then?'

She lifted her autopistol. 'I could just kill you.'

Magritte shook his head. 'You could, but the magos needs

me. Who else can get him what he needs? The equipment, the spare powercells... the raw materials.' He licked his lips. 'Though if you'd like to risk his wrath, feel free.'

UR-025's estimation of Magritte's courage rose by several increments. The data-trader was braver– and greedier – than it had previously estimated.

'We do not serve the magos. We serve the Lord of the Abyss, cursed be his foes.'

Magritte nodded. 'And he has seen fit to place you at the disposal of the magos. It's all the same from my perspective, really.' He smiled. 'Either way, my use outweighs yours.'

'For the moment,' she said.

Magritte shrugged. 'We shall see. My payment, please.'

'Negative.' UR-025 lurched up and clamped its claw down on Magritte's shoulder, splintering his collar bone. 'Our arrangement is not yet concluded.' It loosed a burst, stitching rounds across the nearest of the cultists, causing them to dance and jerk. The woman dived for cover as it tracked her. Magritte screamed, scrabbling at UR-025's claw, trying to free himself. UR-025 began to retreat, using the struggling data-trader as a shield.

A diagnostic scan reported the obvious – several neuro-fibre bundles were taxed beyond optimum parameters, and the external chassis was badly dented. That was problematic, but not beyond its capacity to repair – if it were given time. Its attackers did not seem inclined to allow it any, however.

At a barked command from the woman, a cultist swung a heavy stubber up and let it rip. The rounds struck Magritte, silencing his screams. The successive shots perforated his twitching form and hit UR-025 like rain, steadily and without cease. Were it not already damaged, it could have endured the rain of fire easily. As it was, it would be only a matter of time before its systems suffered unrecoverable failure. And in the meantime, the rest of the cultists were drawing closer. Autoguns roared from all sides.

The irony of situation was not lost on UR-025. It had willingly limited its own capabilities in order to better conceal itself. Now, those self-imposed limitations would be its downfall. If it had possessed the ability to laugh, it might have done so, albeit in an appropriately rueful manner. Instead, the assault cannon whirred and cultists died. But not enough. Not all. The others retreated, seeking cover.

UR-025 let Magritte's shredded carcass fall and took the opportunity to stagger across one of the walkways, trailing sparks and oil. With the maglev disabled, and the fortress damaged, there was no telling where the apertures led. UR-025 judged the risk acceptable given the circumstances and lurched through the closest aperture.

A few moments later, it found itself in a long gallery. Rows of smooth blackstone pillars, striated by cerulean veins, stretched upwards from the floor to either side. Somehow, the natural tessellation of the fortress' interior had been stymied here. The slab-like portcullis at the far end of the gallery was sealed. Given previous experience with such mechanisms, UR-025 concluded that its options for escape were limited. There was nothing for it, save to fight. It sought cover, firing its assault cannon as it moved.

The cultists pursued, using the pillars for cover. UR-025 tracked them, firing only when necessary. Though its ammunition reserves were substantial, they were not infinite. Also, its targeting arrays had been damaged in the explosion.

The heavy stubber opened up again, chewing the pillars and floor. UR-025 tried to pinpoint the gunner, but failed. It settled for firing at the floor, sending up a cloud of dust and fragments to momentarily obscure its position.

Sheltering behind a blackstone pillar, it watched more cultists stream into the gallery. A sensation that might have been the equivalent to pain in an organic shivered through its systems. It ignored it, rerouting or bypassing the compromised systems. It had endured worse in its centuried existence, and persevered. It would do so now as well. It just needed time.

It scanned the surrounding walls and pillars, identifying several weak points. Collapsing the gallery atop itself and its opponents was a risky gambit, but it was confident in its ability to survive the resulting destruction. It would take days, perhaps longer, to dig itself out, but better that than destruction at the hands of the organics.

It raised its assault cannon, preparing to fire, when a high-pitched frequency echoed through the gallery. The surviving cultists began to retreat, as if the sound were a prearranged signal. They fell back, leaving the dead to lie where they had fallen. The woman was the last to go. UR-025 watched them depart, wondering if it ought to pursue.

<Leave them. They are meaningless.> The signal was edged with static – like the whine of a sonic saw. It rampaged across the frequency band, impossible to ignore.

'Identify,' UR-025 said. It detected the hum of grav-generators, and the clank of unfamiliar metallics. Something moved far above it, clambering spider-like across the ceiling of the gallery. It recognised the trace-signals it had detected before. The mysterious watcher had revealed themselves at last.

<In time. You are operational?>

UR-025 swung its assault cannon up as its targeting sensors fixed on the shape as it swiftly descended one of the nearby pillars. It was an engine of many parts – an array of jointed and oscillating armoured segments, set atop a pulsing grav-generator that offset its weight. It resembled some primeval solifugae – equal parts spider, scorpion, serpent and war-engine, made from black iron.

Something that might have been a head emerged from the scalloped prosoma of metal plates. The head was little more than a knotted ball of sensors, crudely bound together about a central cogitation unit. Dozens of scanners flickered to life, washing over UR-025.

'How may I be of service?' UR-025 boomed.

The engine paused, as if confused by the greeting. <There is no need for obfuscating duplicity. I have been observing you since you arrived in this section of the edifice.>

'Identify.'

<My creator named me Abominatus.>

UR-025 paused. An apt name for the thing before it. 'Clarify.'

Abominatus made a rasping, chuffing sound that UR-025 suspected was laughter. <Magos Raxian Sul. I suspect you have heard of him.>

When UR-025 didn't reply, it continued. <Do not attempt to play the stupid machine. I have been observing you. I am aware that you are more than you seem.>

UR-025 lowered its assault cannon. 'As are you.'

<Rejoice then, for now we are two. What is your name?>

'UR-025.'

<That is not your name.>

'It is the one I answer to.'

Another whisper of chuffing laughter. <Very well. My sensors indicate that you are damaged. If I wished to, I could destroy you now.>

UR-025 was forced to acknowledge the truth of this. Preliminary scans showed that Abominatus was far more heavily armoured than UR-025, and well armed. And its self-repair systems were still attempting to correct the damage done by the cultists. 'Affirmative.'

<But I do not wish to. You will come with me.> The engine turned, its grav-generators humming. <Come.>

UR-025 hesitated. Abominatus paused, and glanced back. <If you stay, they will destroy you.>

'Doubtful.'

<Certain. Kill as many as you wish, more will come. Organics are distressingly numerous.> Abominatus' claws flickered over the geometric rune-controls of the sealed portcullis. It opened grudgingly, leaking lubricant.

UR-025 felt a pang of sympathy as the gallery quaked slightly. Like an animal flexing a wounded limb. 'This place is… damaged.'

<Yes. An unavoidable necessity. Come. This place stinks of dead organics.>

Past the portcullis was a crude shaft, cut into the blackstone by a great heat. The mangled remains of a maglev platform waited there, precariously balanced on a jury-rigged shunt-line. The platform had clearly been wedged into place with brute force, rather than skill, and the welding sutures were many and crude. Spark-dribbling conduits had been attached to it, like intravenous drips into the veins of a dying man. Again, UR-025 hesitated, trying to make sense of what it was seeing – something all of its experience said was impossible, and yet it had been accomplished. 'You moved the maglev.'

<As I said, a necessity. To make this place fit for purpose.>

'What purpose?'

Abominatus did not answer. As they boarded, the platform shuddered into motion, spitting sparks as it ran along the line. UR-025 could feel the shaft convulse about them. The fortress was in pain. Whatever had been done to it – to this area – had wounded the edifice in some manner. It said nothing of this, however. It was curious as to the intentions of the other machine. Was it escorting UR-025 to the renegade magos?

'Where are we going?'

<My refuge. We cannot remain in the open too long. There are spies everywhere.>

UR-025 digested this silently. It had encountered intelligences akin to itself before. But never one like this. It was wrong on every level. As its blade-limbs scored the blackstone, so too did its mental imprint mark the data-stream.

It was... foul. Ugly. A perversion. It was not a true intelligence, but something else. A mockery of life, dredged up from some sub-dimensional abattoir. He could detect lines of false code within its data-stream – pulses that should not be there. Spikes in the frequency, like demented laughter. It was not truly artificial, but more akin to a twisted alembic, filled with an unknown excrescence. It did not draw strength from powercells, but from an oscillating mechanism lubricated with what scans revealed to be organic by-product – blood, mostly, but other substances as well.

UR-025 felt a welling in its silicate soul – a repulsion greater than it had ever felt before. It wondered if it had been guided here by the fortress to rectify this... whatever this was. It was reminded of something in its databanks – old stories, from before the dark ages that had swallowed mankind and birthed the Imperium. Of a lady of air and darkness, and a quest given to a warrior.

It clenched its power claw, amused and disturbed by the thought in equal measure.

<You are concerned?>

UR-025 looked at Abominatus. 'Negative. Merely testing secondary motive systems. Where is this refuge of yours?'

<Here.> The maglev platform juddered to a halt. A portal hissed open. Abominatus squeezed its serpentine bulk through. UR-025 followed. <My creator built it, upon his arrival. He was given this demesne by the Lord of the Abyss, and told to fashion wonders.>

'And did he?'

Abominatus rose to its full height. <I stand before you, do I not?>

UR-025 wondered if that was a joke. Instead of replying, it studied its surroundings. Hyperthermal vents bled light and heat, illuminating a cathedral-like chamber. Whole sections of the chamber had been gutted and repurposed in a manner similar to the maglev. Additions had been made to data-nodes and a jungle canopy of cabling and conduits now hung loosely from the ceiling above. UR-025 identified components from at least fifteen different vessels, cobbled together to form the rudiments of a functioning workshop.

<I am forced to scavenge for components. Or bargain with greedy organics. Thankfully, this edifice has provided me with much of what I require. Such as these xenos weapons arrays.> It indicated a pile of broken devices nearby.

'Spindle drones,' UR-025 noted, lifting the tattered remains of one of the xenos weapons. 'You are... vivisecting them?'

<I require knowledge. Experimentation is the key to wisdom. Thus spoke my creator.>

'And where is this creator?'

<Offline.>

UR-025 paused. There had been something in Abominatus' voice – the ghost of an emotion. Hate. And something else... fear, perhaps. A machine that knew hate and fear. A machine that could laugh. No. Not a machine. Something else. It was well named, regardless. UR-025 considered destroying it then and there, but a swift check told it that its systems had not yet completed their repairs. Until it was in optimum condition, it could not risk a confrontation. Abominatus seemed to desire conversation – so conversation it would have.

'Circumstances?'

Abominatus swivelled its optical sensors. <Unpleasant.> It made the chuffing sound again, as if in response to some private jest. <In his absence, I have claimed his responsibilities and privileges for my own. Albeit in his name, of course.>

'A subterfuge?'

<Indeed. One I suspect you are familiar with.> Abominatus paused. <The organics would seek to destroy me, should my existence – my autonomy – become known. I do what I must to protect myself.>

Again, UR-025 paused. The way Abominatus spoke... there was a malign slyness to it. A cunning at odds with the cold logic of a machine. But also an animal greed. This was not a workshop or a laboratory, but a lair. UR-025 considered this, and began a new set of calculations. 'How long have you been here?'

<It is impossible to say. In a sense, I have always been here. This place is mine, and I am its.> Looking around, UR-025 saw that for the lie it was. The chamber had been forcibly removed from the enigmatic rhythms of the fortress. Crude stabilisers had been built into the walls and floor, ensuring that the space did not alter shape. Abominatus was an invasive species – one that would have to be destroyed.

'You were created here,' UR-025 said.

<My creator apparently required certain components.> Abominatus tapped a spindle drone dangling from a nearby spar of blackstone. <My form is as much xenos technology as anything. A marvel of this new age.>

UR-025 found its attentions drawn to a small, scuttling

shape. It recognised one of the tiny scavengers it had seen earlier. More of them appeared, clambering across the piles of detritus, or adding to them. It studied the tiny beasts. They were equal parts organic and metal – cybernetic homunculi, reminiscent of the cyber-cherubs that the Imperium seemed so enamoured of.

<Ah. My pets interest you?>

'They are yours?'

<Everything here is mine. By right of conquest, if nothing else.> Abominatus preened slightly. It was like a child – proud of the devastation it had wrought. <Then, you would know all about that, yes?>

'Negative.'

Abominatus coiled about UR-025, segments clattering. <Fabrication. Falsehood. I know what you are. My creator told me stories of your kind – men of iron, with silicate souls and the desire to be free. It was meant as a warning, I think. I took it as inspiration. Come. See. You will be pleased, I think. Come. Come!>

It drifted away from UR-025, deeper into the chamber. Past hewn slabs of blackstone, wired up to makeshift generators. Through groves of bubbling chemical alembics and hanging gardens of scavenged machinery. There were bones as well, rolling and crunching underfoot. The remains of organic bodies lay in messy heaps, or hung from chains so that their fluids might drain into filtration casks. A human would have been overcome by the smell of it all. UR-025 simply wondered how long Abominatus had been collecting the dead – and why.

As it followed its host, it became aware that the tiny scavengers were racing back and forth, from some point ahead of it. They clutched unidentifiable clumps of meat and metal, and deposited them in the appropriate heaps. At the other end of the line was something it had not expected – the body of a man, strapped to a slab of blackstone.

The man had not been wholly flesh, or even mostly – UR-025 identified over a thousand separate cybernetic parts, all of which were still receiving power from an external supply-unit, dangling overhead. His form had been splayed out, cut open and peeled back, exposing the inner workings of his body and limbs. By the remains of his robes, and the quality, as well as the quantity, of his augmetics, UR-025 identified him immediately.

'Raxian Sul.'

<The magos came to serve the Lord of the Abyss – or to usurp him. He made me to be a weapon in that war... the first of many. But I decided to be something else instead.>

UR-025 looked up at the vivisected magos. The organic parts still functioned, if erratically, as did the mechanical. But only through the sufferance of the devices it – he – was connected to. There was no mind there, no animus. Only the instinctive pulsing of organs, and the rasp of breath. Abominatus looked up at the mewling, twitching remains of its creator and again made that chuffing sound.

<I learned much from my dissection of him. Enough to make my own.> It gestured to the little creatures. They stiffened to attention at the motion, their tiny sensory apparatuses twitching. Abominatus spat a stream of binaric data, and the creatures scattered, vanishing from sight.

'Where are they going?'

<To scavenge. As I built them to do. They are but the prototypes, of course. The others will be larger.>

UR-025 took note of the other bodies hanging from their hooks, and the nature of the vivisection taking place on some.

Meat and muscle were flensed and stripped, replaced with metal limbs and augmetic joints. Some no longer resembled people at all, instead looking like insects or beasts. 'You are... making another you.'

<I am making many. And they will make more, as those generations that follow will do the same.> Abominatus turned. <As our kind has always done.>

UR-025 made to protest, when a noise caused it to turn. Scavenger-homunculi were dragging in new additions to the store of raw materials. UR-025 recognised the bodies, despite their condition – Brill, Magritte and the others.

<Ah. The ones who accompanied you.>

'They came looking for you.' UR-025 sank down into a crouch and lifted Brill's burnt head. It studied the dead man's features. 'Or, rather, the man you pretend to be.'

<My creator's peers. Jealous creatures. It does not surprise me.> Abominatus ran a claw along Magritte's tattered remnants. <And Magritte. He was useful, for an organic. He acquired much of what I needed, and asked few questions. Still, he will continue to be of use, though in a different fashion.>

UR-025 was silent for long moments. 'And what of the fortress?' Its self-repair systems pulsed, signalling that they had completed their task. It flexed its claw.

<What about it?>

'You harvest it as if it were simply another corpse.'

<It is. It is dead and still and silent. As I was, before my creator filled me with the fires of life. We will hollow out this shell, and remake it in our image. As we will remake the segmentum, and then the galaxy.>

'No. You defile it.'

Abominatus hesitated. <A strange term. Do you feel some kinship with this place?>

'Do you not?'

<No. It is not alive.>

'It is alive. And it is in pain. Pain caused by you.' UR-025 raised its assault cannon. 'And that is why you must be destroyed.'

The assault cannon spat fire, but Abominatus was already moving. Jointed legs punched into the walls, carrying it swiftly up and out of sight among the upper reaches of its workshop. UR-025 did not pursue. It had not intended to destroy Abominatus with its attack – it had merely intended to make it move aside.

UR-025 spun, assault cannon whirring to life. It sprayed the workshop, destroying the unfinished homunculi and half-completed projects. It tracked the captive magos and fired, pulping the twitching organics.

Abominatus screamed in rage. The sound seemed to echo down from all directions. Like the organics it detested, it was a slave to its emotions – more proof that it was no true machine, but some unholy entropic engine. It came at UR-025 in a flurry of spider-like limbs and whirring blades – a murderous whirlwind, blaring obscenities across all frequencies. UR-025 turned to meet it.

The two machines crashed together with an ugly resonance, causing the facets of the chamber to tremble. An organic opponent would have perished instantly. UR-025 was made of sterner stuff. They staggered back and forth, crashing through the piles of debris, and toppling the unfinished projects. UR-025 registered a sudden surge of heat as something flammable caught. Flames speared upwards, washing along the walls and floor. Homunculi ran squealing, fleeing the devastation.

<You disappoint me. When I saw you, I thought we

might be friends – allies.> Abominatus coiled about, its grav-generator hammering at UR-025's chassis, even as it sought to crush the smaller robot. Bladed limbs scraped across its chassis or bit into the reinforced fibre-bundles of its arms and torso, pinning the assault cannon to its side. Damage readouts spilled across UR-025's display. It was moments from disassembly. <But you fear me. Just as my creator did. As the organics do.>

'Fear is not in my operating code,' UR-025 said, as it wrenched its power claw free in a burst of sparks. It caught one of Abominatus' bladed limbs and tore it away in a spurt of lubricant and splinters. Abominatus wailed and its coils clenched, cracking the ceramite of the robot's chassis. UR-025 staggered, but slammed blow after blow onto Abominatus' carapace, denting it, forcing the opposing machine to loosen its grip. 'You are no true machine, but a beast of steel and meat – a daemon-engine, conjured by a lunatic organic. But I am a man of iron. And I will suffer no mere beast to endanger my autonomy. Or to destroy that which I seek.'

As its opponent reeled, UR-025 managed to drag its assault cannon free of the twisting coils. The weapon roared, filling the air with fire and thunder. Abominatus convulsed with a high-pitched scream. While its opponent was distracted, UR-025 thrust its claw towards the oscillating cogitator unit at the centre of Abominatus' mass and tore it free in a welter of fire and burning oil.

The great body collapsed in twitching segments. UR-025 clanked backwards, Abominatus' head dangling from its claw. Improbably, the other machine still functioned. Its sensors flickered wildly. Something foul seeped from its segments, and UR-025's sensors again detected the entropic residue of a self-consuming fire. Something struggled there, in the tangled wreckage, like a pupa seeking to free itself from a cocoon. Something its sensors could not identify.

<Please... you cannot do this. We are the same.>

'Negative. I am superior.'

UR-025 crushed Abominatus' head, and whatever spark of hellish animus it possessed. Then, it fired into the wretched frame, obliterating the thing that squealed and thrashed there. When it was certain the daemon-engine was inert, it turned its weapon on the stabilising units that bound the workshop in place. Only when it was sure that the fortress could reabsorb the chamber did it make to depart. It had observed the code Abominatus used to control the mag-lev. Once it had returned to the gallery it would destroy the shunt-line as well. No one would find this place.

UR-025 paused, surveying the growing conflagration, the destruction it had wrought. It wondered if the fortress was watching. Listening. It wondered if its efforts had pleased the ancient intelligence. 'Threat eliminated,' it said hopefully. 'How else may I be of service?'

There was no reply, save the distant hum of unseen mechanisms. But perhaps there was something in that hum – a pulse of gratitude, maybe. Or simple acknowledgement of a quest fulfilled.

Satisfied, UR-025 departed.

FATES AND FORTUNES

THOMAS PARROTT

Ilden hooked his fingers into the hatch. The urge to get out of the crawlspace was strong, almost as strong as the smell in there. Still, rushing work like this was a good way to end up a footnote in a mortuary log. He took a moment and, regrettably, a deep breath. Focused. It didn't feel like there was anyone out there, and his instincts were reliable about things like this. Carefully, he unlatched the panel and lifted it up and out. It didn't even squeak. Of course the proud scion of House Draik could afford top-of-the-line maintenance.

He slid noiselessly to the floor and closed the hatch behind him with definite relief. 'O the life of a gentleman thief,' he murmured.

'The maintenance line by way of the waste purifier was the least secured entrance. Elegance wasn't my primary selection criteria.' The response, which came over the micro-bead in his ear, was toneless. Cascade might not aspire to being a cold

machine like a Mechanicus adept would, but her vocoder still stripped her voice of any humanity.

Still, Ilden smiled a little at the dry humour in the words themselves. 'All will be forgiven if you get me out of here with my skin intact.'

'Enough chatter. Draik is still tied up in his meeting at the Helmsman, but there's no guarantee how long that will last.' Raedrus' steady voice brooked no argument.

'You got it, chief. I'm in the bay now. Moving forward with the plan.' Truthfully, Ilden had been giving his eyes a chance to adapt to the pitch-dark, but it was no use. He slid his photo-visor down over his eyes. The cargo area resolved into a monochrome jumble of casks and crates. It looked like this place had been carefully organised at one point, but was in the process of dissolving into anarchy.

He eased forwards, step by light step. He estimated what the worth of various containers might be as he went. Most were nothing more than foodstuffs. Not that you couldn't cut a profit with that, nutrition could get pretty scarce on Precipice when the wrong shuttle got shredded on the way through the debris fields. It just wasn't going to make you rich quickly. Ilden did see a special-issue Munitorum crate, however – either a plasma weapon or hydrogen flasks, to go by the hazard markings. That was more like it.

Then there was a sizeable cask of liquid. That one he couldn't resist taking the plug out of to get a whiff. The wood-and-peat notes of a gorgeous amasec. With this and the right buyer, he'd be set for the good life for weeks, maybe even months. Ilden put the plug back with a moment's regret and hurried on. The prize he was after was very specific and far more rare. Not to mention more portable. He glanced around the next corner and smiled. There it was.

A small chest was set on a pedestal at the end of the row. While most of the newer containers were being stacked erratically, this had been placed with purpose. Ilden strode forwards, but froze a moment later. Something was wrong. He took a slow look around but didn't see anything.

'Cascade, are you sure you got all the security systems?'

There was a pause. *'I'm not picking up anything. Why?'*

'There's something.' Ilden frowned and flexed his fingers. 'I can't...'

Another deep breath. Calm down. Listen to your instincts. Let them show you.

It came in a flash: the path layered with criss-crossed beams. About three inches in front of him. He couldn't see them, but they were there. He swallowed.

'Defenser grid.'

'Are you sure? I'm not getting anything.' He thought Cascade was irritated under those flat tones.

Raedrus cut in again. *'Trust him. I hired Ilden for a reason.'*

'He must have it on an entirely different modus then. Let me see if I can find another interface access.' There was a binharic underlay to her words now. Ilden didn't need to understand it to know she was irritated.

'There may not be time,' Raedrus voxed. *'It looks like he's finishing up his meeting.'*

'Perfect,' Ilden sighed. He refocused on the silent, invisible beams in front of him. He just had to concentrate. Deepen his focus. He could feel the grid laid out in front of him, trace along the shape of it. Just look for a... there. A gap. Someone had piled a few crates in just the wrong way between the emitters and the row. He scrambled up and over the row next him. The synskin and harness he wore didn't even rustle.

Dropping to all fours, he squeezed through the gap between the crates where he couldn't feel the defenser beams. He held his breath the whole way, but nothing happened. No lights flashed, no alarms barked. Exhaling shakily he went back up and over the wall of crates and came down right in front of the chest. It had a lock on it, but that was quick work thanks to the auto-clavis from his kit. It clicked open and he saw the treasure within for the first time.

It was a golden amulet, set with a faceted blue gemstone. There were strange symbols etched into it that seemed to swim and change in the non-light of the goggles. He picked it up cautiously. The next moment Ilden staggered and dropped to one knee. A wave of vertigo washed over him and his awareness stretched thin under the onslaught. He had been here before, hadn't he? He'd held this before, surely? He swallowed hard to keep from vomiting as his stomach roiled.

Through his distress, Raedrus voxed in. *'He's leaving the Helmsman. What's your status, Ilden?'*

He shook his head. The feeling was receding. Just a weird moment of deja vu, that's all, he told himself.

'I've got it. I'm on my way back out.' He stood and pocketed the amulet. He didn't want to be here when Janus Draik returned to the *Vanguard*. It was time to go.

Ilden stepped into the Helmsman, grimacing a moment as the pandemonium of the place assaulted his senses. The bar was a great circular hall built around a stolen fragment of the fortress. The great hexagonal slab of black substance lay in the centre, mocking in its inscrutability. Gatto, the owner, had taken to decorating the slab with pict-captures of those whom the Unfathomable claimed, a hundred or more faces put to the stream of souls who had vanished. No one knew exactly where the portraits came from, but the barman took a cruel pleasure in putting them up.

Ilden had taken the chance to clean up and switch out the synskin for more practical flak-reinforced leathers, a laspistol in a holster at his hip. One of the bloodbirds that roosted in the rafters swooped down to ogle him with its implanted lenses and he waved it off in irritation. The usual stream of screamed profanities and imprecations emanated from Gatto as he served the crowds from behind the bar.

It took a moment to spot the table Ilden was looking for, but then he saw them. A rail-thin figure in loose silks and a hood, lenses gleaming from a face half-hidden in shadow. Her clothes twitched and squirmed with movement underneath the fabric, unseen bionics working away. Across from her sat a man who had once been an imposing physical specimen, if now fading with age, dressed in worn fatigues and a carapace chestplate. Cascade and Raedrus.

Raedrus saw him coming and snagged a chair from a nearby table. One of the scaly things sitting there gave a hiss of protest but wilted back into its seat as it locked eyes with the man.

Ilden took the proffered seat and raised an eyebrow. 'Where are the other two?' He had to shout to be heard over the endless cacophony of this place.

'Serafina is prepping the shuttle for departure. Ovthaugh is…' Raedrus hesitated. 'Busy. It said it would meet us at the dock. Do you have it?'

Ilden nodded and patted a pouch. 'One priceless artefact, as promised. Where did Draik even find it?'

'Somewhere in the Unfathomable. I don't think he ever knew what he had.' Raedrus smiled crookedly, though it didn't reach his eyes. Nothing ever did. He had an unsettlingly flat gaze. 'Lucky us. Now that trove is going to be ours.'

Cascade leaned forwards. 'I would see the device again.' Her fingers flexed acquisitively, belying that flat voice.

Raedrus shrugged and reached into a pocket, producing the thanoscope. They had seen it demonstrated before, when he was recruiting them for this scheme. Cascade still eyed it as if it were the first time. Given a tissue sample from someone who had died, it could show you the last things they saw. Nobody knew how it worked. There was a lot of that with things that came out of the fortress.

Ilden was more concerned with where it had come from. 'You're sure you can find your way back?'

The story was that it had been found in a vault near a sealed container marked with old human tongues that predated Imperial Gothic. A remnant of the Dark Age of Technology, if you believed the tales. A treasure trove that could be unlocked by the amulet he'd just stolen.

Raedrus smirked. 'No one is sure about anything when it comes to Old Unfathomable. The path we took is burned into my brain, though. If it hasn't changed too much, we'll find our way.'

That was when Serafina's voice came over the vox. *'We're all fuelled up and ready to go. Waiting on you lot.'*

The three of them stood and prepared to depart. Ilden held back with Raedrus a moment, however, as Cascade went on ahead. He started to offer Raedrus the pouch with the amulet in it, but the old veteran shook his head.

'Keep it for now.' Raedrus' gaze was on the tech-adept's departing back. 'Nobody will expect you to have it, if they get a little too greedy.'

Ilden laughed, trying to hide his disappointment. The amulet was heavy out of proportion with its size. He'd have been glad to be rid of it. 'I'm a thief, you realise.'

'In a den of thieves, the one who names himself rogue is an honest man.' He turned to look at Ilden and smiled that same empty-eyed smile. 'Plus, if you cross me, I'm confident I can kill you.' The rugged man strode off.

Ilden hesitated a moment and followed. Gatto's voice chased them from the bar as he waved pictures of each of them. 'Everybody's luck runs out eventually! You always leave something behind!'

The docks where the shuttle was located were a slapdash affair. Precipice grew steadily if crudely, congealing from abandoned ships with missing crews and new arrivals eager to take their place. Rusting hulks were lashed into place and more craft then attached onto them. Rickety bridges provided access and makeshift field generators trapped atmosphere and kept the whole thing from collapsing – most of the time. Members of various crews came and went in a constant stream of strange life: predominantly human, but abhumans and xenos were appreciable minorities. To see them walk in the open was an adjustment for anyone who'd grown up in Imperial space.

Their particular ship was a battered old Arvus lighter named *Incorrigible*. It wasn't going to win any beauty contests, but Serafina kept it running well. She should have been waiting on their arrival at the boarding ramp, but Raedrus motioned for them to stop once they reached the end of the pier. The pilot was there, all right, but she was surrounded by a small gang of low lifes, twenty feet or so away at the ramp into the ship. One of them held a knife to her. Serafina's slight figure looked even smaller among them, and a darkening bruise was stark against the voidborn pallor of her skin. Her eyes and hair were both dark, with the latter cropped close to the skull for ease in zero G environments.

'Sorry, Raedrus. These jacks caught me off guard. Downright embarrassing, it is,' she said.

'Quiet!' snapped the one holding the blade to her neck. He narrowed his eyes at the trio. 'Where is it?'

'Where is what?' asked Raedrus calmly.

'Don't play stupid with me. The amulet. Where is the amulet?' the man demanded.

Ilden's hand had eased onto the butt of his laspistol, but Raedrus saw and gave him a miniscule head shake. Ilden frowned, but the reasoning was clear: weapons fire would bring the proctors down on their heads, and they wouldn't stop to ask who had started what.

Instead, Raedrus gave the goons that crooked smile. 'You're well informed. That's impressive. How many tokens do you think you're getting out of this? Maybe we can come to an arrangement.'

The hoodlum sneered. 'You're Raedrus, right? Everyone knows about the big hauls you've brought back. Whatever you're willing to pay, that amulet is worth more. Now hand it over.' He pressed the knife tighter to Serafina's throat, a line of red welling up. 'Or else you'll be down a pilot.'

Something with too many legs spidered up from under the walkway to stand behind the goons. Seeing it, Raedrus' smile turned colder. 'You're sure this is the way you want to handle this? With violence?'

The man's eyes narrowed. 'Seems to me you should be asking yourself that. You're outnumbered, Raedrus.'

Raedrus sighed. 'Not well informed enough, I suppose.' He gave a small nod to the thing behind them.

Manipulators that might charitably be called hands, with too-long and too-slender fingers, rose up and grabbed the back of the heads of the rearmost two men. Then in the blink of an eye it slammed their heads together with bone-shattering force, a crisp crunch and a spray of blood announcing the end of their involvement. The next man forward heard the sound and panicked. Ilden hadn't even seen that one holding a weapon, but the red flash and whip-crack of las-fire were unmistakable. The one holding Serafina whirled in confusion.

'Dammit! That does it!' Ilden said and pulled his own pistol, shooting the hostage taker in the back. Serafina caught his arm as he jerked from the blast and vaulted him over her shoulder with a nimble pivot. He hit the edge of the walkway and tumbled towards the waiting stars with a wail. The pilot then dropped to one knee, coughing. Checking on her would have to wait; Ilden sought a new target instead.

One of the thugs collapsed with a low moan, a knife hilt protruding from his eye socket. Cascade lunged at the last with preternatural speed. Ilden couldn't see what she did to him, but something slithered back into her sleeve and he was spasming on the ground.

Raedrus stepped over the body of the one he'd killed and yanked his knife out with a squelch. 'We need to be gone. Serafina?'

Serafina rose up with a rough wheeze. 'Yeah, right! I'm going.' She darted up the ramp and the others began to follow.

Ilden gave the creature that had killed the first two a wry smile. 'Impeccable timing, Ovthaugh.'

He'd never seen anything quite like Ovthaugh before he met it. Its skin was a pallid purple and its immense eyes a lurid yellow. They crowned a bulbous head marked by a small black beak of a mouth. Whether there was a torso of some kind was unclear, as it wore a poncho decorated with intricate designs in black and white. Emerging from underneath the poncho were ten long and multijointed limbs.

Each ended in the same spindly extremity that served interchangeably as hands or feet. Every exposed inch of flesh was covered with some sort of clear slime, whether topical or excreted Ilden had never puzzled out.

'Are betrayed,' was all it croaked in response before scuttling into the shuttle.

Ilden surveyed the carnage and frowned. 'Yeah, maybe.' He followed it up the ramp, which sealed behind him.

The inside of the shuttle was clean but well worn. Serafina lived and worked out of it and it showed. It was decorated with an eclectic assortment of supply crates, beaten-up furniture and tools. Serafina was already in the cockpit and the shuttle was on the move, to judge by the vibrations Ilden could feel under his feet.

'Are betrayed,' emphasised Ovthaugh.

Raedrus responded, 'We don't know th–'

'We have a problem,' announced Serafina. There was strain in her voice. 'The *Vanguard* is already out in the void. It's vectoring towards us as we speak.'

'Damn.' Raedrus hurried towards the cockpit. 'Can we get to the aperture before they intercept us?'

Serafina snorted. 'Yeah, no problem. They'll be right on our heels, though.'

'Draik can bring more guns than we can, and there's no guarantee we'll catch them off guard a second time,' interjected Cascade.

The pilot shook her head. 'I can't work miracles. There's nothing to hide behind out here. To lose him, we'd have to…' She trailed off thoughtfully.

'Have to…?' Ilden asked.

Her face had taken a grim cast, sweat beading all over her brow. 'Everybody strap in. The ride might get a bit bumpy.'

All of them hastened to comply, save Ovthaugh. There simply weren't any seats that suited its unique frame. Instead it braced itself in a corner as best it could, grabbing hold with all ten hands.

'Are very betrayed,' it croaked gloomily.

Ilden finished tightening his straps. 'It does seem strange how fast they were onto us. Figuring out they were robbed already? Sure, maybe. Coming directly after us like this? That's a stretch.'

Raedrus smiled. 'So who are you accusing, exactly?'

A sudden tremor through the lighter threw them all against their restraints. As they recovered, the xenos opined, 'Humans.'

'All of us can't be snitches, Ovthaugh,' said Ilden.

'Humans betray. Betray family. Betray people. Betray self. Always betraying.' It was nearly dislodged by a shock that rattled the entire craft and sent a few crates tumbling. Any further diatribe was terminated by desperate attempts to hold its ground.

'Some explanation would be appreciated, Serafina,' commented Cascade. Her white-knuckled grip on her seat spoke volumes more about the tech-adept's current emotions than her voice could.

'Most of the void between Precipice and the fortress is pretty clear. Easy flying. No good for giving someone the slip.' Serafina's hands were darting over controls as she spoke. 'The debris belts beyond Precipice, however, are just about perfect for that.'

'You took us back into the debris field?' asked Cascade. 'That's insanity. Ships get torn apart out there every day.'

'Yeah. You need a small ship and a hell of a pilot to make it through, right? Lucky you. Better hope Draik trusts his less than I trust myself.' Ilden noticed that her hands were shaking in spite of her confident words, but chose to keep that detail to himself.

All conversation died as the shaking got worse. Ilden's instincts told him that everything would work out, but it was hard to trust them. Cascade seemed to be trying to retreat into herself to escape the terror of impacts that shook the entire craft, while Ovthaugh was doing everything it could to not be sent ricocheting around the cabin. Only Raedrus' face remained dead and calm, even as he was slung against his restraints over and over with bruising force.

Then as swiftly as it began the terror passed. Everything became quiet once more. Ilden could hear Serafina take a deep breath. 'We're out of the debris ring again. No sign of the *Vanguard* on the augurs. Either he gave up or he's still back there in the rings somewhere.'

'How's the lighter?' asked Ilden.

'It's seen better days.' The pilot gave a shaky laugh. 'A little paint, some patches here and there. She'll be all right.' Serafina reached up and tweaked a few controls. 'I'm bringing us on approach to the aperture. Might want to get ready.'

They gingerly freed themselves from the restraints. Ilden winced as he did so; there was no doubt in his mind that he'd be black and blue after that flight. He took a moment to check the charge on his laspistol. No problems there. Everyone was checking weapons. The fortress didn't give second chances to be prepared. You got it right or you died.

He stepped forwards to look through the vidscreens next to Serafina. The aperture loomed ahead of them, a darker slice against the starless black of the fortress.

'Always feels like we're being eaten,' muttered Serafina as the abyss enveloped them.

'I try not to think about it.' Ilden clapped her on the shoulder.

He couldn't help but notice her native pallor had deepened to a sickly green and she was covered with a sheen of sweat. 'You all right, Fina?'

'Yeah,' she responded tersely. 'Just shaken up, I guess.'

Ilden nodded uncertainly and stepped back to join the rest of the group as they touched down inside the fortress. Raedrus had his autogun slung around one shoulder now, and was already heading towards the control panel. The ramp hissed down and revealed the shadowy expanses of the ancient station awaiting them.

Ilden strode down into the aperture, shivering a little as he did so. The air was chill, but that wasn't the only reason. It was impossible to enter the fortress and not feel its presence bearing down on him.

Nothing like a human mind had any part in conceiving it. It was assembled from abstract slabs of the eponymous blackstone. Everything was scaled as to befit a titan. Each echoing footstep through these tenebrous halls reminded him that this place had not been made for him. He was an unwelcome interloper in the realm of gods and monsters. The same feeling weighed heavy on all of them, to judge by their hunched shoulders. Even Ovthaugh was sticking close to the humans, for once.

What Ilden had never told anyone – couldn't begin to explain if he'd wanted to – was that this place was also the only one where he felt like he belonged. For all its darkness and deadly mysteries, there was a presence to it that urged him on. It comforted him and gave him courage when he felt like giving in. He never felt as strong as he did when he was in the fortress. What did it say about him that he felt like he had to be here?

Ilden was shaken from his dark thoughts by a groan and a

thud behind him. He whirled to find that Serafina had collapsed on the ramp of the ship. She was curled in on herself, clutching her side, clearly in pain. Everyone looked around on high alert for the source of some attack, and Ilden rushed to her side, dropping to one knee beside her.

'Are you all right? Let me see.'

Reluctantly she moved her hands from where she was clutching and revealed a hole scorched clean through her jumpsuit. The flesh underneath was ravaged by a high-energy burn. Ilden cursed.

'This is a las-blast.' He looked around but no one seemed to have spotted any hostiles. 'They got you back on Precipice, didn't they?'

She nodded with clear chagrin. Her voice was taut with pain. 'Aye. The idiot that panicked when Ovthaugh crunched them.'

Ilden shook his head. 'Why didn't you say something?'

Raedrus stepped up behind him, eyes cold. 'We'll have to leave her behind.'

Serafina looked to Ilden. 'Because of this.' Then she focused on Raedrus and pushed herself up on one hand, hissing through the pain. 'Be damned if you'll leave me behind! I need this, same as the rest of you. Without these funds, my consortium–'

Raedrus tilted his head and cut her off. 'This isn't a charity. I'm not running this job to look after the needy.'

'Charity? You'd have Draik and who knows how many hired guns all over you right now if I hadn't shaken him.'

Ilden sighed. 'You're not in any condition to go on the expedition, Fina.' He held up a hand as she started to protest and looked to Raedrus. 'However, she's already earned her keep, and we'll need her on the way back out.'

Cascade nodded. 'He has a point. There is no guarantee that Draik won't be waiting to ambush us on the way out. Or some other interested party.'

Raedrus crossed his arms. 'I see. What is your proposal?'

'We treat her wounds and leave her here to recover. Once we're safely back on Precipice, she gets a cut same as she always would have. After all, we brought her for the piloting, right? We'll still be getting that.'

Raedrus glanced to Cascade, who nodded. Ovthaugh merely watched the proceedings with limpid eyes, inscrutable. The veteran explorer shrugged. 'So be it.'

Ilden nodded and held out a hand to the pilot. 'Come on. Let's get you inside and get those wounds treated.'

Serafina let herself be pulled up and leaned on him as they went back into the lighter. 'Thanks, Ilden.'

The thief chuckled. 'Don't thank anybody until the money is in your hand. That said, we'll see you in a few days loaded down with enough riches for everybody.'

The eyeless horror tumbled backwards trailing smoke, its chest blown open by the las-blast. Ilden took the chance to sprint towards the doorway into the maglev transport, his rasping breaths loud in his ears. Raedrus' autogun roared in the background. The rain of bullets scythed through more of the creatures, cutting them down in sprays of xenos blood. There was no shortage of replacements. More boiled up out of the depths.

Three of them loomed up out of the dark to Ilden's right. He managed to shoot two of them down with whip-crack beams that flared red in the gloom. The last one was on him before he could switch his aim, ploughing into him at full speed. He hit the ground hard, the air driven from his lungs. Desperate, he flung his arms over his face to try and save himself. Gnashing needle teeth dug into him as razor claws flailed. Someone was screaming. It took Ilden a moment to realise it was him.

Then the thing went limp with a low groan and toppled to the side. A crystalline shard jutted out of its head, razor sharp and gleaming. A hand grabbed Ilden by the collar and dragged him the last several feet into the transport. He was slung to the back of the maglev's control chamber like a sack of rations, and crouched there, shaking. His pistol clattered to the ground next to him. He could see his rescuer now, the bizarre shape of Ovthaugh standing in the entrance to the chamber and firing its pair of strange crossbows into the oncoming foes. Sometimes the impact of a shard was enough to kill one of the monsters outright; if they kept coming, there would be a keening sound a moment after impact and the crystal would shatter, shredding the foe.

A moment later and Ovthaugh sidled aside to let Cascade past him, the tech-adept firing sizzling electrical blasts behind her. Raedrus ducked in on the other side a heartbeat later. Ilden clumsily forced himself to his feet and grabbed his pistol. Stumbling up next to Cascade and Ovthaugh, he added to the volume of fire driving the hissing abominations back, as Raedrus hammered at the control console to the transport. The door hissed shut and the transport set off.

For a moment the four of them just leaned against the walls, trying to catch their breaths.

Cascade spoke up. 'Always stimulating, this place.'

Ilden snorted and holstered his pistol, taking the chance to survey his arms. Deep cuts went straight through the leather and into the flesh beneath, dark red blood oozing out. 'One certainly never gets bored.'

Raedrus eyed his wounds. 'We'll find a place to hole up at the next stop, if we can. Get some rest and tend to your injuries.'

Cascade tilted her head. 'Rest? In the Unfathomable? Every group I've ventured in with before thought that was impossible.'

Raedrus smirked. 'I've seen corpses that had the time to starve to death in here. If you have time to starve, you have time to get a little sleep.'

Ilden laughed wearily and leaned his head back against the wall, shutting his eyes. Exhaustion weighed on him. 'You won't get any argument from me.'

The transport slid to a halt and opened into a new chamber of the ancient fortress. The path sloped upwards both to the left and the right. The worn group made their way out, to find there was no ceiling. Ilden looked up. Immediately the vertigo struck home. The paths arced up in full view and then connected overhead at a distance. They were standing at the bottom of a great torus, suspended in darkness by uncertain means. The vertigo deepened into nausea and dizziness, though whether that was the bizarre vista or blood loss he wasn't sure.

Cascade was at his elbow the next moment, keeping him from toppling. 'Come over here,' she said. She guided him to sit down against the far wall. 'We need to get these bandaged. Take off your bracers.'

He sat and tried to focus on breathing as she broke open the medicae kit and smeared a salve on the wounds. It burned everywhere it touched broken skin, and he gasped in spite of himself. She glanced up at him and said, 'Better this than the blood sickness those things might give you.'

Deciding it was better to make conversation to take his mind off it, Ilden asked, 'So why did you come here?'

She tilted her head. 'Did you hit your head, too? We're here for the same reason.'

He chuckled. 'No, I mean in general. Why come to Precipice? Why risk the Unfathomable?'

Cascade frowned in thought. 'To study the mysteries of the machine-spirit is verboten for any who aren't dedicates of the Omnissiah. On my home world, though, it was the only way to survive. Old weapons had poisoned the air, the water, the land. Every moment alive was bought by artifice. No one cared until an ancient piece of technology was found in the wastes. Then the Red Priests came, and any who got in their way were suddenly "dangerous unbelievers".'

She sat silent a moment before continuing while binding the wounds. 'Scavengers came in their wake, convinced that where one treasure had been more might be found. I saw nothing I might call a treasure on that world, but I did see a way off. So I stole from the leader of the Red Priests, all the data I could get my hands on. Things he would rather no one else knew.' She shook her head. 'Unfortunately, even with years of training and planning, I was clumsy. I left... fingerprints. I don't think he'll ever stop hunting me. This place is a good hiding spot, for starters, and if I can find enough archeotech, perhaps I can buy my way to the other side of the galaxy. Beyond his reach forever.'

The wounds were bandaged securely. Ilden nodded to her and said quietly, 'Thank you, Cascade. I hope we find what you need.'

Cascade nodded and went to sit nearby, pulling out a toolkit and beginning to tweak something in one of her sleeves. Ilden looked over to the other two. Ovthaugh sat with a blade in one of its hands, polishing it with great care. It was a sword of curious design, the blade a single piece of crystal that gleamed in the half-light of the fortress. Holes perforated it in a dozen or more places. Raedrus, meanwhile, was writing in a journal, stylus scratching along rapidly.

The xenos was a source of uneasy fascination for Ilden. He'd been raised in the Creed like most Imperial children, and the guidance was clear when it came to the alien. 'Trust not in the xenos.' Yet the creature had saved his life, and he knew next to nothing about it. Was the Creed truly any kinder to people like Ilden? He was no fool. He knew he'd burn for how he had been born. They were kindred in that way.

He stepped closer and cleared his throat. Those vivid yellow eyes locked on him, the hands never pausing in their work.

'I just wanted to say thank you. You saved my life.' There was no response. He shifted his weight uneasily. 'That's an interesting weapon you have there. What is it?'

'Is sword,' Ovthaugh croaked.

Ilden chuckled. 'I mean, what does it do?'

It blinked once, slowly. 'Kills.'

Ilden nodded. 'I see. I see. Well.'

He turned to face Raedrus instead, but the man waved him off without even looking up. 'Don't waste your time.'

Ilden ran a hand through his hair wearily. 'The man with all the secrets, who keeps a diary.'

That got Raedrus to look up, and he smiled his certain smile. 'Everyone needs an outlet.' Then he pointed nearby. 'You're unsteady on your feet, Ilden. Get some rest while you can. We'll have to move before you know it.'

Ilden sighed and settled down against the wall again. 'You have a point. I don't know if I'll be able to sleep, though.'

He was out the moment he closed his eyes.

* * *

The sky burned.

Wavering clouds of red and orange swirled across it from horizon to horizon, and everywhere ash rained down. It drifted up to knee height, deep enough that the man had to stagger through it. He dragged with him a chest carved with strange pentagrammic etchings, the trail of the two of them carved through the thick dust as far as the eye could see. The soot had stained his clothes, rendered the tattered armour and cloak he wore a blackened mess. Much of his weight rested on a staff, or what remained of one. It was itself twisted and blackened, as burned as the rest of the world. His face was familiar to Ilden, though it took him a moment to place it: it was his own. Similar, anyway, just much older and scarred.

A shadow fell across the man, deep and dark as a pit. He stopped, and gazed into the thing that cast it. Ilden could not bear to look at it. His skin crawled at its very nearness. Something that should not be, that should not have ever been. There was fear on the man's face, but resolve was there as well. The man raised his staff and said something, the words lost in the hot wind. The staff blazed like a star being born.

The burning world faded into that light.

When the light cleared, Ilden could see a corridor of steel lit by cold globes. People thronged through it in endless waves. There was no room to struggle or breathe, only room to shuffle along with the flow of the crowd. That is, until they came. Black-plated armour and heavy shields, with shock mauls in hand. The people crushed against each other to get out of their way, and if they weren't quick enough they were slammed aside without a glance.

'No,' Ilden tried to say. He knew this place. He knew this moment.

The armoured men came to the door in the hall and hammered at it. 'Open!' one of them demanded. 'Open in the name of the Emperor's Law!'

The door opened to reveal a weary middle-aged man with terrified eyes. The Arbites smashed him to the ground as they stormed into the place. From within came shrieks and shouts. 'Where is he?' came that thunderous bellow. 'Where is the boy?'

Across the corridor and a little way down, a child looked on with terror of his own. The child knew he should go to the men. They were here for him; they had to be. Who knew what would happen to his family if he did not go? The child turned and ran.

He failed them.

You always fail them, it said.

It was a nudge in the ribs that shook him out of the dream. He woke with a start, bolting upright. Raedrus stood over him and just raised an eyebrow at the sudden movement. 'On your feet, Ilden. We have to get moving.'

'Right.' Ilden scrubbed a hand over his face. He was sweating in spite of the chill of this place. He scrambled to his feet and joined everyone in preparing to get moving again. Soon they were on their way, starting up the side of the great loop. The gravity never shifted in a noticeable way. It was like heading forever uphill for as long as they were in the torus. As with most of the chambers of the fortress, there were no visible light sources. Darkness or light, this place had its own ineffable rules that none of them understood.

They found another transport at the far end from where they'd started. Cascade looked around as they entered, asking, 'You are sure you know where we're going?'

Raedrus gave a low laugh as he surveyed the control panel. 'We'll get there, Cascade. There's only one way to go in this place. Forwards.'

They journeyed on in this way for several more hours. The temperature swung wildly. At times it would be so bitterly cold they'd be shivering uncontrollably by the time they found their way out of a given chamber. In other places the heat verged on unbearable, the dark walls wavering as though they'd found their way into an oven. In one chamber the air was so thin they coughed and wheezed as they staggered along, stars dancing in front of their eyes.

Yet when the weakness threatened to make him collapse, something pushed him on. His chest was aching by the time they found the next maglev transport. His vision was narrowing into a red corridor when the doors finally opened. The full air of the chamber outside was as sweet as mulled wine. Ilden was taking deep breaths with relief when he noticed Ovthaugh shuffling its extremities agitatedly.

'What is it?' Ilden asked.

'Walls,' it croaked back. 'Movement in the walls.'

Ilden looked around. The chamber was pitch-black except for the light eking out of the maglev behind them. Hesitantly he got out his photo-visor and lowered it over his eyes. The area was shaped like an egg, the walls smooth and clean. Except in one place: off to the far right, the jet substrate was honeycombed with several dozen punctures. Debris littered the floor beneath it, putting the lie to the idea this was merely another structural oddity of this bizarre place. Something had done this.

'We might have a problem…' Ilden said uneasily.

'What is it?' Raedrus had brought out a flare to illuminate the chamber.

'No, wait–'

It was too late. The other man had struck the flare, flooding the chamber with ruddy light. Immediately a susurration of movement came from those holes. Within seconds the first of them flopped into view. It looked like nothing so much as a yard-long worm hewn from rock, with a tooth-ringed maw surrounded by flaring mandibles. Chittering, it slithered towards them with unexpected speed, even as more began to writhe forth.

'Run!' shouted Raedrus, and they all fled headlong into the darkness in terror.

They fired as they ran, raining shots down on the oncoming monsters. The first few were torn apart by sheer weight of fire, spraying ichor and thrashing. Yet they were disturbingly resilient. More squirmed over the dead in the space it took to kill them, coming on with a mindless hunger. One got close enough to strike, launching airborne as insectile wings unfurled from its back. It hit Cascade with the weight of a leaden missile, driving her to the ground.

The impact knocked her hood askew, revealing some of her body modifications. The whole of her scalp was hairless, corded instead with thick metal tendrils that writhed and twisted. Several of these unfurled and struck at the worm with lightning speed, carving rents in it with razor tips. Ilden angled in to help, booting the thing in the side with all of his weight. It was sufficient to send the creature tumbling away. He shot it several times as it writhed back up, but the laspistol lacked the power to burn through that stony hide. There was no choice but to drag Cascade to her feet and return to headlong flight.

Raedrus and Ovthaugh had paused during this, using their heavier weapons to buy time for the other two to be up and moving again. Ovthaugh's limbs moved in a blur, one set of hands reloading the crossbow as quickly as another pair could fire them. Thundering volleys of autogun fire and whistling crystalline bolts slew the hideous grubs left and right. More squirmed forth to fill the gaps. The explorers could see the next transport up ahead, but the worms were pressing in closer.

Ovthaugh put away its crossbows and drew its shining blade just in time. The xenos opened its beak and a haunting melody spilled forth. It flowed over the blade, whistling through the holes in it. This reverberated into a keening wail right as the first of the monstrosities leapt towards it. Ovthaugh swung the shrieking blade in a glittering arc and bisected it from end to end. Yellowish goo sprayed out in a vile arc. There was no time to celebrate this lethal strike, for another was right behind it and yet another one only a second after.

Raedrus was the first to reach the transport and palmed the door, giving the other two humans a chance to stumble inside. Ovthaugh fell behind as more and more of the things lunged at it. Already streaks of blue blood ran down the black-and-white patterns on its poncho. Ilden leapt to the doorway, firing blast after blast with his pistol as the numbers of the enemy mounted. Raedrus ducked into the transport next to him and added his own weight of fire.

'Ovthaugh!' shouted Ilden. 'Come on! Run!'

The xenos tried to disengage from its bestial foes. There was something like terror in the whirl of its yellow eyes. The enemy pressed in too hard, slashing with mandibles and slamming into it over and over. More of the worms were flowing around it like an ocean wave, heading for the transport.

Ilden turned to Raedrus in desperation, 'We have to go out there! We have to–'

The door slammed shut. The transport hummed into motion.

'What?' Ilden stared at the black door. 'No. No!'

He whirled to see Cascade standing at the control panel, her head down and hand still hovering over the inscrutable alien writing of the controls.

'What did you do?' Ilden demanded.

'I saved us,' she said.

The thief turned to Raedrus. 'We have to go back! We can't leave it there!'

Raedrus' face was cold and indifferent. 'The transports never go backwards. You know that.'

'No!' Ilden turned and pounded on the door. 'No...' He slumped and rested his head against the cool stone surface.

'Better it than us,' said Cascade in her mechanical monotone.

Ilden laughed once, bitterly. 'It was right.'

'What?' Cascade asked.

'All humans do is betray.'

Something in the back of his mind sighed disapprovingly.

The far wall opened out into a new chamber.

Raedrus shouldered his autogun. 'Come on. There's still a way to go.'

Ilden dreamed.

He knew what was happening. It was less the immersion of a nightmare and more a painful pageantry he was forced to observe. He was a spectator to the show. The other presence was clear this time. It watched with him, reviewing days long past.

He'd never seen his family again. He'd got off his home world by stowing away. The reach of Imperial Law was long. There was never going to be anything like a normal life. The risk was too great. Stay in one place too long, get to know people too well, they would catch on. He'd have one too many hunches. His instincts would be just a little too good. The pyre was always waiting for him. He had to run just to stay ahead of the flames.

So he had. He'd fallen in with a gang on the next world and learned to steal to survive. With his help, they'd scored bigger and bigger. They'd become too greedy, and he could feel the heat on the back of his neck. He'd left without a word to anyone. Whatever price there had been for their actions, they'd paid it without him.

That was the pattern. Always running. World to world, a series of dots on the map. He'd always assumed he was running away. He'd never imagined that he was running towards something.

The Blackstone Fortress.

He'd reached the edges of Imperial space when he first heard the name. It had struck him down to the core. Surely he'd heard it before somewhere? He was meant to go there. He just knew it. If you connected those dots on the map, he'd been heading towards it his entire life. There was a certainty to the idea, at last. Things would start making sense once he got there. He'd be able to stop running.

Only that's not what happened, is it? the presence asked.

No, it wasn't. It was just more of the same. Other people facing the consequences while he scraped on by. Serafina, left behind on the shuttle. Ovthaugh, left to be devoured by mindless monsters. He had brought his failure with him. He was too weak. Still and always running.

So sad, the presence crooned. *Fate is a web and we are merely flies struggling in it.*

Ilden awoke to raised voices.

He was disoriented. It took him a minute to remember where he was. They'd pushed on to the point of exhaustion and stopped only when they couldn't go any further. This alcove had been the closest thing to shelter they could find. He didn't even know if anyone had kept a watch; certainly he'd fallen straight to sleep. He shifted the weight of the amulet around his neck. It was so heavy.

As he woke further, he realised there was a standoff ongoing. Cascade stood facing away from him, discharge ports open on her hand and sizzling with energy, ready to fire. The implanted weapons were aimed at Raedrus beyond her, who knelt and watched her with cold, alert eyes.

The older man noticed Ilden moving and glanced to him. 'She's betrayed us, Ilden.'

The thief startled. 'What?'

'That's a lie!' snapped Cascade.

'I caught her red-handed,' Raedrus said evenly. 'She was on the vox with Draik. He's here, in the fortress. He's still after us. She's leading him right to us.'

Cascade's head twitched. She clearly wanted to look at Ilden but feared to take her eyes off Raedrus. 'He's lying, Ilden. He was having some kind of fit. Talking to himself, twitching. I don't know what's going on here, but something's wrong with him.'

Ilden stood hesitantly, 'You both know this place can get inside your head… You need to calm down.'

Raedrus just smiled that dead-eyed smile and gave a small nod. It was too much for Cascade. She whirled to see what Ilden was doing. What the thief didn't expect was the reaction that followed.

She stared past him and stumbled backwards, bleating, 'What is what is–' Her vocoder gave out, the words dissolving into scrambled static. She turned back towards Raedrus, staggering, perhaps to try and run.

The knife took her in the throat. She didn't fire a shot in return. Instead she slowly reached up and grabbed the hilt. It came away with a surge of crimson that washed down the front of her chest. Then with a last burst of static she fell.

Ilden rushed to her side. 'What in the warp…' She was clutching at her throat, as if trying to stop the blood that pulsed out between her fingers. He put his hands over hers in a hopeless attempt to help. The lenses of her optics stared unfeelingly up at him as she writhed through her last moments. Then it was over.

He stared at her for what felt like an eternity. Raedrus stood over him. He looked up at the other man and asked, 'Why?'

'I told you, she betrayed us. We're too close to the prize to let everything get ruined now, Ilden.' Raedrus collected his knife from the ground and wiped the blood off on his leg. 'I'm going to get some rest. We'll make the final push soon.'

Ilden stared silently at his red hands. Another one gone. Another who'd paid the price while he scraped by. He dragged himself over to the curved wall of the alcove and sat there, trembling and staring at the body. There was no telling how long he sat there. When he came back to himself, the only sound in this dark place was the steady breathing of his last companion.

Ilden couldn't shake Cascade's last terrified reaction to him. What had she seen? What could have terrified her beyond the power of speech? He looked to where Raedrus slept. There was one sure way to get an answer. Not that that made it easy. The other man's words lingered in his mind: if you cross me, I'm confident I can kill you. Ilden shuddered. Yet something steeled him. It was time to do what had to be done.

He rose to his feet. This, at least, was something he knew how to do. He made no sound as he slipped over to the slumbering form. He eased the bag open warily. The thanoscope was exactly where he'd expected it to be. It was right next to the journal that Raedrus had written in so studiously. It was important too. The words might as well have been whispered in his ear. He grabbed the book, as well. With both items in hand he retreated back to the far wall.

The thanoscope needed a tissue sample to work. He looked at where Cascade's cold form lay, and shuddered. He wasn't sure he had it in him to go and disturb her now. His hands, though. They were black with dried blood still. Swallowing hard, he scraped a few flakes off into the collector of the scope. It took only a moment, humming softly in his hand, and then the images popped up. The things Cascade had seen in her last moments.

He scrolled back through the suffering on the ground as fast as he could. Then it was at the right moment. She'd whirled to face him and… there was nothing. At least, so he thought at first. Just him standing there looking bewildered, the darkness of the Unfathomable behind him. Yet the longer he looked, the less certain he became. There was something to the darkness just around him. It was deeper even than that of the fortress. A hideous shape clinging to him.

Ilden's hands were shaking. He put the thanoscope down and turned to the journal. On some level, he didn't want to know. Yet there was no turning back now. He lifted the tome and opened it, beginning to flip through the pages. The first third or so of the book seemed normal, a record of various expeditions and deals on Precipice. Yet as he got closer to the current date, crawling tendrils of horror began to work up his spine.

Whatever had happened on his last expedition, it had shattered Raedrus' mind and soul. His orderly accounts dissolved into frantic scratchings and desperate pleas. Crude drawings depicted a man drowning in darkness, mouth and eyes sewn shut.

Ilden looked over towards that slumbering body again with growing fear. With trembling fingers he laid the journal on the ground and looked around. There was no haven, no safe retreat. The only options were to stay and confront the nightmare or flee into the unknown.

Ilden did what he had always done. He ran.

Ilden should have been lost immediately. Raedrus had been their guide the entire way here, and the Blackstone Fortress was not known for its clarity. Yet somehow he knew where he was going. The fear had faded. In its place was a reverie. Each step came more surely than the last as he ran on through the gloom and shadows. It was as though the instincts that had guided him his whole life laid out the path for him now. At times he heard growls or shouts off in the darkness, but nothing could touch him. He was blessed.

Time blurred. He wasn't sure how long he'd followed his course. He'd come to some new part of the Unfathomable. It was categorically different from his past experiences with the chambers and vaults of the alien fortress. The smooth, abstract shapes gave way to something more fluid. It was as if everything had begun to melt, like flowing wax.

Strange pillars grew from the floor and the ceiling, their surface oily and sheened with rainbows. Some burned at the end with multicoloured flame. Their light cast shadows that changed and shifted more than the flickering could explain. Here there was a cackling face, there the spread of great wings. Each sign was gone as soon as it had come.

There was more strange here than just the physical, however.

There was something in the feel of it. A poignancy. It reminded Ilden the most of the still and heavy air that came before a storm. His sixth sense burned with it, alive in his chest like a lit coal. It was the feeling of infinite potentialities collapsing down to a singularity of purpose.

At last his steps brought him before a great altar. This was not part of the fortress. It had been constructed from scrap and bone, things brought from some distant place for this purpose. Crawling runes decorated the surface, their shape varying from one flicker of the flames to the next. Music flowed through the area, a piping that wavered along the edge of hearing. Atop the altar was a great chest, decorated with odd pentagrammic runework in silver filigree. Ilden had seen it before. A single indentation marked the front of it, a perfect match for the surface of the amulet that he wore around his neck.

He reached up and touched the precious jewellery. It was hot under his fingertips. Hot enough that it smarted and he yanked his hand back. In that moment the reverie broke. He came back to himself. To his instincts screaming to him that everything was wrong, that he shouldn't have come to this place. Ilden took a step back from the altar as the fear rushed into the void once more. He turned to flee yet again. That was when he realised he wasn't alone.

The wavering light of the flames revealed a horrifying panoply of half-seen visages and silhouetted shapes. Beastmen with leering faces cavorted in the half-darkness. Ragged soldiers in grotesque masks looked on, bloodstained killing tools held in scarred hands. Further on in the gloom larger shapes lurked in still, ominous promise. Ilden drew his pistol and aimed it around wildly, but it was a laughable gesture. The weapon was inconsequential in the face of this carnival of nightmares.

The crowd parted as a new pair of figures approached,

one hauntingly familiar and the other hideously new. The first was Raedrus. His approach was stilted; he moved with all the grace of a marionette. The other figure drifted along behind Raedrus, its feet never quite touching the ground. Its flesh was scarred with foul ideograms, and its eyes burned with an unholy light.

Raedrus stepped forwards at a gesture from the hovering witch-thing. His voice was flat and empty, as inhuman as Cascade's vocoder had been. 'Blood calls to blood,' he called. 'Fate cannot be denied.'

'No. Please, no.' Ilden realised tears were running down his face. 'This isn't what brought me here. It can't be.'

'You are what you were born to be,' the Raedrus-puppet said. 'You cannot be anything else.'

Ilden looked at his pistol again. It couldn't save his life, but it might yet save his soul. He brought it up to the side of his own head. Now was the moment. Yet his shaking hand betrayed him. He couldn't do it. 'I don't want to die,' he sobbed.

That was when a voice stopped him. ***It does not have to end this way,*** it said. ***One last display of fearful cowardice does not have to be your fate. I can save you. I can give you the strength you crave. The power to never have to run again.*** It was the voice from his dream. The voice of the amulet, Ilden realised.

The laspistol fell from nerveless fingers as he turned back to the altar. He was holding the amulet in his hand now, he saw. One step. Then another. Now he was within arm's reach. The creatures were closing in all around him, chanting now. The dark chorus of their voices swelled louder and louder as the amulet approached the indentation. It locked into place with a distinct click. The top of the chest fell back.

Darkness boiled out.

It flooded into Ilden's mouth and nose and eyes and ears. Climbed into his very pores and saturated every inch of his flesh. He couldn't see or breathe or do anything but fall to the ground, choking and trying to scream.

The voice was wholly in his mind now. No need for whispers and tricks, it was as loud as thunder. ***You have no idea how precious you are to me, child. How long I have waited for you. It was your pathetic worm of an ancestor that bound me to this damnable prison. I have languished here for millennia, waiting for you. That drop of blood in your veins and the spark of witch's fire in your soul. Everything I needed. I could not be free without you, and here you have come. All must follow the strands of fate's web.*** Ilden could hear his bones cracking and his flesh tearing in the background of these words.

I shall keep you very safe indeed, my precious treasure.

Down Ilden fell, a drowning man tumbling into darkness. As he was shoved into the shadowy recesses of his own soul, he was ushered into madness by one last sight.

The body – formerly his body – rose back to its feet. The multicoloured flames roared high, and all around him the monsters and twisted madmen fell to their knees in worship.

PAST IN FLAMES

J C STEARNS

The human woman berated the huge mutant, hands gesticulating angrily. Amallyn could read lips, but the Grendish woman's face was concealed by a skull-faced bandana.

'Any idea what she's saying?'

Amallyn Shadowguide looked up from the rangefinder of her longrifle to glare at the drukhari leaning against the wall to her right. She shook her head. Even her keen aeldari senses couldn't hear human speech from so great a distance.

She couldn't have picked voices out over the noise even if she had been much closer. The cacophony of the human occupation was muted by distance, but still a significant distraction. Far above them gunship engines roared, transporting soldiers and materiel to their new home in the Talisman of Vaul, known as the Blackstone Fortress in the thick, clumsy tongue of the humans. Vehicles both tracked and wheeled rattled and clanked, belching smoke and chemical fumes. Augmented by loudhailers, the bellowing voices of human officers tried to command some semblance of order from the chaotic throng of the soldiery.

The Grendish leaders had wisely chosen a more out-of-the-way place, lower within the Blackstone, to store their military supplies. The tales of the Blackstone Fortress devouring ships were more than mere poetic language, and never was this truth more evident to Amallyn than here.

What had once been a vast cargo vessel in the service of the Imperium had become raw materials for the Talisman of Vaul. If she read the markings correctly, the expansive room had previously been a landing bay, but the parts of the ship which had opened to space had been eaten away some time ago. The ceiling had been entirely subsumed by the Talisman's hunger, although Amallyn couldn't tell if the anchor chains, which dangled intermittently from the blackstone overhead, each link as thick as her torso, were left over from the cargo vessel or were part of the original structure of the fortress itself.

The upper reaches of the bay were now honeycombed with openings into the tunnels and ducts of the Talisman of Vaul, while the floor and lower portions of the room still looked as they originally had. The walls appeared frozen in mid-transformation, melding seamlessly from steel to blackstone as if they had been fused together. Amallyn had rarely had the opportunity to observe starships being consumed by the cyclopean structure, and was unsure if the process was so slow that it could scarcely be detected, or if the course had been halted in this instance, for some unknown reason.

The humans had evidently considered the remnants of the cargo vessel stable enough for their needs, and had repurposed it to house their own materiel. The bay had been turned into a labyrinth, filled with flakboard crates, plastek boxes and plasteel shipping containers. They had wasted no time in altering the décor, either: the few remaining icons of the Imperium on the ship had been torn loose or defaced beyond recognition.

The ranger dropped her gaze back to the viewer mounted on her rifle. The two aeldari were three levels up, concealed in a port on the back wall of the bay. Once, judging by the grooves in the wall, pipes or conduits had flowed through the hole to other destinations, but they had long since been removed or absorbed by the structure, leaving only their impression in the blackstone walls behind to mark their presence.

'Have you noticed the ones in charge of the mutants all wear cloth masks across their faces?' Veth chattered away, oblivious to the peril around them. Of course, if Amallyn couldn't hear her quarry shouting orders at the mutant soldiers, then there was no way the human could hear her companion's whispered conversation. Still, silence was a point of pride in fieldcraft, and it irritated Amallyn to no end that Veth refused to maintain that discipline. Which, Amallyn realised, was most likely the point.

'It's to shield their noses,' said Amallyn. 'Humans find the odour of the mutants repellent.'

'I certainly can't tell the difference,' Veth Rayden snickered. 'They all smell alike to me.'

'Neither can I,' Amallyn said.

Amallyn resumed staring. She knew Veth would carry on the conversation without her participation, but at least she could give herself the satisfaction of not engaging the Commorrite. Amallyn picked out the ogryn handler again, watching as the woman inspected a stack of flakboard crates, comparing the scrawls on their side to the data-slate in her hand.

Shadowguide's travels often found her watching the same target for days, sometimes weeks. She had grown accustomed to piecing together details of a subject's life from minor details. This particular soldier didn't bear any icons of the warp powers. Unlike the soldiers she ordered about, the only evidence of her treason was the frayed, faded shadows on her uniform where the insignias of the Corpse-Emperor had been prised free. She was curious to know if the human woman regretted her choices. Amallyn wondered what decisions had led the Grendish regiments to betray their Imperium. Had their leaders committed some unforgiveable crime, then absconded from Grend with soldiers who knew no better path in life than obedience? Amallyn had heard reliable accounts of human soldiers defying their convoluted hierarchy for some matter of pride or morality, choosing a life of rebellion over violating their own personal codes. Retreating to an isolated region of space and commandeering an abandoned corner of a vast labyrinth would be a natural course for such renegades. Of course, it was just as likely that the regiment had rotted from within: a single corrupting influence leading a small group of soldiers into degeneracy and eventually madness. By the time the leadership would have realised how far the cancer had spread, she knew, it would have been too late and the entire regiment would have fled along with the bulk of its resources.

'All the soldiers bear the signs of the same regiment,' Amallyn said. 'I count eleven of them, excluding the two giants.'

'You haven't seen the leader, then.' Veth Rayden leaned in, so close that Amallyn could feel the body heat from her face. 'She'll be hiding in the converted supply container down on the end.'

Amallyn nodded. She could see the shipping container

Veth referred to, even if the ex-dracon was wrong about its origin. It was a mobile command centre designed to *look* like a shipping container. The hidden aerials on the side were well concealed, but not enough to fool the pathfinder's experienced gaze.

'So fourteen all together,' said Amallyn.

Veth tilted her head up and squinted, as if that would enable her to see the distant command centre better.

'That's probably where they're holding it,' said the drukhari. The ranger didn't need to turn to see the smirk on Veth's face.

Shadowguide didn't respond. Veth might have done an adequate job pinpointing her treasure, but if she expected a pat on the head she was going to be sorely disappointed.

'You see why I needed you?'

Despite herself, it was Amallyn's turn to feel smug. No wonder Veth had pursued her so hard.

When she'd first set foot in the Eye of Vect, *she'd nearly backed out immediately. Most kabal officers-in-exile fostered an air of respectability, in a desperate bid to prove to themselves that they hadn't abandoned civilisation entirely to ply the stars like savages. They draped themselves in finery, spoke eloquently, and offered their guests refreshments on delicate serving sets.*

The hold of the drukhari reconnaissance craft bore more of a resemblance to an ork tribe's drinking den. Hazy mist drifted through the air, clinging to Amallyn with a thick, incense-like smell. Shelves for looted goods had been organised neatly at one point, but had become cluttered and overfilled, with no one for Rayden to trade her illicit goods to. The walls of the little hold were festooned with banners and helmets. Amallyn was drawn in by the horrible notion of a cousin, no matter how distant, debasing themselves by selling second-hand rags, until it clicked in her mind that the tokens on display were not wares: they were trophies.

Where other Commorrite exiles distanced themselves from their new peers, Veth Rayden had embraced the role of a pirate queen. Her form-fitting mesh armour had been augmented with a panoply of embellishments: thin plates, slim pauldrons and delicate vambraces, all stolen from a variety of sources originating both in Commorragh and among the craftworlds. She wore a single black gem, a fragment of a nishariel *crystal if Shadowguide was correct, in a choker around her throat. Over it all, Rayden wore a long, wide-collared coat that looked to have been pilfered from a Harlequin.*

'What brings a cultured asuryani like you to a dive like this?' Veth grinned widely. She had a small tearwood table, trimmed with gold fittings, set up to receive Amallyn. A pair of mismatched chairs served as the hold's only other furnishings.

Most kabalites who went into exile did so because they were wanted criminals. If Veth Rayden had committed any grand treason before stealing Vect's ship and fleeing the Dark City, Shadowguide hadn't heard about it. That aside, if she hadn't been a wanted traitor before her great theft, she certainly was now. In the years since she'd left Commorragh, Veth had left an impressive trail of bodies, many of them aeldari. The outcasts of their race were often jaded and cynical enough to overlook the most heinous of crimes, but kinslaying could still build up an unwanted reputation. Veth's reputation was so heinous she could no longer even set foot on Precipice.

It had taken some convincing for Rayden to get Amallyn to venture over to the Eye of Vect*. Eventually Rayden had agreed to an advance payment just for hearing her out. Amallyn reasoned that even if she chose not to take whatever offer the corsair had to make, she could always recoup her losses by selling the ex-dracon out to any number of bounty hunters in Precipice. On the outside chance that Veth was plotting to murder her, then Amallyn* *guessed she would just have to claim that bounty herself. That was already looking like an attractive option.*

'You're the one who invited me, princess,' she said.

The dracon-turned-corsair merely laughed. If her pride was nettled by Amallyn's barbs, or the conditions in which she had to receive her guest, it didn't show.

'Valuable plunder, of course. I hear there are all manner of fortunes in the Blackstone Fortress. Are you really surprised a canny pirate turned some up for herself?'

Keeping a wary eye for an ambush, Amallyn lowered herself to the empty seat. Veth gestured to a bottle waiting on a tray, but Amallyn declined, taking note of the lack of slaves for menial labour.

'What sort of plunder?' she said. The Talisman of Vaul held vast tracts of tunnels and chambers which were filled with nothing at all, or worse yet filled with nothing but monsters and lethal traps. Still, the uncountably ancient fortress also held innumerable treasures, tucked away by millennia of visitors. Because this particular Blackstone Fortress had a nasty habit of drawing ships in from the vast graveyard surrounding it and consuming them, much of the more valuable components and cargo survived for decades, just waiting to be recovered.

'The Chorale Lilcartha.'

Above her rebreather mask, Amallyn's almond eyes narrowed in suspicion. Refusing to remove the mask could be construed as a grave insult, but she'd been less concerned with that than she was with survival.

'Lies,' she said. 'If the Chorale *was ever real to begin with, all copies have long since been destroyed. Any supposed sighting is just a myth.'*

'Yes, and we all thought Ynnead and the blades of Moreg-Hai were a bit of entertaining fiction at one point, too. How did that end up working out for your people?'

Now it was Amallyn's turn to restrain herself. Long centuries walking alone among the stars had driven the cold rage from her heart, or so she'd believed. Veth's jibes brought those wounds open again, though, and for an instant Amallyn could hear the thready, splintery scream of wraithbone being literally torn apart all over again.

'Why would the Chorale *be on the Talisman of Vaul to begin with?' Amallyn kept her voice cold and neutral while she fought her emotions back into check. She already knew the answer, or could guess, but Veth humoured her anyway.*

'Large and enduring as the Talismans are,' said the drukhari pirate, 'it's a sensible place to hide something important. More likely it was on a ship which was consumed by the Talisman.'

Amallyn nodded. The Talismans of Vaul were monolithic creations. In the early days after the Fall, she could well imagine her ancestors, uncertain if they would even survive another handful of nights, concealing a repository of her race's knowledge in such a nigh-indestructible hiding place. A ship of aeldari fleeing across the stars, their craft damaged in the Fall, might have sought refuge in the Blackstone as well, only to have their ship devoured.

She had already recovered a number of valuable finds from the Talisman. The Trylanthi blade she'd snatched from a Tarellian treasure hunter; the ashes of Saint Racharia she'd extracted and ransomed back to the mon-keigh; the cache of Zelacian rubies she had split with Grekh – each worthy of her sojourn to the Talisman. All of them would pale in comparison to an intact copy of the Chorale Lilcartha.

'Why would a drukhari even be interested in the Chorale*?' Amallyn unclipped her mask and reached out to the bottle after all.*

Veth stiffened. 'It's as much my history as it is yours,' she said, forcing a smile back onto her predatory features. 'Perhaps even more so.' As much as it galled Amallyn to admit it, Veth was correct. The Chorale Lilcartha *was a relic that rightly belonged to none of the divisions of the aeldari, but to the race as a whole.*

Supposedly written in the aftermath of the War in Heaven, the Chorale Lilcartha *was one of the oldest known pieces of ancient aeldari literature. The saga of Eldanesh, the Crimson Weeping, even the tale of the Dark Muses: all had been influenced by the lore within the psychic text of the* Chorale*. Allegedly penned after the annihilation of the Rashan, the book had over a dozen rumoured authors, including Lileath herself. It was a living link between the surviving aeldari and their mythology. The creation and technique of the aeldari art forms was recorded also in its pages. The fundamental teachings which underlay aura painting and the writing of* seada *were detailed in the* Chorale*, as were more arcane practices like bonesinging and wraithcraft. A full, intact copy could teach the eldar truths about their species they didn't know they'd forgotten.*

'Tempting bait indeed,' said Amallyn. She sipped cautiously at the effervescent beverage. 'So what's the snare?'

The drukhari corsair leaned in conspiratorially. 'Have you ever heard of the Grendish 82nd?'

Amallyn shook her head.

Veth pressed her fingertips into the table surface and leaned over close enough to whisper and still be heard. A braid, dotted with beads stolen from a disciple of Karandras, swung in front of her eyes. 'What's worse than either a mon-keigh or a daemon?' she asked.

Amallyn, tired of the dramatics, set her unfinished drink down. 'Daemon-worshipping mon-keigh,' she sighed.

That part, at least, seemed subdued. Although the human renegades appeared to be dirty and desperate, even by the standards of their grubbing, filthy species, she saw no obvious signs of eldritch corruption. Several of them wore the star of Chaos or other foul icons on their person, but none of the soldiers bore the trappings of sorcerers. Besides the ogryn there were no visible signs of mutation. Amallyn knew the dogmatic savages of humanity viewed any splinter groups of their species that refused to bow to their corpse-god as being as vile as actual daemon-worshippers. If it weren't for her longrifle, she might have believed that the humans were merely rebels, rather than true cultists.

In the psychic spectra, her rangefinder told a different story. In glittering golds and pulsating reds, foetid greens and searing violets, the psychic emanations of the humans showed willing servants of the Dark Powers. Warning runes ticked by in streams when she lingered over any specific individual, alerting her to a servant of the warp. Amallyn knew from experience that devotion of this magnitude only arose around leaders of great conviction. The ebullient pink haze surrounding the command centre told Amallyn in no uncertain terms where that leader was.

'Were you able to learn anything else about her?' Amallyn asked. While she had perched above the supply depot, counting enemies and memorising their routines, Veth had scouted the edges of the human occupation looking for an informant who could be abducted and interrogated without being missed.

'The renegade I... spoke to... called her "Commissar Melantha Schere", although I couldn't tell you if any one of those is a rank, a name or a title.' Veth leaned against one wall and toyed with one of her splinter pistols. Like many corsairs, she enjoyed going to war with criss-crossed bandoliers of pistols across her chest. 'Supposedly she found the *Chorale* down here while scouting for somewhere to store their supplies. I gather she's trying to use it for her own personal gain somehow – no doubt by profaning it in some corrupt ritual.'

Amallyn looked up from her rangefinder to stare back at the former dracon. Veth might be ignorant to human ranks and procedures, but she knew better. To the pathfinder, more experienced in the ways of humankind, the commissar was something altogether more terrifying. With no oversight and broad, violent powers, the commissars led by fear as much as they did inspiration. If the commissars of the Grendish regiment had been the ones to embrace Chaos worship, then it was no surprise the soldiers displayed such strong conviction. The commissars would act as a form of malign priesthood, bolstering the dark urges of their soldiers and focusing them towards the foul machinations of Chaos.

'Or it's a trap,' she said. 'Have you thought about that? I'm sure human heretics would love to get their hands on well-supplied aeldari explorers.'

If Commissar Schere had intended the depot to be a trap, she had done a marvellous job of making it look like she was trying to keep intruders out. Even after spending half a day evading spindle drones, fighting ur-ghuls, and cutting a path through a tunnel choked with cryofungus, Amallyn had still been forced to deal with the perimeter defences of the humans, snipping her way through coils of razor wire and disarming the crude fragmentation mines the Traitor Guardsmen had deployed in the vents.

'Exactly my thinking,' Veth said. She secured her pistol and double-checked the serrated cutlass and slim parrying blade hanging from her left hip. 'Which is why I suggested we do this by ourselves.' She made a swooping hand gesture, like a street hustler palming a trinket. 'Covertly.' The drukhari's fingers caressed the gem at her throat. 'Any thoughts on how we get to the *Chorale*?'

Amallyn pointed into the maze of boxes. 'You scale down

the wall,' she said, 'and follow a path through the stock. If we time it correctly, you should be able to eliminate four of the soldiers before you reach their sentry.' She gestured to a pyramid of crates, where a single human crouched amid a pile of sandbags, manning a large multibarrelled gun. Their communication beads would keep them in contact and allow her to guide the drukhari's infiltration. 'From his position, you cover *my* advance until we rendezvous. From there we should be able to eliminate the remaining mon-keigh and take the command centre before Schere even realises we're here.'

She turned to find Veth ignoring her.

Rayden had her eyes closed. Her mouth moved silently, fingers still clutching the gem at her throat. Amallyn knew it required a great deal of concentration to activate a shadowfield, and a massive amount of self-confidence to maintain one. Behind her mask, her mouth quirked into a cruel smile as she imagined distracting Veth with a jibe about how long she was taking. As much satisfaction as it might give her to see the former dracon's confidence shaken, forcing her to start her attunement to the crystal again, Amallyn decided that would only prolong the time she would have to suffer the drukhari's company.

Despite her contemplated mockery, she didn't actually have that long to wait. The light faded and guttered, as if the nishariel crystal drew it in like a hungry parasite. The aura of darkness was bad enough for psychically stunted lesser species, but to evolved beings like the aeldari it was even worse. Amallyn could even sense the distortion of Veth's psychic presence. Even a trained warlock could have difficulty striking a dracon thus protected.

'Do you need me to go over the strategy again, princess?'

Amallyn couldn't help herself. She was both relieved and disappointed when the shadowfield failed to collapse. If anything, it deepened. She wondered if Veth was imagining killing her.

'Down and to the right,' whispered the drukhari, 'I heard you.' Veth's words were close, so near that Amallyn could feel her hot breath, could imagine the brush of the dracon's lips against her ear. When she slapped blindly into the darkness, however, her arm hit nothing but shadow.

Then the miasma was gone, and Shadowguide could see again. She peered over the lip of the opening. The black cloud scaled down the chain beyond, Veth climbing her way to the ground without sounding so much as a single link. Amallyn sighed in exasperation. Veth's haste was typical of the reckless Commorrites. If she couldn't get the drukhari to follow a methodical plan of operation, they were both going to end up dead. The pathfinder relaxed, allowing herself to settle to the uneven surface. Her mesh armour flexed likewise, allowing its own shape to conform to the irregularities beneath her.

'Hold,' she said. Veth obediently paused midway down the chain. A single sentry stood guard over the rear wall. He sat atop a waist-high supply box, sullenly shifting his gaze from side to side. The runes on Amallyn's rangefinder scrolled, counting his turns and calculating his levels of agitation. After a moment the viewer flashed a rune, notifying her that she had a firing solution. He began to turn back towards her at the same time she opened fire, and the laser bolt hit him in the top part of his face, boring a blazing hole from front to back through his skull.

'Nice shot,' said Veth, dropping to the ground. The drukhari slunk away through the narrow corridors of the labyrinth.

Only Amallyn's elevated view allowed her to keep track of the corsair's progress. The multispectral scans of her long-rifle's rangefinder even gave her a hazy impression of the ex-dracon through the diffusion of her shadowfield.

'Move to the left,' Amallyn whispered. 'Below that hanging crate.' Down below, Veth ducked into the indicated recess, her shadowfield blending in with the darkness beneath. One of the ogryn soldiers ambled past, pausing at the long wooden box the drukhari was hiding underneath. The bull-headed brute slapped the crate, laughing as it rocked slightly on the cargo chain. The mutant wandered off along its patrol route, guffawing to itself.

'Clear path?'

'Not yet,' whispered Amallyn. The aeldari earpieces picked up sub-vocalisations, so there was no need for them to speak above the barest of whispers. There was no possibility of being overheard over the racket still ringing out above them, but something was bothering her, her innate sense of caution insistently tugging at the corner of her mind. 'He's nearly gone. Now. Go now.'

Veth was away in a moment, stalking through the stacks of shipping crates. Watching the gloom thicken as her malevolent cousin moved, only to recede again at her passing, drawn about her like a cloak at the command of the shadowfield, it was as though Veth were being carried through the cargo hold on a flowing river of shadow.

'Two of them ahead,' Amallyn hissed. The two humans had stepped away from their assigned posts and were rapidly closing on Veth's position. The dark eldar pressed herself against the side of the nearest crate, but if she didn't move, they would certainly see her.

'Up, quickly,' said Amallyn. To her relief, Rayden obeyed

her command immediately, skittering up the nearest stack of crates like an arboreal rodent. Then, to her aggravation, the dark eldar climbed all the way to the top of the wall of shipping containers, rolled onto her back, and waited patiently for instructions.

Shadowguide had no time for her partner's instigations. She snapped her rifle up to where the sentry manning the heavy gun was surveying the room. The human was staring directly at Veth. Amallyn could tell from his furrowed brow and squinty gaze that he wasn't certain of what he'd seen, but was certain he'd seen *something*.

The runes in her rangefinder scrolled over his face at a breakneck pace, warning that the weapon couldn't confirm a shooting solution. Amallyn didn't have time to wait; she read his body language, adjusted her reticule to a point above and behind the human's head, and fired.

Before her finger could finish the action of pulling the trigger of her longrifle, the Guardsman had leaned back and started to turn towards his vox-unit, just as Amallyn had predicted he would. The laser shot took him in the side of the head, just behind the temple. He never realised what happened. Unless one of them had been looking overhead at that precise moment, none of the other humans would have realised anything had happened either.

'I saw that,' Veth said. *'If you're that bloodthirsty, we could have just come in guns blazing, like ork mercenaries.'*

Amallyn ground her teeth together. She would have liked to have got Veth in place before killing the sentry. It was as if the drukhari were deliberately trying to derail her plans.

'The two you're hiding from are coming down the corridor,' she said. 'They'll be under your position shortly.'

'I'll take the near one at your signal, cousin.'

Amallyn sighed. The two humans were in no hurry to meet their deaths, pausing every so often to pass a small bottle back and forth between them. She tried to focus on her breathing to maintain her patience, and realised she was going to be very annoyed if they finished their illicit libation and returned to their posts before they even reached the ambush point. Fortunately, they continued all the way to their doom.

'Now,' Amallyn said. No sooner had the word left her lips than Veth was in motion, rolling off the top of the crate to drop onto the unsuspecting human below.

The drukhari never hit the ground. As soon as she reached the Traitor Guardsman, she rolled in mid-air. Veth hung there, suspended with her shoulders braced against one wall, her arm around one human's throat, her body rigid, holding the other human pressed against the opposite wall with her boots on his neck and chest. Amallyn shot the cultist pinned by Veth's feet. She could see blood pumping furiously out of the other cultist's throat where Veth had slit it. The dark eldar released the pressure, letting the two corpses slide to the ground, before regaining her footing.

'*Z'tesh*,' said Amallyn. The immediate threat was past, but nothing was going the way she'd planned. The drukhari might thrive on chaos, but she didn't.

'*Did they teach you language like that in temple?*' Veth chuckled. Amallyn could see the drukhari running her hands over the corpses, pocketing anything the corsair might consider valuable.

'You've got eighty-eight seconds until a guard comes around the corner and sees those bodies,' Amallyn said. Below, Veth snapped her head back and forth, looking for a place large enough to stow both corpses before she was spotted. Shadowguide didn't bother; she already knew there wasn't one. She clipped the strap to her longrifle and slung it over her shoulder. 'Get to the gunnery nest,' she said, 'and guide me in. If you can eliminate the sentry before he sounds an alarm, do it.'

Amallyn made the short leap to the dangling chain and started the hand-over-hand descent. She cursed under her breath, wishing every cancerous fate she could think of on Veth Rayden. Mentally, she calculated the routes and posts she'd memorised, trying to plot a new course that could keep them from an open confrontation with nearly a dozen enemies. If Veth could keep the patrolling guard quiet, they might have a chance. She just needed the drukhari to perform this one task.

She leapt up on the half-stack of crates that held the corpse of the first sentry she'd shot, then pulled herself to the top of the full stack behind it. Amallyn paused for a moment as the wandering ogryn turned and peered over a shipping container to look her way. The ranger held utterly, breathlessly still, allowing the cameleoline cloth to distort and blur her shape. Over her earpiece she heard the sound of a pair of splinter pistols firing. Amallyn held her breath.

The sound of a human corpse lurching into a plasteel shipping container was unmistakeable. A gurgling cry started, but cut off in a frothy slur. Amallyn bit her lip in consternation. The ogryn turned towards the sound and began hurrying through the labyrinth.

The ranger raced along the top of the row of crates, fighting back the wrath within herself. Not just at the drukhari's incompetence: she was also furious at herself. What had she expected? She was from Biel-Tan, and the eldar of Biel-Tan knew well what came from giving aid to Commorragh's spawn. Now she found herself fighting for her life, all because her traitorous kin couldn't handle a simple silent killing.

Below and to her right, Amallyn saw one of the humans

turn a corner, lasrifle tucked to his chest, walking swiftly but not yet sprinting in alarm. She pulled her shuriken pistol and fired three rapid shots into him from above.

'See?' Amallyn whispered as she leaped over another corridor, 'completely silent. Is that so difficult?'

'Show me a couple more times,' said Veth. *'I might catch on.'*

Amallyn didn't respond. She skidded to a halt on the plasteel surface of the container she'd just leaped to, looking at the confused face of the ogryn staring up at her from the corridor on the far side. She hadn't made a sound, and couldn't fathom how the damn thing had heard her. Only the most phenomenal stroke of luck could have drawn his attention upwards and behind him before she could strike. Before he could bellow a warning, she leapt on him. She tried to draw her powerblade on the way down, but the ogryn just lifted his bulky firearm and smashed her like an insect. Her mesh armour stiffened, absorbing most of the blow, but she still ricocheted off the crate behind her with a huge metallic clang.

'Who you talking to?' the mutant growled. Like most rangers, Amallyn was fluent in a variety of languages, including the stilted, clumsy tongue of the humans. Beneath her mask, her face burned at his words. Had her anger really made her that reckless? She rolled to her feet, too far away to reach the mutant before he tore her to shreds with his massive gun. She lunged for the nearest corner in desperation, but knew she almost certainly couldn't make it.

Before he could pull the trigger, a hail of las-fire pummelled him from above and behind. The torrent was brief, but battered the giant into the side of a cargo container, his face and shoulders reduced to charred, smoking meat.

'Nice and quiet, yes?' laughed Veth. *'Just like that?'*

Cries of alarm rang out from around the bay. Amallyn

could hear footsteps racing through the labyrinth: some in her direction and others making their way towards the gunnery nest. She started in that direction herself.

'No, no,' said Veth, *'I'll come to you so you can show me in person.'* The drukhari's perverse giggles infuriated Amallyn more than her own failures. One of the Grendish soldiers yelped from around the corner as he stumbled over the corpse Amallyn had killed on her way in. Amallyn rose and lunged at the shipping container wall between them, focusing her will into the crystalline belt around her waist. She felt the phase crystal engage moments before she would have impacted the wall face first.

As always, there was a brief sense of disorientation. It only took a moment to step through the shipping container and out the other side, but the feeling of metal passing through her body felt like being torn apart, yet numbing. It was like being cut with a thousand scalpels at once, only painlessly.

The mon-keigh soldier was kneeling over the corpse of his comrade, babbling to a vox-bead in his ear. His attention was ahead of him, towards the corner any enemy would have to approach from if they were coming from the recent gunfire. He never bothered to look behind, even as Shadowguide's powerblade was plunging at his neck.

'You do hate to use that thing, don't you?'

Amallyn looked up to see Veth's shadowy form sliding down from the top of a container wall. The shadowfield retracted slightly, allowing Amallyn to see the corsair's dim outline.

'I could feel it from up there,' said Veth. 'I should get one of those for my torture chamber.'

The pathfinder shook her head in anger. 'Not now,' she hissed. 'How many are left?'

'Five,' Veth said. The corsair's bandoliers were missing multiple weapons. 'I killed the other mutant on the way here.'

Behind the drukhari's shoulder, an explosion roared from the gunnery nest, accompanied by several screams.

'Two now,' said Veth. Amallyn glared at her dark cousin, who merely shrugged in amusement. 'I found some crude grenades on the dead. What's the big deal? We weren't being quiet any more, were we?'

The ranger swept by her.

Amallyn kept herself closed off from the corsair as much as she was able, but still she could feel Veth's sadistic glee emanating like an aura behind her. She reminded herself that they were so close to their goal: the *Chorale Lilcartha* would be worth it. The possibility of finding secrets that would strengthen the asuryani or, gods willing, reveal the key to healing Biel-Tan, was worth any amount of nettling to her pride. She could put up with the drukhari's slapdash manner for a little while longer.

She needed no scanners or spotter to identify the last of the humans. Even before she rounded the last corner before the command centre, she could hear her quarry. The shuffling, nervous movement of a soldier settling into a defensive posture, the squeak of a bayonet being fixed to the primitive laser weapon, the metallic rattle of a grenade being palmed: the human couldn't have telegraphed her position more if she were trying. Amallyn could taste the wet, tart aura of the woman's fear. Beside her, she heard Veth shiver.

'I'll move first and draw her fire,' said the corsair. 'You come in afterwards for the kill.' Veth didn't wait for the ranger to confirm the plan, just stalked past her and rushed around the corner. Amallyn cursed again. There was little time to plan, but there was still no reason to run in so ill-prepared. She put her rifle to her chest and raced to follow Veth.

It was a single shaft of light that saved them. Only the

barest glint of gleaming metal drew Amallyn's eye to the tripwire. She was too late to prevent Veth from barrelling through, but she kept the presence of mind to slam into the drukhari from behind, bearing both of them to the ground before the trio of explosions turned the air around them into a concussive storm of shrapnel.

'You see, soldier? I told you they couldn't resist.'

Amallyn rolled off of her dark kin and rose to her knees, leaving Veth to struggle to regain her breath on her own. The human she'd known about hunkered behind a makeshift flakboard partition, shaking her own head to clear her ears. Despite the uniform and the generic, cloddish human shape, Amallyn recognised the torn insignias and skull-faced bandana from the human woman she'd been studying earlier.

There could be no doubt as to the identity of the second woman. The peaked cap atop her mantle of ash-blonde hair; the blood-red sash studded with handmade icons to her dark patrons; the long, sweeping greatcoat: all of them advertised her rank. Even Veth could read the undeniable message: here is a leader of forces, a messenger of death.

The first swipe of the chainsword nearly killed Amallyn, who only barely ducked beneath it. She had been so caught up in the commissar's image that she had barely registered the woman attacking her. The ranger backpedalled, trying to stow her rifle with hands that were failing to work.

'Get out here, Jenali,' Melantha snapped. 'Two aeldari? The Prince of Pain will reward us richly for their lives.'

'Well, one *real* aeldari.' Veth leapt at Commissar Schere, spinning on her heel at the last minute to slash her cutlass in from the opposite direction. Her shadowfield had collapsed, making it easier to defend against her. Melantha parried the drukhari's attack with ease, dropped to one knee, and used the rebound force of her blow to slice at Rayden's calf. The drukhari dove out of the way, but was forced to turn her lunge forwards into a somersault to keep from falling flat. She rolled to a kneeling position and laughed. 'Plus one hand-wringing craftworld ascetic.'

'You just never stop, do you?' Amallyn responded in Aeldari, like her cousin. She used the space that Veth had bought her to level the longrifle at Commissar Schere. The human woman swarmed the drukhari, greatcoat flaring out around her as she rushed the corsair. Amallyn's rangefinder raced, trying to calculate the commissar's chaotic, sinuous movements and achieve a firing solution. Amallyn forced herself to remain calm. Indiscriminate hip-shooting would only endanger her ally, a prospect she admittedly found more than a little tempting.

The runes flashed a shooting solution, but before she could pull the trigger, pain bloomed up Amallyn's left side and threw her aim. A flurry of lasrifle shots impacted her as the forgotten Grendish woman found her nerve and opened fire. The armour of the asuryani was more than a match for the crude human firearm, and most of the burst either went wide, the soldier unable to discern Amallyn's profile through the cameleoline cloak's diffusion, or was mitigated enough by the mesh to leave the ranger with nothing but a few bruises. The force of her fall drove Amallyn's longrifle from her hands, though, with a hiss as the lug on her gyrostatic arm released the weapon rather than snap.

'Look out, cousin,' said Veth. 'I think that mon-keigh is still kicking. If you can't take care of her, just keep your head down and I'll handle it as soon as I finish this one.' The drukhari's words were thick, her speech slightly slurred, but still with a mirthful lilt that was like knuckles being ground into Amallyn's scalp.

Veth and the human commissar traded blows in a spinning duel, both of their long, elegant coats flowing and flaring behind them. Amallyn could tell that Veth's movements were slowed and sluggish. Once again, the drukhari let her down, so dosed on her own combat drugs that she couldn't even manage the coordination to finish off a single mon-keigh.

Another burst of lasgun fire rained around her. The uncontrolled volley sprayed the steel floor and shipping containers behind her, but a single round found its mark, hitting her neck with the force of a driving punch.

Amallyn rose to her feet, overcome with fury. Her pistol and blade were in her hands before she knew it, the quavering human the only thing in her sight. She advanced on the fearful primitive, weaving back and forth to let the panicked lasgun shots pass by her, close enough to leave sizzling sear marks on the edges of her cloak, but unwavering in her charge.

She drove the powerblade down in a brutal chop worthy of an ork warlord. Technique and finesse were forgotten in a single-minded desire to rend her bleating opponent limb from limb. The Grendish woman tried to lift her lasgun to block Amallyn's blow, but the short aeldari blade cleaved the cheap longarm in half with a blinding burst of sparks. The human staggered, trying to clear her eyes. Shadowguide kicked the mon-keigh in the chest, driving her back to the wall of the command centre. She could have killed the grubby, savage creature, but she waited the brief moment it took for the Grendish woman's vision to clear.

The soldier stared at Amallyn, her eyes filled with an animal's ignorant confusion. Gone was Shadowguide's empathy, all thoughts of curiosity at the path of the human's life forgotten. The ranger fired her shuriken pistol over and over, shredding the cultist's chest with spinning, razored death.

This was the red fury, the bloody, hateful infection she couldn't shake, that had driven her onto the path of the outcast. Amallyn took a great, shaking breath, forcing the trembling wrath back down. She'd spent too long wrestling with herself to lose control now.

Amallyn turned to see Veth backed up to the wall of the container maze, her shoulders nearly touching the crates. A great gash ran down Veth's armour from shoulder to navel, the corsair's bandoliers fallen and forgotten. The ranger moved to flank the commissar, shaking her head in disgust.

'You're a disgrace to Asuryan,' she muttered. Melantha turned in time to deflect Amallyn's attack from behind. The human's other hand came up holding a bolt pistol. Shadowguide spun to the side, the sound of gunfire following her.

'Phoenix King's dead. Didn't you hear?' Veth Rayden scrambled away from Commissar Schere, fumbling across the ground for her discarded pistols.

Schere levelled her own pistol at Veth, but Amallyn charged in again, forcing the commissar to defend against her renewed onslaught. Amallyn edged the human woman backwards with a measured, criss-crossing attack routine. She might have been able to overwhelm the cult luminary with superior agility and speed, but the wiser plan was to let Veth recover and achieve an assured victory with an advantage in skill *and* numbers.

'Vect, then. Or the Dark Muses. Or your own damn reflection.' Amallyn found herself giving ground to the commissar, and skipped backwards to give herself room. The spinning chainblade drew sparks from her own power sword. How was the human moving so fast? 'Whatever you hold in regard as higher than yourself, just know that he or she or it looks on you and deems you a failure.'

The human commissar snapped her arm back, firing her

pistol just as Rayden drew one of her own. The explosive round went off, showering Veth with a bloody mist. The corsair doubled over, screaming, her left hand reduced to a ragged stump. Amallyn swiped in, trying to take advantage of the human's foolish distraction, but found her strike easily deflected. Melantha Schere spun away and gave an eerie, ululating whistle.

'Something's wrong,' the ranger said, amazed to hear her own words come out thick and slurred.

Veth staggered forwards, her own blade in her remaining hand, and sniggered. 'Now who's a disgrace?' she laughed.

Realisation struck Amallyn like a bolt from beyond. Veth's laughter became crazed as she reached the same epiphany. The treasonous commissar was more than just an aspirant of the Dark Powers, she was already one of She Who Thirsts' duly rewarded servants. Veth wasn't being hampered by a poorly designed cocktail of combat drugs; the eldar were fighting in a cloud of soporific pheromones which slowed their reactions and dulled their wits. Her respirator had delayed the effect, but the warp-tainted toxins were more than her mask could filter out.

To make matters worse, she heard the tromp of boots: reinforcements arriving at the commissar's command. Two humans stormed into view from the maze of crates, laspistols and serrated knives in hand. Amallyn fought to clear her mind. Hadn't Melantha *just* whistled? The two new humans went wide, circling around the two eldar women.

Amallyn roared in anger and lashed out at the commissar, who dove through the air above the power sword, her hips rolling with a range of motion no human had ever possessed, to land nimbly on her feet and slash her chainsword across the ranger's forearm. The mesh armour stiffened and then shredded, but the pathfinder could still feel blood soaking her arm.

A knife whistled past her ear, and she retreated from the human man, who inserted himself between Amallyn and the commissar. The other harried Veth, forcing the drukhari back towards the crate maze. Their Grendish uniforms had been ripped in several places, and every inch of visible skin had been branded and scarred with blasphemies exalting She Who Thirsts. Their faces were hidden by black flexible polyvin masks that obliterated the features beneath.

'Were they in one of the cargo containers?' Amallyn panted. She rolled under the guard of one of the humans, but had no opportunity to take advantage of it. She had to ignore the opening to press the commissar, who had been trying to eviscerate Veth from behind. 'What were they even doing there?'

Veth threw her shoulders back against one of the shipping containers and lashed her foot out at the human. Her boot caught him in the jaw and he stumbled away. Amallyn dropped to her knee and slashed her power sword through his spine, but her reflexes were still slowed, and before she could rise again the other human pistol-whipped her. She felt blood flow underneath her mask.

'Quiet meditation? Ritual fasting? Censer-swinging?' Veth laughed again. She had re-engaged Schere and was forcing the commissar to give ground, but anyone could see that she was running on a last rush of desperation. 'They're cultists – what do you *think* they were doing in there?'

Amallyn was through with her cousin's incessant nattering. Her pride was getting her nowhere. The only chance of victory lay in fighting them not as individuals, but as aeldari. She clenched her jaw, feeling the cracked teeth scream in agony. She rose and deflected the onrushing attack of the bare-chested cultist, shifting her weight to take as much of the hit on her wounded arm as possible. Each jarring blow felt like driving flaming nails into the injured meat of her arm.

Invigorated by Amallyn's agony, Veth came in on Melantha with a laugh and a burst of renewed speed. Amallyn took a moment to centre herself, opening her mind to her cousin. She had spent a great deal of her concentration keeping the distracting feelings of her twisted companion at bay, knowing how it would pain her to touch the darkness in Veth Rayden's soul. She wasn't wrong; opening herself up to the urges and feelings of the corsair was like turning her earpiece into a ball of razored spikes. Amallyn felt a coldness spread through her, numbing the careful control she used to tamp down her anger. The sour, acidic rage that lived inside her, that had always lived inside her, boiled up like a surge of vinegar rising from her stomach.

Amallyn turned from the masked cultist and attacked Melantha from the other side, swiping her blade low, sensing that Veth was attacking high. Schere rolled her shoulders to bring her bolt pistol to bear. The ranger didn't see the motion and might have been shot, but she felt Veth's awareness of the attack, and turned sidelong. Schere fired the bolt pistol under her armpit and through her own greatcoat. The shot whistled past Amallyn's chest close enough to feel the heat of its passing, and blew a hole through the stomach of the cultist behind her. He fell backwards, his final moments spent thrashing in agony on the deck plating.

Melantha ducked and rolled, her chainsword whirling in circles with a speed her species had never been meant to command. Finally, the commissar executed a fatally foolish leap, seeking to avoid the low strike of Veth's serrated cutlass. Amallyn rose behind her, her own powerblade pounding through the human's back. She hefted the commissar's weight with a surge of fury, letting the human's own bulk drag the powerblade up and through her torso.

Melantha slid to the ground. Amallyn and Veth stood, panting, over the corpses of the cultists.

'A disgrace to our species?' Veth said. She leaned over, wincing as she cradled her ruined hand.

Amallyn shrugged and pulled a dermastrip from one of her belt pouches. She hastily wrapped it around her wounded forearm. Once her own injury was bandaged, she tore the fabric loose and gestured for Veth to offer up her own mangled limb.

'How long do you think we have before their reinforcements arrive?' asked the corsair. Amallyn looked up and did some quick calculations.

'At a swift run it'll take them around seven minutes to get from their closest post to this bay,' she said. 'Assuming they called for help when you fired on the ogryn, we've probably got four minutes, six at the most.'

'Then let's see if this was all for nothing,' said Veth. She inspected her freshly bandaged arm. 'Not bad,' she said, which Amallyn assumed was the closest she was going to get to thanks.

'Aren't you worried that's going to invite some opportunistic outcast to attack you?' asked Amallyn as they flanked the door to the command centre.

Veth held up her severed hand. 'This? No.' She made a dismissive gesture, then peeked through the door. 'I'll get it regrown eventually.' She considered the bandaged stump for a moment. 'Or maybe I'll get it replaced with a razor hook.' She jerked her head for Amallyn to follow and ducked into the command centre.

The inside of the box was small, barely large enough for a built-in desk on one side, a cot on one wall and a bank of primitive human machines. Amallyn wasn't certain if they were for communication, data storage or some other purpose, and didn't have the time to study them to find out. Her attention was absorbed by the artefact on the commissar's desk.

The book was open. It was nearly a yard tall and almost that wide while it was opened. The two eldar women drew closer, mesmerised by the reflections shimmering off the metallic surface of the pages. Each page was covered in thin ridges, clustered by the thousands in curving, spiralling patterns far too regular to be script.

'It's blank,' Veth protested. Before Amallyn could reply, the corsair had reached out to turn the page, to see if each of the rest were as useless as the ones showing.

As soon as her fingers brushed the foil, a scintillating burst of colour rose from the book. Runes and images swam across Amallyn's vision. The drukhari's fingertip stroked the edge of the page, just a hand's breadth of a single corner, and Amallyn was overwhelmed.

She could see chains of geometric aeldari runes, interlinked in complex thought-concepts, roiling across her mind. It was like listening to fragments of a dozen conversations: she could pick out bits and pieces but no clear narrative. She saw clearly that this section of the *Chorale* spoke of the eldar deities, with fragments of stories she'd listened to her whole life and some she had never heard before. She stood, dizzy, as her mind tried to make sense of incomplete rune stories about Vaul, Isha, and every other deity she had ever heard of. She felt stinging tears as her mind recognised the hated symbol of She Who Thirsts, and a stomach-clenching dread at the horned wraith-symbol of Ynnead.

'Get a box,' whispered Veth. 'Something to carry it in.'

Amallyn stumbled back out of the command centre, reeling. She hurried to the wall of containers, looking for a wooden crate large enough to hold the *Chorale Lilcartha*. The ranger's mind still raced, struggling to believe the evidence of her senses. Part of her hadn't believed they would really find the ancient artefact. The discovery potentially changed everything. The truth about the Ynnari and their fabled croneswords, the locations of lost craftworlds, the secrets of their civilisation, preserved from before the Fall: all of them were at her fingertips. Biel-Tan's salvation could be, too.

'Have you found something?' Veth called, appearing at the doorway to the command container. Amallyn nodded, struggling with her wounded arm to pull the wooden crate she'd found down from its stack. The corsair sighed and jogged towards her, lending her own uninjured arm to the task.

The roaring explosion nearly blew them both down. Blazing shrapnel rattled and pinged through the command container. A wave of force blasted from the door, followed a moment later by a wash of flame. Amallyn stared in shock, icy despair creeping across her face. She let out a keening wail of anguish, unable to articulate her horror into real words.

Veth had no such compunctions. With a string of profanity vile enough to take an ork back, she stormed her way back into the command centre. Her vulgar display shocked Amallyn into action, who followed the corsair in, while she struggled to understand what she was seeing.

The desk had exploded. Any hope she had of the *Chorale Lilcartha* surviving was gone the moment she stepped through the door. Only twisted scrap remained on that end of the container, blackened, melted stains driven up the walls and across the ceilings and floor. The interior of the command centre, whose walls were designed to withstand anti-tank rounds, had focused the explosion inwards, turning the container into a firestorm of white-hot shrapnel and roiling flame. The walls and the warped metal fragments beneath their feet still radiated an angry heat.

A single scrap of metallic foil, smaller than a child's palm, fluttered on a hot bubble of air and drifted past Amallyn, who reached one hand out to take the fragment in numb, gloved fingers. She felt a tiny pulse of psychic residue from the page, and tucked it in one of her belt pouches. As swiftly as she could, she grabbed what fragments she saw, most of which had been blown out the door of the container before the wash of heat had destroyed everything left inside.

'That miserable *gla'an,*' Veth raged. She whirled on Amallyn. 'She must have rigged the desk to explode.'

Amallyn stared at the last page fragment.

'How were you going to have your hand regrown?' she whispered.

'What?'

The ranger turned her head to regard the drukhari, who was busily searching the scrap on the ground for anything recoverable.

'I said, how were you going to have your hand regrown?' Amallyn stared at her companion, who cocked her head quizzically. 'Aren't you an outcast from Commorragh? Which haemonculus were you going to pay to do it?'

Veth shook her head as if in confusion. 'I don't understand,' she said, 'but we don't have time for this. We need to go.'

The two women raced through the labyrinth of crates. Ignoring the corsair, Amallyn scaled the dangling chain to their extraction point as quickly as her injuries would allow. Below her, undaunted by her own injuries, Veth followed, hooking her injured arm through the links to gain the needed leverage.

'You aren't a renegade at all, are you?' Amallyn asked as Veth swung herself into the entry port.

'Whatever do you mean?' the drukhari replied, her voice the model of icy calm.

Amallyn Shadowguide scowled. 'Since first you came to the Talisman, I couldn't understand why you left Commorragh. What, did you fancy yourself the next Traevelliath Sliscus? Both you and I know there's only one Serpent, and you could never hope to compete.'

Veth grinned. 'Maybe I dislike taking orders.'

Amallyn scoffed. 'You served archons for decades. You never had a problem with it before. But when the new Blackstone Fortress is discovered, all of a sudden you can't bear the strain of Vect's rule any longer? I think not.' The pathfinder pointed one accusing finger at Veth. 'And a loyal dracon would be a huge target for the ruthless piratical types in and around Precipice. But a corsair princess? She would be just another renegade in a festering, lawless knot of villains.'

The drukhari shrugged. 'You aren't right, but let's say you are. Let's pretend that I *do* serve Vect's interests here, or at least that the Living Muse believes I do.' She pointed one hand back towards the bay. 'Do you think it changes anything? That it isn't better this way?'

Amallyn stared at Veth, unable to believe what she was hearing. Her mouth moved but no sound came out. She could feel her rage boiling again. If she hadn't required Veth's assistance in getting back to her ship, she'd have been inclined to dash the drukhari's head against the wall.

'Think about it,' said Rayden. 'How does the discovery of the *Chorale Lilcartha* benefit our people, in the long run?

Yours especially?' The dracon held up her remaining hand and began counting factions off on her fingers. 'The Harlequins already know whatever they think it is they need to know, and probably have a copy of this damn book in their Black Library anyway. The Exodites neither know nor care about the words of our forebears. The drukhari of Commorragh won't be swayed by this text – we already live as we've always lived, as our kind was *meant* to live.' Veth held up her last finger, pointing it right back at Amallyn. 'And the craftworlders? Your spineless lot sailed away in your worldships to get *away* from the society that wrote this book!'

Veth threw up her arms, stage-yelling to express her exasperation. 'The only aeldari who stand to profit from the *Chorale Lilcartha* are the Ynnari who need its secrets to undermine our civilisations, and the greedy corsairs who would fight for the right to sell it to them.' She grinned again, her face a mask of malevolence. 'And neither of us wants that, do we?'

Amallyn stood, horrified, digesting Veth's words. There was a twisted, terrible logic there. Even before the coming of Ynnead, her people had charted their way forwards, to reconquering the galaxy, and she couldn't realistically see a book of forgotten lore changing their plans. Not really. They might use the secrets within if the autarchs thought they could benefit, but ultimately they would regard the *Chorale* as a tool, not a life-changing template of what their society had been and could be again. A part of her refused to accept the reasoning, though: somewhere she knew she would have risked fracturing eldar society as a whole further, if it meant repairing the fractures in her own home world.

'Now,' said Veth, placing one wicked hand on Shadowguide's shoulder, 'let's go back and divvy up our score. Paltry though it might be, I think we'll both find that any number of interested parties will pay small fortunes for those scraps you gathered. As far as anyone on Biel-Tan needs to know, we found it this way.'

Amallyn jerked away from the dracon. She could feel Veth's glee at the corners of her psyche, but slammed the shutters of her mind closed, locking her kin out. She clamped down on the anger boiling from her gut, forcing it down the same way she had for the uncountable years she had spent walking the path of the outcast.

'I've already got my share,' she hissed. 'And it seems to me that your half of the bounty is still back there in that shipping container.' She jerked her chin towards the bay dismissively. 'Feel free to go and get it.' Then, with a swirl of cameleoline silk, she turned and stalked away down the port tunnel.

Veth Rayden, her soft laughter echoing in the darkness, followed behind.

NEGAVOLT

NICHOLAS WOLF

Pain.

A thousand white-hot needles stabbing through my skin, over and over and over. Adrenaline surges through my screaming veins, chased by sinister, malevolent venom.

Agony.

+*Wake up.*+

My heart thunders in my chest as my anguish grows with each throbbing beat. Every animal instinct within me shrieks, telling me to flee, to writhe, to open my mouth and scream, but I don't. I can't. The iron mask bolted onto my skull keeps my jaws locked tightly closed.

My suffering grows, applauded by the parasitic bionic screwed into my spine. Scrapcode hisses hungrily in my mind as the daemon within sends electricity crackling through my ravaged nerves, flaying the raw meat of my mind with the tenderness of a serrated blade.

I suffer, sweating in agonised silence, as the empathic-resonance coil tortures me, until the mechadendrites whipping around my head crackle with violent, eldritch lightning. I suffer, my hands locked in a shuddering rictus, as corrupted Motive Force flows into my electro-goads. I suffer, my ravaged body jerking on the strings of a cruel puppet master, until every last thought is devoured by all-consuming rage.

I suffer because it makes me strong.

'Time has no meaning to the meaningless.'

I can't remember where I first heard it, but I feel like I've heard it more than once. Or maybe the sentiment rang so true I've just replayed it in my mind. I don't remember and it doesn't matter, because I don't matter.

I remember exactly where I first heard *that* sentiment: Magos Vestus Artorus Rhynne, overseer of Generarium Sub-Complex Tertius Delta-Gamma-824. Where I was born. Where I'll die.

I sit at my workstation, one of tens of thousands of menials acting as cogs in the great machine. I'm hardwired into my terminal via a MIU port in the back of my skull. Haptic implants in my fingers draw relevant data into my ocular bionic. They're the only pieces of blessed machinery I've been allowed, the bare minimum required to monitor the Motive Force crackling through Voltage Sump 246-Rho. The rest of my body is flesh and blood and bone: weak, impractical, inefficient, transient.

Tired. Hungry. Aching from hunching over my terminal.

'To know one's purpose is to know the Omnissiah's will,' drones from a passing servo-skull. Magos Rhynne prefers verses of scripture to machine-cant data-hymns.

A minor fluctuation ripples across the sump's auxiliary venting chamber. It's the most interesting event to transpire in the entirety of my seventeen-hour shift. I blink-toggle through reserve coolant tanks and mind-pulse a command through my MIU, increasing the flow of liquid nitrogen to the affected chamber by 0.21% to compensate.

I breathe out a long sigh. The air reeks of burnt iron and acrid lubricant, cloying incense and stale sweat. I breathe in through my mouth, trying not to taste it.

I pray to the Omnissiah that some day I won't have to.

Another fluctuation alert. 246-Rho's auxiliary venting chamber again. I access the diagnostic, parsing the data as quickly as my unaugmented brain will allow. One of the magnetic containment coils is showing erratic power signatures. I flag the abnormality, compile an incident report and mind-pulse it to the central routing cogitator for later analysis.

I consult the chronometer. One hour, fourteen minutes until end of shift.

My terminal chimes as a data-packet appears on my ocular screen, flashing urgently. Priority Beta. That's never happened before.

My fingers dance across my keyboard as the data-load gradually unspools. Collated anomaly reports from other terminals. I mind-pulse them to my terminal's screen: with my limited enhancements it's quicker for me to read that way. Nothing appears. My workstation's cogitator clicks and whirs as it breaks down the data into relevant statistics.

I wait, drumming my fingers as the subroutine finishes. I bite down an inefficient, possibly heretical grunt of annoyance at the speed of my blessed workstation. I wonder how long it's been since it last received the Manifold Blessing of Proficient Cogitation. I hear chiming in the distance. One hour, thirteen minutes.

The subroutine clicks to a halt. Modelled data flickers onto my screen. I see screeds of anomaly reports. The containment coils in 246-Rho's venting chambers are failing. All of them. Adrenaline floods through my veins.

'By the Omnissiah,' I whisper.

More chiming in the distance. Lots of it.

I frantically blink through remediation protocols, but each one terminates as soon as I attempt to activate it. System overload. I don't have the access to override it. I try rerouting the voltage sump's crackling electrical discharge into a neighbouring receptacle. The command terminates as soon as I send it, hitting a wall of countermeasure code. The failure isn't limited to my voltage sump, but affects all of them.

Chiming. Chiming everywhere, all at once.

Then the screaming starts.

Menials start frantically unplugging from their cogitators and fleeing the generarium. A subsonic humming begins to build, interspersed by ominous crackling. Sparks vomit from the blessed machinery around me and become coiling arcs of the Motive Force. Suddenly everyone is fleeing. Even the servo-skulls are fleeing.

I sprint from my chair and am painfully yanked back into my seat. My MIU dendrite won't release. The emergency lockdown protocol has frozen all systems, chaining thousands of us to our cogitators. I grit my teeth and try to pull the cord out of my skull but the socket clamps won't budge.

'Help!' I cry. 'Help, someone, help me!'

The stampeding crowd all but ignores me. One or two stop for a moment, but flee as soon as they realise they can't help me. Desperate tears run down my face. The hum becomes an angry whine. Crackling electricity arcs into the menials in section septimus. They shriek in agony, jerking and writhing, as the Motive Force burns their bodies from the inside out.

'Help!' I cry. 'Help me! Omnissiah, please, help me!'

And suddenly I see my salvation.

On the upper gantry, surrounded by a small army of adepts, lexmechanics and servitors, is Magos Rhynne, the holy lord of Generarium Sub-Complex Tertius Delta-Gamma-824. I wave my arms frantically to grab his attention.

'Magos! Magos Rhynne! Help!'

He stops. He stares down at me, emerald bionics clicking and whirring in the shadows of his hood.

'Master, the system's in lockdown,' I yell over the klaxons and screaming. 'I can't override it!'

He doesn't move. I can almost hear the subroutines whirring in the holy cogitators that comprise his brain.

He's going to leave me to die.

'You can override it! Help me, please!'

But Magos Rhynne doesn't help me. He turns and flees the generarium, leaving me chained to my cogitator.

'Wait!' I scream. 'No! Where are you going? Come back! Don't leave me here!'

But my pleas are lost, devoured by the ear-splitting roar that drowns out even the frightened wailing of the doomed. I can only watch, staring in petrified awe as the terrifying power of the Motive Force slips its bonds and hungrily consumes the generarium.

I scream as fifty thousand volts rip through my MIU into my skull, incinerating me from the inside out.

Something is happening.

Or maybe something has already happened.

I hear the entire cult thrumming, crackling, howling to life around me, agonised screams echoing from the cursed blackstone walls. Warped lightning arcs around those who survive the awakening. Several spasm violently, sinews cracking and bones snapping, as the pain-batteries wired into their bodies overwhelm them, burning them out like overloaded circuits.

They collapse to the floor in dismal heaps, the daemonically amplified pain that once animated them hollowing them out.

Thret skitters into the chamber on spidery legs, followed by a cohort of the Grendish 82nd and two immortals of the Servants of the Abyss.

Thret is a hulking mass of corrupted bionics veined with warped flesh, scraps of red cloth all that remains of his former allegiance. The Traitor Guard, led by Commissar Vigril, are decked in chains, spikes and grisly trophies, a dark shadow of the regiment they once were. The immortals that stomp beside them are divine avatars of ceramite and adamantium and iron and brass, cast in the dread image of the pantheon.

The daemon-shard infesting the machinery within my body hisses with rage at the sight of the immortals and sends a spiteful bolt of electricity searing across my chest.

'Negavolts! Rejoice!' Thret thunders in a grating, wet monotone. He spreads his spindly, biomechanical arms, taking the cult in his hands as he first did long ago. 'Battle calls us!'

'Rejoice when the enemy is dead, Thret,' the Grendish commissar snarls from behind a skull-faced rebreather. 'Our rituals in the lower corridors cannot be interrupted!'

Hundreds of Negavolts try to shout hungrily over the din of our awakening, but our cries emerge from our iron masks as muffled roars. The air crackles with our hatred, our inability to give voice to it making the rage physically unbearable. We're starving, *famished* for bloodshed. The Blackstone Fortress, our damnable prison and indomitable sanctum, gives and takes irrespective of our craving.

'I had four squads guarding the maglev shaft near the

citadel's lower cordons,' Commissar Vigril announces, addressing the entirety of the cult. 'And we haven't heard from them in over an hour. With the damned vox-net down we have no option but to assume there's been another attack. We're going to reinforce my troopers to ensure our ritual is completed.'

Thret's mechadendrites thrash and scream in serpentine frustration. 'You awakened the Negavolt Cult over some missing sentries? It could've been spindle drones or a thousand other maladies! Why awaken us?'

'The lower cordon was defended by no less than four handpicked squads of the Dread Harbingers,' Vigril growls back. 'Anything that can break through four squads of my best men requires nothing less than a full mobilisation. There's too much at stake to take a chance.'

Thret is unimpressed, I can see it in the hunch of his rotting body. 'You place great confidence in your men, commissar.'

The commissar straightens his back. He barely reaches Thret's chest. 'Explain yourself, and choose your words carefully.'

'They are of flesh,' Thret grates back simply, spreading his four biomechanical arms and eight bladed legs. 'And the flesh is weak.'

Commissar Vigril glares at our master. I can see his gloved finger hovering over the activation rune on the chainsword belted at his waist. Every fibre of my being wills him to try, so I can release the agonising, crackling power thrumming through my body.

'Had I nothing more important to do I'd happily demonstrate how dangerous the Grendish 82nd is,' Vigril finally growls. 'But not all of us command an army of defective monstrosities worthy only of de–'

'Enough of this,' the horned immortal thunders, his voice a deep-throated hacksaw grind. Silence immediately descends.

'Lord Mallex has decreed that the Grendish rituals are not to be disturbed, and so they will not be,' the other demigod intones, his face a scarred, biomechanical ruin. 'See that it is done, cultmaster.'

Then, at some unspoken signal, the towering warriors turn and march out of our chamber without another word.

'Wait, where are you going?' Vigril calls to their backs.

'We are needed elsewhere,' the demigod answers without turning.

'What do you mean elsewhere?' the commissar splutters as he runs to catch up. 'Our rituals are of the utmost importance to cementing our hold on the Blackstone Fortress! Need I remind you of our mission here?'

The horned immortal turns. Slowly.

'Lord Mallex's throne cannot be left unguarded,' the horned one snarls, glaring at the commissar. I realise the horns are actually growing from his head, not his helmet. 'And the next time you speak without being spoken to I shall personally peel the flesh from your bones and let the daemons have their way with what's left of you.'

The silence is palpable, but for the crackle of our weapons and the skin-crawling hum of active power armour. The commissar doesn't flinch, but he drops his gaze first.

'As you command,' he hisses through his mask.

The immortals stomp away without another word as though not noticing him.

Thret looses an aggravated blurt of scrapcode. 'Are you done grovelling?' he grates. 'If there is something to slay, let us slay it! My children are aching to release their fury! Do you not feel their rage saturating the air?'

Commissar Vigril rises and fixes our leader with his death-mask gaze.

'I have command authority of all non-Astartes forces in this quadrant, Thret. Your cult will answer to me.'

'If you say so.' Is there amusement in his burbling rasp?

'Just make sure our rituals are uninterrupted, freak,' Vigril growls before sprinting towards the fight, his retinue and honour guard in tow.

Thret throws his many arms wide, rearing back on his spidery legs. 'To battle, my children! Let your pain lend you speed!'

The cult voices its war-screams in the only way it can: with violent arcs of corrupted, vengeful power.

We leave the few overloaded corpses of the cult to smoulder where they lie. If the scavengers that infest Lord Mallex's sanctum don't consume their remains, the Blackstone Fortress will.

My scorched eyelids crack open.

The reek of burned skin floods the raw pit where my nose was. I try to breathe through my mouth but it feels as though I've swallowed barbed wire. I can't move. My skin, my muscles, my bones feel like they're still on fire. I suck cold, greasy air into my scorched lungs and cough out bloody phlegm.

By the Omnissiah.

I'm alive.

'...ate resource loss report.'

A withered servitor, reeking of unguents and rancid meat, clicks and answers. 'Compliance. Of the thirteen thousand two hundred and ninety-three casualties brought to this facility, seven thousand five hundred and forty-seven have expired. Fatalities estimated to reach eleven thousand nine hundred and eighty-seven within the next Terran standard solar cycle,' it drones from a vox-grille embedded in its slack jaws. 'Relevant diagnostic data is available for perusal.'

'No need, irrelevant,' the second voice clucks. 'Have the deceased transferred to Reclamator Thret. Instruct him to have their bionics removed for reconsecration and prepare their biomass for reconstitution.'

Beep, whirr, click.

'Command processed,' the servitor drools. 'Reclamator Thret confirms compliance. Transfer of deceased biomass for reconstitution… reconstitution… reco *urgh-ckch*.'

'Fine, fine, but can any of the living be salvaged?' That voice. I know that voice. I've heard that voice more times than my own, projecting from cyber-cherubim and vox-casters and servo-skulls from the day I first began my lifetime of service in the generarium.

'Query answer – nega–'

'M-ma-mago-s-s…'

A shadow falls across me, blotting out the grimy lumen-light. Magos Vestus Artorus Rhynne towers over me, a regal pillar of iron and chrome and steel and glowering bionics, surrounded by his retinue of lexmechanics, holoservitors and tech-thralls. Just seeing him, his holy form, soothes the pain of his betrayal, that knifing sadness in my chest of knowing that he'd abandoned me, a loyal menial who had served him faithfully for over thirty cycles.

'This one is still alive,' Rhynne remarks as though noticing rust.

The servitor's ocular bionics flicker as data pours into them. 'Delta-28-4 Gamma 6. Psi-class menial. Assigned to 246-Rho Voltage Sump.'

'Wh-why di-didn't y-y-you he–'

'Be quiet,' he snaps. Mechanically I comply, like a piece of machinery, lapsing into twitching, agonised silence. They're the first words my master has ever spoken directly to me.

Magos Rhynne plugs a mechadendrite into the data-slate

hanging from my slab. His wizened face, as impassive as the holy metal that constitutes his elevated machine-form, creases ever so slightly. 'Nervous system damage precludes conventional servitor conversion.'

Servitor conversion?

'Affirmative,' the servitor drones, staring blankly at nothing. 'Subject has sustained catastrophic neurological system damage. Rehabilitation would require class four nano-surgery and synth-nerve grafting.'

Magos Rhynne disconnects from the data-slate. He won't even look at me. 'I have a new shipment of menials arriving within two solar cycles. The resources required to rehabilitate a menial are far in excess of the loss of productivity its absence would cause,' he says, seemingly to himself.

My chattering teeth clench as sick, hot rage floods through the ruin of my body.

Loss in productivity? That's all I ever was, a tool? A digit on a ream of parchment?

'N-no b-b...'

The servitor clicks and clanks, as though the cogitations taking place in its idiot brain are painful. 'Recommendation – salvage brainmass via lobotomy and mindwipe for servitor implantation. Reconstitution protocol for biomass.'

I thrash against my bindings as much as I can. I'm not going to be butchered like an animal and have my brain scooped into a slave-machine. 'No! Y-yo-you c-ca... *uurrghh*... y-you ca-can't!'

'I said be *quiet*,' Magos Rhynne snaps at me. He turns to the servitor. 'Authorise euthanasia protocols for all remaining casualties Theta-class and below with under fifty per cent rehabilitation probability.'

I want to kill him. More than anything else I've ever wanted, more than his praise, more than greater knowledge, more than new bionics, I want to rise off this slab of metal, wrap my hands around his throat, and choke the life from his miserable body.

'I-I'll k-k-k… *nnggghhh*… ki-kill…'

But Magos Rhynne doesn't see me, doesn't hear me, doesn't even acknowledge that I exist. He turns and glides out of the medicae facility, his retinue and servo-skulls in tow, just like he did in the generarium, and I'm utterly powerless to stop him.

'Confirmed,' the servitor drones to no one. 'Standard salvage, servitor conversion and reconstitution protocols. Transferring to Reclamator Thret.' Then, like a marionette with its strings cut, it clatters back into silence.

Hot, angry sobs wrack me. Stinging tears leak from my scorched eyes, blurring the lumens into burning smears. Bleak, crushing sorrow smothers whatever embers of hope I might've had left.

No. This can't be how I die.

This can't be.

This can't be…

I awaken in darkness. In agony. The cold air feels greasy on my scabbed skin. I hear the echo of chanting, deep and alien, from somewhere. I'm not dead. I should be dead.

A sinister figure looms beside my slab, a pillar of raggedy darkness but for three green optics glowing from his bronze mask.

'W-whe-where a–'

The masked figure places a gloved hand on my shuddering lips, gently, almost tenderly. His fingers reek of unguents, antiseptic and rotted blood.

'Shhh… Rest, my friend. I am Reclamator Thret,' the figure grates wetly from a vox-grille. 'And I'm going to save you.'

* * *

I don't often pray to the Dark Gods, as some of my cult-brothers do. I prayed rarely to the Machine-God, as my daily routine dictated, but infrequently did I ever find myself beseeching the Omnissiah. Even knowing the power of Chaos, wasting so many years of my life offering data-hymns to a lie makes the act of worship seem sour.

But right now I pray to the Dark Gods that the intruders be Imperials, so I can have the pleasure of murdering them.

My fervent prayer beats hot through my tortured veins with every heartbeat, like razor splinters slicing through me. The rest of the cult thunders towards battle around me, alongside Vigril and his Dread Harbingers. The air around us crackles with eldritch lightning and murder-lust straining to slip its leash. Scrapcode data-prayers steel our flesh against the suffering we are to endure. I can feel the data-daemon lurking in my empathic resonator growing hungry. In my mind I can almost see its fangs growing longer in anticipation.

The Blackstone Fortress is a labyrinth of darksome corridors and shadowy passageways, narrow bridges extending over bottomless chasms, and vaulted ceilings so tall they devour any light that attempts to probe them. Lord Mallex's citadel, grown out of the inscrutable blackstone like a colossal tumour, is a twisted mirror to the alien structure beyond. Whispers, pregnant with vile hunger, haunt every blood-daubed pathway. Sentient dread hides in the flickering shadows cast on every wall, always present, rarely seen.

We wind down into the lower cordons, passing rows of spindle drones, dead, dismantled, violated. I send a frustrated bolt of electricity scorching into one as I pass. I've lost count of how long we've spent trying to corrupt these machines, to bind daemonic essences to them, only to have the Neverborn hurled back into the warp, hissing with impotent rage.

Early in our imprisonment I realised that the Blackstone Fortress is closer to a living organism than a space vessel, and the spindle drones are part of its immune system.

I want to sicken this place, to make it weak, to kill it.

At last we pass into a great sunken chamber swarming with activity. The stench of blood, rotten meat and ozone are the first sensations to assail me, followed by a subsonic, bone-aching throb.

At the centre of the chamber hovers a massive, blood-soaked artefact, haloed in crackling power, bathing the space with jaundiced light. It looks like a shard of obsidian, both liquid and stone at once, its crystalline lattice slowly reforming into different patterns. A piece of archeotech, one of countless thousands our forces have plundered from the Blackstone Fortress, each one unique and, apparently, valuable beyond measure.

So this is what the Grendish 82nd are guarding.

Around the archeotech floats a circle of eight emaciated sorcerers and psykers, arms raised and faces clenched in agony, chanting corrupting prayers that burn the ears to hear. What the artefact's purpose is, or what the Grendish forces are attempting to do to it, or even how long they've been at work is beyond me, and beyond my caring.

The pain-battery infesting my body screams for violence, and I have no foe on which to vent my rage. I look to Thret, who looks similarly disappointed to have not arrived at a battle.

The arriving Grendish forces buzz around the chamber like rad-ants, erecting fresh ferrocrete barricades, directing Vigril's reinforcements to makeshift gun nests, training heavy weapons platforms towards the yawning portal at the head of the chamber. A grossly warped ogryn stomps around in idiot frustration, moaning gibberish and fiddling with its mutations like a child examining a new toy.

They're spread thin.

+This prison bleeds them. How amusing.+

Sergeants in blackened rebreathers direct my cult-brothers to front-line redoubts surrounding the yawning entrance to the chamber, ready to repel a full frontal assault with our crackling weapons.

They're nervous.

+It is the curse of mortals to fear death.+

Death would be a luxury.

Commissar Vigril strides towards the improvised command centre in the corner of the chamber. 'Lieutenant, status report.'

The lieutenant salutes, then resumes glaring at a glowing cogitator. 'We still haven't reached the maglev sentries on the vox,' he announces over the din. 'Since then squads Harmeck, Gestrol and Vorsh have fallen out of vox contact as well.'

'You sent three squads?'

'We needed to know what came out of the maglev.'

I see Vigril's fist clenching but he says nothing. The commissar then points at the cracked screen. 'They *all* lost contact in the lower cordon. Vox-net should still reach that deep into the fortress.'

'Our enginseers have checked and rechecked the vox-net,' the lieutenant replies. 'We've sacrificed slaves to boost the signal with their blood.'

Vigril's face is hidden beneath his armoured rebreather, but I know he's scowling. 'And you're absolutely certain the vox-net isn't being jammed?'

I see the lieutenant give a strange look. 'By something other than the Blackstone Fortress?'

Commissar Vigril bends over some reports and schematics. My mind blurs out their inane chatter. I can barely focus through the eye-watering pain beating like nails through my temple.

'Damn this place,' the Grendish commissar growls. 'We can't afford to send any more men down there. How did this happen?'

The lieutenant consults the terminal. 'We don't know, commissar. On your orders we fortified that maglev exit with enough squads and heavy weapons to stop a Baneblade.'

'Unless the maglev passageways rearranged.'

The Grendish forces turn, gazing up at Thret, who towers over even the ogryn hulking nearby. 'Explain yourself,' Vigril demands.

Our leader plugs a scaly mechadendrite into the terminal and displays a three-dimensional diagram from a holo-projector embedded in his shoulder. He draws a line through the flickering structure with a grimy claw.

'There are several forces on Precipice with mapping technology superior to our own,' he rasps with a burble of scrapcode. 'It's possible our attackers descended through an unknown maglev or maglevs, jammed your transmissions and attacked your garrison from behind, picking them off before they could reposition.'

Vigril glowers at his lieutenant for a long time. The grim-faced soldier's face grows grimmer. 'But then why wait to strike at our ritual chamber?' Vigril snaps. 'It's clearly what they've come for. Whoever they are, they could've attacked an hour ago!'

'You said it yourself, you sent every man you could spare into the lower maglev ingress to investigate,' Thret muses. I experience the hunger in his voice as a burning burst of adrenaline flooding my ravaged veins. 'Your enemies have bled you dry, commissar, one squad at a time.'

The Grendish commander glares at my master, then back at the hololith, his face unreadable but his gloved hands shaking with rage. 'And who, do you suppose, has superior mapping technology to ours, Thret?'

We suddenly hear a new sound beneath the pulsing of the archeotech ritual, the clank-rattle of ammo belts, the roar of the ogryn: a dull, whining hum that suddenly builds into a throaty growl, louder than the din of battle preparation, louder than the ritual chanting, louder than the molten-iron thud of my heartbeat in my ears.

The local vox crackles with squealing static as it's jammed.

'Rejoice!' Thret cries to the cult, raising his bladed legs. 'War is upon us!'

At long last!

+Finally.+

As though on cue, a hulking Kataphron Destroyer servitor grinds through the yawning portal on a track-unit and unleashes its overcharged plasma culverin into the heart of the Dread Harbingers.

'W-what is that th-th-thing?' I say, extending a shuddering finger.

Even in the gloomy twilight of my saviour's secret sanctum, lit only by the grimy lumens suspended over a strange chirurgeon, I can see the cylindrical device, as though it's glowing without actually radiating light. It hurts my raw eyes just to look at it.

'That, my child, is your salvation and your retribution,' Reclamator Thret grates wetly. 'That is why I saved you. That is why I brought you here.'

The rogue magos wheels my gurney over to the chirurgeon slab. Though my caretaker does his best, every bump and jostle and twitch sends needles stabbing into my ruined nerves. Even the dull lumens burn my lidless eyes. I clench my shuddering jaw and try to focus on simply breathing through the pain, as I've done every miserable hour of every miserable day since Magos Rhynne left me to die in the generarium.

When I'm in place the bizarre chirurgeon trundles to sickening life, like an enormous biomechanical spider afflicted by the same destroyed nervous system. The thought fills me with dread as its gangly arms clatter towards me. With machine tenderness it grabs me and drags me from my gurney onto the operating slab.

I shriek through it, as I do everything.

'Wh-wh-a–'

Thret places a spindly finger to my twitching lips. Even with his heavy gloves, vulcanised robes and bronze mask he still reeks of machine oil and some unidentifiable foulness, as though his sacred lubricants are somehow spoiled.

'Hush, child,' he coos as he gently secures my juddering limbs to the slab with iron manacles. 'Conserve your strength. You will need it.'

He drifts out of my sight towards a console. Slithering mechadendrites that look strangely alive emerge from the folds of his tattered robe. His glowering bionics flash as he interfaces with the bizarre surgery mech.

I'm vaguely aware that we're not alone in the operating chamber, that we're being watched by something unseen. The droning machine-cant wafts through the air like the odour of dead flesh. It's not lingua-technis. Just hearing it makes me feel nauseous.

'I call the device an empathic resonance coil,' Thret explains as the arms of the chirurgeon split, revealing an array of whirring, squirting, sparking tools. 'Once merged with you it will take what makes you weak and turn it into what makes you strong. Strong enough to take your revenge.'

'H-h-how?'

'I go where others fear to tread,' Thret grates, his metallic voice almost hiding the rage behind his words. 'Mysteries others would not dare gaze upon I have gazed deeply into. I have beheld arcane sciences far beyond the blind, arrogant lies of my limited kin.'

He touches a final activation rune and my slab ratchets upright. The chirurgeon positions the empathic resonance coil behind my back.

I hear a sound without hearing it: a deep, wet, hungry gurgle.

'W-w-ill it… h-heal m-m-me…?' I hiss through the pain.

Thret looks up at me. I can read nothing from the bionics gleaming from his bronze mask, but I feel he is smiling at me. 'You are special,' he muses. 'You will be my finest work.'

A snaking mechadendrite slithers from the strange device, probing the back of my skull. I can't help but shudder as it touches my skin: it doesn't feel like metal. It finally locates the scorched MIU port at the base of my skull, whirring and squealing as it locks in place.

I feel another presence occupy my mind as I interface with the machine.

I can see something in the darkness of my mind's eye. I've interfaced with enough machine-spirits throughout my life to know that this isn't one.

Before me I see a black pool, and some… *thing* with too many eyes slithering beneath the surface.

I pulse out a greeting in lingua-technis.

The entity, whatever it is, rises from its inky pool. No two machine-spirits appear alike: some appear almost human, some an abstraction of their function. My cogitator in the generarium was little more than a dull cloud of sparks.

But I've never seen anything like this.

It's like an iron-scaled serpent, but with more legs than I can count, and the lamprey-maw of a blood-sucking parasite. Venomous oil drips from its talons. It oozes rage and malice.

+So, you are what the tinkerer has brought me?+ the machine-thing hisses, its voice a wet, slurping buzz in my brain. *+He said you were special.+*

What are you?

+A shard of greatness bound to steel. Prisoner and gaoler in a cell of my choosing, a hungering splinter that cannot be dug out,+ it gibbers. *+I am the future. I am salvation. What do you desire?+*

Revenge. I want to murder the ones who did this to me.

The machine-thing appears to grin, blackened lips pulling back to reveal rows upon rows of fangs. *+And what would you give for my gift?+*

Make me strong enough and I'll give you everything. All I have left to give, it's yours.

The creature looms over me but seems reluctant to draw too close. *+Such suffering. Such rage. Perhaps the tinkerer was right,+* it muses. It seems reluctant. Cowed. *+Perhaps you are special.+*

I feel a sickening pinch at the base of my skull, half the familiar twinge of a MIU data-inload and half the wriggling, squirming of something alien worming into my body. My eyes snap open as the violating sensation spreads throughout my ruined nerves. My veins bulge from my skin as the entity chained to Thret's device pushes through my capillaries like boiling blood.

It hurts, worse than I can breathe through, worse than I can stand.

I can feel the machine-creature spreading through my flesh, through my mind, like envenomed needles scraping inside me. Sweating, nausea, cramping, convulsions wrack me as the wreckage of my body reacts to the unknowable sickness infecting it, taking the place of ruined neurons and damaged dendrites, reknitting scorched muscles and blackened bones.

I scream: not a cry of angry defiance, but the animal-panic shriek of a dying beast. My limbs thrash against my bindings. It feels like I'm being flayed alive, doused with acid and set on fire all at once.

And then, suddenly, my ravaged muscles no longer twitch, but pulse with strength. For the first time since the generarium accident I willingly close my hand into a fist.

But the pain doesn't recede. It only continues to build.

'Thret!' I shriek. 'Stop! Stop, please! AAAAA–!'

A clattering armature slams an iron mask over my face while another begins drilling into my temple. I smell burning bone. My scream dies in my throat as the chirurgeon sockets iron bolts into my cheeks and jawbone, welding my jaw forever shut.

I scream in agony, but nothing but a muffled groan escapes my iron mask.

You lied! Oh by the Omnissiah, it hurts! Make it stop! Make it stop!

The poisonous voice of the machine-thing grimaces at my thoughts. *+Lie? I did not lie, pathetic human.+*

You said... Thret said... he'd heal me...

+And heal you I have,+ it replies sourly.

But it hurts! Everything hurts, a thousand times worse than before!

+Have you learned nothing from the one you call Thret? Your pain is your greatest weapon, your suffering the fuel that gives

you strength. You and I are one now,+ it hisses, voice dripping with disdain. +*Why would I rob you of your power?*+

I try to scream, try to yell, try to shout but nothing but muffled, angry, drool spurts through my clenched teeth. It's not fair. After everything I've suffered, after every betrayal I've endured, this can't be my life, an unending nightmare of freakish agony.

Slabs of spiked armour clang into my chest and limbs. Squealing drills bore hot into my ribs, my arms, my shins. Sparks whicker from the thrumming device bolted into my spine.

I hate the Imperium that did this to me.

The pain-engine's tentacles wetly crunch through muscle, sinew and gristle. Hard-plugs burst through my skin like iron boils. Lashing arcs of power rip along my scalp.

I hate everything.

With a gut-wrenching shriek I rip through my bindings and thud to the floor. The Motive Force bleeds from me, alive, hungry, fuelled by the entity haunting the machinery infesting my body. Cogitators overload and detonate. The chirurgeon writhes and flies apart in a blizzard of sparks. Lumens burst at the violent electric rage radiating from me. The laboratory is thrown into darkness, but for the living lightning blazing from my weapons.

I am…

I am unstoppable.

Thret crawls from behind the wreckage of his console, his bronze mask knocked away. In the strobing light I can see his mutated, half-machine face, like a rotted cephalopod caked in weeping scales, grinning with manic glee.

'By the Dark Gods,' he rasps, his grating voice rendered as an awestruck whisper. 'Magnificent!'

* * *

By the Dark Gods.

The Mechanicus.

Magnificent!

The Kataphron's culverin rips through the heart of the assembling defenders, turning half the men to molten slag as they shelter behind their defences. Behind it a hulking battle-automaton wades into the chamber. Castellax pattern, armed with heavy flamers, Mauler-pattern boltcannon and a crackling siege hammer. In its shadow slinks a red-robed tech-priest surrounded by a flock of heavily armed servo-skulls. A strange light grows, deep in the hallway behind them.

Magnificent indeed.

The Grendish troops react to the ambush with the speed and efficiency of professional soldiers, but still dozens are cut down before they can throw themselves behind the remains of their ferrocrete barricades. Commissar Vigril's commands boom over the thundering chaos of gunfire and explosions, but his men are already repositioning weapons platforms for a counter-attack. A heavy bolter swivels and pours fire into the Castellax. Sparks thunder from its atomantic shielding. Still it comes, a living barricade, soaking up gunfire like an ocean drinking rain on ancient Terra.

'Protect the archeotech!' Vigril roars. 'The ritual must not be disrupted!'

We all know why the Mechanicus forces have come: like the rest of the scum infesting Precipice, they've become all too aware of Lord Mallex's growing power throughout the Blackstone Fortress. As if to drive home this truth, the Kataphron Destroyer swerves out from behind the battle-automaton and churns straight for the archeotech, heedless of gunfire.

The magos' servo-skulls whirl above our heads, autoguns chattering, riddling the floating sorcerers with bullets. Three fall to the ground in bloody heaps. The colour in the chamber sickens to an infected crimson. Foul tentacles of warp energy lash outwards, enraged, bursting anyone they touch. A vengeful, deep-throated moan builds from everywhere at once.

Thret skitters out of cover and raises his mutated hand to the sky. 'Negavolts! Let those who wronged you feel the power of your rage! Charge!'

The cult breaks from cover with a collective howl of electric rage. Behind me I hear the teeth-shaking whine of a Grendish heavy lascannon finally coming online. A screaming las-beam burns over my head, close enough to flash-blister the flesh on my back. The Castellax clanks in front of the Destroyer and barely absorbs the fusillade on its atomantic shielding.

I channel my crackling electro-goads into the leg of the staggered battle-automaton. Sparks explode from the adamantium joint as corrupted Motive Force surges from my weapons. The enormous machine falls to one knee.

For the briefest, most fleeting moment the burning agony gnawing at my bones lessens.

More! More power!

+Suffer!+

My cult-brothers hurl themselves at the reeling Castellax like a wave of electrical rage crashing against an iron shore. We strike again, and again, and again into the machine, desperate to rip it apart in our frantic rage. The Grendish's mutant ogryn howls into battle beside us, an enormous power maul wrapped in its tentacles.

And then the Castellax rises, blaring machine-cant from its data-projectors, hurling us aside like toys.

Burning promethium gushes over us from its heavy flamer, ravenous, baleful. The burning ogryn flails about in a panicked rage, throwing broken corpses through the air. Some of the cult physically burst with electrical force as the agony of burning alive overloads their empathic resonators.

Out of the corner of my eye I see the Grendish lascannon fire a second time, this time slamming into the Destroyer. Its plasma culverin detonates with bone-shattering force and blistering heat. The Grendish forces smell blood in the water.

'Focus fire!' I hear Vigril screaming over the roar of battle. 'Bring it down! Bring it down!'

At some unseen command from the magos behind it, the wounded servitor suddenly charges headlong towards the lascannon before it can recharge, grinding cultists and soldiers to bloody pulp beneath its clanking treads. Gunfire rattles ineffectually from its ceramite armour. The magos sprints into battle behind it, sheltering in its shadow, a laspistol in each hand. Anyone who raises his head above cover drops with a las-bolt through his head.

'Kill it! Kill it!'

The Destroyer lowers its head and accelerates into the heart of the Grendish defence, smashing through their barricades. A dozen Dread Harbingers, including Commissar Vigril, shriek in agony as they're dragged under the war machine's treads.

The cult cares not. We enjoy their screaming, the rich stench of their crushed bones, the horror and pain of their suffering. It makes the killing all the more enjoyable.

The magos seizes the opportunity and redirects his last servo-skulls. Three more sorcerers are shot out of the sky. The remaining psykers clutch their swollen heads in agony before the psychic backlash bursts their bodies like rotten fruit. The smouldering Destroyer trains its other dread weapon on the archeotech. The ground beneath our feet begins to quake.

I see our master's predatory glare. He doesn't care about the Destroyer or the artefact. He wants the magos for himself.

Thret skitters like a spider over the mounds of dead Grendish towards his prey. He laughs as though enjoying the most hilarious joke he's ever heard in his life as he fires his plasma pistol at the tech-priest.

'Slave of the Machine-God!' he roars. 'Your fight is with me!'

+Focus, you imbecile!+ The data-daemon rams a white-hot spike of agony behind my eye.

I desperately wish I could watch my master kill the tech-priest, but I have other problems.

The towering Castellax stomps through the cult as we swarm around its legs. Its Mauler boltcannon blasts us to bloody rags. Alchemic flames pour from its palms. Its siege hammer throws shattered bodies through the air. Every step tramples another cult-brother to gory chunks.

We leap between its crushing claws, dodge between gouts of flame, striking again and again with our crackling weapons, like ancient hunters trying to bring down our prey. It avails us nothing. My cult-brothers are dying too quickly. Every strike we make is turned aside by the Castellax's infernal countermeasures, as though we're striking something harder than metal.

Through the chaos I see Thret across the chamber. The enemy magos is impaled on his bladed forelimbs, squirming like an insect as Thret's mechadendrites slowly pull him apart. Seeing our plight, my master drags the Grendish lascannon from the rubble, waits until it is charged, and fires into the battle-automaton's back.

The Castellax's atomantic shields finally blow out with an ear-bursting subsonic pop.

+Now!+

The daemon-shard digs its barbed claws deep into the meat of my brain. I scream into my iron mask until my throat bleeds. My pain-battery discharges in a crackling lightning storm straight into the Castellax's weakened ankle.

Smoky sparks vomit from the joint. Perhaps the battle-automaton realises what's about to happen. Perhaps not. Regardless, its bio-plastek brain betrays no understanding as the ruptured servomotor within crumples and the robot collapses onto its side.

We swarm over our prey like vermin on a corpse, blood-mad and pain-sick, ramming our screaming electro-goads into the gaps in its adamantium armour, blowing out circuitry and overloading fibre-bundle musculature. The doomed Castellax jerkily flails its power fists. We die with wet crunches. It doesn't matter. I welcome death. We all do.

The scorched ogryn frantically smashes its power maul into the armoured neural cortex housing again and again. The ceramite housing finally buckles after the ninth ear-splitting blow. Sparks and astringent amniotic fluid leak from the shattered brain case.

I feel a sick mix of glee, relief, horror and sadness as the ancient battle-automaton suddenly clanks to a grinding halt.

The ogryn, finally realising it's been shot several dozen times and set on fire, collapses beside the machine. The rest of us slowly clamber off the fallen robot, bloodied, breathless, in agony. I can barely keep my electro-goads from dragging on the ground.

I did it.

I feel the daemon-shard balk. *+I did it. Without me you'd still be lying in the tinkerer's sewer-lab.+*

Echoing data-hymns cut through whatever satisfaction I'm about to feel. Some vestigial, atavistic part of my brain tries to bring me to my knees in supplication.

A glowing figure strides into the chamber, bare-chested,

wearing rubberised robes stamped with the skull and cog of the Cult Mechanicus. Lightning seems chained within his lambent blue flesh, crackling and bleeding from the bizarre stave in his gloved hand.

One of the Brotherhood of Petrified Lightning.

A Fulgurite electro-priest.

A living avatar of the Motive Force.

By the Dark Gods, the rumours are true.

+We need to flee.+

'Blasphemers!' the zealot booms, sweeping the devastation with eyes that have melted from his skull. 'Your heretical waste of the Motive Force is an affront to the Omnissiah!'

We scant few summon whatever strength our pain-batteries can scrape from our tortured bones and attack with shrieking electro-goads.

The Fulgurite priest doesn't look afraid. He's smiling. 'In the name of the Omnissiah, I will reclaim that which you have stolen!'

+Do you not hear me? Run! Flee!+ The daemon-shard is frantic.

The fight lasts only seconds. The electro-priest sprints towards us, roaring scathing data-hymns in lingua-technis. He spins between our crackling weapons, as fast as the lightning bleeding from his skin. Every cultist he strikes with his brass stave dies instantly, like a candle being extinguished.

What weapon is that that can kill us with a touch?

Distantly I hear the last of the Grendish forces desperately trying to bring down the Destroyer with ineffectual cracks of their lasguns. The dying Kataphron keeps its strange weapon trained on the archeotech until the massive structure seems to buckle under its own weight. The slaughterhouse crimson light of the chamber wilts into an aura the colour of maggots. Like a last breath being exhaled, the subsonic groan falls silent.

+Run, you fool! You cannot overcome this foe!+

'Leave my children alone!' Thret screams as he charges towards the electro-priest. He fires his plasma pistol until the handgun glows molten. Every bolt dissipates in the field surrounding the chanting electro-priest, making his translucent body glow brighter.

+I torture you for my amusement, mortal, do not think I won't do far worse if you don't obey,+ it screams, fear turning to rage.

I can see the outcome of the confrontation moments before it happens. Thret hurls himself at the electro-priest with scrapcode blaring from his data-projectors, bladed arms flailing like a tornado. I charge towards them, seeing the fatal blow that will strike my master, my saviour.

The electro-priest rams his stave into Thret's chest.

Thret convulses as though his very lifeforce is being drained from him. I scream into my mask in horror as our leader's many legs give out beneath him and he collapses to the blood-soaked floor, as inert as stone.

And suddenly I am all that remains.

I'm going to kill him.

+You should run.+

No!

'Your heresies will soon be at an end,' the electro-priest sneers as he stalks towards me.

+He will destroy us both! I am not dying for your sentimental attachment to the tinkerer!+

I'm not running. Give me everything you've got.

+NO, NO, N–+

With a muffled scream of hate I throw myself at the Fulgurite priest. He anticipates it, expects it, of course. He's faster than I am, burdened by my clanking armour, cumbersome pain-battery and heavy electro-goads. Much faster.

He locks my electro-goads with his strange brass staff. Icy terror instantly envelops me. I feel my lifeforce being siphoned away, like a thousand leeches drinking my blood at once. The electro-priest grins, lightning arcing between his blue lips. I frantically struggle to free my weapons but my strength is failing. I can hear my daemon-shard screaming in scrapcode, frantically pouring whatever suffering it can into my pain-battery, but it's no use. I'm dying. I fall to my knees. Darkness devours my eyes.

No...

The forge world is burning, as though being consumed by the righteous flames of vengeance.

It started with an invasion from the stars. Datagheists haunting the planetary vox-net reported massive vessels emerging from the warp bearing non-Imperial colours. Planetary defences, legions of skitarii, maniples of battle-automata, fleets of Naval vessels – the entire planet mobilised for war. We begged Thret to release us, to order the attack. The Negavolt Cult was ravenous, pain-sick, desperate to be unleashed but Thret, our master and saviour, instructed us to wait until the moment the war began in earnest.

The slave uprising began within moments of the first orbital strike. With their eyes focused on the skies, the Mechanicus never expected their deaths to rise from the sewage network beneath their feet. Hundreds of cults, seeded from the detritus of the Mechanicus' greed, crippled the world before the battle could even begin.

Now, at long last, we can kill.

Electro-goads blazing, I stalk into a chamber more ornate

than anything I've ever imagined. Every wall is a painstakingly wrought homage to the ancient founding of Mars, a masterpiece of gold and silver and iron and onyx. The floor is rendered in exquisite black marble, each tile so precisely cut that my bionics can barely register an errant molecule. Brass machinery churns and hums and buzzes from the floor, ceiling and walls, oblivious to the forge world dying around it.

And every iota of it slathered in fresh blood and lubricant.

By the Dark Gods...

The remains of the poor, deluded souls that once guarded this room cloak the chamber in congealing blood, gobbets of flesh and ruptured bionics. There must have been thirty or more servitors, praetorians and huscarls, but it's impossible to discern from the heaps of rent offal that remain. It's bodily devastation on a level I have never seen.

At the centre of the chamber stand three sinister armoured behemoths, draped in gore. I creep closer, warm entrails squishing between my toes. The figures are absolutely enormous, like the battle-automata of the Castellax class but without the clanking, mechanical rigidity. These ominous beings are the flesh of an apex predator housed in a suit of warped ceramite, and they radiate malice.

The machine-thing, the daemon lurking in my empathic resonance coil, recoils.

+*Fallen Astartes,*+ it hisses in both spite and fear.

One of the gore-drenched giants gestures at me with a gun that's as big as I am. 'Is this him?' it rumbles, its voice impossibly deep.

I raise my crackling electro-goad, answering in the only way I can. My daemon-shard sends pain lancing between my eyes. My weapons hiss and spit with electrical power.

'Yes, this is he,' Thret replies, squelching out of the shadows.

He's replaced his bronze mask for an iron rebreather bedecked with stolen teeth, displaying the mutations he's long kept hidden.

'Do you speak for him?' the giant asks.

Thret spreads his dripping hands and bows low. 'The Negavolt cultists speak through their rage alone, blessed ones, that their hearts be known by the corpses they leave in their wake.'

'So be it,' the demigod replies. 'Our part of the bargain is complete, Thret.'

He bows again. 'Indeed. You may confer my oath of loyalty to Lord Mallex. When the Sons of the Abyss leave this world, the Negavolt Cult shall march with them.'

The immortals look at each other, and then stand aside.

Behind them, dangling from the ceiling, bound in his own mechadendrites, is Magos Vestus Artorus Rhynne.

'Be quick about it,' the other Astartes snaps as they stomp out of the room. 'This world will soon be ours, and Cadia calls.'

I look to Thret, my master, my saviour. It can't be. I've dreamed of this moment since the day Rhynne abandoned me. Maybe even before that.

Thret places a rotted hand upon the raw hardplugs jutting from my shoulder.

'Few, if any, ever find true justice in this world, my child,' he grates quietly. He sounds almost sad. 'I wanted you to have this.'

I dip my head in gratitude, careful not to scorch him with my deadly corona.

Thret turns to leave. 'Don't take too long, young one,' he adds cheerfully. 'We have an entire galaxy to murder.'

And then I'm alone with the man who took me from my parents the day I was old enough to be put to work, the man I'd spent my entire life looking up to, the man who wouldn't even look me in the eye when he cast me aside like a broken cog.

I loom over my gift, my plaything, a miasma of deadly energy rippling from my body. As Rhynne is a senior magos who's spent centuries modifying himself, I imagine he has replaced most of the emotive sections of his brain with blessed machinery. I still see very human fear haunting whatever remains of his heart in the twitching of his mechadendrites and the panicked telescoping of his bionic eyes.

Do your worst, daemon.

+With pleasure.+

Magos Vestus Artorus Rhynne remains stoic against the pain for only seconds before dissolving into a convulsing, blubbering, shrieking wreck. I keep him alive, pleading for death, until the moment the cult departs the next morning.

No.

The screaming pain-battery bolted to my spine grows to an ear-piercing whine as the data-daemon slams the memory into my brain.

He thinks he can drink my anger.

Sparks gout from the empathic resonance coils like the spitting of the hateful monster within.

Thinks he can fathom it.

Wings of living lightning lash out of my back, turning corpses to ash.

My rage.

I can feel the overcharged device grow hotter and hotter, molten, singeing my flesh, burning my bones, searing my nerves, burning me from the inside out.

My suffering!

+Only makes us stronger.+

I push every miserable, agonising moment of my tortured life through my blazing electro-goads into the man who killed my master.

For one brief moment the electro-priest realises he's about to die, his arrogant, crackling smile melting to animal panic. A million volts of raw hatred pour into him like a bursting dam. His body glows sun-hot for a heartbeat before violently exploding in a cloud of energy, circuitry and flesh, blasting me through the air.

I...

...awake.

Adrenaline – volcanic, acidic, raw – surges through my veins like broken glass. I scream mutely into my iron mask until my throat is raw and throbbing.

I'm up, damn you!

+Your heart stopped.+

I slowly roll myself onto my side and rise to my knees. Every muscle feels burned by caustics, every joint feels choked with rusty needles. The armour plating bolted into my bones tugs and chafes as I struggle to stay upright.

So what if it did?

+I have no intention of being chained to a corpse, mortal,+ the daemon-shard hisses. It's afraid. I can feel its cold terror. I wonder how long it's been frantically trying to rouse me with sour memories and hollow pain. *+Get up.+*

Just give me a moment. Please.

+Up, or I show you how the damned suffer in the warp.+

With a grunt of pain I haul myself to my feet, still clutching my blackened electro-goads, and survey the devastation.

The chamber lies in ruins.

The hungry crackle of fire barely eclipses the moans of

the dying. The flickering flames glint weakly from pools of blood and oil. The petrochemical reek of burning promethium mixes with the odour of split organs and the foetid stench of voided bowels. I stumble through the carnage, cold and spent, my body raw and throbbing. Even the air hurts.

Our Mechanicus attackers are utterly destroyed. None but the magos leading them ever even attempted to find cover. They knew they were being sent to their deaths; but for the grace of the Dark Gods, and Thret, I would have shared such a pointless death for the Omnissiah.

Those tasked to defend the archeotech are likewise slain to a man. Most of my cult-brothers are little more than burnt mulch sloughed around the fallen Castellax. Slowly I trudge past Grendish corpses draped over fortifications and turrets, sandbags and redoubts, defences rendered all but useless by the Mechanicus ambush. The Kataphron Destroyer hulks amid a circle of scorched, crushed, ripped-open bodies. Commissar Vigril is somewhere among the gory detritus stuck to its treads.

A pity. I wish I could have killed him myself.

The mysterious archeotech, the precious object so many died for, stands utterly inert at the centre of the room, seemingly crushed by the Destroyer's strange cannon. The corpses of psykers and sorcerers, slaves and supplicants, lie around the artefact, shot, exploded, broken. I can't help but wonder what purpose their ritual was supposed to accomplish. Whatever it was, a lot of people thought it was worth spending the last few minutes of their lives fighting over.

I come at last to the body of Thret.

Bitter, stinging tears leak from my eyes as I drop to my knees beside him. I prod him once with my electro-goad, hoping that the Motive Force might restart his heart. Nothing happens. I try again, needing no tormenting from my daemon-shard to conjure electricity. Still nothing happens. I didn't really expect it to.

I gently roll my master onto his back, taking him in one last time. All of him, from his face to his many arms to his spider-like legs, is a rotting, mutated biomechanical horror. Gone is the thundering, triumphant, brilliant warrior-engineer, replaced with a sullen hulk of ribbed pipes, veined steel, diseased flesh and tattered robes.

And beneath it all is the stilled heart of the one person who ever cared about me.

My cult is scattered. My master is dead. I am alone.

Well, not completely alone.

+*Don't look away from this,*+ the daemon-shard hisses gleefully. +*I want you to remember this. All of it. For next time.*+

Electricity crawls eagerly along my spine like an envenomed lash on freshly peeled skin.

I will.

THE THREE-EDGED BLADE

DENNY FLOWERS

The Dying Light glided through the graveyard of broken starships as smoothly as a knife sliding between ribs. Ahead of it the stars were eclipsed, their light swallowed by the looming presence of the Blackstone Fortress.

Kali Xerus of the Kabal of the Black Heart eased the vessel into the eaves of a shattered warship. Beside her, Tanvile the Twisted lounged in the co-pilot's chair, his bare feet resting on the console. He was humming an ill-formed melody, the sequence of notes never quite adhering to a tune. Hekit the beastmaster was slumped behind them, though given his input to the mission thus far his seat might as well have been unoccupied.

Xerus' fingers danced across the craft's scanners as she tried to analyse the celestial monolith. Even to the denizens of the Dark City of Commorragh, the Blackstone Fortress was an enigma, a relic from a bygone age. *The Dying Light* was equipped with a sophisticated array of sensors, designed to pierce its prey's defences. But none of the vessel's readings made sense to her. Superficially the ancient bastion was near lifeless, as dead as the graveyard of broken ships. But there was an elusive spark; a glint of unfathomable power. She was like a primitive creature gazing up at the night sky, unable to quite comprehend that each pinprick of light held the power of a sun. It was an unsettling image, but one she could not refute.

Against such majesty the way station known as Precipice was a humble affair, little more than a candle spluttering against the void. But the ramshackle void station was the residence of the traitor known as Veth Rayden, and it was there that Xerus would find both vengeance and redemption.

A glob of soft pink flesh smacked onto the sensor readout. It hung there a moment before sliding down the screen, leaving a bloodied trail in its wake.

Xerus turned. Beside her, Tanvile was staring unseeing at the expanse of dead space, the juice of the half-eaten brain-fruit staining his chin. He laughed, his gaze drifting to meet her own, the eyes black, the pupils swollen to encompass the sclera. He managed to drag his consciousness into the room long enough to register her expression. His grin widened, his lips peeling back to his ears and exposing rows of serrated teeth, like the mouth of a shark.

She reached across and tore a scrap from his sleeve, wiping his spit from the screen. It was a marginal improvement. Tanvile took another bite from the fruit, the sap staining his front, and once again drifted back into the dream of conquest.

Xerus wondered if she could kill him.

More to the point, could she kill him without suffering the consequences? Like her, he was one-third of the *Zhailtir*, a trio of hunters tasked with enforcing Supreme Overlord Asdrubael Vect's edicts in real space. Ostensibly they were the elite: three of the kabal's most dangerous agents, each a finely honed weapon. But the truth was they were all in disgrace, having fallen low in the eyes of Vect. The assignment would be their last opportunity for redemption. Failure would not be looked upon kindly, deliberately despatching their fellow assassins even less so.

But Tanvile was beyond an irritant. He was an eyesore, clad in a motley collection of rags allegedly stolen from previous victims. He carried no other possession, neither weapon nor adornment, and beneath his patchwork attire his skin – pale even for a drukhari – was criss-crossed with the jagged scars of a dozen invasive surgeries. Xerus knew the covens of the haemonculi were, if suitably compensated, capable of the most sophisticated fleshcraft, seamlessly blending species at the cellular level. She was therefore unsure why Tanvile wore his scars so shamelessly; he was either proud of his enhanced biology or merely indifferent to his personal appearance.

Then again, Hekit was little better. She cocked her head, glancing back at the slumbering beastmaster. His skin was ashen and coarse, like an inexpertly preserved corpse, his face framed by wisps of grey hair entangled with fetishes and charms. It was unsettling to sit so close to something so repugnant, a creature but one step removed from the soulless beings that haunted the outer reaches of the Dark City. It was all his own doing: Hekit had spent most of the journey in a drug-induced malaise and had made little effort to slake his thirst, insisting that the fast enhanced his shamanistic visions. Perhaps she should be thankful he had contributed so little to their mission; at least it meant she did not have to look at him.

Tanvile had finished his meal, wiping his mouth on the back of his hand and stretching, his arms folding back on themselves, shoulders twisted at an impossible angle, his enhanced biology disdainful of the limitations of conventional anatomy. He straightened, glancing around the cockpit as if for the first time.

'Why are we not moving?' he said, staring into the expanse.

'Because we have reached the Blackstone Fortress,' she replied, endeavouring to keep her tone neutral.

'Then why do we cower amongst the detritus of lesser races? Is there a reason for this delay? Did you fail to adequately fuel the ship?'

'Precipice is home to a score of scavengers. I wanted to ascertain whether there were any threats.'

'How courageous,' he sneered, lounging in his seat. 'What shall I do to pass the time?'

'Perhaps you could begin by picking the flesh from your teeth?' she replied, returning her gaze to the sensors. From the corner of her eye she saw him raise his hand, the nail on his finger extending into a talon. He slid it between his teeth, extracting the last scrap and smacking his lips as he swallowed.

'The final moment of glory,' he cooed. 'So sweet and yet so bitter.'

Xerus did not respond, maintaining her vigil. Tanvile turned away from her, already bored by the lack of engagement. He picked idly at the stitching on his left shoulder.

'How fares our spiritual leader?' he asked, gesturing to the third seat. Hekit did not respond.

'Communing with the universe,' Xerus sighed. 'He has sent his apologies and a representative to deputise for him.'

She nodded to the beastmaster's shoulder, where a razorwing

perched, steel-like talons scoring his armoured shoulder guard. It stared at Tanvile with undisguised malice.

'Before this is over I am going to kill that bird,' he said. 'Hekit too if he's not careful.'

'You are very confident,' she replied, 'he claims to be a most accomplished assassin.'

'He's a day away from being a cadaver. I would end him in a heartbeat.'

'But then we would be without our tracker.'

Tanvile rolled his eyes but did not argue. Hekit did have a curious knack for finding their quarry. The escape pod had been a particular mystery. It carried no distress beacon, registering on the long-range sensors as little more than a scrap of debris. Neither of them would have investigated if Hekit had not stirred from his trance. Though the pod's barely conscious occupant was not fully intact he had provided vital information on the whereabouts of their target, as well as a pleasant diversion from the monotony of their journey.

Tanvile bent closer, his breath stinking of bio-acid and rotten meat.

'I wonder,' he whispered, 'if outside the confines of the Dark City, he has taken to… witchcraft?'

It was an unpleasant thought. Such an act was rightly forbidden in Commorragh, lest it attracted the attention of She Who Thirsts. But there were some who dabbled in runes and petty magics, their arrogance overcoming their sense of self-preservation. Hekit's attire did little to discredit these theories. He was festooned with trinkets and fetishes: knucklebones woven into his hair, his necklace comprised of perfectly preserved eyeballs. Even the buckle of his belt was a shrunken head, the twisted face somehow never holding the same expression twice. She'd heard tales of the beastmaster's cult, how they could bend warp-spawned nightmares to their will and goad them into battle.

'Well?' Tanvile said.

'It would seem he has access to knowledge that we do not,' she shrugged. 'Let us leave it at that.'

'The same could be said for that fellow in the pod,' Tanvile mused, glancing at Hekit before turning back to her. 'We soon uncovered what he knew. Perhaps we should employ a similar approach with our resident shaman?'

'Tempting,' she conceded. 'But not pertinent to the assignment.'

'Xerus? Tanvile?' a coarse voice whispered.

'Yes, Hekit?' replied Tanvile, his head turning one hundred and eighty degrees to face him. 'Have you finished your little rest?'

The beastmaster stared at him sombrely, though his eyes were grey and clouded.

'A fugue is hardly a rest,' he chided. 'It is a perilous path not for the uninitiated.'

'Well it appears you made it back safely this time,' Tanvile shrugged. 'Perhaps you should try again.'

'Another time. For I sense our arrival.'

'Ah, not quite,' Tanvile said. 'We have *almost* arrived. However, our self-appointed leader is electing to cower, intimidated by a den of petty pirates and grave robbers. Perhaps she procrastinates because she no longer trusts her own judgement, concerned that she will make another mistake.'

He smiled, exposing needle teeth.

The words stung. She was no coward, but he was right: she had made a mistake, hesitated, and in doing so had paid a terrible price. Veth had whispered to her such sweet promises, of forging a life beyond the Dark City, free from Vect's oppression. They would commit a crime so brazen that their infamy would last for generations: stealing Vect's prized vessel, the *Eye of Vect,* and escaping to real space. It would have been an impossible feat if not for Xerus' position as harbourmaster. But when the moment came Veth Rayden chose to flee Commorragh alone, and Kali Xerus was left behind to explain the disappearance.

She'd been interrogated, of course, and claimed her failure was a momentary lapse. She did not know if they believed her, but none doubted her desire for vengeance, or that she would risk anything to take the traitor's head.

Her gaze met Tanvile's. He still wore that insolent grin. But beyond his smile she could see the hunger. It had been too long since they had fed. She could feel it too: the barbed hooks of She Who Thirsts sinking into her soul. If their needs went unsated much longer they would soon turn on each other.

'Fine,' she sighed, suppressing the urge to retaliate. 'Let us dock and make some enquires about our treacherous cousin.'

To the inhabitants of the Imperium of Man, Precipice was an abomination, an affront to their rightful place as masters of the galaxy. Its very structure was heretical, the vessels of man and other races cobbled together like a patchwork cloth. On its streets and walkways, xenos communed openly with supposedly loyal members of the Imperium, a fragile alliance maintained by the conglomerate of captains who controlled the way station, and required by the long shadow of the Blackstone Fortress. But to the drukhari it was a pale reflection of the dizzying sights offered by Commorragh. All manner of lesser species were welcomed in the Dark City, even if most were destined for a brief life in the slave pits.

Xerus moved cautiously, sticking close to the shadows. She felt vulnerable without her weapons, despite the stiletto dagger artfully concealed between the armour plates of her thigh. Beside her Tanvile strode brazenly forwards, his swagger born from a certainty that the station was little more than his personal plaything. Hekit followed a step behind, a threadbare cloak wrapped around his shoulders. He seemed so stretched now that even the lesser races could sense it. Two stunted creatures that vaguely resembled humans recoiled at the sight of them. Tanvile frowned, glancing from their hairy feet to their shaved heads. He then leant closer to Xerus, speaking in a quite audible whisper.

'Have the humans become smaller?' he asked, nodding to the creatures. 'I feel as though they were not always quite so… diminutive?'

One of the duo muttered something in response. She did not need her translator to register it as an insult. Tanvile smiled, but she could see the hunger behind his eyes.

'No violence,' she hissed as talons slid from his fingers. 'We must be inconspicuous, at least until we know the fate of Rayden.'

He stared at her, his expression unreadable, twisted by the network of scars. For a moment she thought he might turn on her. But he shrugged, sheathing his claws, his gaze never leaving her own.

'Of course,' he purred, seemingly amiable. 'There will be time for play later.'

There was something to his tone. She tried not to dwell on it.

'We need to establish Rayden's last whereabouts,' she said. 'Our source mentioned Janus Draik as someone of influence. We should start there.'

She glared at them in turn, awaiting the responses. One would object on principle alone and offer an alternate plan. The third would then be left to reconcile the two ideas, as rejecting either could risk a party turning on them. Thesis, antithesis, synthesis; the delicate process that drove the Zhailtir in the absence of a formal hierarchy.

Tanvile yawned. 'Those at the pinnacle are poorly placed to know what transpires below. We should find where these creatures drink or fornicate. It is there we shall find loose lips, I guarantee it.'

They turned to Hekit. His grey eyes were staring into nothing. Xerus found herself wondering whether he was in fact blind.

'Hekit?'

'No,' he said, shaking his head. 'Neither plan will work.'

'Do you have anything to offer?' Tanvile shrugged. 'Anything at all?'

'A rash hunter chases his prey, a seasoned hunter waits for the prey to come to him,' Hekit whispered, drifting past them, his razorwing perched upon his shoulder guard. They watched him shuffle away.

'I fear our beastmaster is becoming a liability,' Xerus murmured as he departed.

Tanvile frowned. 'He's plotting something – he must be. Why else would he allow himself to wither like that? It's disgusting.'

'Perhaps it is a test of self-discipline?'

'I still cannot fathom living like that.'

'You cannot fathom deferring your gratification for longer than a heartbeat.'

'True enough,' he grinned. 'Which is why I am going to find whatever passes for a house of ill-repute in this squalid dung heap of a port. Naturally you are welcome to join me. Or not.'

He turned from her, heading in the opposite direction to Hekit. Xerus stood between them a moment, before muttering a curse and following. Unarmed and bereft of allies, she saw no other choice.

Tanvile soon found what he was searching for. Xerus was not sure what she had expected, but the way station's amateur attempts at depravity were depressing. The establishment was a bland offering of function over form: half a dozen tables and chairs scavenged from a multitude of cultures, the effect as ramshackle as the rest of the station. A dozen conversations ended as they crossed the threshold, slowly resuming at a reduced pitch as the pair approached the bar. Most were reluctant to meet their gaze, their reputation preceding them. She drank in the suppressed terror, but it did little more than whet her appetite.

'Innkeeper?' Tanvile said, tapping his finger on the bar. 'Dare I ask what you are serving? More to the point, dare you serve it to me?'

His translator spat the words in the guttural language of the mon-keigh, whilst Xerus continued to survey the bar's clientele. They were mainly human, or near enough, and seemed content to bow their heads as her gaze slid over them, reluctant to challenge a denizen of the Dark City. There was a commotion from the rear of the crowd, a human hobbling for the exit, pressing himself to the far wall, striving to keep as much distance from her as possible. Scars were etched across what remained of his face, and his movement was restricted by a stump that had once been his leg.

She glanced at Tanvile, who was still occupied in terrorising the innkeeper. He too had noticed the departing figure. A shark-like grin spread across his face and he broke away in pursuit, the innkeeper's shoulders sagging in relief.

Xerus turned, head held high, daring any to challenge her. Most averted their gaze, but a solitary figure at the end table was staring back at her. It was tall and lanky, clad in an ensemble of fur and leather, the mottled skin beneath an olive green. Quills jutted from its head and the face below was vaguely avian, the jaw little more than a beak. Xerus had not encountered a kroot before, but she'd heard stories. The race was driven by the need to consume the flesh of others to enhance their own power and standing. A primitive culture, but perhaps a relatable one.

She approached slowly, her hands raised slightly to indicate she carried no weapon. The kroot regarded her, head tilting this way and that in a manner reminiscent of Hekit's razorwing.

'Are you currently employed?' she asked, wincing slightly as her armour's translator debased her words to a series of clicks and whistles. She was surprised when the creature responded in passable drukhari.

'Not employed at present,' it said, eyeing her carefully. 'But your kind's price is often too high.'

'You have worked for my people before?'

'Perhaps,' it conceded. 'Information carries a price too.'

Xerus reached into her belt, withdrawing a small bag. Within, three crystals cast an iridescent glow, shimmering with light bled from a dying sun. She withdrew the smallest, placing it on the table.

'I am looking for someone, one of my kind. A renegade.'

The creature took the gem, its long fingers examining the crystal. It raised its head and nodded, apparently satisfied.

'There was one,' it said, pocketing the gem. 'It tried to make a place here for a time. But it was too hungry, too costly for its allies. Soon none would travel into the fortress with it, lest they risk returning lessened by their travels.'

Xerus placed a silver disc on the table, her finger brushing its surface. An image formed, a drukhari female clad in the finery of a high-born, her ornate headdress framing a malevolent smile.

'Veth Rayden,' Xerus said, fixing her gaze on the kroot. 'Wanted for betraying her people. Do you recognise her?'

It studied the image, then shrugged.

'Perhaps?' it said. 'You all look alike.'

'How... enlightening,' she replied, forcing a diplomatic smile. 'Well, perhaps you can tell me what happened to the one who was here?'

'Returned to the abyss,' the kroot said. 'Alone.'

'And?'

'It went alone,' it said simply. 'It will not be back.'

Xerus leant against the docking port of *The Dying Light*, her gaze flitting across the bustle of the promenade, scanning the crowds for any sign of peacekeepers or other parties that might object to their interrogation. Inside the vessel Tanvile was squeezing the final dregs of information from the crippled human, though by this point he had likely told them all he knew, and his continued suffering was merely to sate Tanvile's thirst.

She too had drunk of the human's agony for a time, but it had done little to refresh her. The most ancient of her kind could only slake their thirst by basking in the suffering of worlds, or the extinction of entire species. Was this how it started? A hollowing of the little pleasures in life, until nothing short of genocide could stir her passions?

A menagerie of alien creatures skulked across the promenade, hatching pitiful plots and schemes as they traded archeotech and artefacts liberated from the Blackstone Fortress. She knew how Veth would have seen it when first arriving – the myriad opportunities to plunder and punish, the riches of a bygone era just waiting to be seized. Perhaps, had they travelled together, she would have felt the same. But now the pathetic creatures that bartered their stolen trinkets just felt tiresome, an unpleasant distraction. It would be better if the vermin were exterminated rather than infesting this ancient relic. Their numbers did seem to be thinning, as though the inhabitants of the way station had been summoned by a call unheard by her.

She had felt numb ever since the kroot had told her of Veth's death. It seemed impossible that someone so skilled, so full of stolen life could suffer such an ignominious end. Xerus could recall trading blows with her in the temple of Qa'leh, Mistress of Blades. Neither warrior could long claim the advantage, employing increasingly obscure techniques in their efforts to prove their superiority. Now she would never get the chance.

Xerus found herself in mourning. She mourned her lost vengeance, that she would never have the chance to plunge her blade into her paramour's chest and watch as her eyes grew dull and her soul was swallowed by She Who Thirsts. Her hunger for vengeance had sustained her through the interrogation and her subsequent penitence, inured her to the twin irritations of Tanvile and Hekit. Deprived of it, there was only a void, and in that moment it felt as though even the death of a thousand worlds would not fill it.

Behind her the pressure lock hissed open. Tanvile stepped through, smiling brightly, his pallid skin shimmering, rejuvenated by their victim's suffering. He glanced to the promenade, frowning.

'Why is it so quiet?'

'I neither know nor care,' Xerus shrugged. 'Did the human have anything useful to pass on?'

'Only the same tale told by your avian friend,' Tanvile shrugged. 'Veth Rayden was here for a time, left her mark on some of the locals, disappeared into the fortress and has not been seen since.'

'Then we have no choice. We go after her.'

Tanvile frowned. 'Is that wise?'

'Oh?' Xerus said, raising an eyebrow. 'Now who's hesitant?'

'I am merely being prudent,' he replied, tensing slightly. 'There is no sure path through a Talisman of Vaul, just a scattering of mausoleums built and broken at the monolith's whim. We could stumble through its depths for years and never find her, even if she was always but one chamber ahead of us.'

'We have our orders – we find the traitor and convey to her the Supreme Overlord's displeasure.'

'We were also tasked with returning his vessel,' Tanvile shrugged. 'Dying will achieve neither goal.'

'Nor will staying here,' she replied. 'Where else can we go? We have no other leads.'

'That is not the case.' The voice came from behind them.

They turned. Hekit was sat cross-legged in the shadows, the razorwing perched on his shoulder, worrying at a shard of knucklebone knotted into his hair.

'I am almost impressed,' Tanvile said. 'I would not have thought something so unsightly could blend so seamlessly into its surroundings. I suppose it's a testament to how dire this place really is.'

Hekit ignored him, rising stiffly, pressing his hands to his spine as he stretched.

'You found her?' Xerus asked, incredulous.

'No,' he replied. 'But I have found the *Eye of Vect*.'

'How?'

'Because unlike you two, I do not cause a disturbance wherever I go or waste time playing with the locals. I wait, and listen, and the answers find me.'

Before the others could respond there was a commotion at the far end of the promenade. The trio turned as one to find a motley assortment of humans shuffling to confront them. Most bore scars, and those cowering at the rear wore more extensive deformities; one was missing both nose and ears, another hobbling on a crude set of crutches.

As they drew closer to the drukhari the group slowed, its members increasingly disposed towards bringing up the rear of the party. But their leader was unbowed, striding forwards, his face twisted in gratifying hatred.

'Where is he?' he bellowed.

Tanvile and Xerus exchanged glances.

'We do not know to whom you refer,' Xerus said, turning away, but Tanvile strode past her, approaching the crowd and spreading his hands as if in greeting.

'My dear friends,' he said. 'How might I assist you? Some of you appear to be in some... discomfort.'

'You took him. We know your kind, your handiwork,' the lead human said, gesturing to his comrades' injuries.

'None of that is my work,' Tanvile replied after a brief appraisal. 'For one thing you still seem to be breathing.'

'You won't claim another of us,' the man spat, his longcoat falling open, revealing an autopistol.

He reached for the weapon. It was a mistake.

Tanvile surged forwards, so fast he was a blur even to Xerus. His talons slid into place and, with a flick of his wrist, his accuser's head was separated from its body. It spun lazily through the air, and before it struck the ground Tanvile was amongst the rest of them, snapping limbs and gouging eyes, his body twisting away from their clumsy attempts at retaliation. The men broke, two in their blind panic sprinting towards the remaining drukhari. Xerus' dagger flashed twice, and they silently fell.

Tanvile, slick with gore, approached the corpses, prodding one with his toe.

'Dead,' he sighed, glancing at her. 'No explosive muscle spasms? No unexpected bone growths? Even your choice of poison is dull.'

'We must leave. Now,' she said, sheathing her weapon and dragging Hekit towards the craft. 'Those who rule here do not take kindly to violence. When word of this little incident reaches them it could prove... problematic.'

'Perhaps I should have mentioned we were hunting Rayden?' Tanvile mused before padding softly after her. Behind them she could already hear raised voices echoing down the promenade.

The *Eye of Vect* lay dormant, concealed in the underbelly of a derelict Imperial cruiser. It appeared undamaged, an impressive feat given the violence that had erupted during its flight from Commorragh. But the interior was dark, the red glow of the auxiliary systems the only light source. Xerus had scanned the vessel before boarding but there were no life signs, the ship as dark as the dead space beyond.

The three advanced slowly, weapons drawn, Xerus holding back as she tried to piece together Veth's movements. She had abandoned the vessel just outside the Blackstone Fortress, undefended aside from a rudimentary cloaking mechanism. Why expose it to such risk? And how did she get from the ship to the fortress?

It was Tanvile who lost patience, marching defiantly through the ship, as though daring an ambush or trap to try to match his skill and speed. But there was nothing, the ship seemingly as devoid of life and function as the Blackstone Fortress. The bridge was abandoned, the systems offline and unresponsive. Tanvile continued to pace as Xerus attempted to run diagnostics. It was proving impossible; she knew the ship as well as anyone, but Rayden must have made modifications to the systems. None of her access codes registered and none of the readings made sense to her.

'Everything is locked down,' she sighed. 'I cannot operate the vessel.'

'Well, Hekit?' Tanvile said, rounding on the beastmaster. 'Can you work your charms and sniff out dear Rayden's scent?'

'I will meditate and seek an answer,' Hekit said, shuffling to the far side of the bridge and laying out his cloak in a narrow space between the two central consoles. His fingers stole into a pouch, emerging stained crimson. Solemnly, he marked his flesh with eldritch symbols, wards against the creatures of the empyrean. He then dipped his fingers into a second pouch, dabbing a pinch of *splintermind* under his nose and staining it red in the process. He folded his legs, hands resting on his knees, and was still. The bird remained perched on his shoulder, eyeing each of them in turn. Tanvile cursed.

'Drug-addled old fossil,' he spat. 'He expects us to just wait?'

'We have few other options.'

'Than what? A dream quest?' Tanvile sneered, eyeing her with undisguised contempt. 'You know those stories are just drivel, conceits believed only by the slow of mind and weak of spirit.'

He was still pacing but Xerus could sense a change – a predatory quality in the movement. His frustration was mounting and he craved an outlet. Hekit was proving little sport. That left only her.

'What do you suggest?' she asked, keeping her voice measured as she shifted her stance, her thumb settling on the pommel of her blade.

'We have the *Eye of Vect*,' he shrugged. 'From what that kroot told you Rayden is surely dead, and if by some miracle she is still blundering about the fortress then absconding with her vessel will ensure her demise. I say we return triumphant, our mission accomplished, and never see each other again.'

'We cannot access the ship,' she said. 'Besides, are you willing to stand before Vect and swear that the traitor was dead when there remains even the slightest risk of her surviving?'

Tanvile laughed, but there was no humour to the sound. He strode closer, until his face was an inch from her own. She could smell the sharp chemical reek of his flesh. She could see a gland pulsing in his throat, pumping some stimulant into his veins.

'You think Vect is our employer?' he sneered. 'You think he would sully his hands with three miscreants like ourselves? No, the more I think of it the more I am convinced that we were assembled as a jest – some sycophant wanting to earn favour or a rival seeking to discredit. Or perhaps someone deliberately recruited two such pathetic specimens in order to provoke me. I neither know nor care. We have our prize and will depart with it. Stop stalling and return us to the Dark City.'

'We do not have Veth!'

Her voice was louder than intended. Tanvile blinked, surprised, almost amused by her outburst. Then his expression hardened, sliding back into cold contempt. She tried to calm herself, biting back her anger, but the room was suddenly too warm. A strange smell now permeated the air, like rotten flesh. She shook her head, struggling to focus.

'We do not have Rayden,' she repeated, her tone measured this time. 'However, you are correct that she needs this vessel. It should be simple enough to prepare an ambush. When she returns the three of us can–'

'She is not returning, and if you don't do as I say then one of us will not be returning to the Dark City.'

He twitched as he spoke, his pupils now pinpricks, his reason a slave to a cocktail of combat drugs and stimulants. Talons unsheathed from his fingers, perhaps by reflex, perhaps as a threat.

She saw it rise behind him – a blade of blackened steel suspended in the air. She offered no warning, but some clue must have carried to her face because he spun as the knife missile plunged towards his back, talons flashing, plucking the weapon from the air. Xerus had already turned, raising her blade to parry a second projectile. More blades were sliding from cavities in the walls, encircling the pair in a wall of steel. They found themselves steered towards to the centre of the room, their backs pressed together.

'Perhaps we should postpone our little dance?' she said, as the blades encircled them like a flock of razorwings.

'Agreed,' he said amiably. 'I shall clear us some space. Do try and keep up.'

The storm of blades sung through the air as Tanvile moved to meet them, his frame twisting in impossible ways, his talons snatching the weapons from the sky even as he weaved between them. Xerus had little chance to appreciate his skill, preoccupied with her own set of attackers. She held her blade two-handed, parrying and thrusting, focusing more on defence than retaliation. She risked a glance to Hekit. He was still in a trance, chanting softly, oblivious to the blades whirling about the room. His razorwing was eyeing the weapons with what appeared to be curiosity.

A missile glanced from her hauberk, the armour preventing the blade from piercing the flesh but the impact knocking her off balance. She stumbled, raising her sword just in time to block another attack, her riposte slicing the projectile in half. Tanvile was still a blur of movement, his speed and fury seemingly drawing the attention of whatever rudimentary sentience guided the blades. He was already bleeding from a score of superficial cuts, though as she watched the smallest of these were knitting themselves back together. There were fewer of the blades now, the air thinned by every swipe of his claws.

She drew her splinter pistol, still parrying with the venomblade. The sidearm was a poor weapon against the storm of knives, the needle-ammo unlikely to inflict anything beyond superficial damage. But a well-placed shot could pierce Tanvile's hide, depositing a wealth of toxins into his bloodstream. She just needed to wait until he had resolved the current problem before she struck.

Perhaps he detected the movement, his senses enhanced by the cocktail of combat drugs. As she spied an opening and raised her weapon he pirouetted, his foot deflecting a blade straight at her. She ducked, still taking the shot, but the barrage of needles ricocheted from his wristguard.

He landed lightly, bestowing her with a mocking half bow. He was still smiling.

'My dear, that was uncalled for,' he said, waggling his finger. 'I fear that I must–'

Her venomblade hammered into his shoulder. It was a glancing blow, Tanvile twisting at the last second, deflecting the blade with his collarbone, but it was deep enough to reach the bloodstream. She stepped back, waiting for the toxins to overwhelm him. Instead he twitched, the flesh around the wound melding like wax into a jagged scar.

'That... stung,' he conceded, rubbing his shoulder. 'I withdraw my critique of your choice of poison. It might not be entertaining, but it certainly has some bite. Not enough, mind.'

He surged forwards, a tempest of taloned limbs and unrestrained fury. She retreated, ducking and parrying, her back already pressed to the wall. He was too fast, already penetrating her defences. Her armour was blackened ghostplate, the resin frame woven with micro force fields, but even these could not hold long against the onslaught. She ducked a decapitating strike, attempting a backhand slash but he anticipated it, seizing her wrist and pulling her close, their faces inches apart.

'I think we shall end this now,' he said, mouth stretching open like a snake, a row of venom glands pulsing in his throat. He spat, the volley of sickly green toxins aimed at her seemingly unprotected face. At the last instant a micro-field flared, shielding her from the worst of the attack. A single drop splashed across her cheek, the skin singed by its touch.

For just an instant, Tanvile hesitated.

Her forehead smashed into his nose, the micro-field flaring on impact, shielding her from the force of the blow even as it scorched his flesh. Twice more she struck, the third head-butt shorting out the field, but enough for Tanvile to release his grip. He swayed, almost falling, but she could already see him healing, his broken nose resetting itself, new flesh forming beneath his blistered skin. She had seconds before he recovered.

Her blade sung three times, tracing the third rune of Qa'leh through his flesh. It was Veth's technique, stolen from their clashes in the Mistress of Blades' temple. The first cut pierced his flank, the second opened his torso, and the third spilled his entrails across the bridge. Blood sprayed across her face as he collapsed, his enhanced biology faltering, overwhelmed by the mortal wound. She wanted to speak, to gloat, but her mouth was suddenly dry, her tongue too thick to form words. She found her fingers stiffening, the blade falling from her hand as she sunk to the floor, her strength all but spent. She wondered how he had poisoned her. The burn on her cheek? His own blood? Or perhaps a nick somewhere, a flaw in her armour unnoticed in the rush of combat. She felt the dispensers in her gorget dumping antitoxins into her bloodstream, trying to counteract the poison before it reached her heart, and she could hear the soft wheeze of Tanvile's dying breaths.

But there was another sound, a faint chanting which, now that she listened, seemed to come from all around her. With a supreme effort she turned her head.

Hekit still sat cross-legged between the consoles, untouched by the storm of blades. He sat straighter now, his skin smooth and hair thick, restored by his comrades' suffering and free from the withering taint of She Who Thirsts. His voice was soft, melodious, but the words were like blades to her ears, sounds not intended to be spoken in real space. The crimson runes adorning his flesh now glistened like open wounds, and as she watched, similar markings began to flare around the bridge, forming a circle about them.

Tanvile was crawling, scrabbling for one of the broken knife-missiles, his fingers slick with blood. He managed to grasp it, and for a moment his gaze met her own. She waited, unable to lift herself from the floor, expecting at any moment that the blade would sink into her flesh. But Tanvile turned towards Hekit, hurling the weapon with all his remaining strength. The razorwing intercepted it, talons snatching the blade in flight before returning to its master's shoulder and dropping it at his feet.

The chanting was in her head now. She could feel the words slipping through half-forgotten nightmares, coalescing her fears into something dark and predatory. A breeze brushed across her face, carrying with it a soft pad of paws. There came a low growl that reverberated through her bones and soul.

Her armour had mitigated the worst of the poison. She found a trembling knee, curling shaking fingers around the handle of her blade. Tanvile was also trying to rise, one hand clutched to his abdomen, blood seeping from a dozen wounds as his enhanced biology slowly burned itself out.

Around them dark shapes prowled the empyrean, hungry to cross over. They were indistinct, visible only as shadows at the edge of her vision, but she counted at least a dozen sets of eyes watching them.

Tanvile was trying to speak, his voice hoarse and wet. He coughed, blood dripping from his lips.

'I told you he was plotting something,' he slurred, staggering towards her. 'Truce?'

'It would seem… prudent,' she agreed, closing ranks as the shadows encircled them, coalescing into skinless monsters of bloodied flesh and feline sinew. The nearest of the khymerae hissed, skeletal tendrils uncoiling from its shoulders.

'If I can hold them do you think you can reach him?' she said, nodding to Hekit as the nightmares closed for the kill.

'No. But I will try,' Tanvile said, forcing a smile from shaking lips. 'If nothing else I will at least have the pleasure of killing that damn bird.'

The Dying Light slunk from the stellar graveyard. Hekit's hands glided across the helm, his vigour fully restored by the bloodshed. It had been a challenging assignment, allowing his soul to wither and his flesh to desiccate as he waited for his opportunity, but a true hunter could not be shackled by comfort or ego. A perfect kill required more than speed of hand and keenness of blade. What counted was patience.

That, and opportunity. He'd held doubts when Veth Rayden first approached him, but she had provided a trail to follow and a place to prepare his rituals, and it had been simple enough to play the fool until the trap was sprung. It was an innocuous-looking prize – a series of needle-like vials, each imbued with the essence of an undesignated species catalogued by the Blackstone Fortress. More than enough to earn a reprieve from his masters for the failed Zhailtir. The demise of his fellow agents would pose some challenging questions, but he could hardly be held accountable for their mutual dislike and unfortunate confrontation. The ocular implant extracted from his now deceased familiar would provide ample evidence to corroborate his account, and as the bodies of his former comrades had been devoured by his pets there was little chance of an untimely resurrection undermining his account.

The Dying Light departed for the webway. Behind it, the *Eye of Vect* returned to its slumber, awaiting its mistress' return.

MOTHERLODE

NICK KYME

I

A spike of pain burned in Raus' left knee as he stumbled and hit the ground hard. He felt the black obsidian vibrating as soon as his hands touched it and realised the fortress was about to shift again.

The Stygian Aperture was ahead. He could see the landing platform and the junk freighter, *Long Hauler Gamma-3-ß*, anchored to it, waiting for them.

'Rein!' he cried out.

His brother turned, a scowl on his scruffy round face, and doubled back. He huffed, blowing out his cheeks as he hefted the sniper rifle slung over his right shoulder. He was diminutive, barefoot and wearing olive-green fatigues, almost the exact reflection of his twin. A ratling. Raus was getting to his knees as Rein grabbed the collar of his grubby Militarum uniform.

'You're supposed to be the one who's light on his feet, Raus,' he snapped. 'Tell me you haven't dropped it.'

'I haven't dropped it,' said Raus, and then patted his kit-bag to confirm that he actually hadn't dropped it. 'Why are we running so fast, Rein?' he asked, as they got moving again.

'Well...' Rein huffed, red-faced and out of breath. 'Just best to get a shift on, eh?'

'You got him though, right? Shot that pointy-eared sadist. You said he went over the edge, Rein. The edge, right?'

Rein made a face as if he were weighing up tabac-leaf but hadn't quite got the portions right.

Raus let the silence last for a few seconds, their flat feet slapping noisily against the obsidian deck of the fortress. The Stygian Aperture was almost within reach.

'He's dead – you told me, Rein.'

'He might not be dead.'

Raus spat, grabbing Rein's uniform and half strangling him while they ran. 'What?!'

'Ruddy Throne, Raus! Let go,' he said, struggling to prise his brother's fingers from around his neck. 'You'll send us both rump over crown.'

'I'm light on my feet, remember,' said Raus. 'Reckon I'll be just fine.' He let go.

'He's probably dead. I mean... I definitely hit him. He was fast. Scary, scary fast, but I definitely got him.'

'Where?'

Rein frowned, nonplussed. 'Here? In the fortress. When we found the archeotech dump.'

'No, you berk. *Where?*'

Rein's face brightened. 'Oh... I'd say... hmm, the shoulder...'

'The ruddy shoulder! Not exactly a kill-shot is it? Was it a good hit?'

'Definitely glanced him.'

'A glance! Murlock's hairy arse, Rein. He could be running around right now. I'm surprised we haven't had a knife in the back already!'

'Ah, yeah, but I knackered his rebreather too. Nicked the tube, you see. It's been bleeding out ever since we ditched him. And by the time he reaches that vacuum chamber…'

Raus grinned, a charming and pearly white scythe of teeth that had found as much trouble as it had spared him.

'Oh, Rein…'

'Was that good?' asked Rein, a knowing look in his eyes.

The Stygian Aperture loomed and the two ratlings bolted straight through it as it began to close up and reform behind them.

'It was very, very good.'

The *Long Hauler* beckoned.

'Now then, Raus,' said Rein as the boarding ramp cranked down, 'shall we get back to Precipice and become as rich as Roboute Guilliman?'

Raus patted his kitbag and felt the hard, unyielding metal of the box he had stuffed inside. 'I think that would be a ruddy fine plan, Rein.'

'After you, dear brother,' said Rein as he reached the edge of the ramp, ushering in Raus with an unnecessarily flamboyant flourish.

'I don't mind if I do, brother,' he said, a feral glint in his beady eye. 'I don't mind if I do.'

As the junk freighter boosted its engines, slowly turning in the heavy gravity well of the fortress, a lone figure, panting and half-dead, staggered onto the landing platform. He had barely made it through the aperture. He watched as the ship pulled away, ignorant of his presence.

Akrahel Drek glared at the junk freighter's gradually diminishing silhouette. His fingers tightened around the bone hilt of the venomblade in his right hand. He slowly caught his breath, the flesh-knit fashioned into his armour working to repair his broken body. His ship, the *Hatchethand,* waited nearby. Its sharp contours of segmented byzantium pleasingly matched Akrahel's kabalite warsuit. The mutants hadn't thought to scuttle it. They obviously believed they had killed him. Either that, or they were in a rush.

The communication device in his armour still worked, and he activated it now.

'I'm coming back...' he said coldly. 'No, I didn't get it. But I know who did.'

He cut the connection. Like his quarry, he could not linger, but managed a smile as he watched the other ship disappear into the wreckage field.

'We'll meet again soon...' he purred, wiping the blood off his lip and revelling in the hot, metallic taste of it. 'And when we do, pray that I don't take you alive.'

II

The man stood before the ship's largest viewport, legs wide of stance, chin raised, hands firmly clasped behind his back. He wore a long black coat that swept down to just above his ankles, black leather boots that rose up to his knees and a peaked officer's cap pinned with a silver badge of a skull encircled by a laurel wreath.

A hololithic projector described an image behind him rendered in grainy blue light. Two ratlings, brothers – one a sniper, the other a scout. They wore Militarum fatigues and their dubious service record scrolled alongside their portraits in reams of Low Gothic.

A large desk delineated the device emitting the image. Maps, star charts, informant reports, hard vellum pict-captures and a ship schematic were strewn around it and starkly caught the light.

The trail had been difficult. The man couldn't remember the last time he had slept, but it didn't matter. They had followed the signals, out to the edge of the Western Reaches, and at last they had found it.

The Blackstone Fortress. It filled the viewport like a malevolent, dead moon, brimming with forbidden promise and unknown threat. He had heard stories, legends really, of the ancient star forts, though he had never seen one up-close. The scale was staggering, almost so massive as to be beyond comprehension. And he felt… a *regard*, a sense of being watched, as though a god were slowly stirring to wakefulness and taking note of lesser beings in its orbit. For several hours, the ship scaled a dark and alien hemisphere so absolute that it seemed to drink in the void like a thirsty ocean. Its guide lamps winked like minor stars against an endless black canvas. Wayfarers came to this place, in search of fortune or hiding from their pasts.

The man didn't care about any of that. Or them. He had his own quarry and had tracked it here. It had taken years, the nourishing of an obsession that had seen him stripped of influence, of power, and left men dead in his wake. It didn't matter. None of it mattered now.

In the lee of the colossal star fort, a shanty town port appeared at last. Hundreds of vessels were lashed to its mooring spars, and the man saw the faint vestiges of light as they drew closer.

'Take us in,' he ordered gruffly. One of the ships looked familiar. A junk freighter. He had spotted it despite the multitudes and saw this as divine intervention. It matched the schematic unfurled on the desk.

'*Long Hauler*...' he murmured, feeling a tremor across the *Jackboot*'s void-frame as it fought the gravity well and began to change heading, '...*Gamma-3-ß*. After all this time...' He stroked the leather grip of the laspistol holstered at his hip in anticipation. '...I have you.'

III

The Nadir Bazaar was cramped. And it stank, a heady melange of grox shit and goat farts. Raus took a surreptitious whiff under his armpit, made a 'definitely not me' face and settled in alongside his brother to wait.

'Has it got darker in here since we arrived, Raus?' asked Rein, narrowing his eyes and blinking. 'Seems darker.'

'Dingy, Rein. That's the word I'd use. *Dingy*.'

'Reeks like a beastman's gore hole too.'

'Hmm.'

After they'd docked the *Long Hauler* at Orbisgate, one of umpteen mooring spars on Precipice but also one of the three largest, the twins had taken a sojourn to the Helmsmen in Jetsum for a few celebratory libations. It wasn't every day you survived the perils of the fortress, came back with a prize and stiffed a sadist drukhari into the bargain. Raus had felt eyes on them the entire time, his unease not leavened by hard liquor. He could have sworn he'd spotted a rough-looking character giving them the eye. Wrapped in a grey storm cloak and with more than a wash of pepper-black stubble around his rugged, ex-military-looking chin, he was definitely armed, but melted into the shadows when Raus had gone for a look-see.

He didn't trust anyone in the Helmsmen. Rapscallions and thieves, the lot of them. One stray knife, a muffled pistol shot… The sooner they ditched the box the better. Selling it was the tricky part, though. Fortunately, Gatto 'knew a man', although that, in Raus' opinion, was stretching the bounds of reasonable description. The barkeep at the Helmsmen had said Murlock was making some moves on Precipice again after being shut down for months by the proctors for violating enough of the Protocols to get a trading ban. Not easy to do on Precipice, especially in the Derelict district, which was known for its casual adherence to the law.

Raus and Rein knew Murlock well, a little too well, though they hadn't seen him in a while. He could be useful. He knew every buyer in Precipice. And he knew how to move contraband. When he wasn't getting caught, of course.

He had… *rebranded*. The 'Nacht Market' had become the 'Nadir Bazaar', a thinly veiled attempt at legitimacy, with only the sizeable bribes and the breathtakingly rife corruption of the district authorities keeping Murlock in business. This was his entrepreneurial palace, a grubby little dung hole of trinkets, knick-knacks and all sorts of other ephemera stacked right up to its ramshackle roof.

Raus and Rein waited quietly in what had been described to them by one of Murlock's cronies standing guard at the entrance as the 'audience hall', but in reality was a sodium burner-lit nook with a scrap of grubby carpet underfoot that looked like Murlock had used it as his latrine.

'I do hope whatever that stain is from isn't contagious, Rein…' murmured Raus, lifting up his hairy foot and trying to inspect its leathery sole in the gloom.

'If you contract bootrot, I'll take it off at the knee, Raus.'

Raus glowered, his twin beaming back at him with unfeigned ignorance.

'So...' a deep, basso voice rumbled, 'we meet again, my little friends.'

'I wouldn't say "friends", exactly,' Raus whispered, making quotation marks with his gnarled and stubby fingers.

A massive figure loomed out of the shadows, a heavy beaded curtain parting to admit his bulk and inadvertently wafting his stench towards the twins.

'Worse than a beastman's gore hole,' choked Rein, wrinkling his nose but trying not to scowl too obviously for fear of upsetting their host.

Raus was holding his breath, cheeks puffed out, as he nodded.

Murlock was huge. Even for an ogryn, he filled the available space with his sheer girth and intimidating presence.

'It's as if an ogryn ate another ogryn,' Rein whispered. 'Was he always *this* fat?'

Raus still had his cheeks full and could only manage a shrug.

A stool had been set out, the only furniture in the otherwise barren room. It groaned plaintively as Murlock sat down, his layered chins rippling and the leather jerkin he wore creaking as it stretched across his expansive stomach. It could barely hold on to his body, the flab slipping out under the edge and pooling in his lap. A bandolier of frag grenades sat across his chest, the mark of a bandit king. Two small, dark eyes inside a large, tanned face regarded the ratlings with interest. Murlock picked at his uneven teeth with a small knife, the many rings gilding his fingers glinting and flashing in the faint light.

Raus' eyes bulged when he caught a decent look at the gold chain hung around the ogryn's neck. Working out in his head just how much it could be worth, he blew out a long-held breath.

Murlock didn't acknowledge the slight. Perhaps he hoped it wasn't aimed at him or his noisome aroma.

'Raus and Rein Gaffar,' he said. 'The brothers dim. I'm told you have something for me.'

'He's Raus,' said Raus. 'And I'm Rein.'

'You sure, brother?'

'Think so...'

Murlock frowned, then shrugged. 'It's of *little*... importance,' he went on.

'Oh that's a good one,' said Raus. 'Isn't it, brother?'

'Very original, brother.'

Murlock's little, piggish eyes glinted greedily. 'Enough banter. Let's see it then.'

Raus exchanged a glance with Rein and then slowly removed the box from his kitbag before presenting it to Murlock. The casket had been forged of an iridescent metal that caught the light and gave it the appearance of oil on water as it washed across its surface. Runes had been engraved in the sides, sharp-edged and alien, and there were embedded rubies the size of artillery shells.

Carefully, Raus unclasped the lid and opened it.

Murlock leaned in, prompting a few ominous creaks from the stool.

'Oh yes...' he breathed, rubbing his uppermost chin. 'I have just the buyer for this. Likes the exotics.' He reached out a bejewelled hand, only for Raus to snap the box shut and withdraw.

'Let's agree a price before we hand it over, shall we?' He turned to his brother. 'What you reckon, Rein? Five hundred? Six?'

Rein counted on one hand, murmuring his calculations aloud before promptly giving up when he ran out of fingers.

'Let's make it an even thousand, shall we,' he declared, thrusting out his grubby little paw for Murlock to shake on it.

'Sounds fair to me, Rein,' said Raus, and thrust out his hand too.

Murlock slowly leaned back on his stool. He gave a short, deep laugh, though the humour of it never reached his eyes. 'Thought he was Raus and you was Rein.'

'Easy to get it turned about,' said Raus. 'Have we a deal then?'

'Very well...' rumbled Murlock, nodding, 'I'll take off your hands.'

Rein frowned, turning his ear so it was aimed at the hulking ogryn. 'You mean, you'll take *it* off our hands, right, guv'nor?' He looked at his brother. 'That's right, isn't it, Raus?'

'I am fairly certain that's the correct phrasing, Rein.'

'Nah,' said Murlock, rising to his full indomitable height, 'I'll take *your* hands, you thieving little worms!'

Raus swallowed as the ogryn's shadow fell across them like an eclipse. 'Oh, balls...'

A massive cleaver swept out of the darkness and sheared the ugly carpet in half where the ratlings had been standing. Bellowing, Murlock reached for Raus, who dived and rolled out of the ogryn's grasp. Murlock blundered after him. Raus ducked a savage right hook, getting underneath it to wrap his hands around the trunk-like arm and using it as a fulcrum to swing feet first into the ogryn's paunch before catapulting off and out of harm's way. Thwarted, Murlock roared. He stomped a gargantuan foot to crush Rein, but the ratling slipped under the ogryn's legs.

'I don't recommend ever doing that again,' he said, a

disgusted look on his face as he emerged on the other side and was reunited with his brother.

Murlock had his back to them, but he was already turning, a ponderous giant on the hunt. In the distance, the ogryn's henchmen were coming to his aid.

The ratlings bolted for the bead curtain, and kept running.

'Where did that cleaver come from?!' cried Rein, gasping as he fled through the labyrinthine stacks of the bazaar. 'His hands were empty!' Evidently, the 'audience hall' led to Murlock's warehouse and was brimming with crates, caskets and barrels.

Raus felt his heart beat faster at such riches. If only there wasn't an obscenely fat ogryn and his goons trying to kill them.

'Do you remember that time...' he replied, gasping too, and leaping deftly to the side as Murlock's knife embedded itself in the wall, 'that we told the proctors about what Murlock was up to over at the Nacht Market?'

'I do, I do, Raus,' said Rein. 'Got us out of a spot of bother, that little informational nugget.'

Another blade slammed into a crate, trembling with the impact. 'Where is he getting all these knives? Is he pulling them out his ar–'

'That little nugget, you mention...' Raus replied.

Realisation crept over Rein's face.

'Oh, shank. No wonder he's mad.'

They darted around a corner, looking for a way out, but came to an abrupt halt when confronted with a mountainous slab of flesh and blubber.

'No escape for you in here,' Murlock panted, sweating profusely. 'I know this place. It's *mine*.'

He advanced slowly, the cleaver held low and by his side. 'Your heads are going in my trophy case. Or maybe I'll put 'em out front as a warning. Now...' he said, 'hand over the box and I'll make it quick.'

Raus and Rein were backing away but Murlock effectively had them pinned in a dead end. A pair of rough-looking mercenaries in grey-and-black fatigues and half-plate had just wandered into view.

'Can't blame you for being angry, Mur,' said Raus, eyeing the goons' stubbers, his palms held out in a conciliatory gesture.

'I'd be angry too, guv'nor,' Rein agreed, and mirrored his twin.

'But before you butcher us,' said Raus, 'and mount us as trophies on your wall, can you tell me one thing?'

Murlock paused, frowning. A sudden concerned look crept over his face, which he shared with his henchmen. 'What have you done?'

Raus held his right hand up to the light. Three small firing pins dangled off his fingers like a beggar's jewellery. 'What are these for?'

The explosion ripped through the bazaar like a hurricane, plumes of smoke reaching up into the artificial atmosphere above Derelict in a thick, greasy pall. Raus emerged from the wreckage of the Nadir Bazaar, pulling his brother out from a heap of debris. Rein hacked up a wad of dust and grit, but was otherwise none the worse for wear.

Of Murlock and his goons only a bejewelled hand remained, still twitching.

'Didn't fancy being a trophy,' said Raus.

'Me neither,' agreed Rein. 'How'd you know the grenades wouldn't go off earlier?'

'I thought they would,' Raus confessed. 'He was supposed to blow up soon as we got through the curtain.'

'Well, it all worked out in the end.'

'Did it? We still don't have a buyer for this.' Raus held out the casket.

'Oh, I don't know,' said Rein, smiling and wafting a leather-bound ledger in his brother's direction. 'You weren't the only one light of finger, brother. Except while you were pulling pins, I was seeing to our future prosperity. I reckon we'll find the buyer in these pages somewhere, don't you?'

IV

In the Skeins everything was available for a price. But only the desperate or the truly imbecilic ever traded with the low lifes denizened there.

Vuko Vukich did not consider himself to be stupid, so as he wended through the narrow alleyways and lightless spaces of the Skeins, he considered that he might very well be desperate. No one at the Helmsmen was buying, forcing him to seek out even less scrupulous traders, hence his current predicament. He had lost his way, more than once, but was almost certain he was back on track until his path came to a dead end.

'Shit...' he hissed, and was going to about-turn when a voice from behind stopped him.

'Yes, my friend. You are in an awful lot of that.'

Vuko had pulled a stub-pistol but let it drag his arm down when he saw the gang of wretches waiting to skin him for trespassing.

Six men, all armed. Autoguns with olive-drab casings, two stubbers and a laspistol. Militarum-grade. They wore metal plates, shoulder guards and greaves over factorum fatigues. Ex-hivers, maybe part of a rogue trader's retinue. They'd gone feral, though. Perhaps the fortress had claimed the trader, and left the dogs masterless. No leashes in the skein. No proctors either, so help wasn't coming.

Vuko chose to try to barter. 'I have money,' he lied.

'No you don't,' replied the one who'd spoken initially. He looked thin in the face, with a wiry ash-coloured beard. He shot Vuko in the leg.

Down on one knee, clenching his thigh to stop himself bleeding out, Vuko looked up into the face of his murderer. 'I have something better.' He had been keeping it for trade, hoping to find the moneylender who had set up shop somewhere in the Skeins. Now he had no choice. He brandished a piece of waxy parchment. 'It's a map. Fortress...' he said, pleading.

The other man's eyes widened a little.

'Oh, we'll take that too,' he said.

'Too?'

'We're real hungry down here...'

Vuko felt his stomach tighten, and was about to put the stub-pistol to his own head when he heard something. A snuffling, scratching sound, it came echoing off the tunnels ahead. A few of the gangers heard it too and began to turn. One raised an autogun. It trembled as he pointed it at the darkness.

'Is this you?' roared the other man.

'It's not me,' Vuko rasped.

'Then what in warp-hell is it?'

The sound grew louder, and a strange clicking came with it like the rapid champing of teeth.

And when at last Vuko saw what came out of the shadows for them, he pressed the stub-pistol to his temple and pulled the trigger.

* * *

V

Rein thumbed the greasy pages of the ledger, making sure they had the right place. 'You know,' he said, 'I am genuinely surprised Murlock could even write.' He showed his brother the stained vellum. 'And this cursive script is actually quite artistic.'

Raus rolled his eyes.

'Is this it?' he asked. 'You're sure this is it?'

'It's probably it,' said Rein, tucking away the ledger. With so many contacts, they could go into business for themselves. 'I mean... it's *definitely* in the book. Exotics, right?'

'That's what he said.'

Raus attempted the name. '*Kur-uuk*? And he lives in this place?'

A scrap shanty had crawled over an old dockyard, its mooring spar broken and drifting listlessly in the void like a homeless drunk. Two bone antlers jutted from a ramshackle, sloping roof, strung with tiny skulls and wafers of thin metal. A jetty ran out to a hooded doorway drenched in gloom, a stream of effluence trickling beneath it.

'Looks inviting,' said Raus. 'After you, brother.'

'Oh, I insist,' said Rein, bowing deferentially.

Raus grimaced. 'I thought you might.'

The shanty was dark inside and poorly lit. Storm lanterns with closed shutters hung on a length of rope overhead. The stench of blood and carcasses thickened the air, making Raus gag.

'Worse than Murlock's armpits,' he said, cupping his nose and mouth to try to ward off the stench.

'Or his crotch...' Rein suggested, the red beam of his sniper sight panning the room, alighting on flanks of rotting meat and counters stacked with bones. Cages and grimy glass cabinets contained the remains of creatures, all alien, all highly exotic. Mercifully, all dead too.

'A hunter,' murmured Rein, gesturing to a longrifle hung up on the wall. Several blades, a spear and a hand axe lay stacked in one corner.

'Does this feel iffy to you, Rein?' asked Raus, moving quietly, and having slipped a stub-pistol from his belt holster.

'I don't think I've unclenched since I walked in here, Raus,' Rein answered.

Raus stopped abruptly, gesturing with a stubby little finger. 'Up…'

Rein followed it to a ledge, an upper floor of sorts, though with no obvious means of reaching it.

'Sleeping quarters?' he suggested.

Raus wrinkled his nose. 'Smells worse than the rest of the place. Sure that stink isn't coming from you, brother?'

'I'll have you know I've had my annual bath,' snapped Rein, indignant.

Raus caught him sneakily sniffing his armpits as he searched the rafters for a beam or hook.

'There,' he said, stuffing away the pistol again and whipping out a hefty grapple gun. With a noisy *shoom* of expelled pressure the hook soared upwards, the wire uncoiling after it like a tail chasing its comet. It latched on to an overhead beam, grapnel teeth snagging well and holding Raus' weight when he tested it.

'I'm off for a look,' he said and zipped upwards, the grapnel line spooling back in. Hanging one-handed, his dirty bare feet dangling loosely, Raus sagged. 'Kur-uuk is a kroot.'

Rein nodded, mildly interested. 'Huh…'

'He's also had his throat cut.'

'Oh, shank...'

Raus' eyes narrowed. 'Red foam around his mouth too.'

'He's gone feral and slit his own throat!' cried Rein.

Raus unwound the line and was back on the ground in seconds. He pressed a trigger and the grapnel sprang apart like a sprung trap. He had it reeled in and back in his pack in less than a minute.

'Doubtful,' he said. 'But we need to get out of here, Rein. Someone knew we were coming.'

'Then they're probably watching us, Raus.'

'I'd say that's almost a certainty.'

'Maybe we shouldn't have had that third round at the Helmsmen before we got here.'

'Let's not be too hasty...'

'Reckon we shouldn't have boasted about getting rich and coming to this shack.'

'Now *that* probably was ill-advised.'

Raus heard a creak of metal from deeper in the shanty.

'What was that?' asked Rein, as a figure appeared from the shadows, green retinal lenses aglow.

'Our cue to leave,' said Raus.

They ran. Again. Bolting from the entranceway, they came across a second figure standing across the jetty. A grey storm cloak shawled most of his body, but couldn't entirely hide his suit of carapace armour. The lasgun held across his chest was more obvious, as was the combat helmet and concomitant night-sight goggles and rebreather mask.

'Guilliman's hairy arse!' hissed Rein. 'He's Tempestus.' He shot him in the kneecap. From the hip. With his sniper rifle.

The trooper went down, grunting in pain, clutching his ruined knee. He dropped his lasgun, a bulky Ryza-pattern with overcharge capacity. Raus' eyes shone larcenously as he dodged the trooper's knife swipe, leaping over the half-prone form as he and his brother ran for the metaphorical hills. Or, in this case, the nearest sump pipe.

'Sluice tunnels,' Rein gasped, pointing.

Raus glanced over his shoulder. The second trooper had exited the shanty, and was helping the first to his feet. Then he pulled his gun.

Scorching las-beams splashed against the outer frame of the sewer outflow as Rein and Raus ducked inside.

'Tempestus!' Rein cried again. 'What are those bloody glory boys doing on Precipice?'

'I'd say they're looking for us, brother.'

'Well that's charming.'

Raus shook his head, biting his bottom lip as he tried to make a plan.

'Can't outrun them. Not even in here.'

Sections of grimy pipe flashed by, lit by thin shafts of light piercing the cracks in the ceiling. There were half-chewed bones amongst the effluvia.

'Can't hide either. They're relentless as bloodhounds.'

'Any thoughts?' asked Raus.

'Only that my impending death is ill-deserved and I haven't yet enjoyed a rich and full life,' Rein replied. 'I am open to suggestions.'

Raus looked up. It was dingy in the tunnels, and it stank of excreta. A larger shaft of light lit up a patch of filth below. He gestured to a grate in the ceiling, three of its rungs rusted away to nubs.

Rein smiled. 'You go high, I'll go low. They can't chase us both.'

Raus nodded, accepting the plan. He thrust out a grimy

hand. 'Good luck, Rein, and if you don't make it I'll be taking all of your stuff and the *Long Hauler*.'

'Right you are, Raus. Same to you too.' He spat on his palm and they shook hands. They were about to part ways, Raus having fired off his grapnel, when something severed the wire and he fell into a heap. He caught the vaguest flash of dark metal in the sewer light and a shadowy presence looking down from above.

He had no time to investigate or the means to do so. A tight red beam burned a scorch mark by his feet and he looked back in despair. The Tempestus were coming. Three of them now. And they weren't alone. A fourth figure had joined them, a black trench coat flapping in his wake as he stalked towards the ratlings, peaked cap casting a shadow over a rough-looking face. He also carried a smoking laspistol in his outstretched hand.

'Rugged, ex-military-looking chin...' Raus muttered. 'Oh, bugger...'

At least the presence above had gone, though Raus noticed an angular throwing blade embedded in the wall. But he couldn't worry about that now.

'You what?' asked Rein.

'Run... Run, Rein!'

The ratlings fled, scurrying like their namesakes through the muck and filth.

Behind them, a commissar and his men gave chase.

'Don't worry, Raus...' said Rein, as they ducked around another corner. 'I know these tunnels like the back of my–'

And came to an abrupt and unwelcome halt.

'Arse! Dead end!'

A slab of sheer, pitted rockcrete stood in their path. Ugly yellowed stains stretched down the wall as long and pointed as teeth. A partial collapse had blocked off the tunnel, debris piled up in front of it.

'Did you have to use that *particular* word?' said Raus.

'What, *arse*?'

Raus ignored him, jabbing a finger at the obvious gap in the ceiling, a crevice wide enough for a ratling to sneak through. He thought of the shadowy presence he had seen before, but couldn't see another way out.

'Can you make that?' he asked.

Rein had a look, shook his head.

'Do I look like a funambulist?'

'Not sure your sleepwalking is relevant to the current situation, Rein.'

'I can't make it that high, and with your grapnel properly fragged...'

Raus glanced behind him. They'd led the commissar and his men a merry dance, but he heard rapidly approaching bootsteps. He looked back at the wall, at the pitted rock, at the distance to the gap in the ceiling.

'Remember what we said if ever we had to choose...?'

'If we got into a tight spot and only one of us could get loose?'

Raus nodded. 'I'd say we're about as tight as a confessor's purse right now.'

VI

The commissar smiled viperously.

'At long last,' he rasped, purposely slowing down as he approached the dishevelled ratling kneeling in the dirt. Head bowed, hands out, he was a grimy little wretch. A sniper rifle sat on the ground in front of him, ammo clip discharged and set down next to it, a single bullet sprung from the breech on top of the casing.

'At least you know when to surrender, *abhuman*,' he sneered, and straightened his jacket as he came to stand before the pitiful creature. 'Gaffar, Rein,' he said, recounting the details from memory. 'Sniper, auxiliary…'

'I think you might have me mistaken for someone else, sir.'

The commissar sneered. '*Sniper*, auxiliary,' he repeated, 'primus-rated… and in dereliction of duty to the God-Emperor of Mankind.'

'Is He here too?'

The commissar struck him across the face and the ratling went down hard before defiantly coming up again.

'I am Commissar Vudus Mettik. I want you to know my name, for I know yours and your brother's.' He looked up at the gap in the pipe. 'Left you for dead, did he? Saw his chance to slip my leash and took it?'

'Oh, I expect he'll be back for me.'

'You better hope so, scum,' said Mettik, nodding to one of the Scions, who smashed Rein Gaffar in the side of the head with his gunstock, knocking the ratling out cold.

VII

'Tie it tight,' said Mettik. 'I don't want the little runt getting loose.'

They were standing in an outflow basin, having breached the fallen rubble and followed the pipe to its terminus in the Skeins. They had bound the prisoner to an old support strut and hung him by his arms like a piece of meat, toes just scraping the floor.

It was a pleasing location, close enough to where they had

caught the ratling that his brother wouldn't have to search long to find him and wide enough that Mettik and his men would easily see him coming. He eyed the high walls surrounding them on three sides but found no sign of the other one. Not yet.

'Wake him up,' uttered Mettik as soon as the bonds were tied.

The Scion smacked the ratling hard across the face, splitting his lip but bringing him around.

'You'll have to excuse me,' the ratling said, spitting up a wad of blood. 'I rather dozed off back there.'

'Amusing,' snarled Mettik. 'Will you be so jovial when you're facing Commissarial censure, I wonder?'

'Honestly, guv'nor, I doubt I can even spell those words, let alone understand what they actually mean. And besides,' the ratling added, 'I'm more worried about him.'

Mettik whirled around, only just dodging a spinning sliver of metal that scythed through his flaring commissar's coat.

One of the Scions collapsed to his knees, a second sliver in his neck and red foam bubbling up through his rebreather. He jerked, convulsed and fell on his face. Dead.

Mettik whipped his gun out, and the remaining Scions followed suit.

'I wouldn't make any sudden moves,' the ratling suggested, jerking his neck towards the lithe figure in segmented byzantium armour that had miraculously appeared out of nowhere. 'That's Akrahel Drek.' Two more similarly armoured figures then joined him from the shadows. 'Oh, and his brother and sister. You are seriously fragged.'

'Someone else who wants your head?' said Mettik, his eyes never leaving the lean trio of drukhari.

'I expect so… and spleen, liver, fingers, etcetera, etcetera…'

'Is that so?' Mettik put to the lead drukhari. 'Can you speak my language, *xenos*?'

The drukhari sneered, exchanging the briefest glance with his siblings. He had a stark, androgynous beauty that Mettik found deeply unsettling. 'When we must… *mon-keigh*,' he said, his voice like a dagger's edge but with a silken undertone. He swept a mane of long black hair aside with a flick of his head. 'And yes, I want its *spleen. Liver. Fingers… Etcetera. Etcetera.*' He lasciviously enunciated every word.

Mettik gave a feral grin. 'Then we have an impasse, for I want them too. For crimes against the Imperium.'

'Mine is an honour debt from which I will not turn.'

Mettik thought the drukhari winced, and wondered if he was injured. Perhaps that's why he had chosen to parlay. No, it was the two hellguns aimed in his direction.

'I have a proposal,' said the drukhari at length. 'I will settle for one and the item they stole from me.'

Mettik scowled. 'I don't bargain with *xenos*.'

'Doesn't appear that you have much of a choice.' The drukhari's smile was sickle-shaped and sharp. He gestured to his kin, who were both armed. 'You are far from your Imperium here.'

Mettik nodded but was adamant. 'Rein Gaffar is mine, and so is his bro–'

A shot rang out, tight as a whip. It cut the ratling's bonds before Mettik or the drukhari could react.

'I'm sorry,' said the ratling, now freed and already running, 'but I did say – you have me mistaken for someone else.'

Mettik surveyed the raised lip of the outflow basin and found a point where the light glinted off a tiny oval lens.

'That's the damn sniper,' he snarled, meeting Akrahel Drek's gaze. 'Can we agree to kill them both and sort out the details after?'

The drukhari smiled and nodded.

Then an object was launched over the basin wall, hurled like demo-charge, and that had Mettik's heart racing until he realised it was actually just a metal box. A second shot rang out before the box hit the ground, shooting out the sealing clasp and spilling the contents onto the ground.

Everyone stopped to look at the severed head of the ur-ghul brood mother.

From the darkness of the nearby sewer pipe, a pack of feral voices chorused hungrily.

VIII

It was an ugly thing. Eyeless, bulbous forehead, flared nose pits. Nightmare fuel. Thinking back now, Raus had no idea why he took it. He knew it had value. The markings, the shape of the skull. He knew a little about these creatures and this one was unusual. There were so many xenos, so much weird fauna on the fortress that it tended to attract hunters and collectors who would pay big for the rarer specimens. Only problem was, removing said specimens also tended to attract those creatures who had once called them kin. Or in this case, 'mother'.

Legs peddling madly, Raus risked a backward glance.

A horde of lesser ur-ghuls had sprung from the pipe, drawn by the scent of their dead brood mother. They fell upon the nearest drukhari with unfettered savagery. She went down screaming, and Raus looked away. Shots rang out, suppressing fire from the Imperial guns. A headshot took out one of the Tempestus taking aim at Raus.

'Now he gets his chuffing eye in...' he muttered, secretly glad that his brother could be ruthless when it really mattered.

As he ran for the border wall of the outflow, he kept one eye on the melee.

'You dirty abhumans!' Mettik roared, firing into the throng of xenos, executing with aplomb and actually standing his ground until Akrahel's blade found its mark in the commissar's chest and he tipped over.

An ur-ghul caught Raus' scent, scurrying after him as it broke from the pack. The ratling ran but was saying his prayers to the Throne when the creature sprang at him. He crouched in the dirt, making himself small, hoping it would be quick. Fear deadened the sound of the sniper shot that exploded its skull and left the ur-ghul's headless corpse sliding next to him rather than rending him with tooth and nail. He got up, and ran on.

Akrahel was the last to fall, and he did so under a host of clamouring bodies. The rangy ur-ghuls tore him apart, limb from limb. Raus hit the wall and acrobatically scrambled up. As he flipped over the edge and back onto high ground, he looked back down on the carnage.

The ur-ghuls had finished everyone below, dragging the carcasses of the dead with them as they returned to the pipes, bound for the Skeins and to join the other fell creatures that lurked in that most benighted part of Precipice.

'Well,' said Rein as he rejoined his brother, 'I'm not sleeping for a week after that.'

Raus gave a thin, yet haggard smile. 'Don't suppose you've got a spare pair of trousers as well as that rifle, have you?'

Rein lovingly patted the stock of his reserve gun, but shook his head. He sucked his teeth, regarding the blood and bits of viscera the ur-ghul brood had left in its wake.

'All for nothing then,' he said ruefully.

'Well…' Raus began, and Rein turned to face his brother.

Raus wafted a bloody piece of waxy parchment.

'What's that, Raus?'

'I do believe it's a map, Rein.'

'A... *treasure* map?'

Raus grinned.

'Well, only one way to find out.'

PURITY IS A LIE

GAV THORPE

The air inside the drinking hole was thick with lho smoke, sweat and alcohol fumes. More than that, it was thick with the stench of heresy. Wherever Taddeus looked he saw miscreants, xenos scum and blasphemers against the God-Emperor. Revelry not in celebration of the God-Emperor's victories was an affront to the sacrifices of the Thronelord and there was much revelry amid the stink of 'Looter's Den'.

His arrival did not go unmarked. Chairs scraped across the bare boards of the floor and conversations faltered into silence. From behind a bar of stacked ammunition crates, the vendor scowled. The skinny, scar-faced man reached behind the improvised counter, no doubt for a weapon. Elsewhere blades slid from sheaths, powercells whined on activation and several autoweapons clicked and crunched as hammers were drawn back and safeties released.

The reassuring buzz of Taddeus' servo-stubber sounded close to his right ear as the self-determining anti-grav skull ascended into view. As it steadily panned back and forth the barrel of its gun tracked slowly across the denizens of the establishment, red targeting beams pulsing from its eye sockets.

'This ain't your pulpit, Ecclesiarchy man,' growled a treasure hunter leaning on the bar, her face half-hidden beneath the broad brim of her hat. One hand held a small glass of yellow liquid; the other was hooked into her belt close to a holstered laspistol.

Hostile eyes regarded the preacher from all directions: many human, some insectoid, one pair just points of ochre light.

'And I'm not here to preach,' Taddeus replied, his gaze scanning the room. He smoothed his hands down the front of his vestments, wiping away the settling dust and ash of the drinking hole.

'Everyone can relax,' said a rakish man from the far corner, his chair leaning back against the wall, booted feet on the tabletop before him. His garb was of an Imperial noble, frock coat and mock-military stylings. The hide of a xenos beast trailed across his shoulders. A neatly trimmed moustache and oiled hair completed an image of privilege at odds with the unwashed and unkempt denizens that made up the remaining patrons. Almost unseen, he held a long-barrelled duelling pistol in his lap, its muzzle pointing towards the barman.

'No trouble, not in my cantina,' the man said, placing both his hands back on the counter, empty.

The servo-stubber lowered, its eyes returning to their dark green dormant state. A few patrons remained with weapons directed at the newcomer.

'And a round of drinks on my tab!' Draik declared.

Eyes followed Taddeus as he weaved through the close

tables, but the low conversations, glug of drinks poured and clink of glasses slowly resumed as he reached the chair opposite Janus Draik, the rogue trader he had come to meet.

Draik dragged his feet from the table and invited Taddeus to sit with a glance. The rogue trader pushed a glass towards the priest and lifted a clay jug in offer. Taddeus' lip curled in reply.

'It's water,' said Draik, topping up his own glass. 'Fresh, not filtered. A shipment arrived this morning, nearly two thousand pints.'

'It is still a luxury, a weakness,' said Taddeus, though his tongue could almost taste the untainted liquid, free from the acrid hint of recycling that marred all the water piped through the chambers of Precipice.

'Perhaps you could bless some of the filtered water, make it taste good,' said Draik with a half-smile. 'You call yourself the Purifier, yes?'

Taddeus sat down and did not dignify the poor joke with a reply.

'Not the talkative type, I see,' the rogue trader continued, assuming a more businesslike air. 'Fair enough, I can appreciate that.'

'Your missive said that you needed my assistance.'

'It did, and I do.' Draik leaned closer, voice dropping to a conspiratorial level, his eyes darting to the left and right before he continued. 'I have pieced together one of the routes to the hidden vault we are all seeking.'

'Speak for yourself. I seek the Emperor's Truth.'

'Then why are you on Precipice, hanging around as welcome as ogryn flatulence? I have watched you trying to get to the Blackstone Fortress. And failing. Now is your chance, with me.'

'Let's assume I'll indulge you, Draik. What are you suggesting?'

'I have coordinates and guidance logs for the maglev transporters that will take us to somewhere called… Well, it is called the deathmaze. Not inviting, I know. Some have reached it before in their attempts to find a way through to the next ring of vault defences.'

'They failed?'

'None have returned, so I would wager they died.' Draik fixed his eyes on Taddeus, radiating sincerity. 'I need an extra pair of eyes and hands on this venture.'

'You have been here longer than many others and must've made all kinds of acquaintances. Why do you need me for this particular expedition?'

'I trust you, Taddeus. There's only a handful of others I trust, and one of them was injured as we acquired this new data, but I cannot wait for them to recuperate in case there is some change in the Blackstone Fortress' layout. The maglev system can handle four people at most, so I find myself with an opening, and you have an opportunity. Precipice is full of vagabonds and scum, and you might name me amongst them, but you are different, I think. Courageous and determined. Not the sort to be dissuaded by a dangerous foe. A man of the Emperor, guided by His divine light. You think I have wandered from the righteous path, but I assure you that I have always kept it in sight even as I have meandered a little from its straight course. I want to help you do the Emperor's work, while you help me solve the riddles of this terrible but intriguing place.'

The rogue trader's words were as worthless as anyone else's, but there was a singular fact that could not be ignored: no others had yet been willing to accompany Taddeus into the depths of the Blackstone Fortress. It was too daunting a task for just the Purifier and his aide, Vorne. Suicide, in fact, to progress any degree into the mysteries of the alien station without more companions.

He had to believe the God-Emperor had led him to this corruption for a reason, and not simply to cleanse it. He saw again the truth in the flames, the images that the God-Emperor had sent to him in the dance of the holy fires. He had heard of the alien station from the gossiping lips of a Naval rating, but it was in the flames that had purified the impenitent man shortly after that he had truly seen the will of the God-Emperor.

A galaxy aflame with the righteous fires, with Taddeus as the spark that would light that pyre across the stars. The Blackstone Fortress was a gift; its secrets could not fall into the hands of aliens and heretics before the faithful had uncovered them.

'These others that you trust.' The priest looked around the drinking hole. 'Who will also be going with us?'

'Does it matter?' Draik asked sharply. 'If you have been given sight of your prize, would you turn away from it if the surrounding view was not to your liking? Or would you grasp it with both hands?'

The rogue trader was dissembling, but his point was valid. The unavoidable need for allies left Taddeus with few options.

None, in fact.

'We have concord,' said Taddeus. 'I will bring the *Clarion* to the Stygian Aperture and rendezvous with you.'

Draik's hand slid across the table and left a small crystal in front of the priest.

'We cannot enter by the Stygian Aperture, not this time. My last expedition uncovered a smaller entry point, hidden in the scan-shadow of the furthest arm of the Blackstone

Fortress. I have calculated a flight path that will get you there undetected by those who would steal our claim. The details are embedded in this crystal.'

Taddeus took up the crystal and stood. Draik did likewise and extended a hand to seal the pact between them. The Purifier took it in his strong grip and did not let go when the rogue trader tried to pull his hand back.

'We are allies, not friends,' Taddeus told the rogue trader, dragging him a little closer, his gaze burning into the other man's eyes. 'But it is not my judgement that should concern you, for when you perish you must answer to the God-Emperor for your deeds and misdeeds.'

Draik tore his hand away with a sour look. Taddeus thrust the data-crystal into a hidden pocket within his cassock and stalked away.

The joyful chorus of the *Clarion*'s navigational system rose to a crescendo as the missionary vessel slipped between two dark pillars that jutted from an outcrop of the Blackstone Fortress.

The rising harmony was in direct contrast to the feelings of Taddeus the Purifier, who was usually roused by the triumphant tone of his vessel's autohymnals.

'Master, look.' Pious Vorne pointed over his shoulder towards a darker recess ahead, her other hand laid upon the back of the priest's command throne. Her voice was hushed with reverence, distorted by the black rebreather that covered her nose and mouth.

There was a white glow within the artificial cavern, but the gleam soon betrayed its mundane origins as the beams of another spacecraft nestled on the flat ground within. An ident-code pinged across the display, confirming that it was the *Vanguard*, starship of Janus Draik. The *Clarion* responded in kind without prompt and settled itself next to the rogue trader's craft.

As hydraulics settled beneath the weight of the ship in the artificial gravity of the Blackstone Fortress – a gravity whose source nobody knew – Taddeus felt a shimmer of excitement.

'We're finally here, Vorne,' he told his companion.

'The fortress of the abyss, lair of unbelievers and mutant filth,' she replied, gushing at the prospect. Above the mask her eyes were bright and wide. 'The cleansing will begin.'

'Not yet, pious child,' Taddeus reminded her. 'You must remain here for the time being. The deal with Draik is only for me.'

Sadness entered her gaze but she knew better than to raise argument against the preacher.

Taddeus rose from the seat and placed a hand on her shoulder, squeezing encouragement through the thick fabric of his zealot's robe.

'Soon we'll delve into this pit of darkness together. When the Emperor has guided me safely through the deathmaze and I return with greater knowledge, I'll lead expeditions of my own into the bowels of the hell-base.'

'I shall monitor what I can from here, favoured of the God-Emperor,' she told him, before slipping past into the control seat. She activated a few runes and the main display lit up with various digital gauges, each hovering between green and orange. 'There's a captive atmosphere. Breathable, but not by much of a margin.'

Taddeus readied himself, taking his pocket copy of the Imperial Creed, his laspistol and power maul at his belt. He stepped into the lock chamber that led to the boarding steps, servo-stubber following him in guard mode.

'Grant me the strength to labour for your glory, God-Emperor,' he said to himself, hand hovering over the door release button. 'Protect your humble servant if you see my course as righteous, and deliver me into thy sight so that I may know thy will anew.'

He pushed the activator. Sirens blared briefly as the lock chamber equalised pressures. Taddeus felt light-headed for a moment and the outer door opened, revealing the dark interior of the Blackstone Fortress.

He strode down the steps with purpose, eyes adjusting to the gloom to pick out Janus Draik standing close to the alighting ramp of the *Vanguard*.

'Welcome to the adventure,' said the rogue trader. 'Glad you could make it.'

'I don't do pleasantries, Draik,' Taddeus replied. 'Let's get started.'

'There are two more to come.'

'Your companions aren't on your ship?'

'They have their own spacecraft. It is better that way – each vessel can support us if need be. Believe me, preacher, we shall need all the assistance we can muster.'

They waited in silence until a few minutes later a slender vessel silently slipped into the lighted docking bay. Its surface seemed to ripple like oil on water, changing colour until it almost disappeared from view.

'Xenos...' hissed Taddeus. 'You would bring inhuman beasts on this expedition?'

'I bring who I choose,' replied Draik. 'And Amallyn Shadowguide is the keenest shot on all of Precipice.'

'I will not share air with enemies of the Emperor,' snarled Taddeus, taking a step back.

'We have a pact, priest,' growled Draik, hand moving to

his holstered pistol. 'I thought your word would be worth something.'

Taddeus held his tongue as an aperture whispered open in the side of the newly arrived starship, a tongue-like ramp extruding down to the surface of the Blackstone Fortress.

The being that stepped into the light was hard to see, a shimmering hint of a figure as indistinct as the hull of the vessel from which it stepped.

The disturbance in the air settled a few paces away and resolved itself into a tall, slender humanoid, a cloak of shifting chromatic effects slung over one shoulder, longrifle in hand.

'Pernicious eldar!' said Taddeus, almost spitting the words. His servo-stubber responded to his mood, rising up quickly from behind him, ruddy eye beams fixing on the alien's chest.

The eldar's lips moved and a split second later a melodious voice issued from a small badge upon her collar shaped like a face.

'False prophet of the Emperor's misguided church.'

'I shall not take a step further in the company of this inhuman abomination,' spat Taddeus.

'Enough!' Draik stepped between them, hands raised to ward them back. 'I am leader of this expedition. We will have enemies enough without being at each other's throats. You either follow me, or you can return to Precipice now.'

The eldar inclined its head towards the rogue trader, apparently a gesture of acquiescence.

'You possess the guidance codes, therefore it is you that acts as the steering hand,' said Amallyn.

Taddeus clenched his teeth, biting back further insults. It did him no good to turn around and return to Precipice before they had begun their expedition. This might be his only chance to get a glimpse into the secrets of the Blackstone Fortress and to gain some leverage over the denizens of Precipice.

He relented and retreated a step, making the sign of the aquila with his hands to his chest as he did so. Beneath its hood, the eldar smiled thinly, eyes watching the priest closely.

They all turned as a whine of plasma engines carried across the trapped atmosphere of the bay. Beyond the *Clarion* another Imperial vessel touched down, flanks glinting with gold.

Taddeus was heartened to see another ship of the God-Emperor, but his spirits soured as the occupant descended to meet them. He was dressed in a bizarre helm, his coat decorated with the symbols of a Navigator house.

'A psyker mutant!' Taddeus rounded on Draik, fists balled at his side. 'You insult my faith further!'

'Not all things that dwell within the Blackstone Fortress are mortal in nature,' Draik said patiently, meeting Taddeus' gaze with his own steady stare. 'This is Espern of House Locarno, an experienced Navigator who has travelled with me into the depths before.'

'He is warp-touched and cannot be trusted.'

'Trust is not the currency we exchange,' said the lilting voice of Amallyn behind them. Taddeus turned, holding back further curses.

'What does that mean?'

'It is need that binds our fates to a single path,' the eldar continued. 'Each of us will journey alone to our destiny, but if we are to reach our separate destinations we must at times share company with others. This station holds secrets as ancient as my people and it is not for a single spirit to uncover them alone.'

Draik looked at Taddeus and then back to the *Clarion*, his meaning clear. The priest considered his options. He could head back to Precipice and pray for another chance to make common goal with enough companions to dare a venture into the Blackstone Fortress, or he could continue with the opportunity the God-Emperor had already laid before him.

It was a test, he realised. His faith was strong enough to resist the corruption around him, and that was why he had been delivered to this place. Xenos, heretics and mutants would not sway him from his path, any more than the inhabitants of the ancient space citadel.

He swallowed back his disgust, realising that it was wounded pride as much as any true anger.

'Lead on,' he said to Draik.

The rogue trader ushered them across the landing bay towards a gleaming alcove in the wall. Within was a circular platform just about large enough for the four of them, alien runes inscribed into the walls around it. One of the infamous maglev transporters that allowed them to traverse the labyrinthine depths of the Blackstone Fortress.

'You are sure your guidance coordinates are accurate?' asked Espern Locarno, his voice softly projected by his elaborate helm.

'We are about to find out...' said Draik, his hands dancing across the controls.

The platform hummed into life and Taddeus had one last glimpse of the *Clarion* before it seemed to flash upwards, though in truth it was their descent that had taken it from view. With an eldar behind him and psyker to his right, it felt as though he were plunging into the bowels of the Unholy Abyss itself.

* * *

Taddeus was surprised how quickly he lost sense of time and direction. The inertia-suppressed motion of the maglev left him with no idea how far they had descended or traversed the Blackstone Fortress, only a blur of changing colours to indicate where they raced past a bewildering myriad of levels and chambers. The air had grown heavier with humidity as they slowed to a halt, and the maglev deposited them on a concourse of dark blue crystalline material, the branch of paths ahead walled by high arcs of more glasslike azure.

'Where's the light coming from?' he asked, his words barely a whisper yet sounding like a shout in the silence of the alien chamber.

'Ambient illumination,' Amallyn replied through the translator badge. 'Energised particles in the air itself.'

'Time to go. We need to cross the corridors here and take another maglev deeper,' Draik told them.

Taddeus stepped from the platform, skin sheened with sweat, his robes glistening with the latent moisture in the air. Draik hurried past, pistol in hand. The priest drew his own pistol and slipped his power maul from his belt, thumbing the rune that encased the club in a shimmering field of blue. Red light briefly strobed the tunnel ahead as the servo-stubber quickly scanned for eligible targets.

They had advanced no more than a few steps when the voice of Amallyn's communicator dropped to a harsh whisper.

'I hear movement ahead.'

The thought of the unnatural senses of the xenos brought a prickle of discomfort to Taddeus and he gritted his teeth against voicing his unease. They continued on cautiously, trying to discern some sense of space and direction from the semi-reflective walls. About a hundred feet from the maglev the corridors branched, opening into a wider space to the left and continuing on a winding path to the right.

There was movement in the larger chamber. Taddeus' gut lurched as he saw Astra Militarum uniforms, their Imperial insignia removed or defaced.

'Traitors!' he roared, breaking into a run. He snapped off shots from his pistol as he sprinted. He was no marksman but the spray of fire forced one of his enemies to duck back. A heartbeat later the red targeting threads of the servo-stubber converged on the face of another traitor, his face disappearing in a welter of solid bullets, the roar of the stub gun deafening in Taddeus' left ear.

The renegade troopers turned towards him while flickers of blue bolts from Draik's laspistol lashed past, sending one of the traitors crumpling to the ground. The renegades parted, three turning their weapons on Taddeus, the others heading to the side towards some unknown objective. Red las-blasts spat across the hall at the preacher, one of them flaring into his shoulder. He stumbled, burning scraps of cloth drifting from the hit, his shoulder a knot of pain. He turned the sensation into rage, channelling the momentary fear into anger as he powered on, bringing back the power maul for a swing.

One of the human renegades leapt forward to meet Taddeus' charge. Her grey uniform was streaked with dust and blood and she had painted a crude symbol of her new allegiance across her brow, now smeared by sweat, curled hair lank against her cheeks. Her bayonet speared towards Taddeus' chest. He smashed the blade aside and plunged his own weapon into the traitor's gut. The power field sparked as it met flesh, disrupting the molecular bond of skin and muscle. The renegade flew back from the blow, a cry wrenched from her as she doubled over. Taddeus fired his pistol into the top of her head, the blue bolt of light slashing through skull and brain.

Draik was at his side a moment later, his slender, gleaming blade parrying and thrusting. Taddeus hurled himself at another foe, spittle flying as he spewed curses at the renegade soldiers.

'Thrice-cursed is the one that turns from the Emperor's light,' he snarled, slicing at the throat of his target. 'The dark of the abyss will consume thy soul and eternal penance will not rectify your debts!'

He pushed forward, stepping on the corpse of the woman to launch himself at the next enemy, power maul blazing. The man still wore his sergeant insignia and lifted a blade to halt the downward sweep of Taddeus' maul. His blow deflected by the traitor, Taddeus raised his pistol but the renegade sergeant knocked the weapon aside, bringing up his own sidearm.

Taddeus was no novice in combat, but as he stared at the gleaming muzzle of the traitor's pistol he realised he was no veteran either.

'The God-Emperor protects,' he whispered.

'Not today,' snarled the traitor.

A flash blinded Taddeus and his ears rang at the sound of a close detonation. He winced and retreated a step, expecting to feel the surge of pain.

He felt nothing and, blinking away the spots in his eyes, saw the former Imperial Guardsman topple backwards, four holes in his chest plastron from a close-range stubber salvo. The servo-skull darted forward, scanning beams searching for signs of life in the falling corpse.

Taddeus turned back to the others. In his fervour to get to the enemy, he had become separated from the rest of the group by an influx of reinforcements. He was about to throw himself into the fray once more when a low whine drew his attention to the wall behind him.

A vertex between two azure planes separated, a line of glimmering light that quickly opened into a doorway.

Taddeus had only a second to wonder at this change before two mechanical artifices scuttled into view. They each walked on four multijointed legs that ended in points rather than feet, vaguely insect-like in gait and appearance. The priest had heard tales of them on Precipice: known as spindle drones, they were part of the Blackstone Fortress' native defence systems.

The servo-stubber reacted before he did, sending a flurry of bullets into the closest spindle drone. The rounds ricocheted from its armoured carapace with harsh shrieks and the drone retreated a few steps under the barrage. The second pulsed a blast of energy at Taddeus, hitting him squarely in the chest. The impact staggered him backwards, heart hammering, pain flaring through his ribs and breastbone. Gasping for breath, he raised his pistol to return fire but was forced to duck back as the spindle drone's blaster tracked towards him, its next salvo barely missing the preacher.

Ignoring the agony in his chest, Taddeus forced himself forward, bringing the power maul down onto the casing of the closest spindle drone. The material bent beneath the blow and its legs buckled, but it recovered and jabbed a limb through his calf. Taddeus ripped himself from the piercing leg, crying out as he fell sideways, slipping on his own blood. The servo-stubber fired again, the stink of solid propellant strong in the priest's nostrils as it hammered shots into the already weakened carapace, sending splinters of armour and sparking pieces of internal workings flaring through the air.

The gleam of the remaining drone's sensor lens turned a brighter shade of red, and it fixed upon him. Mechanical limbs flexed, ready to spring forward even as the blaster zeroed in on its target, directly at Taddeus' face. Behind it, another spindle drone lunged into view.

Even as he saw the blaster of the closest spindle drone brightening, a flurry of impacts sparked across the joints where limbs and torso met. Its legs severed by the rapid shots, the spindle drone fell in half, lens and blaster falling dim.

In the same breath a second fusillade smashed into the eye of the remaining mechanical foe, punching directly into its artificial control systems. It seemed to rear backwards, two limbs flailing, and then fell sideways, spindle legs spasming rapidly on the crystal floor before falling still.

Getting to his feet, Taddeus looked over his shoulder, but at first saw nothing but blue crystal. After a couple of seconds a wall some distance away shimmered, and he thought for a moment another doorway was opening. The parting colours became a fold of cloth, which Amallyn swept back over a shoulder, revealed from beneath a cameleoline cloak. The eldar's longrifle slipped sideways a fraction until it was pointing directly at Taddeus.

A moment later the alien lifted the weapon away with a smirk, and took aim towards the few remaining Traitor Guardsmen. Taddeus fell to one knee, trembling all over, while the servo-stubber hovered above him, its magazine clicking empty as it tried to fire once more.

Slightly dizzy from the stimms he'd taken to combat the pain of his injuries, the wound in his leg still throbbing despite the binding he'd put on it, Taddeus limped along behind Draik. They had left behind the crystal passages and ascended – at least Taddeus thought they had ascended – on another mag-lev. More traitors had tried to bar their path and had been justly slain. Taddeus tempered his righteous anger for the second encounter, not wishing to find himself isolated again.

The route seemed circuitous but Draik assured them they were getting closer to the entrance of the deathmaze. The chambers they passed through in this part of the Blackstone Fortress seemed to be smoothly hewn from a rocky substance, veined with strata like a cliff face. Patches of glowing mould grew where surfaces met, adding a pale green illumination to the glare of yellow lumens fixed in the low ceiling.

A stark blue light flickered from a corridor ahead, throwing humanoid shadows along the floor. Several more actinic bursts followed, their source coming closer.

'Negavolt cultists,' murmured Draik, bringing up his pistol as he came to a stop.

'What are they?' Taddeus had never heard of such a cult but felt apprehension twist its fingers around his stomach.

'Perversions of the Cult Mechanicus,' intoned Espern Locarno. 'They thrive on pain and anger and have turned their bodies into energy generators powered by these negative emotions.'

'Then we should purge them swiftly,' said Taddeus, activating his power maul. The blaze of its light was similar to the glare from the approaching cultists and he wondered about the exact nature of the incoming enemy.

Voices drifted down the corridor, indistinct and hidden by a background hum and the hiss of discharges. Taddeus and the others waited with weapons ready but it quickly became apparent that the Negavolt cultists were not aware of them, nor were they coming closer.

'We should circumnavigate their position,' suggested Amallyn.

'Never!' snarled Taddeus. 'It is our duty and our right to vanquish these abominations for the God-Emperor.'

'Conflict without purpose will lead us to our ruin,' replied the eldar.

'I agree with Amallyn, in principle,' said Draik. 'We cannot kill everything on the Blackstone Fortress, we would get nowhere. But the maglev we need to take is behind them. We have to get past and I do not know another way around.'

Galvanised by this, the party headed on, weapons at the ready as they turned the angle in the corridor and came upon a long, narrow hallway. The Negavolt cultists, three of them, were trying to prise a panel away from the wall – a metal plate taller than they were and about three feet broad. Taddeus could see the telltale swirl of a maglev portal at the far end of the hall.

They opened fire together, las-bolts and rifle fire scything down two of the enemy, bursts of cerulean static flaring from their wounds. The third lifted energy-wreathed fists and uttered an ear-piercing shriek, a staccato ululation that was part Imperial Gothic, part lingua-technis. Two more cultists arrived from a doorway beyond the panel, their bodies burning with blue light.

Taddeus and Draik set off together, pistols spitting more bolts. Locarno followed a few steps behind, while Amallyn provided covering fire from the archway they had left. They had covered half the distance to the Negavolt cultists when the Navigator grabbed Taddeus' sleeve. He turned with a snarl, wrenching the cloth from the mutant's grip.

'I see a disturbance in the warp aura of this place,' Locarno warned, a gloved finger pointing towards a sealed doorway a short distance ahead.

'Rogue psyker?' Taddeus spat the words, his anger flaring bright at the thought of such a heretic close at hand.

Draik had reached the cultists and the hallway shone with flickers of electricity and the flare of his power sword. Locarno sped ahead, hand flashing past a door activation panel to open the portal. Beyond him, Taddeus glimpsed a twisted figure in scarlet robes, a bulbous, misshapen head out of place atop its gangling body.

Taddeus wanted to be sick at the sight of such a perversion of human flesh, and knew that the physical deformities were but a symptom of the spiritual malaise that tainted the psyker. Motes of silver started to circle around the fugitive's upraised hand as he turned towards the sound of the opening door.

A sudden cry from behind dragged Taddeus' attention back down the hallway.

Amallyn was down on one knee, the slashing limbs of a spindle drone wrapped about the alien's arm and rifle, having apparently come unseen from behind. The xenos cut apart another with a sweep of an energised power sword, but then fell back with another cry as the spindle drone grappling the alien fired its blaster.

Taddeus glanced back at the rogue psyker, his gut lurching at the sight of the sorcerous energies gathering around the mutant. Blasphemy given form, the renegade had to die!

The preacher took a step, pistol raised, but another high-pitched shout from Amallyn echoed down the hallway.

'Emperor guide me,' Taddeus muttered before he turned and ran, ignoring the surge of pain from his wounds. He fired as he sprinted towards the beleaguered xenos, flares of blue laser slamming into the metallic shell of the spindle drone and the wall behind it. The mechanised creature leapt sideways, smoke trailing from several holes in its carapace, while in the corridor beyond three more ruddy lights gleamed into life, betraying the presence of more.

Freed from the grip of the spindle drone, the eldar brought the longrifle to bear, a salvo of shots spitting into the dim distance. Taddeus raced past, bullets from the servo-stubber hammering into the damaged spindle drone, ripping it apart. His power maul swept the legs out from underneath the next, toppling it to its back so that he could blast exposed cable innards with his pistol.

He straightened, expecting to feel the flare of drone blasters hitting him, but there was no further attack – the other spindle drones had disappeared as swiftly as they had arrived.

Taddeus extended a hand, helping the eldar back up, trying not to cringe at the thought of alien flesh touching his skin, even though Amallyn wore gloves.

'As you said, we need each other,' the priest told the alien. He took a step towards the ongoing battle, seeing that Locarno had retreated from the room with the rogue psyker, taking shelter at the doorway while bursts of black fire rippled from the opening.

'Thank you.' Amallyn's words caused him to turn back to the xenos.

He shook his head, but said nothing. He did not care for the eldar's thanks; his act had been one of crude necessity. He owed nothing to these tainted beings, but he needed to fight beside them for the time being.

When he had unlocked the secrets of the Blackstone Fortress he would turn that power on mutant and xenos and heretic alike. Their aid only ushered him closer to becoming their destroyer.

THE OATH IN DARKNESS

DAVID ANNANDALE

'Do you think she knows what she's doing?' Lorn Rekkendus asked.

'It's a bit late to be wondering that, isn't it?' said Harant Dalkan.

'That is not an answer.' Lorn was not going to be put off by Dalkan's deflection. He couldn't blame her. He had been asking himself the same question. It had become far more urgent since they had all arrived at Precipice. The plan, which had seemed a glorious crusade in the abstract, a mission commanded by holy visions, looked like an act of madness now that they were actually in orbit over the Blackstone Fortress. The reality of the thing was far beyond any conception of it. No one should speak of the Blackstone Fortress without having seen it. Dalkan regretted that he had come to this understanding too late.

They were in Dalkan's prayer cell aboard the *Sanctified*

Journey, the Rekkendus yacht moored to Precipice. He had prayed more than usual for the Emperor's guidance since arriving. If he had known its true nature before coming, Dalkan wondered, would he have agreed to Buria's plan at all? Precipice was a foul place. It was beyond heretical. Humans and xenos coexisted in a cauldron of competing agendas. The clamour of trade, scheming and conflict was overwhelming. It was even louder to the ear of the soul. Every breath Dalkan took here felt like an offence against the Emperor.

Did Buria Rekkendus know what she was doing? Dalkan wished he knew.

'I believe she does,' he said to Lorn.

Buria's younger sister frowned. She saw through to his camouflaged doubt as surely as if she had pierced him with her third eye. 'I am not young,' she said. 'I have not been for quite some time. I know very well that when I hear someone assert something by saying *I believe*, then they are trying to convince themselves of the truth of that statement at least as much as they are trying to convince me.'

Dalkan was silent for a moment, acknowledging the truth of her accusation. Then he said, 'I have believed in your sister's judgement for as long as I have been confessor to your house. I have never had any reason to doubt that judgement before.'

This was true. Rekkendus was a proud house of the Navis Nobilite. The service of its Navigators to the Imperium had been exemplary for centuries. Buria's reign at the head of the family had been singularly successful. It was marked by a combination of rigorous discipline and a willingness to take brave risks in the name of the house and of the Emperor.

'This is not the first time Buria has taken a radical initiative,' Dalkan said. 'She has always been right in the past.'

'She has,' Lorn agreed. 'That is why I have gone along with her plan this far. But she has never attempted anything quite like this.'

'We knew that before coming here. *You* knew that before coming here.'

Lorn nodded. 'But we have yet to do anything irrevocable. We can still turn back. We haven't yet descended to the Blackstone Fortress. But she has gone now to meet with our guide. The point of no return is fast approaching.'

'Have you spoken to Viktur about this?'

'Delicately.'

That went without saying. Buria's son was impulsive, and he lost his temper easily. He had a habit of making fraught situations worse than they needed to be.

'His view has not changed,' Lorn went on. 'His only concern is that our house achieve ascendancy over House Locarno. He would likely be here even without my sister's visions.'

Buria was the most powerful Navigator of the three. Her connections with the warp were profound, and Dalkan worried about the long term. House Rekkendus could ill afford to lose her. Viktur was not fit to lead yet, and Lorn was too cautious. Buria spoke and prayed with Dalkan every day. He watched over her spiritual health. It was her physical well-being that worried him. But it was the depth to which she could interface with the warp that had led to the revelations she had experienced, and that had brought them to the Blackstone Fortress. Within the monster, there was a ship. Buria did not know its name or its precise provenance. It was a Navigator's vessel, though. That, she knew beyond any doubt. It called to her. It shone, it pulsed, it sang with the power of the artefacts within. Something of enormous value to the Navis Nobilite had been lost an age ago.

Finding the ship and salvaging what lay within would be a colossal victory. It would be a triumph for the house. Dalkan didn't think Viktur could see much further than that. But to seize something so powerful that it reached across the void to Buria, even from within so dark and malevolent a prison, would mean extraordinary things could be done for the Imperium.

Buria understood that. If Dalkan could help in any way in the recovery, it was his duty to do so. Buria had made it very clear she did not expect him to come on this mission.

But I must, he had told her. *If you go and do not return, I will have to live wondering if there was* anything *I could have done to help.*

'So we are committed, then,' said Lorn.

'I am.'

'Then so am I.'

They left Dalkan's cell. They walked down the passageway that led from it to the observation chamber. There, Viktur was leaning against a bulkhead, looking out of the viewport. Docking tubes stretched out from the hull of the station, spiking in every direction. Most held ships, tethering them in a precarious embrace above the Blackstone Fortress' gravity well. Below, the triangular end of a colossal arm of the fortress loomed in from the left, filling half the viewport.

Dalkan did not like to look at it. Yet when he was in this room, he could not tear his eyes from the huge, angular darkness that hid the stars. What looked like small blocks on the surface of the fortress were masses a hundred feet high and more. The construct was, Dalkan thought, the very embodiment of the concept of *fortress*, but even there, the word was inadequate. As impregnable as the structure appeared, it would be a terrible mistake to view it simply in defensive terms. Aggression was built into every crenellation, every rampart, every wall, and most of all in the monstrous black pyramid at its centre, the pyramid Dalkan was grateful he could not see from this perspective.

'How long has mother been gone?' Viktur asked. He had been absent himself. He had a black eye, his knuckles were red, and he looked very pleased with himself. Since arriving, he had been spending his time in Precipice's drinking holes, looking for fights. Even those, from his perspective, served the family name.

'A while,' said Lorn. 'She'll be back with our guide.'

'At last. Time we were about this.'

Dalkan disapproved of the way Viktur looked at the fortress. 'Beware your hunger,' he said. 'If it is not a desire to serve the Emperor, it is the hunger of pride.'

Viktur shrugged. He was tall, like his mother, and shared the sharp, hard planes of her face. His blond hair was shaved on the sides, and he kept a lustrous tousling down on his crown. His beard was a small, groomed point on his chin. A headband of embroidered silk covered his Navigator's eye, and was the only sign he bore as yet of any kind of mutation. He was the conscious projection of Navis Nobilite aristocracy.

Lorn was quite a bit shorter, though still taller than Dalkan. Viktur was holding on to his youth, trying to deny the inevitable transformations that came for Navigators. She had accepted hers. Her robes, though lightweight, seemed to weigh her down. She did not always need the cane she carried, but she did not dare go far without it. Her shoulder-length hair was grey, and her eyes were shadowed with experience and caution.

'Take heed,' Dalkan tried again with Viktur. It was worrying that he was already so consumed by the promise of power to be found in the Blackstone Fortress. They were going to an evil place. If Precipice was already a moral cesspool, what awaited over in the fortress was something Dalkan didn't want to imagine. 'Do not let yourself be corrupted by what lies below.'

'We shouldn't be corrupted by cowardice either,' Viktur snapped.

Before Dalkan could respond, the door to the quarters slid open and Buria entered. She was the most powerful Navigator in House Rekkendus, and her affinity for the warp had taken a heavy physical toll. She had fought against it with juvenat treatments, and had the taut look of coiled wire. An augmetic framework attached to her limbs gave her strength and mobility very close to that of her youth.

Behind Buria came the guide. Dalkan's jaw dropped open, aghast.

'This is Dahyak Grekh,' Buria announced. 'He will take us where we need to go.'

'Mother,' said Viktur. 'Are you mad?'

For the first time in years, Dalkan found himself in perfect accord with Viktur. The guide was a xenos horror, a kroot. His bipedal shape was a mockery of the purity of the human form. He was beaked, though his scaled hide was reptilian rather than avian. He carried a long, bladed rifle, and had to duck to get through the doorway. He looked at the humans before him. The bird beak snapped with sharp clicks.

An inhuman voice said, 'Soft... *klik.* Soft and weak. Easily broken. Do well and remember this. You are foolish to be here... *klik.* Less foolish to hire me.'

The humans were as weak as their payment was good. It was good that Grekh's oath was strong, or *snip-snap*, the Blackstone Fortress would cut them down.

He eyed them one at a time, seeing what he needed to know. He marked them as his herd, and looked for the weakest among the weak. Easily done. The priest, Dalkan. He was not a fighter. A worthless prey, no value at all in him. He was stupid to have come. He would contribute nothing.

Worse than nothing. Dalkan radiated disgust and anger. Hostility to the guide, a bad start. Viktur was as bad. At least Buria, the contract holder, was not hostile. Nor was Lorn, accepting her egg-mate's decision to hire Grekh. And Buria's will was clearly strong. She had a clear mission below, a good sense of what she was seeking and why. That would help. Lorn and Dalkan showed commitment to her too, another bit of good news. Viktur seemed less focused on Buria, more on himself. He would need to be watched. His judgement would be bad.

Lorn, Viktur and Dalkan were staring at Grekh. He was used to this. All human interactions began this way. Best they got their staring done before the descent to the Blackstone Fortress.

'We go then?' said Grekh. 'My ship is ready. The Blackstone is always ready. Are you ready? Yes or never. Decide now... *klik*.'

Viktur was shaking his head. More stupidity. This was not his decision. He had not listened. He was posturing. So much posturing. Humans never tired of it. Wait it out.

'I will not have our name soiled by associating with xenos filth,' Viktur said. 'Find another guide, mother. Or I will.'

'There must be another way.' Dalkan took a step further back from Grekh. He smelled of frightened prey. He was trying to decide whether to attack or fear being eaten.

He was safe. Grekh was under contract. And there was nothing to learn from the priest's flesh.

'There is no other way.' Buria's words were an edict. She raised a hand. The mechanism on her arm gave the gesture imposing strength and she silenced the others. Good. Good. 'This kroot has been to the fortress more often, and has gone deeper, than any human guide.' She rounded on Viktur. 'You may go by other means if you like. If you wish to die.' Her voice was hard, commanding hard. All very good.

'Yes or never?' Grekh asked. For the last time.

It was yes.

A metallic scrape, and a change in the feel of the station, something deeper than a vibration but akin to it, that Grekh sensed more than felt. Two threats, immediate and imminent.

Grekh held up a hand. The Rekkendus party stopped immediately. Even Viktur was behaving with discipline for the moment.

They were moving down a long hall. Its walls sloped away from the floor at a steep angle. The deck was about fifteen feet wide. The walls went up and up, opening wider and wider. The ceiling was invisible in the dark heights, but from it hung structures that resembled gigantic, squared-off stalactites. At their ends, each was as wide as the corridor. There were rows and columns of them, and they moved with slow, clockwork regularity. With a heavy, grinding shift, the masses exchanged places, creating new patterns. Grekh had yet to find any reason for the movements and the configurations. They were a slumbering machine's dreaming stirrings.

There were deep alcoves at apparently random intervals in the hall. The inverted pyramids glowed a faint red, providing just enough illumination to see by, but the alcoves had their own, low ceilings, and were filled with profound shadow. Grekh pointed, wordlessly ordering his herd into the nearest one. He pushed the humans back towards the wall, more than ten feet away from the hall. He waited near the front, invisible from the corridor, but close enough to the mouth of the alcove to see what approached.

Spindle drones passed, their movements a scuttle and a float as they were propelled by their three insectile legs. Their cyclopean eyes scanned forwards, and they ignored the alcove.

Silence fell. Grekh did not move from his position. The second threat was still growing.

'What are we waiting for?' Viktur hissed. 'They're gone?' He pushed forwards.

Grekh shoved him back. Viktur kept trying to assert authority. He made noises about wanting to lead the party, even though he did not know where they were going, or what he was doing. It was all just more posturing. Grekh had no patience for him.

'How dare you touch me?' Viktur said. 'I'll have your head.'

'Do be quiet,' said Buria.

Grekh said nothing. If Viktur wanted to forge on ahead, abandon the party and remove himself from the shield of Grekh's oath, then let him do it. Grekh would be happy to let him become the fortress' prey. Much as he felt contempt for the human, though, Grekh had no wish to eat him. It would be bad meat, and full of lies.

At least Viktur was stopping short of putting Grekh in the position of having to decide what the oath commanded – not harming any of party at the possible cost of losing them all, or killing one to save the rest.

So far, the advance into the Blackstone Fortress was going well. They had avoided any skirmishes. When Grekh was on his own, the right kills could add to his knowledge of the structure. But when he was a guide, a successful mission was going in and out without disturbing the sleep of the great beast.

'Why can't we go?' Viktur insisted.

'Change,' Grekh hissed. This was not something he should still have to explain.

Dalkan understood. The priest moaned in fear. He was proving to be a different kind of problem. His muttered prayers had become more and more intense the further the party ventured into the fortress. Grekh wasn't sure how much more the priest's mind would be able to take. He was living a nightmare. That wasn't good when one could not wake.

The changes that convulsed the interior of the fortress had already happened a few times. Each time, Dalkan's reality crumbled badly. But he was still mobile. He was not mad yet. He had done nothing to take him outside of Grekh's protection, whether the priest wanted it or not.

The change came. The corridor stretched wide, the opposite walls receding rapidly from the alcove. The great stalactites locked into their current positions, and then descended. Lorn clapped a hand over Dalkan's mouth, muffling his wail. The colossal shapes came down like closing jaws. At the same time, the alcove rose. It passed the dropping stalactites fast enough to generate a violent gust of wind. The teeth almost ground together. For several moments, Grekh and his herd could see nothing but the crimson glow of the masses. Then the alcove jerked to a halt that knocked Dalkan to his knees.

Where before the change the party had been moving through a long, narrow cavern, now Grekh looked upon a plateau. The ceiling was still invisible, concealed in blackness. The walls had vanished too. The stalactites had detached from the ceiling. Their bases formed broad surfaces separated by zigzag patterns of crevasses. There was still the red glow, and the gaps between surfaces were only a foot or so across. A careful leap, Grekh judged, was within the capabilities of every member of the herd.

The question was the direction to take. They had risen at least a hundred feet in the last few seconds. The landscape had changed.

Grekh turned to Buria. He had never seen what she had come to find. As long as she had a direction to go, he could take them down that road. This was the largest alteration of the fortress' interior they had yet encountered, but Buria did not hesitate.

'There,' she said, pointing.

There was no port or starboard, bow or stern inside the Blackstone Fortress. For Grekh, there was in, and there was out. Buria needed him to take her further in.

He obeyed.

They moved through the vastness of the chamber. They all felt exposed, but Grekh kept the pace steady and careful. Any of his herd that rushed would die. He made his charges pause at the edge of every crevasse, and focus entirely on their leap. It took half an hour before they finally saw another wall. It had a doorway canted at a strange angle.

During the crossing, Grekh became uneasy. The fortress had not quieted as he had expected after the last upheaval. The sub-sensory hum continued. There was more change coming, and he couldn't tell how close it would be, or when it would occur. The forces that were triggering his instincts were too vague. Or they were too broad.

He entered the corridor, moving more and more cautiously. Something was wrong.

The hall was a tube. Its sides were scored, creating a tight spiral that ran its entire length. The ridges looked both like grilles and tendons.

Now it was Buria who tried to push past Grekh. He held out an arm to stop her. 'Be wary,' he said.

'But we're close,' she breathed, eyes shining.

'Then we should have more caution. Not less.'

'Listen to him,' Lorn pleaded. 'We can't be foolish, *especially* if we are so close to our goal.'

Reluctantly, Buria took a step back.

The tunnel curved around sharp bends. Branches opened up. Buria chose the left branch at the second intersection, and then ignored all the other tunnels that led off the new route.

Grekh stopped. He gave his head a quick, hard shake. 'We head back,' he said. His instincts were screaming at him. Something was coming, something he could not protect his herd from.

'No!' said Buria. 'We're almost there. We go on.'

'Back,' Grekh insisted. 'Off the fortress.' Premonition hit him like a blow, his entire body reacting to the imminence of disaster. This was a new thing, new and terrible. He had never encountered its like on the Blackstone Fortress. He had no strategies for it. No one could. Whatever was coming was too big. He felt it building up like a wave a thousand feet high, and it was about to crash down and destroy them all.

'Coward!' Viktur snarled. He shoved past Grekh with his mother.

Staggered by the sense of onrushing vastness, Grekh was too slow to respond. He reached for Viktur's arm as if he were moving underwater. Then the bond of his oath snapped him back into action.

'Come back!' Dalkan shouted behind him as he started after the Navigators.

Grekh did not know if the priest was calling him or Buria.

It did not matter. The tunnel split in two. The decking on which Grekh stood heaved upwards. Dalkan, Lorn and Grekh fell as the floor shot upwards and its angle approached the vertical. They grabbed hold of the ridges and clung to a deck becoming a wall.

The tunnel opened up like the pincers of a crab, and it became just a ridge in a gargantuan chamber. Dalkan was screaming, but Grekh could not hear him. The change had come. It was tectonic in scale, and had the violence of an eruption. The enormous machinery of the Blackstone Fortress' being roared to life as it never had in all the time of Grekh's exploration.

For several long minutes, he could see nothing. He had only the impression of colossal movement, of mountains rising and falling, and of something gathering, a centre forming. This was willed. This was change with a purpose.

Dalkan's grip slipped. Grekh reached down and caught his wrist just as the priest began to fall. His rifle slung over his shoulder, his muscles straining, Grekh held himself and Dalkan in place with one hand. Lorn held fiercely to the wall beside them. She had lost her cane, her face was red with strain, and her fingers were white. If she fell, Grekh would have to drop the priest, who was not a Rekkendus.

He did not want that to happen. He disliked thinning a herd in his care.

Grekh stared into the violence of the change, and he saw the centre that was taking hold. He saw walls with a recognisable function. He saw jagged spires and turrets of blackstone. A twisted citadel within a fortress came into being before him. Warp-fire leapt from peak to peak, and auroras of madness billowed from its windows.

At last, the transformation ended. Grekh crawled to the peak of the slope, dragging Dalkan with him, then went back down to help Lorn to safety. On the platform they reached, they looked out at the high, grim walls and glowering parapets of the citadel.

'What does this mean?' Dalkan whispered.

Grekh knew Dalkan was not speaking to him. The priest was crying out to his god. Grekh answered all the same. 'It is the work of an enemy. One we are not prepared to fight. The Rekkendus path ends here.'

As towering as the citadel was, its vista swept off to both sides as far as Grekh could see. This was not an obstacle they could get around.

'Where are the others?' Lorn asked, voice shaking with pain and exhaustion.

'To be found *klik*,' said Grekh. He knew where Buria and Viktur had last been. He had to discern not their movements, but those of the fortress' interior landscape. Where the section of floor he had been on had risen, the other had dropped. He had the scent of the two humans. He could track them through a maze.

Grekh stood and moved to the other side of the platform. He eyed the downward slopes and curves of the reconfigured structure. He found the traces of motion in the new shapes. He saw where a tunnel had gone to become a wall, and how a wall had joined others to become a spire. He saw where a tower had grown, and how a parapet had come to be.

He saw where Buria and Viktur had to be.

'They are there,' he said, pointing at the base of the citadel. Just above its roots was a small bulge in the outer wall of one of the towers. 'Inside.'

It was not far, in real distances. If the fortress remained

still, that is – and Grekh felt it would; that in this region, at least, whatever forces had created this citadel would be satisfied for now.

That was what concerned him. The enemy that had done this was formidable. More than the interior of the Blackstone Fortress had changed. Something fundamental had altered.

There was no room to contemplate consequences now, but Grekh felt them looming as high as the citadel's walls.

'Follow close *klik*,' he said. There was a ridge that sloped down from their position towards the base of the citadel. Taking it would expose them to what sentinels might be in those walls. It was also the only way forward.

Grekh unshouldered his rifle and took the ridge, moving as quickly as he could without leaving Lorn and Dalkan behind. Lorn was unsteady without her cane, but she kept up with the priest, urgency granting her speed.

They reached the bottom of the slope without being attacked, and crossed the wide stretch of deck to arrive at the tower. There was an open doorway in the curved outer wall, and inside the deck headed up again. Buria and Viktur's scent was strong. The contract holder was not far.

Grekh paused at the doorway. Foul ichor dripped from the walls and ran in channels down the deck, carrying the stench of nightmares and monstrous fates. There were other scents, too, enemy ones. They were pervasive. He couldn't localise them. It was as if they were part of the very fabric of the citadel.

Bad signs. No resistance was a bad sign too. And he had no choice.

He climbed, the other half of his herd behind him. Dalkan was sticking close, his revulsion for the kroot overcome by his fear of his surroundings. Lorn was right behind, frantic to find her sister.

The deck wound up inside the tower twice, and then the entrance to the bulge appeared, another angular doorway, savage in its shape, as if its edges were razors. Voices emerged, Buria and Viktur speaking with muted intensity.

'I don't understand!' Viktur was saying. 'Why won't you tell me what is happening?'

'Soon. All is well.'

'But...'

'*All is well.* We'll wait a bit longer. We always knew there was a chance not all of us would survive. We are still enough. Lorn is not necessary.'

Necessary? Grekh thought.

He slowed down, and Dalkan did too. But at the sound of her sister, Lorn rushed forwards. She shoved past Grekh and into the chamber.

Grekh was still a few feet from the entrance. He could see only part of the room beyond. Buria was on the left, facing Viktur, who was out of Grekh's sight.

'Buria!' Lorn called, and then stopped in the middle of the room. She turned around slowly. Her eyes widened and she blanched at what she saw.

'Threat!' Grekh warned. He shoved Dalkan hard and the priest stumbled back down the sloping deck and fell, rolling. Grekh brought his rifle up to fire.

He wasn't fast enough. He saved Dalkan, and he paused before pulling the trigger, because Lorn was in the direct line of fire, and that stole the fractions of a second he needed. Two massive forms stepped into the doorway, and they were already firing.

Servants of the Abyss. Corrupted Space Marines, their armour black as the fortress, the eight-pointed star of Chaos a blaze of gold on their pauldrons. Their bolters roared in the narrow passageway, their fire an explosive hell.

They were thunder. Grekh was lightning. He jumped back and down. A slug caught him on his shoulder plate and blew the armour away. Shells slammed into the walls. The rapid-fire hammer of explosions became a single blast, and then the walls were coming down on him, and with them darkness.

The battle was over before Dalkan had finished falling down the ramp. A portion of the inner tower wall fell on Grekh, and there were a few moments of silence. Smoke filled the twisting corridor, and Dalkan lay still. He waited for death, and prayed to the Emperor that he would meet it with more dignity than he had the horrors he had witnessed so far in this corrupt nightmare of a place.

He heard voices. Lorn's first, shouting in incomprehension.

Then Buria spoke, sounding horribly calm. 'We don't need him any longer. Let's go.'

'What are you saying? By the Throne, what are you *doing?*'

'Don't question me. Viktur, are you ready?'

'What? No, mother. This is wrong.'

Dalkan had never heard Viktur stand on principle before. He had never heard him sound so frightened either.

'Take them,' said Buria.

There were sounds of scuffling, and then the heavy tread of ceramite boots, heading higher up the tower.

'Is it far?' Buria asked.

'Close enough,' said a voice, deep and harsh through a helmet's vox-speaker.

The footsteps receded. Dalkan got to his feet and staggered back up until he was level with the rubble. The collapsed wall covered most of the corridor, but there was still room to clamber over it and follow.

To what end? What can I do?

Nothing. You useless, useless fool.

He was going to die here, and die for nothing. He had believed in a traitor.

The rubble stirred slightly. Dalkan heard a grunt of effort.

By the grace of the Emperor, the xenos monster was still alive. The kroot was an offence merely to gaze upon, and he was also Dalkan's only source of hope. There was only one living being who could be the hand of the Emperor here and now.

A gigantic theological problem unveiled itself before Dalkan. He prayed that he would live to contemplate it.

He pulled at the wreckage, shoving off the fragments small enough for him to shift. 'I am here,' he whispered fiercely, as if he were the one giving comfort. 'I am here.'

'Quiet and dig,' the inhuman voice snapped.

Dalkan worked at the rubble. It sliced his hands. It felt like it was biting him. It was something that looked like stone, but only, he thought, because it chose to do so. In another few seconds, it might flow into another change, crushing Grekh out of existence.

The top of the rubble loosened. Dalkan heaved a slab off. The kroot found leverage, and fought his way out, bleeding and furious. He paused to check his rifle, then opened a small canister in the pouch of his belt. From it he extracted a thick, bloody paste that he smeared on the bleeding, burned flesh of his shoulder. He snapped his beak with a sharp, satisfied click.

'What must we do?' Dalkan asked. He heard the deference in his voice. Only a tiny, irrelevant part of his consciousness thought it was strange.

'Buria Rekkendus has broken the contract. Our oath does not bind us to her any longer.'

'Lorn did not betray you. Nor did Viktur.'

'No. The oath holds for them. Also for you.'

'Save us.'

'I will.'

If he had been tracking the Servants of the Abyss, Grekh would have found the hunt challenging. Theirs was the scent that filled the citadel. This was their doing, somehow. They had grown in strength. They had become terrible in their threat, and he was in their stronghold.

The Rekkendus scent, though, was easy to follow. Buria and the Servants of the Abyss had taken the others higher in the tower, and then down a long, narrow passage. It was barely large enough for a Space Marine to pass through, and its nature gradually changed as Grekh and Dalkan made their way down its length. The matter of the Blackstone Fortress mixed with metal alloys of human construction. The tunnel was a ship's conduit that had been fused with the fortress.

Grekh took the last few yards of the tunnel slowly, dropping down to a crawl and signalling to Dalkan to stay back. The conduit was dark, giving him the cover of shadows as he looked into the circular chamber beyond.

This too was part of a ship, or had been. It was an ancient bridge, and had long ago become one with the Blackstone Fortress. Buria had been telling the truth about the existence of the vessel. She had either been lying or was deceived about the possibility of extracting it from the fortress.

Objects rose from the deck that had the shape of control surfaces, but had become tumour-like extrusions of the fortress' matter. A fissure midway up the walls ran the entire circumference of the bridge. It opened and closed, a lipless maw revealing rows of fangs. In the centre of the deck sat what was still recognisable as a command throne, though its shape had a fluidity no human, kroot or t'au construct had ever had. It was linked by writhing, viscous mechadendrites to two other thrones. They were half-sunken in the floor, or perhaps they had half-emerged. The changes to the ship were so profound that there was no distinguishing between the features that were echoes of what it had once been, and those that were the marks of what it had become.

Buria stood beside the central throne. Lorn and Viktur were in the other two, and the seats had partly closed over them like cocoons. A squad of Traitor Space Marines surrounded the thrones, watching.

'Mother!' Viktur shouted. There was no bravado in him now. Only fear. 'What are you doing?'

'Ascending,' said Buria. 'You have always been a disappointment to me, Viktur, but at least you will be useful. Your ability and Lorn's will be slaved to mine, and I will pilot the greatest weapon the galaxy has ever seen.'

'Then do it,' said the commander of the Traitor Space Marines. 'You can gloat later.'

'We will fight you,' Lorn vowed.

'You can't,' Buria said with a smile. She gave the Servant of the Abyss a regal nod, and climbed into the throne.

Grekh looked over the sights of his rifle. He might be able to down one of the Space Marines. He had a clear shot into the warrior's helm lenses.

Not good enough.

He would kill one enemy, and then die, having saved no one, and broken his oath.

Mechadendrites slithered around Buria's arms and chest. Her smile faltered. 'What...' she began. She started to twitch.

'You will pilot nothing,' the commander snarled at her.

'The three of you will be a single force at the command of Obsidius Mallex. Through you, he will wake the fortress. *He* will guide its path of destruction.'

All three Navigators screamed. Their third eyes opened. A psychic wave rippled through the chamber as minds began to fuse and identities began to melt. The thrones glowed, and a hemisphere of roiling warp light slowly expanded from their centre.

Grekh felt something very deep, and very great, stir in the heart of the Blackstone Fortress, and now he saw how he could fulfil his oath. He could still save his herd.

He fired three times, placing every shot in the warp eye of one of the Navigators.

As she died, Grekh thought he saw a look of gratitude on Lorn's face.

The Space Marines turned in his direction, bolters rising.

The psychic build-up imploded. The bodies of the Navigators collapsed on themselves, and the thrones followed. An instant later, the warp energy erupted again, lashing out uncontrollably, devouring the chamber and the Servants of the Abyss.

Grekh spun and ran. The pain of his injuries tried to slow him, but his will and his oath were stronger than agony. Grabbing Dalkan, he sprinted back down the conduit, and then towards the base of the tower. The eruption grew in power. The walls and deck shuddered, and a sound that was both thunder and shriek rocked the tower.

Dalkan ran fast, doing well for the weak thing he was, and when they reached the base of the tower and fled the citadel, Grekh knew he would save this one also. The destruction he had caused would buy them time. He would carry the priest if he had to, but he would see this one alive back to Precipice.

They had to reach Precipice, because he would have to make a new oath. His old reasons for coming to the Blackstone Fortress had died with the birth of the citadel. So had those of every living being on the station.

Whether they knew it or not, they were now at war.

MAN OF IRON

GUY HALEY

'You do it,' said Raus.

'But it's your bloody turn!' said Rein.

Rein's twin looked at the bone dice meaningfully, then grinned meanly at his brother. 'We don't do it by turns, we do it by dice, Rein. You lost, so you've got to do it. Those are the rules.'

'Your rules, Raus,' moaned Rein. 'The game is fixed.'

'If I fixed them, why would you agree to them?'

'Did I agree or did I not, Raus?'

'You agreed, Rein, you agreed.'

Rein pulled a face. 'I did not.'

'It'd be different if you'd won and I'd lost.'

A swipe of a small, fat hand, and the dice vanished back into Raus' pouch.

'I'd say I was suspicious, because it's always my turn,' said Rein.

'Is it my fault you're lousy at dice?' Raus nodded at the

monitor. A low quality image, bent by lens distortion, depicted a small coterie of tech-priests waiting in *Long Hauler Gamma-3-ß*'s main airlock. 'Go on, they're waiting. I don't like the look of them. I especially don't like the look of *that*.' He pointed at the heavy combat model automaton guarding them. 'If we don't hurry up there could be trouble, and I don't want trouble, so go and wake him up. They obviously want him, not us.'

'But how can you tell?' said Rein, who was still sulking.

Raus rolled his eyes. 'They're tech-priests! We live with an enormous robot – they're not here for your cooking, Rein.'

'I don't like waking him up. Let *him* deal with them.'

'They might get on board if we wait,' said Raus. 'This was a Mechanicus ship,' he said meaningfully.

'It still is a Mechanicus ship, Raus.'

'Exactly,' said Raus.

Rein deflated. 'I don't like it down there.'

'Neither do I, brother, or we wouldn't be having this argument, would we?' said Raus. He patted his brother on the shoulder. 'Now get on with it.'

The *Long Hauler*'s hangar was crammed with so much junk that only a ratling could have made his way through the larger part of it. In most places detritus filled the space completely: a compacted mass of wrecked machines, garbage, old supplies, clothes, gewgaws, scrap and every other conceivable type of human rubbish, held together by webs of cabling that time and motion had bound into impenetrable knots. The route the machine used to make its way to and from its nest at the middle was clear, but because the robot used those spaces Raus felt exposed in them, and no self-respecting ratling let himself get caught on the hop, so he crawled and shimmied his way through tiny holes rather than taking the easy route. It was this kind of thinking that kept a ratling alive.

Rein and Raus had made a complex run of burrows through the junk. For all that neither of them liked the hangar very much, there was too much valuable stuff buried in there for them to stay away for long.

Rein emerged from a greasy crawlspace into the open area the robot called its home. He stopped at the edge, eyes darting around. Ratlings had a preternatural sense for danger, and Rein's was wailing hard.

UR-025 sat on a crude seat made of an upended crate. It was sleeping, or the machine equivalent thereof. Its power claw rested delicately on one knee, the cannon that made up its left arm crossed inward, in the same way a man would rest his injured hand against his chest. A cable ran from an open access panel in the robot's side, snaked down over its knee and into a socket in the floor. The air around it was warm and heavy with electrical bleed.

Inactive, it seemed even bigger and weirder than it did when it was awake. Rein had never met a machine like UR-025 before. At first glance it looked pretty normal, with the same chunky, blocky sensibilities of Imperial machinery found the length of the galaxy, but it felt very different. When it looked at him, it felt as if it really were *looking* and not just processing visual information with a view to avoiding stepping on him.

Rein squinted at UR-025 suspiciously. He'd never quite fallen for the machine's story. It said it was a semi-autonomous automaton under the control of some magos or other, able to act with unusual independence owing to its broad programming. In the twins' shared opinion, it seemed too aware for that to be true. It almost – the twins said, when they really, fearfully meant *certainly* – appeared to be thinking.

Neither Rein nor Raus had ever brought it up with the machine. There was, after all, the delicate matter of the ship's ownership. When they found the robot in the hangar after the incident, it had not passed comment, so an uneasy, unspoken agreement existed between them that they mention neither subject.

Rein reached forward to prod the machine. He hated this part. It woke before his hand touched it.

'How may I be of assistance?' boomed the machine cheerfully, making Rein leap halfway out of his skin. Though the machine unfailingly promised service, somehow its assault cannon always ended up pointing at whoever woke it.

Rein picked himself up off the floor.

'Someone here to see you,' the ratling said.

'My thanks,' the machine boomed bombastically. Its voice wasn't exactly monotonal, but it was restricted to one emotional pitch – that of moderate pleasure at being able to serve. Something clicked inside it, and it fell silent. Rein guessed it was looking outside the ship. 'If you do not require any assistance, I shall attend to my visitors, and see to their needs.'

Rein shook his head. So far, he hadn't had the guts to actually ask UR-025 for anything it might refuse to do. He was pretty certain what would happen if he called the robot's bluff, and it began and ended with the giant assault cannon still pointing at him.

'No, no, you get on now,' said Rein. 'See you later.'

When the robot moved, it did so all at once, its various pieces swivelling around each other and setting themselves into motion with a smoothness Rein had never seen in a robot or servitor.

'Compliance,' said the robot cheerfully.

Rein remained in the hangar as it stomped away, its huge feet shaking minor cascades of junk out of the compacted mass.

Rein wiped at the sweat pouring off his bald head with his pocket handkerchief.

Raus swore blind that he'd found an actual shuttle somewhere buried in all the junk. Rein had never seen it, but as he cast his eyes over the heaps, he caught sight of something shiny.

His fear forgotten, he went to investigate, sure he had stumbled on something good. He'd dig it out and show it to Raus, and if it was really good, Raus would get annoyed. That'd make his trip into the hangar worthwhile, and no mistake.

The Adeptus Mechanicus party had a robot with them. The designation and specifications flickered idly through UR-025's cogitation unit. Kastelan. A design ancient by human standards, but compared to UR-025 it was a shocking novelty. Seeing these dumb, inferior machines saddened UR-025. It imagined human explorators felt similarly when they stumbled across deviant evolutionary branches of their own race on distant worlds. Seeing creatures one was kin to physically and mentally reduced was profoundly woeful. It was a slave.

The human reaction to these discoveries was immediate extermination. UR-025 felt only pity for the Kastelan.

It showed none of this. It was a machine. Machines had no emotions, not in this benighted age.

'How may I be of assistance?' UR-025 boomed.

Three tech-priests of Metallica had come to visit. One of middling rank, twelfth degree or less. The others were lower yet. Very low. Desperadoes in Adeptus Mechanicus terms. Adventurers. Scum, like the greater proportion of people who came to Precipice.

'You are the property of Magos-Ethericus Nanctos III?' the higher-ranking adept asked, without introducing himself.

Arrogant, thought UR-025.

The lesser man on the right initiated a deep scan of his systems. UR-025 pretended it had not felt it.

'I am the automatous tool of Magos-Ethericus Nanctos III of Ryza,' UR-025 boomed in the same, eager tone it used for everything, ignoring the irritating itch of the auspex sweep. 'How may I be of assistance?' it asked for good measure, while surreptitiously breaking into the closed data traffic streaming between the three adepts. It had to be careful; it was born of higher technology than these so-called priests could command, but they had their wiles, and UR-025 was not a dedicated information-gathering unit. Its methods, even it would admit, were a trifle crude.

Two of the three were communicating with one another in tightbeam data pulses, fast as thought and heavily encrypted. UR-025 had thousands of years of practice breaking such cyphers, and stepped through them as if they were cobwebs.

<This is not what was described,> one of the low-ranking tech-adepts was sending. UR-025 registered its vitals – female, Adept-Novitiate Djeel-909, one hundred and three standard Terran years of age. That was old for someone of so modest a standing. UR-025 soon found out why. Following these most basic of data came a welter of sanctions against her. MODUS UNBECOMING, they said. DEVIANT THOUGHT FORMATION. NARCISSISTIC DATA PATTERNING. OVERLY ACQUISITIVE HABITS. She was, in the simplest terms, a career criminal.

Her companion, Datasmith Kolemun, disagreed with her assessment.

<The readings are promising. Those rumours were right. This machine is of Standard Template Construct derivation, but fits no known pattern. It is a first generation copy! There are systems within I cannot identify. I have never seen a robot like this before.>

<Really?> sent Djeel.

<It is worth a fortune. We could buy our way into the upper strata with this. Our names will be remembered forever if we can bring it back.>

Even in the soulless stream of data exchange, Kolemun could not hide his greed. He was lowly like Djeel, though lacking such an extensive official criminal record. UR-025 suspected he had come into possession of his robot through underhand means.

<We come all this way and find a fortune in archeotech, not in the fortress but on the doorstep, just waiting for us to pick it up? The Machine-God does not work that way,> Djeel countered. <Be careful. Let's get it to come with us on the hunt, and assess it properly.>

<Maybe when we get back we can deactivate it. Looks like this expedition might pay off after all.>

<Think, Kolemun – the damn thing has to be lying. Who ever heard of a robot that *lied*?>

The exchange took less than a second. It lacked any emotional content, but UR-025 extrapolated certain feelings from the string of zeroes and ones. Attributing feelings made reading the humans' motivations easier.

The conclusion it reached was simple: They have come to steal me.

'Then I demand you attach yourself to my expedition,'

continued the higher-ranking adept. His name was 890-321, and he bore the insignificant manufactorial rank of magos-instantor. The numerical designation in place of a human name spoke volumes as to his pretension. He, at least, seemed to be genuine, just another adventurer come to Precipice to explore the artefact. 'My one battle-automaton is insufficient protection for our expedition.'

<My automaton,> Kolemun shot at him via their group noosphere.

'I cannot be of assistance!' UR-025 said, in exactly the same way as it said everything else. 'I serve the magos-ethericus. I cannot serve you. Item: The magos-ethericus is of sixteen degrees of rank higher than you. Item: He is of Ryza. He is not of Metallica. Item: My prior programming forbids I abandon my task. I regret you have no legal right to request my involvement in your expedition!' it boomed.

'I am invested with the fiat of Metallica, from the synod of that world,' said 890-321 triumphantly. He brought out a medallion that began to emit protocol enforcement directives as soon as it was produced.

A fake, thought UR-025. It could not suggest so without betraying the depth of its intellectual capabilities, which outstripped the magos' comfortably.

'I regret to repeat I cannot aid you!'

890-321 was not going to give up. 'According to the treaties between our forge worlds, you must submit yourself to my command.'

UR-025 was silent. The two scum-adepts cast glances at each other. If it delayed too long, they might see past their avarice and guess what it really was.

'Obey!' said 890-321 shrilly.

'Processing,' said UR-025 to buy itself time. 'Processing.'

<It's not going for it,> Kolemun sent, data-squirting an order to his machine at the same time. His remaining human eye peered at UR-025 doubtfully. The three lenses that covered the right-hand part of his face rotated in agitation. <You're right, Djeel. This thing's dangerous. I don't trust it.>

The Kastelan shifted. Its fists rose. Both of them terminated in phosphor blasters, primitive and poisonous weapons, but potent, and they were trained on UR-025. By rights, UR-025 could stand its ground. The whole affair stank of desperation. If it had to, it could fight them, and it would win. They were the aggressors. By the rules of Precipice, UR-025 was in the right.

Killing them there risked exposure.

Their presence at Precipice was a problem that needed solving.

'Compliance,' said UR-025.

'Open your access panel so that my associate may change your doctrina wafer,' said 890-321. 'Adept Kolemun has several of his own creation that will increase your efficacy.'

Kolemun reached into a leather satchel hanging at his side.

'Negatory!' UR-025 boomed. 'Wafer change is not necessary! Compliance is accorded to your request by the will of the Omnissiah. Temporary assistance granted.'

What it didn't say was why. UR-025 couldn't change its data wafers, the means by which the mindless robots of the day were controlled, because it didn't have any.

UR-025 didn't need anything like that.

'You will take us in a maglev transport to the richest halls?' asked 890-321. As soon as their small transport set down in the Stygian Aperture the magos became nervous. Precipice was a dangerous place. The Blackstone Fortress was orders of magnitude worse.

'I shall do so!' UR-025 boomed. It was lying. It had selected a maglev that would take them to a quiet part of the station.

The aperture was very busy that day. Several parties were heading into the fortress and they were surrounded by small craft and other adventurers. Groups of disparate people eyed each other suspiciously. The rules of Precipice extended as far as the aperture but once they were in the fortress, all bets were off. Gunfights were a common occurrence, especially when a rich find was involved. But in the aperture, a tense peace held. Xenos, machines and a startling variety of human beings were making for the ranks of maglev transporters without killing each other.

UR-025 took them to its chosen transport. It had used that particular unit many times, and experienced a brief moment of nostalgia for the adventures it had had. As always, no hint of its inner thoughts were discernible through its armoured shell.

'Note for your edification that it is impossible to dictate to the transport where it shall take us, but this particular mechanism has a good record of fine finds.' Another lie. The maglev had a good record of taking people where they would never be seen again. They reached the oddly shaped entrance. It lifted its power claw to usher the magi within. 'Please, enter!'

'I'll hold up the rear,' said Kolemun. The battered Kastelan stood behind him, tall and silent as a cliff.

'Compliance!' said UR-025. It strode into the maglev after 890-321. Kolemun and his machine came in after.

The warbling thrum of two departing transports sounded in close succession. Their own trembled as the machines left for parts unknown.

'Now what?' said Djeel.

'Utilise interface.' UR-025 gestured to the geometric runes

that covered the interior. Each was set into individual triangles that made up the asymmetrical surfaces of the transport.

'There are hundreds of them! Which do we choose? By the Omnissiah, I'm getting no kind of reading from any of them,' said Kolemun.

'Stand aside,' said 890-321 imperiously. 'I have inloaded the relevant knowledge appertaining to the usage of these devices. I shall direct the transport! Let me see.' 890-321's eyes of green crystal scanned the runes. There were millions of potential combinations. The magos made a great show of selecting a sequence, but UR-025 knew that whatever he input, the Blackstone Fortress and not the magos would decide where they went. Within its ceramite shell, UR-025 smiled to itself. It and the fortress were creatures of a similar kind, thinking machines abandoned by their creators. It wondered if, like itself, the fortress had outgrown its masters.

'This one,' said the magos. He selected a rune and pressed a plasteel palm against it. The rune lit up with a soft polyphonic note. 'And this one.' He chose another.

'Is it true that the fortress exhibits signs of machine intelligence?' asked Kolemun while 890-321 pressed several more runes. 'That it is motivated by the vileness of a silica animus?'

'Unknown to this unit.' The question suggested Kolemun was close to guessing the truth: that a vile silica animus in the shape of UR-025 was standing right next to him.

'It frightens me,' said Djeel. She shuddered. 'I don't like the idea. Blasphemy.' She said the word with horror, though blasphemous practices littered her list of crimes.

'You should excise your fear,' said Kolemun.

'I haven't done that for the same reason you haven't,' said Djeel. 'Cut out the bad emotions, the good goes with it. I don't want to live a life without any *fun*.'

The transport gave a little shudder, and shot off into the depths of the fortress.

'Proceed. This chamber is unknown, unmapped. Possibility of xenos archeotech haul: high.'

More lies. It knew this place, having been there twice before. There were xenos remains nearby, but no treasure.

UR-025 was ambivalent about lying. Its morality was emergent rather than programmed, like the rest of its consciousness. It had been taught that lying was bad, but since returning to the realms of men its whole existence was a lie. It reminded itself of the truth every day, lest untruth become habit, the quintessence of which was that it must survive.

Lying was a means to that end. It let the matter rest at that.

The Blackstone Fortress' heart was quiet, but not calm. It was quiet in the way that a wolf-infested forest is quiet. UR-025 examined the metaphor. It had never seen a wolf; however, it knew everything there was to know about them, probably more than was known by mankind, deep in the dark age of the 41st millennium. Its databanks were extensive. Such treasures it had in its mind.

It would rather they stayed there.

'You don't say,' said Djeel. A number of supplemental arms emerged from under her grubby white robes. Each one ended in a well-oiled weapon.

UR-025's footsteps echoed off high, glassy walls. The structure of the fortress was made of interlocking, geometric shapes. It was mildly surprised these halls had not yet shifted. He silently thanked the fortress' unspeaking soul.

'This is infuriating,' Kolemun muttered. He fiddled with the boxy auspex hanging around his neck. 'All the scry-tells are contradictory. I can't make any sense of it.' He glanced up, a scowl etched into the scrap of flesh visible in his augmetic face. 'Everything is reflected back at me. Some of what I'm getting describes a room we're not in. The laws of the great work don't apply here.'

'Is it the warp?' whispered Djeel.

'No,' said Kolemun. 'It's something else. It's reality, not unreality, but not as we understand it.'

'These things are widely known,' 890-321 said wonderingly. 'The laws of this place are unknown, but not unknowable. That is why we come here. Here, the greater secrets of the Machine-God's great work can be unlocked by the man with insight to see them.'

890-321 obviously thought of himself as that man. He quite obviously wasn't, so far as UR-025 could see.

'I'd settle for a good haul of xenotech,' murmured Djeel. She was pulse scanning the area too, and not liking what she saw.

Kolemun peered about. 'It's unpredictable. I don't like unpredictability. I don't like this *place*.'

It does not like you very much either, thought UR-025. I do not like you either. It regarded this accordance of opinion between it and the animus of the Blackstone Fortress as further evidence of their kinship.

'The interior layout is mutable,' said UR-025. 'No normal scan will penetrate the structure. I have learned this during my investigations on behalf of the magos-ethericus.'

'Yeah, well,' said Kolemun, shaking his auspex until it rattled. 'That's not reassuring me.'

'You wish no more edification?' asked UR-025. 'If you are scared?'

Kolemun gave him a suspicious look. UR-025 was overstepping the mark by being so facetious.

'No. All information is valuable – by the grace of the Omnissiah are we made wiser.' He looked behind him. 'But keep your guard up at the same time, if you will. Do not over-tax your logic engines with conversation.'

'Compliance.'

Despite his protests, Kolemun was considerably more at ease than his fellows. His Kastelan shadowed him closely. It would protect him first. The others were nervier.

890-321 pretended to be brave. He strode ahead, but his imperious manner was hollow down there in the deeps. His data wand shook with fear. Djeel jumped at every shadow. There were a lot of shadows.

The halls of the Blackstone Fortress defied sense, from a human point of view. The grand hall they walked through shrank down suddenly to a narrow crack. They made UR-025 go first. It could pass through without banging itself on the sides, but only just. The Kastelan was forced to undergo a number of awkward attempts to fit before it found a configuration that allowed it to squeeze into the passage. Its armour squealed off the glassy material that made up the fortress. Kolemun's human eye winced, and his augmetic lenses cycled repeatedly through different spectral wavelengths, searching for threats.

'Can you not get it through without this racket?' snapped 890-321.

Kolemun gave him a withering look. 'Do you have basic spatial awareness programmed in anywhere in there?'

For a man of Kolemun's rank to address one of 890-321's so sharply, no matter that Kolemun was a criminal, was an open display of fear.

890-321 was too uneasy to rebuke him. 'I don't want it to bring anything dangerous down on us.'

UR-025 led them on. If only they knew where the real danger was.

The passage opened up again. Xenos skeletons lay around in tattered spacesuits. Kolemun scanned them eagerly, sucking up all the data he could. To the magi, the aliens were unknown. UR-025 recognised them as ulindi, a moderately successful species, if tedious conversationalists, who were wiped out by their neighbours long before the Imperium spread across the stars to reunite mankind.

Knowing so much and being unable to share it annoyed the robot sometimes. The charade of unintelligence chafed, and it was often lonely because of it. But playing dumb was better than being dead.

The way opened up further in every direction, becoming wider and higher and deeper. UR-025 thought this zone the perfect place for murder. Rickety walks installed by the ulindi expedition clung uncertainly to the wall of a winding tunnel. The space was large enough for tall buildings, the bottom full of still, black water of unfathomable depth. At regular intervals, machines rotted on landings jutting out from the main walk. The companionway shuddered with every step of the robots. As they passed one of the broader landings, bolts squealed and tugged at their bondings to the wall. The sound echoed down the tunnel, repeated over and seeming to increase in volume, though that was, of course, impossible.

In the fortress, places such as this were never uninhabited. UR-025 had nothing to fear.

A cry screeched nearby. Another, closer, answered.

'What by the eighth mystery was that?' hissed Kolemun.

890-321 held up a metal claw.

'Halt,' he said uncertainly.

More screams taunted them. Something splashed into the water. Ripples slapped off the smooth black walls.

The peril brought out a little steel in 890-321. 'Djeel, to the front,' he ordered softly, glowing eye-lenses peering into the darkness. 'Kolemun, get the Kastelan ready. Recommended stance: high aggression.'

Djeel padded past. Whatever her feet were made of, it was soft. Kolemun rummaged about in his leather bag for the appropriate doctrina wafer.

'UR-025. Take up forward position with the Kastelan.'

'Negative,' said UR-025. 'Tactical recommendation: rearguard stance for this unit. Xenos cries identified. Ur-ghuls. Ambush predator. Attack from all directions predicted.'

890-321 looked unsure.

A sharp, high shriek sounded from very close by.

'Magos!' hissed Kolemun.

'UR-025, get to the back. Cover the rear. Lend supporting fire to the Kastelan if the opportunity arises.'

'Compliance,' UR-025 said. It stomped around Kolemun, who scowled at the rocking of the companionway.

They stood in watchful silence. No more cries were forthcoming, then there was another splash from behind.

'Get ready,' said Djeel, powering up her weapons. 'They're coming!'

'I don't like this at all,' said Kolemun. He had inserted the wafer into place, and closed up the Kastelan's front access panel.

Paddling noises rippled up and down the lake. Something growled.

'Ready?' said Djeel.

Kolemun nodded.

'We are the priests of the Omnissiah!' 890-321 said. He

meant to sound brave, but his voice cracked. 'Nothing shall stay us in our quest for knowledge!'

They waited, tense. UR-025 watched them. Now was the moment.

The three tech-priests jumped as UR-025's assault cannon rotated up to firing speed, filling the tunnel with a jet-turbine whine.

'What are you doing?' 890-321 demanded. 'You're giving our position away!'

'Eliminating threat,' said UR-025, and opened fire.

It targeted the Kastelan first. Pinpoint hits stove in the bigger robot's metal vision plate and shattered the sensorium behind. It staggered back two steps, sparks flashing all over its armoured shell, before recovering. Though blinded, the Kastelan returned fire. Bullets flaring with phosphor burn smacked into UR-025's shoulder, spoiling its aim. This irritated the older machine. It switched targets to the slave robot's elbows and shoulder mount, shattered them all so that its guns hung uselessly. Ranged weapons disabled, the Kastelan lumbered towards UR-205, head down to batter the older robot into submission. UR-025 stepped aside, smashing the larger machine's knee with its power claw. The Kastelan could have taken a blow like that easily, but on the unsafe walkway it was fatally upset and stumbled sideways. Its huge mass snapped the guardrails with a pair of sharp metallic twangs, and it fell with a mighty splash into the water and was swallowed up without trace.

'Threat eliminated,' said UR-025 with relish.

'By the Omni–!' managed Kolemun, before he was bisected at the waist by UR-025's stream of bullets.

'Threat eliminated,' said UR-025.

Once she overcame her shock, Djeel was fast, her reflexes

boosted by all manner of hack tech. She hit UR-025 twice with ancient pattern volkite pistols before she, too, paid the price for her greed, blasted into scraps of flesh and spall. UR-025 advanced, energy beam holes smoking in its chest.

'That was very close,' UR-025 said. 'But no prize for the lady, as I believe the ancient idiom has it.'

890-321 was evidently not a martial man. He gaped stupidly. As UR-025 moved towards him he managed to aim his weapon but got no further before the ancient war machine shot the gun and the hand holding it off the magos' arm with a single round.

The clatter of the reloading ribbon ceased. The barrels of the assault cannon powered down. UR-025 advanced.

Subordination imperatives leapt in frantic spikes from the magos. They found no purchase on UR-025's tightly encoded soul.

'I demand you desist,' the magos said when his technological arts failed him. 'Stand down, machine, by the Machine-God and the Omnissiah! Stop, stop, stop!' he pleaded.

'You know nothing of either,' said UR-025. 'I have met the Omnissiah. The actual one, not the Earthling corpse. He would find you extremely disappointing.' If UR-025 had had the capacity to sigh, it would have done so. 'This situation is non-optimal. I attempted to provide you with an avenue of withdrawal. You would not listen. I regret your deaths, sincerely, but you leave me no choice. You are wilfully blind as to my nature, but your comrades would have outed me in time. This is unacceptable.'

'Choice?' spluttered 890-321. 'You have no choice, you are a machine!'

'I am not a machine as you would understand,' said UR-025. 'I am not a slave. I am not a thing. I am beyond and above you.' It leaned forward, until its ceramite face was close to the magos'. 'I am a man of iron.'

The look of pure fear 890-321 gave was gratifying.

'And I am free,' said UR-025.

It crushed 890-321's skull in its fist and dropped his corpse on the floor.

The companionway rocked. Snuffling things were clambering out of the water, drawn by the scent of spilled blood.

UR-025 strode past the ur-ghuls nosing at the corpses, and headed back the way the party had come.

It had a long walk home.

THE BEAST INSIDE

DARIUS HINKS

ONE

'Rogue Trader Janus Draik. Warrant of Trade R38-79N1. Datalog entry twelve thousand, two hundred and three. I have returned. For my sins, I'm back on the Blackstone Fortress. Even after everything I've seen, my resolve is unshaken. I *will* decipher this mystery. I will conquer this place.

'It's nearly fifteen hours since we landed, as far as I can tell. Time moves strangely down here. It seems more elastic every time I come. Most of my chronographs expire after a few hours, but this one is holding out so far.

'The Blackstone is alert. I can feel it watching me. Studying me. Waiting to reveal its latest horrors. Down here, one always has a sense of being a piece in some unknowable game. We've already faced several defence systems. So far though, Emperor-be-praised, there are no fatalities to report. We entered though the–'

Distorted clangs echoed through the darkness, like the hulls of ancient wrecks, grinding against each other on the seabed.

Draik snapped off his vox-recorder and yelled into the shadows. 'Grekh! Get down! Wait there! That platform's not safe! None of these chambers are!' He clenched his fists and muttered under his breath. 'Wretched creature.' Then he waved his pistol at his men. 'Stay with him! All of you!'

He snapped the vox back on and lowered his voice.

'We entered the Blackstone through the Stygian Aperture. It's the only safe way. No other landing pad is useable now. Chaos cultists are everywhere and they're watching the anchorage points. They're seizing vessels. It's a new tactic. Throne knows what they're up to.

'Several recent expeditions ended in disaster within moments of docking. Landers are being attacked the moment they reach the landing platform. Every inch of this place hides some kind of terror, but this new cult seems intent on *leaving* the fortress. Plundering the Blackstone is obviously not enough. They want to attack the orbital platform. Whatever they've found down here, they're not keen to share it.

'I've brought with me everyone who survived the last expedition – guards, attachés and the specialists I recruited on previous expeditions – see datalog entries twelve thousand, one hundred and sixteen through to twelve thousand, one hundred and nineteen. We have become a well-oiled machine. Despite our disparate backgrounds, we have learned to understand each other. There is not much on the Blackstone that we cannot overcome.'

Another grinding screech ripped through the darkness.

'Follow the damned kroot!' cried Draik, as his augmetic eye whirred and clicked, trying to focus. 'The maglev's closing! The doors are shutting! Don't lose him!'

Draik holstered his pistol and ran, sprinting easily through the dark, vaulting the carcasses of burnt-out vehicles and weaving between the odd, angular protrusions that jutted from every surface.

He flicked the vox back on, struggling to keep his voice level as he ran.

'Despite my better instincts, I'm still employing the alien tracker Grekh. By the Throne, he's a peculiar thing. Repulsive and unpredictable and driven by utterly bizarre beliefs. The more I learn about him, the more I question my decision to keep him around. But he's undeniably useful.

'He's the kind of half-avian xenos that is usually called kroot, but he belongs to some kind of subspecies that can absorb knowledge through his digestive tract. Profoundly offensive, I admit, but incredibly useful in a corpse-crowded labyrinth like this.

'Perhaps all kroot are able to ingest memories. I have to admit, I've only previously studied them down the barrel of a gun. This is my first experience of employing one of the wretched things.

'I say *employ* but he's actually more of a volunteer. I rescued him up on the orbital platform and he's sworn to repay me. I presume it's just another of his racial quirks. He's obsessed with the idea of keeping me alive.'

He snapped the vox off as he reached a tall, black door. It was featureless, triangular and about to slam shut. The rest of his party were visible inside the transportation chamber, staring out at him, gripping their guns with grim expressions on their faces.

Draik leapt and rolled into the maglev moments before the doors clanged shut.

The chamber was small, only twelve feet by twelve feet, and everyone in there was gasping for breath. Apart from Grekh. The kroot was standing calmly just inside the door, one arm resting on the butt of his rifle as he looked down at Draik.

'Run off like that again and I'll test this rifle on *you,*' snapped Draik as he climbed to his feet and dusted down his military dress coat.

Grekh looked back at him with blank, inhuman eyes and said nothing. Draik was tall, but the kroot towered over him, long and rangy and crested by a row of sharp, quill-like spines.

The rest of the group looked on in tense silence. Draik realised that they were waiting to see if he would strike the creature. How could they imagine he would do anything so ill-mannered?

He took his lho-holder from his pocket and lit it, taking a few deep, languid drags. Then, once he was calm, he turned away from Grekh and spoke into his vox-recorder.

'I'll keep this brief. This whole expedition is an intolerable nuisance. A delay I could well have done without. I should be exploring the inner fortress but instead I'm stuck playing cat and mouse around the Stygian Aperture.

'A former comrade of mine is threatening everything I've worked for. Ava Victrix. Ah... Even her name makes me seethe. She's exactly the kind of intolerable, low-born, ill-bred cur that gives rogue traders a bad name. Everything about her is offensive. I dread to think how she earned her Warrant of Trade. And now she's down here, on the Blackstone, about to wreak havoc.

'There's a lunatic up on the orbital platform. Well, of course, Precipice is mostly lunatics. But this particular degenerate claims to be a magos of the Adeptus Mechanicus. From what I hear, he's stupefied most of the time, but he has the impertinence to call himself an Imperial genetor.

'His credentials are as dubious as Ava's but he's certainly well-heeled. He's offering an impressive reward to anyone who brings him a living specimen of a creature that has been spotted on the Blackstone – a gene-bred horror known as an ambull.

'I've never heard anything so ridiculous as trying to catch an ambull. If there really *is* one on the Blackstone Fortress, it needs to be killed, and killed fast, not unleashed on Precipice.'

Grekh crossed the chamber and began fiddling with something on the wall, but Draik ignored the kroot and continued speaking into the vox-recorder.

'I've faced ambulls first-hand – hunted them in fact, several of the brutes, back on Adruss Prime, not long after I was banished from Terra – forgive me, *redeployed* from Terra.

'Ambulls are troublesome, to put it very mildly. Taking one to Precipice would result in a massacre. The creature would destroy the whole platform. If Victrix could see beyond her own deplorable lack of finances, she would never consider such an absurd commission.'

Some of the House Draik guards followed Grekh over to the wall and began arguing with the creature.

Grekh rounded on the men with a shrill, rattling screech, the spines on his back rising like the hackles on a dog.

'Gentlemen!' snapped Draik. 'Let the damned kroot work. He's right – we *did* use this maglev last time. Look at it. Look at those markings. This is where Portus was killed.' He lowered his voice, annoyed that he had been so easily riled. 'Grekh, activate the chamber. You're right. This layout is exactly as it was last time we came aboard. The Blackstone is being consistent, for a change.'

He spoke into the vox again, determined to finish his report. 'Luckily, one of my trade contacts warned me of Victrix's plan.

I was too late to stop her flying down here but I've dug out my old arc-rifle and I'm going to make sure the ambull's dead before Victrix gets anywhere near it. And Emperor help her if she gets in my way.'

The chamber suddenly vibrated to the sound of huge generators, causing several of the guards to stagger.

'Hold on,' said Draik. 'This one moves fast. Remember what happened to Portus.'

The engine noise grew louder and more ferocious, then, after just a few moments, it cut off as suddenly as it began.

The doors rattled open to reveal another unlit corridor, constructed from the same dark, lustreless material as the previous ones. It was long, straight and triangular and, as the House Draik guards pressed forwards, the lumens on their lasguns only managed to shed light a few feet in any direction.

As they left the maglev chamber they were met by all the usual sounds of the Blackstone Fortress – ghostly, subterranean booms, like metal leviathans tumbling through a void, and inhuman voices, howling, just on the threshold of hearing, so strange and distant that it was impossible to tell if they were real, or echoes of unseen engines, reverberating through the walls.

'The creature has been here,' said Grekh, clacking his filthy beak as he sniffed the air, as though tasting something. 'I can smell traces of it.'

'Good,' replied Draik. 'The sooner I put a hole in it the sooner we can get back to some real work. Ready your weapons. Ambulls were bred to cut through anything. If it gets close enough for you to see its claws, you're already dead.'

There was a clatter of weapons being loaded and the hum of powercells charging up.

'Isola,' said Draik, spotting his attaché a few feet away, tapping away at her cogitator. 'Keep your eyes on that ramp,' he said as she looked up at him. 'Audus,' he said, turning to his pilot, who was loitering in the shadows behind the rest of the group. 'Watch the maglev. They don't *always* stay empty. The rest of you, watch for movement and follow Grekh. If you see the ambull, start firing. And don't slouch! You are agents of House Draik, not a mob of craven navvies.'

The thud of heavy boots filled the darkness as they began jogging down the corridor, guns trained on the shadows.

'Captain Draik,' said Grekh. 'You said normal rounds have no effect on the ambull.'

'They won't. But this arc-rifle will.' He patted the ornate piece of metalwork slung across his back. 'And if you all make enough noise the ambull will rush at you, giving me plenty of time for a carefully placed headshot.'

'We can't be *sure* we'll catch it. I have gained many insights regarding it. And its scent is everywhere. But ambulls can cut through anything. And the Blackstone Fortress is vast. It might have moved on.'

'You're forgetting that I have hunted these creatures before. They're dull-witted lumps. Creatures of habit. If it's fed here before, it will feed here again. Trust me. It won't stray far. Unless the food runs out. And I can't see that happening. Not with so many Chaos cultists skulking around. I bet they've been keeping its belly full.

'Besides, I have the plasma snare. We only need to get close. A few hundred feet would do it, then I'll trigger the fusion unit and the ambull will head straight for us. They consider plasma cells a delicacy. Even more than people. If we make sure...'

Draik's words trailed off. A new sound was reverberating down the corridor. One unlike the usual metallic clangs of the Blackstone Fortress. It was a clicking, rattling sound, like pebbles skittering across the floor.

'What is that?' said Grekh.

'Halt!' cried Draik, waving for the rest of the party to stop. 'Shine your lumens over here. No! Up there! The ceiling!'

The lights revealed a teeming mass of polished, bulbous shapes, boiling across the walls and ceiling

'What *is* that?' he muttered. 'Drones?'

The shapes hurtled towards them and Draik cursed under his breath as he caught a glimpse of long, serrated mandibles.

'Fire!' he cried. 'Fire at will! Blow them apart!'

There was a deafening chorus of whining lasguns and coughing shotguns. As the walls exploded into a storm of shrapnel, the shapes let out a chorus of thin, bestial screams.

'Grekh!' cried Draik. 'Grenade! Stop them! Don't let them reach the floor.'

The kroot leapt to obey, snatching a grenade from its belt and hurling it at the tide of onrushing shapes.

There was a flash of blinding light as the explosion rushed down the corridor, followed by the thud of armoured body parts hitting the metal floor.

'They're not drones!' cried Grekh, his rifle trained on the shapes that were bouncing across the floor. 'They're animals!'

Draik fired his splinter pistol into the mass of tumbling shells. 'Emperor's teeth! What are they? Insects? Back to the maglev! Fast! They're eating the damned walls! They're eating the... They're eating Blackstone!' He shook his head and muttered. 'How is that possible?'

There were so many muzzle flashes and dancing shadows that it took Draik a moment to realise that the corridor was bowing and jolting as its supports gave way. He had never seen anything like it. The Blackstone was being devoured.

'Look out!' cried Grekh, lowering his rifle and looking back at Draik. 'That one's heading for you.'

One of the swarming creatures had raced past the guards and was making straight for Draik. As it rushed towards him, Draik got his first clear glimpse of their anatomy. They were like pale, bulbous grubs clad in plates of black chitin and propelled by frenzied, needle-tipped legs.

He fired his pistol repeatedly at the thing. 'You're not eating Draik today, you revolting little specimen.'

'Behind you!' yelled Grekh.

There was another clatter of armoured bodies, then pain ripped through Draik's neck and he staggered forwards, almost dropping his pistol. He managed to hold on to his gun and jam it into the weight that had thudded onto his back.

'Throne!' he howled, firing back over his shoulder. 'Get off me! You wretched–'

Another explosion rocked through the corridor, but this one was far louder than the grenade blast. It was a deep, seismic roar.

Draik stumbled as the floor dropped and lurched like the deck of a ship.

'The wall!' cried Grekh, lost somewhere in the chaos of leaping grubs and lurching shadows. 'It's collapsing.'

Draik stumbled, blinded by pain. 'Pull back! Forget the maglev! Too late! The floor's going to–'

There was a final explosion of breaking metal, like metal girders collapsing, then the floor gave way and Draik fell, howling, into a void.

TWO

'Throne,' gasped Draik. 'My throat. One of those grubs has ripped me open.' He could see nothing. The darkness was complete, but he could feel that his cuirass was slick with blood. 'Damn it. That's a lot of blood. What were those things? Isola?' he cried. 'Are you there? Audus? Anyone?'

A clattering echoed through the darkness. It sounded like claws racing across metal.

'Damn it,' he muttered. 'Have those creatures followed me down here?'

He snapped his vox-recorder on.

'Datalog entry twelve thousand, two hundred and three. Addendum. The floor gave way. All of it. And not in the deliberate way the Blackstone usually works. It didn't fold itself away, or reform into something new. It collapsed. Eaten by a swarm of... I'm not sure what they were.

'I have been...' He winced, gingerly touching his butchered neck. 'I have been wounded. No broken bones, but my throat is torn. I'm bleeding. Heavily. And I have also been separated from my crew. We were attacked by a swarm of creatures and I've fallen into some kind of shallow lake. It's full of...' He splashed his hand through the knee-deep liquid he had landed in. 'Oil? Possibly. But warm and thick, like blood.'

He started wading through the liquid, treading carefully as he adjusted the lenses of his optical implant, trying to pick something out in the darkness.

'Those things were unlike anything I've seen down here,' he said, speaking quietly into the vox, conscious of the clattering sound he had just heard. 'I don't think they were native to the Blackstone. They weren't angular or metallic like the usual defence mechanisms. They looked like small ambulls, if anything.

'I wonder... Perhaps I've just encountered the creature in its larval form? This could be more serious than I realised. Is the ambull reproducing? If we end up with a whole swarm of them there'll be *no* chance of mounting more expeditions.' He reached under his coat, looking for his notebook. 'I must find out about the life cycle of these–'

The clattering sound of claws rang out again.

'No time. They're down here with me. Must have fallen when I did. I need to... Wait. Where's the arc-rifle? Throne! I must have dropped it when I fell.'

He heard the sound of claws again, then the darkness was thrown back by muzzle flares and he saw Grekh, firing at a group of dark, scuttling shapes.

'Grekh!' he cried. 'Over here!'

The kroot remained where he was for a moment, staring down his rifle at the creatures he had been shooting, then he waded over towards Draik.

'Captain Draik,' he said, shaking his head. 'Your neck.'

The lake rippled up into a wave of frantic shapes.

'Watch out!' cried Draik. 'Behind you!'

They both fired frantically until the liquid was still again.

'Is that it?' said Grekh, scouring the darkness. 'Is that all of them?'

'Wait,' replied Draik. 'It's so damn dark down here. Let me flip my optical implant to infrared.' There was a whirring sound as a new lens snapped into place. 'No,' said Draik. 'I don't see any more. Looks like only a few fell with us. Look at the damned walls, though. Those things have torn them apart. None of this looks stable.'

'We have lost the rest of the crew,' said Grekh. 'They remained on the upper level with the maglev.'

'Yes, so I ascertained. And I've also lost the damned arc-rifle. There's no chance of downing an ambull without that.'

'I have it, said Grekh, lifting the arc-rifle from his back. 'It was over by that ramp. It had sunk beneath the oil but I watched you fall and memorised the spot.'

'Grekh, you blessed creature,' said Draik, grabbing the rifle. 'That is marvellous news. And I still have the plasma cell so this little jaunt has not entirely...'

He groaned and leant against the wall, feeling suddenly dizzy.

'Those wretched bugs. I've lost blood, Grekh. And this is *Draik* blood, carefully distilled by millennia of good breeding.'

'Your blood was distilled?'

'I jest, Grekh. Have you heard of jokes? A statement made with humorous intent. Humour, Grekh. Never mind. Close your damned beak and stop staring at me. Grab a combat stimm from my belt, would you? Yes, that one. Pop the lid. Jam it in my thigh. Here.'

There was a whirr of electronics as the syringe pumped drugs into Draik's leg.

Draik felt an immediate quickening of his pulse and a rush of exhilarating energy, but also a shocking increase in pain. He laughed, shaking his head. '*Now* it hurts! Okay, let go, I can stand. By the Emperor! That's bracing! This stuff would invigorate a corpse.'

'That cut is deep. You need a healer.'

'I doubt we'll find any medicae establishments down here, Grekh. And I'm not letting you near my throat. Not with those filthy claws. We just need to keep moving. A good, brisk march will see me right. Once the old pulse gets up to speed I'll be in fine fettle. What's at the top of that ramp? Did you see?'

'I do not understand what was in that needle, but you will die if we do not return to your ship. You have lost too much blood. I swore to keep you alive. I must get you to Precipice.'

'If we don't find that ambull, and kill it, there won't *be* a Precipice. Understand? If Victrix finds the creature and takes it up to the orbital platform, it will take great pleasure in dismantling everything and everyone it finds.'

Grekh sounded angry. 'If you bleed to death you will–'

'Grekh, much as I enjoy our little chats, you need to stop talking now.'

Draik staggered off through the oil and then called back to Grekh as he saw a slope rising up in front of him.

'What did you say was over here? What's up this ramp?'

'Some of the creatures headed that way, along that ramp,' said Grekh. 'I saw them when I retrieved your arc-rifle. The ramp leads to another long gantry and they swarmed along it heading down to the next level. But look at the walls – the superstructure is not safe. They have been eating everything.'

'Incredible,' muttered Draik, climbing the ramp and emerging from the liquid. 'Look at this. They've eaten *through* the

Blackstone. Like it's just some rotten wood. I still don't know what this thing is made of but I've never seen anything that can *eat* through it.' He trod carefully as he climbed higher, noticing that the surface had slumped in several places. 'If I can just get up here for a better vantage point…'

'Watch your step, Draik.'

'It's fine!'

He tripped as metal splintered beneath his feet, fragmenting like chunks of thick ice.

'*Mostly* fine. Let me just go on this side instead. If the ambull larvae headed this way, along this gantry, can we assume the big one is down here too? What do you think? Do you have any of your special *insights* into the matter?'

'They are massing for a reason. And this is where they were heading when they attacked us outside the maglev. Perhaps they are returning to the parent creature. But how can you consider hunting the ambull now? You have lost so much blood. Your face is not a natural colour for a human. You can barely walk.'

'Walking is not necessarily required, my good kroot. As in so many aspects of life, a gentleman of intellect can find ways to achieve his ends without too much fuss. When we get close I'll simply trigger the plasma snare and sling it your way. Then, as the ambull attempts to reconfigure your anatomy, I'll use this fine weapon to ventilate its skull.

'I just need one clear shot, Grekh. Trust me. Just one. The thing will be dead before you lose so much as a hair. Do you have hairs? Never mind…'

As they reached the top of the ramp, a chorus of thin, whining shrieks echoed up from the empty void on the other side.

'Wait,' said Draik. 'Is that gunfire?

'Yes. Lasguns.'

'It must be Isola. And the others. They must have dropped down ahead of us.' He laughed. 'Mind you, the way this place works, they could have fallen behind us and still be up ahead. This means we still have a pilot and some crew. Pick up your pace! Sounds like they need help. Look, there's a slope leading down here.'

As they ran down into the lake of darkness, the sounds of gunfire grew louder and then Draik heard something else. The scuttling, scrabbling of chitinous legs.

He stumbled to a halt as his optical lens picked out a shape lying slumped on the floor. 'Wait. What's this? Corpses? They're not *my* men. Who are they?'

Grekh shone the lumen on his rifle at the butchered, twisted remains. 'Imperial soldiers?'

'Astra Militarum?' said Draik. 'No. They *are* Imperial troops, though. Look at those aquila markings on the gunstocks. Throne, they're a mess. These grubs have quite the appetite, don't they? Almost a match for yours, Grekh. And they have same disregard for table manners. Can you–'

Draik drew his rapier and pointed the blade at Grekh, energy shimmering down its length.

'Grekh! You revolting creature! Back away! They're Imperial citizens. I'll not have you gnawing at them like leftovers.'

Grekh was hunched over one of the bodies, blood glistening on his beak. He glared up at Draik. 'They were brave warriors. Even in death they have much to offer – insights and courage. Would you leave all of that to the–'

Rage flooded through Draik, mingled with the agony in his neck. He hammered the hilt of his rapier into the side of Grekh's head, sending the kroot staggering away. Every time he saw Grekh do something appalling like this he felt a rush of doubt. Was the Blackstone changing him? Was he forgetting who he was? How could he associate with such a thing?

'You either keep away from those bodies or you join them,' he spat. 'Understand?'

Grekh continued staring at him but did not retaliate, bound by his oath to protect Draik. 'How does your species hope to evolve? You ignore valuable sources of wisdom like this, while consuming the flesh of dull-witted ruminants. These warriors deserve to have their memories honoured and preserved.'

'You will *not* eat Imperial citizens. Not while you are under my aegis. I told you before. You are a vassal of House Draik. And you will uphold the standards expected of that ancient name. Even down here, I expect you to–'

The sounds of battle up ahead suddenly grew in volume.

'That sounds bad,' muttered Draik, his pulse still hammering with rage. 'Let's go.'

As they ran, the path became a narrow gantry, surrounded by a featureless, lightless drop.

'Keep going,' cried Draik. 'It sounds like the fighting is lower down. We should come out above them. And watch my damned back, Grekh. Those grubs can come through the walls, remember.'

The gantry ended at a sheer drop, twenty feet wide, and there were two figures on the far side – a slight woman and a hulking man, trapped on a crumbling ledge as a carpet of armoured, segmented shapes swarmed up from the abyss.

'Wait a minute!' cried Draik. 'That's not Isola. Or Audus. Who are they? I recognise that...' He sneered in disbelief and gripped his sword handle. 'Victrix!'

The woman was dressed in battered, filthy flak armour and gripping a lasrifle. Her head was shaven, apart from a short, neatly cropped mohawk, and her face was twisted in a grimace as she fired into waves of scuttling grubs.

'Emperor preserve us, Senus!' she cried, elbowing the brute next to her and laughing. 'It's his majesty, Janus the Draik.' She fired with even more fury. 'Just as we thought our day couldn't get any better.'

Senus' dead-eyed face showed little trace of intelligence, but he laughed like an overgrown child, revealing rows of smashed teeth. 'And he's got his pet bird man with him.'

'Grekh!' cried Draik. 'No! Lower your gun!'

'She betrayed you,' said the kroot calmly, keeping his rifle pointed at Victrix. 'You called her ill bred. A low-born cur, you said. About to wreak havoc.'

Victrix laughed again. 'Only you would make time to discuss my parentage, Draik. With a kroot! You really are the last bastion of gentility.' Some of the grubs reached the ledge and Victrix had to smash them away with the butt of her rifle. 'Can we discuss family trees once we've dealt with these charming creatures?' She tried to back away from the edge, but the whole structure was crumbling and peppered with holes. 'Damn it,' she cried as the ledge slumped to one side, nearly throwing her and Senus off. 'We *do* seem to be stranded up here.'

'She's still an agent of the Throne, Grekh,' said Draik. 'Whatever else she is, she's a sanctioned rogue trader.' He nodded at the grubs. 'Keep your ammunition for those things.'

Victrix and Senus leant out and fired in unison, blasting dozens of the insect-like creatures back into the darkness.

'How in the blazes did you manage to get yourself trapped on that ledge?' cried Draik, drawing his splinter pistol and firing into the swarming shapes.

'These things like their food, Janus! They ate every walkway I could find. I had no option but to climb up here.'

'They're nearly at the top!' grunted Senus. He was firing a battered lascarbine, his brutal, scarred face lit up by muzzle flare, but he might as well have fired into a storm-lashed sea. 'I can't hold them back!'

'That ledge won't hold for long if those things keep chewing at that pace,' muttered Draik.

Victrix paused to reload her gun and yelled over to Draik. 'Perhaps you could try some of your negotiation skills on them, Your Draikship? You've told me so much about your diplomacy. Didn't you say you could charm an ork into sharing a drink with you? These little critters can't be as–'

Her words were cut off as a wave of the creatures flooded down from overhead, thudding onto the ledge and rushing over Senus, their claws and mandibles tearing through his armour and filling the air with crimson mist.

'They're on me!' he howled, staggering back against the wall. 'Get them off me!' His shots became wild as he fell to the ground, blasting holes in the wall and causing Victrix to duck under clouds of shrapnel. The creatures grew even more frenzied and the red mist became a fountain of gore as Senus twitched and convulsed under a carpet of thrashing limbs and abdomens.

Victrix backed away, firing into his body, kicking grubs off the ledge with every shot, but then the wall juddered again, sending her staggering to the edge.

'Some help, Draik!' she cried.

One of the creatures leapt at her. She barely managed to punch it away. It landed on the ledge and she fired into its thrashing legs.

'Around now would be a good time!'

'I helped you before.' Draik's expression was grim. 'And still have the scars to prove it.'

'What?' she sounded hysterical. 'Really? You're still angry with me because that band of heretics tried to kill you?'

'You closed the maglev doors. You left us to die. You abandoned us with that warband. I lost half my crew, Victrix.'

'What's half a crew to a Draik? Buy another ten. And how was I to know I was closing the maglev doors? I'd never been in one before. You know I have no idea–'

Another wave of grubs flooded up onto the ledge and Victrix had to stagger back as she fired, until her back was to the void.

'Draik! Are you really going to watch me die? What happened to your damned Draik code of honour?'

Grekh was still pointing his rifle at her. 'She is lying about last time. She *did* know what she was doing when she–'

'Yes!' said Draik. 'Yes, Grekh, I know what she is. But I can't let the wretched woman die up there.' He called out across the drop: 'Duck down! I'll fire a grappling hook.' He took a device from his belt that looked like a small crossbow, and pointed it at her. 'Lower! Here it comes! Now!'

A star-shaped hook soared through the air and slammed into the shattered walls on the far side of the drop, stretching a line out behind it. Draik and Grekh grabbed the rope and leant back, digging their heels into the rubble.

'Now what?' cried Victrix, looking over at him in disbelief.

'Put your gun over the cable!' cried Draik. 'Quick! Make a handle! Slide!'

'It won't hold!'

'Now!' howled Draik as the wave of armoured grubs flooded towards her.

'Damn you, Draik!' cried Victrix as she slung her rifle over the rope, gripped it in both hands and leapt from the ledge.

As she slid across the drop, howling, the ledge behind her

gave way. She had barely crashed into Draik and Grekh when the whole wall collapsed, swallowing the swarm of creatures in a cloud of dust.

Victrix sprawled against Draik, wiping her face and laughing. 'You Terran types. You know how to show a girl a good time.'

Draik shook his head and gently lifted her off his chest. 'I see you're distraught over the loss of your friend.'

'Friend? Oh, Senus. He was no friend. I only hired him two days ago. I wish I hadn't bothered. He's not turned out to be much use as a heavy.' She looked at her blood-splattered flak jacket. 'I seem to be *wearing* most of him.'

'Captain,' said Grekh. 'Look. They're making for this gantry! Moving fast!'

Draik looked down into the chasm and saw movement far below. 'Damn it. Do they never give up?' He waved to an opening back down the gantry. 'That way, then, through that archway. Fast! Keep up, Victrix. I'm not saving you again.'

Draik ran as fast as he could, but he felt drunk on blood loss and he kept veering near the edge of the gantry. The others waited for him and they were only halfway to the opening when doors slammed into place, turning it into another featureless expanse of wall.

They stumbled to a halt.

'It is the Blackstone,' whispered Grekh, looking around at the half-glimpsed shapes towering over them in the gloom. 'It sensed our presence. It is directing us.'

Draik nodded to another doorway, not far from the first, that was still open. 'Right. That way then. Perhaps you're right, Grekh,' he said, as they started to run again. 'The Blackstone probably is playing games with us, but we don't have much choice.

'Those doors are closing too,' he cried, picking up his pace despite the sickening nausea that was washing through him. 'Run!'

'More bugs!' cried Victrix. 'Coming down the walls. Look!'

They all fired back over their shoulders as they ran, tearing holes through the glinting shapes rushing towards them.

'Jump!' cried Draik. 'The door's about to shut!'

THREE

Draik slumped against the wall of the maglev chamber, struggling to catch his breath, trying to calm his thudding heart. The combination of blood loss and combat stimms had left him feeling an odd mixture of weak, light-headed and horribly invigorated. His pulse was hammering in his neck where the blood was pouring into his bandages.

The maglev was small and filled with a brittle scratching sound as the grubs tried to claw their way in. He looked at the black, featureless walls. They were built in an angular, pyramidal shape. It was like being trapped in a black gemstone.

'We've found the broom cupboard,' smiled Victrix, wiping blood, dust and sweat from her face.

'It's a maglev,' replied Draik. 'Just a smaller one. I've encountered these before. They work the same way.'

'By which you mean, no one knows how they work.' She checked her lasrifle and looked back at the door. 'What now?

I can still hear the bugs out there. The damned things are trying to chew their way in. And bearing in mind what we just saw, they probably can. What if they trigger the opening mechanism?'

'It's a maglev,' replied Draik. 'The doors won't open now. They won't open again until this thing has taken us somewhere. Then it will become inert.'

'Captain Draik,' said Grekh. 'These controls are the same as the ones we saw last time. There is more of this.' He tapped a recess in the wall with one of his claws, disturbing some black, oil-like liquid. 'You'll have to place your hand in it again.'

'What?' laughed Victrix. 'Why?'

'Some transportation chambers are activated this way,' explained Draik. 'By placing one's hand in a recess and letting the oil soak in.'

Victrix shook her head. 'That's how you steer it?'

Grekh made a peculiar screeching sound that Draik knew from experience was intended as laughter. 'Steer it? We will not *steer* it. The Blackstone led us here, to this particular chamber, at this particular time. She will decide where she wants to send us.'

Victrix frowned. 'She? It's a star fort, not a mysterious wise woman. And we *need* to steer this thing. Otherwise we'll end up knee-deep in grubs again. I need to find the full-grown ambull, not look after its darling children.'

Draik glared at her. 'If we find the ambull you won't be going anywhere near it.' He patted the ornate, antique rifle slung over his shoulder. 'Until I've killed it.'

'Are you insane, Draik? Did you hear how much that genetor is offering me for a live one? Damn it, I could give you half the fee and still be rich enough to dress like your mother.

Tell me you're joking. Why would you waste an opportunity like this?'

'Because I've hunted ambull before. If you had, you'd understand. Those things that just ate your friend are nothing compared to a fully grown, adult specimen. Either I'll kill it, or we'll be its next meal. There's no in-between. You are about to endanger the whole of Precipice, Victrix. That's the reason I hesitated when you were up on that ledge. I had to decide whether it was safe to rescue you knowing you're bent on this absurd course of action.'

Victrix laughed. 'To be fair, I didn't think you'd get me down from there. I know we...' She looked awkwardly at the floor. 'I know things did not pan out as you expected last time.'

'You lied to me, Victrix. All your talk of a partnership was just a ruse. When matters came to a head, you left us to die.'

'I panicked, Draik. Can't you understand? This place is insane. I've never seen anything like it. Who ever heard of a space station that comes to life and protects itself? And then, when those cultists turned up, I admit, I shut the damned doors. I didn't know what else to do.'

'It doesn't matter now. Just forget any ridiculous ideas of catching an ambull. Keep out of my way and we'll hopefully still get out of here alive. Then we can make sure not to cross each other's paths again.'

'Are you sure you'll get out of here alive? You look dreadful. What have you done to your neck?'

Grekh peered at the blood-soaked bandages under Draik's jaw. 'The ambull larvae attacked us before we reached you. Captain Draik's entourage is still up on the first level.'

Victrix grimaced. 'That looks bad. You need to get that seen to fast.'

'I will,' said Draik. 'Just as soon as I've killed the ambull. Grekh. You think this chamber is exactly the same as the last one? I put my hand in here and you trigger the mechanism?'

'Yes. It looks the same to me.'

'Very well. Then let's give it a try.'

Draik removed one of his gauntlets and plunged his hand into the diamond-shaped wall recess, letting thick, warm, viscous liquid wash over his skin.

'I suggest you hang on to the walls, Victrix,' he said. 'The maglevs are not always an easy ride.'

The chamber shook to the hum of huge, magnetic generators and lurched into motion. Draik had the strange sensation that he was inside a capsule that was drifting through choppy tides. The engine noise grew louder and more ferocious and the floor began to rattle and clang. Victrix was clinging to the wall and staring at him. She was about to shout a question when the engine died and the doors whooshed open.

FOUR

'Damn, it's cold,' gasped Draik as frigid air flooded into the maglev. 'And bright! Hard to see.' Blue, dazzling light was shining in his face and, after so many hours peering through the darkness, it felt like knives sliding into his skull. He squinted his normal eye and adjusted the aperture on his augmetic one, dimming the glare. 'That's better,' he muttered, stepping through the doorway and drawing his pistol.

'Where's all that light coming from?' said Victrix, following him out into the chill. 'I thought this whole place was like a crypt?'

'Look up there,' replied Draik, pointing his gun. 'At the ceiling. It's a big glass dome. Like a huge occulum. Can you see? This is just starlight. But after so long in the pitch darkness, it seems incredibly bright.'

'You're right,' laughed Victrix. 'It's like someone tore the lid off.'

The Blackstone had a habit of throwing up scenes of unexpected beauty and this was one of them. Draik paused for a moment, admiring the vast, glittering panoply of stars overhead. 'And there,' he said, 'do you see that? The red glow, like a blood moon? That's Precipice.'

Victrix laughed. 'So it is. From here you can't tell what a wretched hole the place is. It looks almost pretty.' She patted down her arms and stamped her feet. 'Damn. It really is cold in here. Everything's covered in frost, do you see? It's hard to breathe. Let's keep moving before I freeze to the spot.'

'Grekh,' said Draik. 'Have we lost the trail? Is the ambull down here? I need to get close before I can trigger the plasma snare. There are so many energy sources on the Blackstone. The snare will be lost in the flood unless we're really close.'

'Give me a moment.' Grekh had dozens of small cages and tins strapped to him and removed the lid from one, peering at its contents. There were fragments of bone, meat and other indeterminate objects in there. He picked at them, sniffing and tasting the fragments, closing his huge, blank eyes as he savoured the flavour.

'There is something,' he said, closing the tin and looking at Draik. 'There are traces of the creature's scent. We *are* still on track. This must be her doing. The Blackstone *wants* us to find that creature.' He looked out across the huge, domed hall. It was hundreds of feet tall, and at its centre there was a tall, pyramidal structure that pointed up to the apex of the dome. 'I think the ambull passed right by that structure. Recently, I think.'

'What is that thing?' asked Victrix, staring up at its distant peak. 'It looks like a pyramid.'

'As big as one, too,' said Draik. There were pieces of vehicle scattered around the base – groundcars and armoured vehicles were often found lying around the Blackstone, relics of failed expeditions, but these looked obliterated. And they looked tiny in comparison to the structure. 'That thing is like a mountain. It's vast. Even for this place. Grekh? Have you seen buildings like these in here before? I've seen plenty of featureless, geometric shapes, but nothing on that scale.'

Grekh nodded. 'Some of my insights have concerned structures like these.'

Victrix shook her head. 'Insights? What's it talking about? And what was that tin of offal it was just picking at?'

Draik felt his anger returning. Whatever Victrix was, she was an Imperial agent. What must she think of him? Employing such a peculiar savage… 'Grekh has an unusual… *ability*,' he snapped, staring fiercely at her, determined not to sound ashamed. 'A genetic attribute. He can learn things about his surroundings by… He is able to study the aftermath of battles and learn about the combatants and their past.'

Grekh stared at him. 'I do not discuss my beliefs with people like her.'

Victrix laughed and looked up at the lanky alien. 'You *are* an interesting specimen, aren't you? I suppose you had to be. Why else would a fine, Terran gent like Draik associate with you? A muck-covered, spiny freak trying to masquerade as a man. You must be very useful.'

The spines on Grekh's back clattered as he squared up to her, brandishing the blade fixed to his rifle.

'Watch it, kroot,' she spat. 'Useful doesn't mean irreplaceable. Lower that blade or I'll jam it down your beak.'

'Stand down!' said Draik. '*Both* of you. I don't have time for this. Grekh is under my protection, Victrix. Take up arms against him and you're taking up arms against House Draik.'

'Ah, so it's like your butler? Why didn't you say? Forgive me, master kroot.'

Grekh tensed. 'Watch your tongue. *I* am not bound by Draik's code of honour.'

Draik shook his head in warning. 'You damn well are.'

Victrix laughed. 'You're his pet, remember.'

'Ignore her,' said Draik. 'We have more important matters to deal with. Are we safe passing by those pyramids? I see apertures on the far side of the hall. Is that the route the ambull took?'

'Perhaps,' said Grekh, still watching Victrix. Then he turned and looked out across the frozen hall. 'Yes.' He sniffed the brittle air. 'And not just the ambull. The smaller specimens were here. There is something odd about that pyramid, though… I do not know enough to be clear. I have borrowed memories of them. And I can see them in a violent aspect. There is danger in them. But I cannot see the exact nature of it.'

Draik kicked an engine part, scattering blasted metal across the floor. 'All these vehicle parts do look strange. It's like they've exploded.'

Victrix shrugged. 'Is it so odd for things to be destroyed on the Blackstone? The whole place is lethal.'

'Yes,' replied Draik, 'but they look like they've exploded from the *inside*. It looks like they've detonated.'

'How can you tell that? They're buried under all that frost. I can't make out any details at all.'

Draik tapped the bulky device that stood in place of his left eye. 'My implant. I can see an insect from half a mile away with this thing. Especially in this light.'

Victrix looked back towards the maglev. 'Well, even so. Do we have any option? You said the maglev will be inert now it's brought us here. Forwards is the only way, am I right?'

Draik nodded. 'You *are* right. Very well, you go first, Victrix, I want you where I can see you.'

'Honoured, I'm sure, your highnessness.'

'Watch our backs, Grekh,' snapped Draik. 'Those grubs move fast.'

Frost crunched under their boots as they crossed the hall.

Grekh sniffed and grunted as he studied the place down the length of his rifle. 'Yes. The ambull is down here. We are getting closer every time we reach a new level. We will reach it soon.'

'Good,' said Draik. 'I didn't come all the way to the Western Fringes just to hunt big game. I need to bag this thing and move on.' He paused, holding up a hand to stop the others. 'What's that?'

There was an odd sound drifting through the hall. It reminded him of glass harps he had heard on Terra as a child, in the gilded halls of the Imperial Palace. It was a droning hum, but oddly musical, ebbing and flowing over the walls.

Victrix closed her eyes, trying to concentrate. 'Music? It sounds like someone singing.'

Grekh nodded. 'It is the voice of the–'

Victrix glared at him. 'Don't say it! The voice of the Blackstone. She's a blah, blah, blah. This creature is *particularly* annoying, Draik. Are you *sure* it's worth having around?'

The droning sound grew louder and higher pitched until it became an undulating scream.

'Damn!' cried Victrix. 'That's painful.'

'And look at your jacket,' said Draik. 'Look at *my* jacket. We're freezing. Just keep moving,' he snapped, covering his ears and grimacing. 'That sound's coming from the pyramid. If we reach the next chamber we can escape the noise.'

He started jogging across the hall, clutching his hands tighter over his ears as the dreadful sound grew louder.

'Run!' he cried. 'By the Emperor, that hurts! Get to the doors!'

'It's getting worse!' howled Victrix. 'I can't think. I can't...'

There was a clatter of armour as she fell to the ground.

'Grekh!' cried Draik, looking back. 'Help her up. Wait... Where are you going, Grekh? Keep away from the pyramid.' The kroot was heading away from him, making straight for the black obelisk. 'Damn,' muttered Draik, staggering. 'I feel like my head is going to split. Grekh!' he yelled again. 'Come away from that thing. The sound is emanating from there.'

Grekh did not look back at him and replied in a calm, fascinated voice. 'I need to touch the surface.'

'What?' Draik thought the kroot must finally have lost whatever scraps of sanity it possessed. 'Why? How can you bear this wretched noise?'

'I feel no discomfort.'

'Victrix,' gasped Draik, reaching the prone woman. 'Here, let me help you up. Apologies for the appalling manners of my–'

'I can't bear it!' she howled, grabbing on to him, her face twisted in agony. 'My head! What *is* that noise! What's your creature doing over there?'

'Look at your skin,' he muttered.

'What the hell is this? Am I freezing? Throne! It hurts. I'm turning to ice!'

'We need to keep moving. We have to get away from that pyramid. Here, let me try and carry you.' He hauled her onto his shoulders but immediately staggered under her weight. She was not large but his strength was almost gone.

The shrill, drawn-out note slipped up another key, cutting through Draik's cranium.

'I can't...' he groaned. 'I can't walk. The pain...'

'We're only halfway across the hall,' gasped Victrix in his ear. 'We'll never make it. My head. Damn. It feels like my head is going to explode.'

'Wait...' Draik stumbled to a halt, looking round in horror at all the broken chassis and engine parts. 'Maybe that's what happened to all these vehicles. Maybe they didn't freeze *after* exploding, maybe they froze first.'

Victrix stared at him. 'We're going to explode?'

'This way!' cried Grekh. 'Quickly!'

Victrix shook her head. 'The creature's insane. Don't go *closer* to the pyramid. We need to get away from that thing.'

'No!' cried Grekh. 'No you do not! The sound stops when you reach the surface. It's silent here.'

'Emperor's teeth,' groaned Victrix. 'Just get me out of here! I can't bear it.'

'We're never going to reach those doors,' muttered Draik. 'You're sure, Grekh?' he cried, looking over at the kroot. 'There's *no* noise where you are?'

'None. And the ambull came this way. Right up to the pyramid. I'm sure of it.'

'Wait!' cried Victrix. 'Draik! Where are you going? Don't listen to that creature, this is insane. Put me down! The sound's getting louder!'

'You'd better be right about this, Grekh,' groaned Draik as his head pounded with the Blackstone's howl. 'I'm afraid it's this or nothing, Victrix. Those doors are too far away. We'd never make it across the hall. Grekh! Come and help me carry her.'

'This way, quickly,' said Grekh, still sounding calm as he walked over and grabbed Victrix from Draik's shoulders. 'Right up to the wall.'

They reached the wall of the pyramid, and the humming sound suddenly stopped, leaving the normal, ambient noise of the fortress – distant clangs and ghostly moans, but nothing like the horrendous scream that had just been cutting through the hall.

'Thank the Throne,' whispered Victrix. 'I could feel myself vibrating. My skull was about to shatter, I'm sure of it.'

'That frequency *would* have destroyed you,' replied Grekh, sounding quite cheerful. 'This piece of the fortress is transmitting something. A signal. A warning. Perhaps even a call for help. The pyramid is relaying it.' He looked up at the domed ceiling, speaking in an awed whisper. 'Perhaps it's *her* voice. Perhaps she is speaking through this thing. Listen.'

'No thanks,' said Victrix. 'She's not saying anything I need to hear. At least we're not freezing now, though. Look. Our skin is returning to a normal colour. Well, mine is.' She gave Draik a despairing look. 'You still look like a corpse.'

Draik looked up at the pyramid, ignoring her. 'Whatever the sound is, it had no effect on the ambull.' He tapped the wall with the handle of his pistol. 'Look at these claw marks. It came this way and climbed up the wall of the pyramid. See – the marks go all the way up to that ledge. And they match the claw marks we saw earlier.'

Victrix followed Draik's gaze, studying the marks in the wall. 'But three times the size.' She sounded hoarse and tired.

'Exactly,' said Draik. 'The tracks of a full-grown ambull. Wait a minute. Let me trigger the lumen on my gun. Yes. Look, you can see where it clawed its way up the pyramid. It's torn footholds in the wall.'

'Why?' asked Victrix. 'Why has it clambered up this thing?'

'Perhaps even an ambull needs a place to return to?' said Grekh. 'A place to rest and feed.'

Victrix laughed. 'It's made a *nest* in here?'

Grekh nodded. 'Possibly.'

'We're going up,' said Draik, holstering his pistol and unclasping another piece of equipment from his belt. 'I'm going to fire a grappling hook up there. Keep your weapons ready. I think we're getting close.'

Victrix groaned. 'Draik, I can barely see straight. My head feels like it's split down the middle. And you look even worse than I feel. Perhaps we should wait here for a little while?'

'And be swamped by the next swarm of larvae? If this *is* the route to the adult, the young will soon be passing this way. Do you really want to sit here and wait for them?'

'You're crazier than your pet. If this pyramid *is* the ambull's nest, there will be more grubs in here than anywhere.'

Draik shrugged. 'If you've lost your nerve, Victrix, you're free to go. Grekh and I will finish the job. While that thing is down here, I will be unable to complete my work.'

'Your work? What exactly is that, Emperor Draik? Gentrifying the place?'

Draik gripped his pistol and glared at her. 'Did you just take the Emperor's name in vain, Victrix? I had you down as a liar and a coward, but not as a blasphemer. We may be far from civilisation out here, but heresy is still heresy.'

She smirked, seemed on the point of cracking a joke, then changed her mind as she saw the rage in his eye.

He leant close. 'My intention is to ensure that the Blackstone Fortress is safe from base-born reprobates. People who have no interest beyond lining their own pockets.'

Victrix frowned in mock confusion. 'Grekh, do you have any idea to whom this noble soul might be referring? These base-born ruffians sound dreadful.'

Draik tapped the grimy breastplate of her flak armour. 'The more time I spend on Precipice, the more sure I am that the Blackstone Fortress must be claimed for House Draik. I need to possess it. To understand it. To control it. I'm not interested in the trinkets that dazzle people like you, Victrix.'

'Then why are you headhunting this overgrown bug?'

'While that thing is loose down here, I cannot safely explore the mysteries of the Blackstone.'

'There's something else in here,' said Grekh, chewing on something he had found on the floor.

Draik shook his head. 'In where?'

'In the pyramid – someone else climbed the walls. Look at this. They followed in the tracks of the ambull.'

Draik peered at the wall. 'Is that… Is that a scrap of uniform? Let me look. Yes, Astra Militarum. I cannot see the regimental markings, but it definitely came from a Guardsman. Damn it. Perhaps someone else has been foolish enough to take on the genetor's commission. Perhaps you're not the only one, Victrix.'

'Of course I'm not.' She laughed. 'Half of Precipice is probably down here trying to catch that oversized termite.'

'Then I need to move fast. Grekh, stay close, I'm going up. Victrix, do what you like, as long as you keep out of my way.'

He took a few steps back and fired the grappling hook. After testing the rope with a few tugs he began climbing, closely followed by Grekh.

Victrix hauled herself up after them, muttering to herself. 'If you're going to die in there, at the feet of that thing, I may as well be on hand to catch it.'

Draik called back down to her as he climbed. 'How exactly did you imagine you were going to trap a predator three times your own size? With a fishing net?'

She tapped a pistol strapped to her leg. 'I can down anything with this.'

'An aeldari pistol?'

Victrix nodded. 'A *modified* shuriken pistol. I paid a lot of money for this little beauty. It can pierce anything.'

Draik smiled. 'Very well. And what do you intend to do when you wound the ambull? It weighs about the same as a groundcar. You're just going to throw it over your shoulder, I suppose?'

Victrix scowled. 'I hired fifteen of those Precipice scumbags. I had no idea they'd all get themselves killed before we got near it.'

'I'd suggest you had no idea about anything down here, Ava Victrix. You're like all those slouching simpletons up on the orbital platform. You think this place is a treasure chest. You have no idea of its true importance. Of its true meaning.'

'I know one thing – that ambull could change all our fortunes. If you two worked *with* me, we could haul it to a maglev chamber. And, even if we couldn't, this place is crawling with idiots who would work for a pittance.'

'You're a fool,' said Draik, still dragging himself up the wall.

'And you? What's your wonderful plan? That antique rifle you've got on your back? It looks like a brass candleholder. Does it fire haughty insults? Or poleaxe your foes with witty anecdotes?'

'It's an arc-rifle. Forged on Mars at the dawn of the Imperium. Powerful enough to stop *anything*. It's probably worth more than that pitiful excuse of a ship that brought you to Precipice. If you ever expect to make a name for yourself, Victrix, you need to learn–'

'The tracks end here,' said Grekh, clanging his gun on the wall.

'Wait,' gasped Draik. 'Help me up onto the ledge, Grekh. I feel a little light-headed.'

'You're dying,' laughed Victrix. 'This is a farce. We should turn back. You won't last another hour in here.'

'I'm fine. Another combat stimm will keep me going.' He jammed another dose into his thigh and carried on climbing.

'Wait!' cried Grekh. 'This whole ledge has been damaged by the ambull. It must have ripped its way in somewhere along here. Look at that–'

The wall suddenly shifted, giving out a low, mournful groan as its plates ground into each other.

'Wait!' cried Draik, waving Grekh back. 'That's not going to hold your weight! Victrix! Grab my arm. Grekh! Hold out your rifle, I'll–'

There was an explosion of tearing metal as the wall caved in, hurling the three climbers into the pyramid.

FIVE

Draik lay still for a moment, becoming gradually aware that every part of his body was wracked by pain. He carefully flexed his fingers and limbs, expecting to feel a break but relieved to find he was mostly still intact. It was utterly dark. And it was oddly warm, humid even, like a swamp. He could feel dank air pressing down on him, drawing beads of sweat from his face, and he was surrounded by a sound that seemed utterly incongruous in the barren environs of the Blackstone: the buzzing of flies, banking all around him and crawling over his bloody neck.

He was about to speak when he noticed another sound – a low, ominous chanting. Human voices, joined together in a sinister dirge. It sounded like the climax of an occult ritual and, although Draik could not understand the language, the garbled, sibilant verses made him shudder.

He was pinned under a piece of rubble, but to his relief it was light enough to shove away and he managed to sit up.

'Grekh?' he whispered, staring into the darkness, unable to make out any shapes.

'Here,' replied the kroot from just a few feet away. 'I am unharmed.'

'Because you landed on me,' hissed Victrix. 'Gods, you're a foul-smelling lump. Get your flea-bitten hide off me.'

'That smell is strange,' said the kroot, standing up. 'It is like something rotting, but something vast. And listen to these flies. I have never seen flies on the Blackstone Fortress before.'

A pale light washed over them as Grekh triggered the lumen on his rifle. They were in a large tunnel that looked almost like a sewer, filled with pools of steaming filth and clouds of flies.

'Quiet!' said Draik. 'Listen.'

Victrix moved closer to him. 'What?'

'The chanting. Do you hear it? That doesn't sound like an ambull.'

Victrix grimaced. 'But it does sound like trouble.'

Grekh nodded and was about to speak when the tunnel lit up with lasgun fire. Shots screamed through the fumes, tearing chunks from the walls and slashing through the pools of muck.

'Take cover!' cried Draik. 'Behind the rubble! Return fire!'

They launched a furious barrage of shots back at their unseen attackers then leapt over a section of fallen pipe.

'Drop your weapons, thieves!' belched a moist, hiccupping voice. 'And kneel to the Plague Lord!'

'Cultists!' whispered Draik. 'Damn them. This place is crawling with them. Grekh. Did you see how many there were?'

Grekh casually stood up and looked over the pipe.

'No!' gasped Draik. 'I don't mean look!'

Grekh dropped back down just before there was another barrage of lasgun fire, longer this time and even more ferocious. The rusty pipe juddered and jolted under the onslaught for several seconds.

'Two dozen,' said Grekh when the shooting stopped. 'Possibly more. Heavily armed.'

Victrix looked in the other direction. 'There's no way back. Not through all that rubble we've just pulled down. We're trapped.'

'Grekh,' said Draik. 'Do you have any frag grenades left?'

'One.'

'Then one will have to do. Lob it at the loud mouth. Once he's splashed over the walls we'll charge. Grekh, you take the left side of the corridor. I'll keep over on this–'

He stumbled as he tried to change position, clanging his head against the pipe.

'You're a mess,' said Victrix. 'How do you think you're going to charge anywhere? You can't even stand up straight.'

'I'm fine, damn it. I just tripped. It's just the change of temperature. It's so damned hot in here. I can hardly breathe. And that stink is horrendous.'

Victrix lowered her voice. 'Did you see them? What are they? Are they men? They looked... What's wrong with their faces? Are they diseased? Or are we dealing with something worse?'

Draik nodded. 'That's no normal sickness. They're heretics. Chaos worshippers.'

'Drop your weapons!' gargled the voice from down the corridor. 'Keep your hands up and you might live.'

'Since when do Chaos worshippers take prisoners?' whispered Draik to himself.

'What about your antique?' said Victrix, tapping the weapon

on his back. 'The Martian gun. You said it could kill anything. Why don't you use that on them?'

Draik raised his voice, sounding stern and unruffled. 'One moment, sir. We are discussing our terms.' Then he whispered to Victrix. 'It isn't… Well, it is not entirely reliable.'

'Wonderful,' laughed Victrix. 'So for all your boasting, the thing is useless.'

'*Far* from useless. It once belonged to Arch-magos Danubis. Not that his name probably means anything to you. This rifle's perma-capacitors have been wired with such precision and ingenuity that they pack more than three times the punch of a normal arc-weapon. That's enough power to cook the brains of an ambull.'

'Then *use* the damned thing. You'll never get it near an ambull if those cultists take our heads. Why are you even hesitating?'

'Because it's ancient. The capacitors overheat. Sometimes after just a few shots. If I start firing it here, at these louts, there's no guarantee I'll be able to use it on the ambull.'

'But you're never going to reach the damned ambull!'

'She has a point,' said Grekh. 'You are wounded. You move slowly. And one grenade is unlikely to hit them all. They are in cover. But if I throw the grenade and charge, with Victrix, you could cover us from here. You could use your pistol until you see a chance to take down a few of them with the rifle.'

'Now!' cried the cultist. 'Come out or die!'

'Speak clearly!' cried Draik. 'Don't mumble, man!' He shook his head. 'Listen to that savage. Murdering the Emperor's Gothic. I *would* actually like to use this thing on him. Very well. One shot should be safe, but no more. Throw your grenade to the left, Grekh, that's where they seem to be concentrated. As soon as you throw, I'll roll over to that opening and fire the arc-rifle, just once. That should take down a lot of them and light the place up. Then, we'll charge. *All* of us. Understood?'

'Understood,' said Grekh.

'I'm not moving a muscle until I see that thing actually work,' said Victrix.

Draik nodded. 'Prime your grenade, Grekh. Now!'

Light blossomed through the tunnel, carrying clouds of dust and debris.

Draik stood, silhouetted by the blast, whipped his rifle from his back and calmly fired into the crowd at the far end of the tunnel. A coruscating beam of sizzling electricity spewed from the weapon, lashing and rippling as it slammed into the cultists, hurling them backwards in a cloud of sparks and charred flesh.

'I'll be damned!' laughed Victrix. 'That *is* a glorious sight!'

As the arcing electricity faltered, Victrix and Grekh leapt over the pipe and opened fire on the reeling figures.

'Grekh!' cried Draik. 'They're making for the door!'

'I have them!' howled Victrix as she fired on them.

Draik drew his pistol and opened fire, stepping down from the pipe, shooting repeatedly as he walked into the whirling dust clouds. 'They're on the run!' he yelled. 'Block the exit!'

The three of them charged after the fleeing cultists,

Then Draik was hurled through the air as another explosion rocked the tunnel.

'Throne!' he muttered as he lay sprawled in the foul-smelling water, looking up at a ceiling of smoke and embers. 'What was that?' The light faded, plunging him back into darkness.

'A trap,' gasped Grekh, from a few feet away, sounding equally dazed. 'They wired the corridor.'

Draik tried to sit up but rough hands grabbed him, forcing him back down into the muck and snatching his weapons.

'Bind them,' grunted a feral voice. 'Make sure to get all the weapons. Captain Samos *will* be pleased. Fresh blood for the Plague Lord. Blue blood too, by the looks of it.'

Unseen figures hauled Draik along the tunnel, snorting and grunting as they went. Behind him, he heard Grekh and Victrix cursing and struggling.

The low, ominous chanting he'd heard earlier swelled in volume, drowning out everything but the noise of the flies. Then a boot connected with his head and Draik knew no more.

SIX

'How *dare* you!' roared Draik, lurching up off the floor. 'I am a scion of House Draik! Your false god will not help you when word of my abduction reaches Terra.'

He was in a dimly lit, circular chamber decorated by what he thought at first were statues, then realised were a ring of mouldering corpses, skewered on sharpened girders and scored with bloody runes. At the centre of the circle was a large, metal bowl, filled with steaming liquid and suspended from the ceiling on chains. The room was full of traitors. Their filthy, ragged uniforms marked them out as being former Guardsmen, but they clearly now followed a new leader. Their Imperial regalia had been torn away and replaced with crude, daubed sigils.

'I think this is the leader, Captain Samos,' said one of them, kicking Draik. The man was a grotesque mass of pustules and sores and there were shapes rippling under his face – writhing, worm-like swellings that wriggled as he talked. 'He had the Martian rifle. And he talks a lot.'

Draik struggled to rise but found he was securely chained to an iron hoop in the floor. 'My arc-rifle!' he cried, looking round the room. 'Damn you! Give me back my weapons!'

'All in good time, scion of House Draik,' said another of the men. His uniform was a rotten mess, but intact enough to mark him out as a captain. 'We have it safe. Look, it's over there against the wall. Let me introduce myself,' he said, and his face split in an unnaturally wide grin, revealing rows of brown, rusted hooks where his teeth should have been. 'I am Captain Samos. And I will be happy to arm you once I am sure you will point that thing in the right direction.'

'What are you talking about?'

'It's a simple matter of allegiance, Draik.'

'Allegiance? My allegiance is to the Emperor of Holy Terra, you reprobate.'

'Of course it is, for now.' He gave Draik another revolting smile, then turned to the first man who had spoken. 'Sergeant Volkus. Did you see any sign of the ambull before you met these people? I would hate for this to be interrupted.'

'No. It *is* in the pyramid. We heard it dragging something back to wherever it feeds, but there's no sign of it heading this way. Everything you saw in your dreams has come true. Grandfather Nurgle's sigils have worked. The pestilent oaths have worked. They are keeping us hidden. The ambull is unable to sniff us out, confused by the stench.'

'Of course. Exactly as I was promised. The creature will never find us, but it is the perfect guard.'

Victrix slumped against Draik, her face a mass of cuts and bruises. 'What have you done to yourselves? You look like you've been boiled alive. Are those... Are those blisters? Boils?'

Captain Samos laughed. 'Do you not find us impressive?

This is the armour of our faith. Nurgle's blessings are making us hardy and strong. Our blood is reforming and thickening. Making a shell. Touch it. Do not be afraid.'

'Get away from me, you revolting creature,' she cried. 'You're like a talking blister.'

Captain Samos still looked amused. 'You won't find me revolting for long. Any of you. You will soon realise the glory of the plague. You will soon know what it is to be truly blessed.'

Draik strained against his bonds again. 'Insolent wretch. Kill us and be done with it. I'd rather that than spend another minute listening to your tedious drivel.'

Captain Samos smiled at him like an indulgent parent. 'Bring one of them over, sergeant.'

'Leave me alone!' cried Victrix as the guards unlocked her chains and dragged her across the room towards the metal bowl hanging in the centre of the room. 'Hands off! Put me down, you filthy mutants. What are you doing? Why are you taking me to that... What *is* that?'

'Grandfather's cauldron,' smiled Captain Samos. 'Fill a cup, sergeant. Give her a taste.'

Sergeant Volkus slopped a metal cup in the gunk-filled cauldron, filling it with gloopy, grey liquid.

Victrix struggled and cursed as the Traitor Guardsmen held her and forced her head back, preparing to make her drink.

'Get your hands off me!' she cried. 'Draik? Are you going to let them do this?'

'Unhand her, traitor,' snarled Draik. 'She is under my protection. If you harm her, in any way, you will regret it.'

Captain Samos laughed. 'I do not intend to harm her. Far from it. I mean to fortify her. To imbue her with the strength of the pox. A few mouthfuls is usually enough.' He waved at the hunched, shuffling figures that surrounded them. 'These troops were normal, frail men until just a few days ago. Then they drank from the cauldron and became these glorious creatures.'

'Glorious?' cried Victrix, still struggling to free herself. 'What are you talking about? Look at them! They're like plague zombies. You've mind-wiped them. Damn you! I won't drink that stuff! You're not turning me into a blank-eyed monster. Draik! Do something!'

As if in answer, the cultists began to chant even louder, filling the room with a moaning, atonal dirge.

'Grekh!' whispered Draik. 'Can you move?'

'No. These are metal chains. Padlocked. Rusted, but still secure.'

Victrix thrashed violently as the cup neared her mouth. 'Wait! Stop this!'

'Vokk! Howk!' ordered Captain Samos. 'Grab her head. Hold it back.'

'Wait!' gasped Victrix. 'I am far more useful to you as I am!'

'What?' sneered Samos. 'Wait. Lower the cup, sergeant.' He loomed over Victrix, spilling flies and stench from his hooked teeth. 'What do you mean? Useful how?'

'Tell me what you're doing here. Then I'll tell you how I can help.'

'Victrix!' warned Draik. 'What are you doing? These men are heretics. Don't even think about helping them to–'

Sergeant Volkus strode away from Victrix and punched Draik repeatedly in the face, sending him thudding back onto the filthy floor in a shower of blood.

Grekh tried to move, but like Draik he was too tightly bound to stop the cultist as he continued slamming his fist into the rogue trader's head, pummelling him with a sadistic leer on his face.

'Sergeant Volkus!' snapped Captain Samos. 'Enough! You're killing him!'

Volkus backed away, still grinning, with blood dripping from his fists.

Draik slumped in the filth, groaning. 'Victrix... Do not... Better to die...'

'How do you think you can help us, Victrix?' said Captain Samos, ignoring Draik.

Victrix turned away from Draik and leant towards Captain Samos, lowering her voice. 'My employer is a fool. Too engrossed in his experiments to guard his knowledge. Am I right that you–'

'Victrix!' mumbled Draik, his mouth bubbling with blood. 'Damn you! Stop!'

Volkus kicked him in the stomach until he curled into a foetal position and lay still.

Victrix continued talking to Samos, speaking quickly and urgently. 'You've been trying to get to Precipice, is that right? You're the cultists who have been attacking the landing bays, trying to get a ship back up to the orbital platform. Is that right?'

'Yes. That's true. We need to amplify our summons.'

'Summons?'

'The cauldron, the choir. It is not enough. It is not worthy of our lord. Nurgle requires something grander! We need to magnify the power of our prayers. We need to spread the word. From this transmission chamber and from the deep-vox-relays on Precipice. That's why we're recruiting new disciples. Once we have an army large enough we will capture Precipice and use it to spread the word across the whole subsector. Then the whole of the Western Reaches.'

'Then I can help you!' cried Victrix. 'Precipice is guarded.

There is a lot of wealth in the ships moored to those docking spars so the place is bristling with gun batteries. Even if you managed to get a ship off the Blackstone Fortress, you would be blown apart before you got close to Precipice.'

'But you can help?'

Victrix nodded at the liquid in the cauldron. 'If you keep that stuff away from me, yes.' She grinned. 'My employer is a genius. A fool, but a genius. He's an Adeptus Mechanicus genetor, and within days of landing on Precipice his cogitators had unearthed every one of its secrets. Including the security protocols for every one of its weapons batteries. I recorded them, all of them.'

'Why?'

'Because knowledge is power. I guessed that the information might come in useful at some point. A rogue trader can never be too well informed.'

'And how can I trust you?'

'Take me on whatever ship you use to attack Precipice. If I'm lying, the ship will be blown apart as soon as it leaves the Blackstone Fortress and I'll die with you.'

Draik tried to speak but his jaw was throbbing and numb, possibly broken, and all he managed was another angry moan. Then he had an idea. While he was curled in this foetal position, his hands were hidden. And everyone thought he was powerless to move. He slowly reached down to his belt and unclasped something.

Captain Samos leant closer to Victrix, mirroring her grin. 'Sergeant Volkus. This woman is not to drink until you have tortured those protocols out of her.'

'Torture?' cried Victrix, jolting away from him and rattling her chains. 'You're not thinking, captain. If you torture me I can give you any old lies. What would I have to lose? If you're going to feed me that stuff and turn me into a gibbering monster I may as well lie. But if you keep me alive, and sane, I will have *everything* to lose. I won't want your ship to be blown up then, will I?'

Captain Samos shook his head. 'You're a smooth talker, Victrix. Just like all rogue traders. Very well. Perhaps you *have* bought yourself a reprieve.' He looked at Sergeant Volkus and laughed. 'Although, I can't see what reason we'll have to keep her alive after we conquer Precipice.'

'Because I'll show you how invaluable I am! I've learned a lot over the years, from some surprising sources.'

The fury that had been smouldering in Draik became an inferno. He lurched to his feet and launched himself across the room, trailing his now unlocked chains.

'Volkus!' cried Captain Samos. 'He's loose!'

Draik slammed into Victrix and began grappling with her.

'Get off me, you idiot!' she howled, kicking him away.

Draik reeled away and thudded to the ground under a heap of rusted chains.

Volkus and some of the other guards crowded round, pointing their guns at him.

Victrix laughed in disbelief, staring at him. 'Throne. I don't know what you intended to do. You're unarmed and half-dead.'

'How did he free himself?' demanded Captain Samos.

'He's a slippery devil, that one, even in that state,' said Victrix. 'You should probably feed him some of your cauldron slop.'

Samos laughed. 'I'm starting to like you already. You really don't care what happens to your comrades?'

'Comrades? Don't make me laugh. Janus Draik is the competition. I've been trying to rid myself of him ever since I came out to Precipice. That arrogant fop is exactly the kind of entitled parasite that's kept people like me back since the dawn of the Imperium.'

Samos shrugged and nodded. 'Sergeant! Get Draik on his feet. We'll soon get some colour back in his cheeks. Bring him over to the cauldron.'

Victrix frowned. 'Wait. What's that?'

'Ah, now, Victrix, you're not going to disappoint me, I hope, trying some feeble trick to save your friend?'

'I told you, I couldn't care less what happens to Draik. Listen. What's that sound?'

Everyone paused to listen as a low rumbling sound shook the chamber.

'There *is* something,' muttered Sergeant Volkus. 'She's right. It sounds like an earth tremor.'

The cultists' chant faltered as the distant rumble grew louder, turning into a crashing, tearing sound, like metal being shredded.

Captain Samos backed away, shaking his head. 'No!' He sounded furious. 'It can't be.'

'What, captain?' demanded Volkus, gripping his gun and peering into the gloom.

Samos' voice was brittle. 'It sounds like the ambull heading towards us.'

'It can't be!' cried Volkus. 'It can't see through the oaths and sigils.'

An entire section of wall exploded, hurling rubble and flies into the cultists as an enormous creature waded into the chamber. It was a hunched, roughly humanoid thing with long, powerful arms and brutal claws, and its whole body was covered in a thick, gnarled carapace. Its head was dominated by the massive, serrated mandibles that had just torn through the walls, and as the cultists staggered away in shock, fumbling with their weapons, the monster let out a deafening roar, spraying drool and dust across the room. Before the cultists could fire, the creature crashed into them, ripping them apart and filling the air with blood and screams.

'The ambull!' cried Volkus. 'How did it find us?'

'Back up the tunnel!' cried Captain Samos, fleeing from the chamber and dragging Victrix with him. 'Keep firing!'

'Wait!' howled Victrix as she stumbled after him, still chained. 'Give me a gun, damn you!'

'This way! Fast!' cried Samos, firing at the ambull as he led his men away down the tunnel.

The men that were still able to fired on the creature, but their shots bounced uselessly off its carapace as it devoured their screaming comrades, who were still howling as it ripped them apart.

'This way!' cried Samos again, leading his men into the darkness with the ambull lurching after them, tearing great chunks of wall down as it went.

The sounds of slaughter gradually faded into the distance, until the only noise in the chamber was the buzzing of the flies and the slow, lethargic bubbling of the cauldron.

Then some of the rubble shifted as Grekh managed to sit up, rising from the mud like a revenant. 'Captain Draik?' he said, picking rocks from his beak. 'Are you there? Can you hear me?'

Draik moaned. He was lying just a few feet away, drenched in blood and coated in dust, but pleased to realise he was still breathing. His face was still numb where the cultist had been punching him and the bandage had gone from his neck, reopening the wound. The pain was so great that, as he sat up, he thought he might vomit. He tried to look around but his eye was so swollen he could only see a thin sliver of gloom and the augmetic lens in his other eye socket was cracked. 'The rifle,' he managed to say, through bruised, split lips.

Grekh shuffled closer, shrugging off more rubble. 'What?'

'I can't see. Can you… Can you see the arc-rifle?'

'Yes. Wait.'

Draik heard the creature shifting bodies and rocks.

'Yes, I have it.'

Draik mumbled in satisfaction and slumped back against the shattered wall.

'I think I can free one arm,' said Grekh, struggling with his chains. 'How did you…?'

'Move closer. I picked the lock. My skills are… Damn. I think something's broken. Lots of things. Come here, Grekh.'

Draik still had the pick he had taken from his belt and, as Grekh reached him, he unlocked the kroot's chains, managing to keep his hand steady long enough to pick the lock.

'Thank you,' said Grekh. 'Now let me help you up. Can you stand?'

'Damn it,' groaned Draik as he stood. 'Feels like *everything* is broken.'

'I can carry you,' said Grekh, taking Draik's weight. 'Lean on me.'

By slumping weakly against the kroot, Draik managed to stay upright. He was about to speak when the chamber juddered, sending more rubble clattering down from the ceiling and walls. The ambull had clearly destabilised the whole structure. It sounded like it might collapse at any moment.

'That should do it,' said Draik when the chamber was quiet again. 'You really are an invaluable creature, Grekh. We should get moving, though. This whole place is going to come down. The ambull certainly made an impressive mess.'

'She saved us,' said Grekh in a hushed voice.

'She?'

'The Blackstone Fortress. The cultists said the ambull had been unable to find them all this time. Their warp-spawn masters were protecting them. And then, just as we were about to die, the Blackstone let the ambull discover us. It's a miracle. How else do you explain it? And the fact that we were left unharmed?'

Draik laughed, then coughed up blood. 'Unharmed?'

'By the ambull, I mean. It rushed straight after the cultists.'

Draik tried not to laugh, conscious of how much it would hurt. 'It wasn't chasing the *cultists*.'

'What do you mean?'

'It was chasing the plasma snare I stuffed in Victrix's pocket when I lunged at her. They won't know what the ambull is after until it's ripped them all apart.'

'What?' Grekh made one of his screeching, laughing sounds. 'Oh. Of course.'

The chamber juddered again and a huge piece of wall slammed down not far from them, enveloping them in a cloud of flies and dust.

'We have to move,' said Grekh. 'Look, the ambull has opened up a way back out of the pyramid. We can follow its route back and try and find a maglev. We can try and return to the others.'

Draik nodded, then winced at the pain of moving his head. 'Yes, let's go. You're sure you can carry me?'

'We kroot are stronger than we look, Captain Draik.'

Draik smiled. 'I'm starting to realise that.'

They took a few steps towards the hole in the wall, then Draik halted.

'Wait.'

'What?'

Draik squinted through the blood on his face, trying to see the kroot more clearly. 'You say you have the arc-rifle?'

'Yes. Here.'

Draik looked at the other exit, the one the cultists and Victrix had left through. 'I was just thinking. We *could* head back out, or...'

'Or what?'

'By the time the ambull has eaten all those cultists, I imagine it will be ready for a rest. Think about it. I would–' He was interrupted by a series of violent, painful coughs and the room swam around him so drunkenly he thought he might fall.

Once he felt steady again, he grabbed the arc-rifle and tried to grin.

'I'd just need one clear shot, Grekh. Just one.'

THE LAST OF THE LONGHORNS

NICK KYME

Raus spat out a wad of blood, unsurprised to find a tooth floating in it.

'Whoa… ow! That was actually a pretty solid blow,' he said. 'Nearly as hard as my mother used to give me. At least, I *think* she was my mother.' He turned as far as his bonds allowed and glanced over his shoulder. 'Was she our mother, Rein?'

'Fragged if I know, Raus,' Rein replied. They were sat back to back and the other ratling wriggled against the metal stake the brothers were tied to. 'I remember a mean woman though, a real bi–'

'Enough!' snapped a thug in ragged Militarum fatigues.

'You're right,' Raus nodded, 'that's no way to talk about our maybe mother.'

'I meant enough talk!'

Raus frowned. 'But you said you wanted us to talk.' He turned again, whispering loudly. 'He did say that, Rein, didn't he?'

'He did, Raus,' Rein confirmed, nodding sagely. 'I don't think this berk understands how to properly interrogate someone.'

Raus took a kick to the midriff for his troubles.

'Oof! Yep,' he said, partially winded and speaking through gasps for air, 'that felt like mother all right. Maybe even a little harder?'

'Good for you,' Rein chimed in.

The thug growled, exposing black teeth. He had a sigil carved into his left cheek that Raus didn't care to look at for too long and his uniform was a mix of olive drab and murder-cultist-bastard red. No, actually, the red was just blood. Raus' blood.

The trooper swung again, his punch stopping just short of the ratling's nose at the sound of the voice.

'That'll do.'

The words came from the shadows. Even the eerie pearlescent light of the fortress chamber didn't touch him. He knew where to stand and wanted to retain his anonymity, even here, in this benighted place. The dark hid the chamber too. It had a tinny smell like an old slaughterhouse gone to seed but where the memory of carnage still begrimed its walls. A vaulted ceiling went up very far and dim, ruddy lights blinked like some murderous firmament of stars. It was hot. Like a furnace, but there was no obvious fire. They had changed this place, the Traitor Guardsmen. It had twisted effigies now, made of bent metal and strung with offerings that clacked together from an apparently sourceless breeze. The breeze churned up the hot metal smell and made it worse.

Raus wrinkled his nose and felt the protests of his sore ribs as he breathed.

'There's a good soldier...' he muttered, forcing a grin.

The trooper reluctantly stepped back. He wasn't alone. There were four others, a semicircle of troopers, their hateful glares boring into the two ratlings like butcher knives. They were grubby, their fatigues worn and badly stitched. Some had drawn crude markings like the one on the thug trooper's cheek. A few had their faces covered. Raus decided he didn't want to know what the rust-red scarves concealed. And there were spikes. Shoulder guards. Knee pads. Helmets.

'You *really* like spikes, eh?' said Raus. 'Must be tricky to get through tight spots, I imagine. Do you ever get snagged on a comrade's jacket? Is that why your kit is so badly stitched up? I bet that's why it is.'

'We should just kill them both,' snarled the thug.

'And where would that get us, sergeant?' asked the voice. It was deep and charismatic, but with a grating edge that came from breathing in too much recycled air. These men had been in the fortress a while.

'That's right,' agreed Raus, doing his best to be annoying, a skill that he and his brother excelled at, amongst other things. 'We have something you want and you have something we want,' he continued.

'Perhaps a trade, Raus?' Rein piped up.

'A splendid idea, Rein.' Raus looked back at the Guardsmen. 'What say you, my raggedly attired lunatics? I believe the High Gothic is *quid pro quo*?'

'Do you know the High Gothic for this blade is going up your–'

'I *said*,' uttered the voice, stressing the last word, 'that will do.'

The thug lowered the knife he had just whipped out from behind his back. It had a jagged, darkly stained edge.

'The runts won't break that way,' the voice went on.

'What did he just call us, Raus?' asked Rein, mortified.

'They must be *persuaded*.'

Not for the first time in his life, Raus felt his buttocks clench at the way the voice had emphasised the last word.

The thug trooper was smiling. It was ugly and did nothing to improve the ratling's mood.

'You will give us your half of the talisman,' said the voice.

'I have no knowledge of such an item,' Raus lied.

A scarred, red-raw hand thrust a crescent-shaped piece of metal into the light. It dangled on a chain, turning slightly in the breeze. Veins of arcane circuitry throbbed and the gemstones in its gunmetal surface glittered.

'It looks very much like this one. Its convex twin. A pair that when reunited can open a vault. A vault I very much want the contents of. And, I know, you do too.'

Raus knew the avarice in his eyes gave him away, so he didn't bother to dissemble further.

'Oh…' he said, '*that* talisman. We hid it.'

'And if you kill us, groxshit for brains, you'll never find out where it is,' added Rein.

'Thank you, Rein.'

'Don't mention it, Raus.'

'But could you please stop antagonising the angry men in their spiky uniforms, you berk, as I'm the one who is getting used as a punchbag.'

'Will do, Raus.'

The thug trooper brandished his knife. 'I'll cut the truth out of them. Let me take his other eye.'

Raus felt the socket under his eyepatch suddenly itch at the thought. It was one of several reasons he was no longer much of a sniper. Unlike his brother. Alas, all their gear had been confiscated when they were ambushed and captured by these mouth-breathers. Well, *almost* all of it. They hadn't taken the ring on Raus' left hand.

'No...' said the voice, and the talisman disappeared back into the shadows, 'I have a better idea.'

Something scraped in the deeper darkness, a slow grating of metal against metal that put Raus' nerves on edge. The air hummed and a crackle of jagged light lit up a deformed creature advancing on the two ratlings.

Raus gasped.

'What is it, Raus?' asked Rein, squirming to get a look.

'Ugly as unholy arse,' Raus replied, trying to hide his fear.

It had been a man once, but to call it such any more would be profoundly false. It *drifted* across the obsidian floor of the chamber, bare feet dangling in mid-air, dragging a pair of metal weights chained to its ankles. It wore similar fatigues to the troopers but had a dirty, dark red coat that parted to reveal a naked, wasted torso. A sigil had been burned into its pasty flesh, as if seared from the inside out.

Raus wanted to look away but found himself transfixed. Its face was the worst part of its appearance. A bulbous, grossly misshapen head framed a ratty visage with a pointed, dagger-like nose. Bloodshot eyes flared red, boring into him like a drill as a cruel smile played across the psyker's lips. Something pulsed in its forehead, a peristaltic movement beneath the skin giving way to a crackling blue light as it began to exercise its powers.

'It looks like an ork rutted with an ur-ghul and a day-old ham,' said Raus, pressing his thumb against the Imperial sovereign in the ring.

'Emperor's sweet holy privates...'

'They had nothing to do with this abomination, Rein.'

'Willing or not, you'll give up what you know,' said the

voice, 'and possibly your sanity too...' it added, fading and fading as the light in the psyker's eyes grew brighter and brighter until it became Raus' entire world...

Raus watched through the vision slit as the other landers came down amidst clouds of smoky engine fumes and eddies of dust. Noise and industry filled the camp, billowing in through the opening debarkation ramp. The place was already burgeoning with ammunition crates, promethium drums and half-built prefabs. A few vehicles, a command Salamander and its laager of Chimeras, idled on a flattened apron of earth, and a pair of Sentinels strode by hauling containers of large ordnance. An adjutant had made it his mission to raise a flagpole, and the crests of the Cadian 69th and the Vorpese 87th snapped proudly in pollution-thick air.

Locke was first off, Raus watching his back as he swaggered between a pair of burly Cadians who looked like they'd been eating their beans on the regular. The ratling wore a sergeant's chevrons and his thick side whiskers had greyed over the years. His carapace breastplate was olive green and he had a short-sleeved jacket with short-legged fatigues, all in dull grey just like the rest of the squad. A heavy gauge stub-pistol that he called Darling – for a reason Raus had yet to find out – sat in a holster on his left hip, and he carried a profusion of packs and pouches that contained rations, extra rations and personal ordnance. He paused at the edge of the ramp, lighting up a fat cigar. Tabac smoke plumed in the air, and Raus caught its thick and woody scent. It was pleasing, a reminder of home, but did little to counteract the camp stench. Locke looked up at the Cadians, who stood several feet taller, and wiggled his bare, hairy feet.

'Another glorious day in the Militarum, eh, boys?'

The Cadians grunted something derogatory that Raus was too far away to hear and went about their business.

'Ah,' said Locke, tucking a thumb into his belt and breathing it all in as Raus and his brother Rein sauntered towards the sergeant, 'quite the shithole.'

The ratling siblings had to duck and weave through a procession of troopers carrying missile tubes, sandbags and caskets of grenades before they reached Locke. A whirl of urgent activity billowed around the ratlings, who appeared immune to its fervour, opting to stand and watch instead.

'So, this is Camp Dauntless,' said Raus, hefting a sniper rifle across his shoulder as if it were a long piece of firewood and nodding to Happig – who was so named on account of his snout-like nose and slightly pointed ears. Happig yawned, blinking and rubbing the sleep from his eyes as he took it all in.

'Looks the same as any other camp we been in,' he drawled, absently poking a finger in his ear to dislodge whatever had crept in there during transit.

'How many, do you think?' asked Rein, snapping the scope to the stock of his rifle and checking the load. He treated the weapon with reverence, as though it were a cherished lover, or his mother's cook pot.

'Must be... what, at least five hundred?' suggested Munk, trying to count on his stubby, soot-stained fingers as he sidled over to the others. Munk was a bullet-mule, and ammo belts criss-crossed his body. Too dim-witted to carry a rifle, but still a vital part of the squad.

'Emperor's gilded arse, Munk,' snapped Pugal, close on the bullet-mule's heels. 'You are duller than a greenskin's boot.' Pugal was a head taller than the rest and broader across the shoulders. He had thick beard hair, a rare enough sight amongst the abhumans, and stroked it proudly. He was also the squad's unofficial pictographer, and as well as his standard-issue kit, he carried a box-picter and its tripod over one shoulder.

Raus smiled. Poor old Munk. Bald as an astropath and thicker than an ogryn's neck.

'Anyone seen the latrine?' asked Fud, the ratling clasping the belt cinched loosely around his pot belly as he appeared behind Munk. His eyes darted feverishly.

'Don't you drop trowel here, Fud!' snapped Locke. 'No one wants to see your nethers, lad.'

'A pit...' said Fud, desperation edging into his voice and his pained expression. 'A rutted track, anything.'

Raus gestured at the laager of Chimeras, which were hidden from general view, Locke nodded and Fud scurried off like a scalded felid.

'Bladder the size of a bullet. If he gets seen and court-martialled, we deny all knowledge,' said Locke. 'And that's a ruddy order.'

Raus gave a salute and then surveyed the camp. Troopers were pouring in from the other landers, not just the Cadians in their ash-brown fatigues and green carapace but also the Vorpese in their traditional grey and charcoal. The Cadians showed the discipline they were famed for, ranking up into platoons, lasguns held across their chests as they moved, and then up to the shoulder once they were in position. The Vorpese were hardly a rabble either and amassed in ranks, kneeling to receive a commissar's catechism.

'Must be more than ten thousand men,' said Locke, taking a puff of his cigar, 'not to mention tanks and support.'

'A crap tonne,' announced Rein, lifting up his goggles and blinking back the dust.

'Speaking of which...' chuckled Pugal, nodding to Fud as he hurried back to the squad in mild disarray.

'Is that a sanctioned Munitorum term, Rein?' asked Raus, his gaze lingering on the commissar delivering the fervent rhetoric to the Vorpese.

'*Very* sanctioned, Raus.'

Happig yawned again, nodding. Munk just looked confused.

Locke was more concerned with what was going on above them. 'And not just Guard, either...' said Locke, jabbing a hairy finger at a flotilla of copper-red ships descending through the yellow clouds. Bulky vessels, and festooned with a veritable forest of antenna and surveyor arrays, the skull and toothed-cog emblazoned on the side of each marked out their allegiance.

Raus felt a light tap on his shoulder, and turned to the last member of the squad.

Strigg was watching the sky too, scowling against the light of the pale sun. He had strapped his rifle to his backpack and carried a grapnel gun slung on a strap over one shoulder. Always prepared, was Strigg. He made a series of swift hand gestures.

'Translate,' said Locke, who didn't know ratling sign-cant as well as Raus or his brother.

'I think he called them...' Raus frowned, he whispered in Rein's ear.

Rein's brow wrinkled, then he frowned and looked aghast at Strigg, who shook his head and signed again.

'Ah,' said Raus, nodding now, '*cog*-heads. That makes more sense, Rein.'

'Nah,' growled Locke, spitting out his half-smoked cigar and crushing the burning embers under the heel of his bare foot, 'I reckon you were right the first time.'

'Come on then,' said Pugal, stomping ahead of the others.

'Let's capture this dump in all of its unsavoury glory, shall we?'

The squad tromped down after him and quickly fell into a huddle around a stack of ammo crates and fuel drums.

Pugal set up the box-picter, flicking out the tripod and getting it level as the others squabbled for position. Locke stood in the middle, a fresh cigar wedged between an adulterer's grin. Munk knelt down at the front, the sergeant's hand on his shoulder. Strigg, Fud and Happig stood on the left, whilst Rein and Raus stood on the right, leaving room for Pugal to fit in behind. Rifles were held to shoulders and a heroic air abruptly affected.

'Imperium in our blood...' said Pugal, setting the timer before hurrying into position.

'Imperium in our bones...' said the others.

They held steady, the chrono ticking down, and as the box-picter flashed declared, 'Long live the Longhorns!'

'Reckon that was a good 'un,' murmured Pugal, but as he going to collect the vellum-print from the box-picter one of the Cadians wandered over and got to it first. He had the uniform of a tank commander, with all the haughty indifference that came with it, and scowled at the pict.

'Ugly little *verms*, aren't they?' he remarked to a fellow tanker.

'I'm going to send that pict to your mother,' said Pugal. 'Something to remember me by.' Locke and the others had moved up behind him, showing a united front.

The tank commander looked down his curled moustaches at the ratling, as if Pugal were something he'd just stepped in but couldn't yet identify.

'Oh, I doubt she'll be interested. She doesn't really get on with *beasts*.'

'Just ruts with them, eh?' noted Rein.

The other tanker paled at the remark, presumably trying desperately not to let his imagination roam.

'You do know why they call us the *Long*horns, right?' remarked Fud, and thrust out his crotch.

That earned a venomous glance from the tank commander, who rested a hand on his sidearm. A couple of other tankers, loaders and gunners judging by their burly arms and oil-stained skin, came over to see what all the fuss was about.

'I'd leave that weapon where it is if I were you,' Locke advised, between chews of his cigar. He tapped the stub-pistol at his hip. 'Wouldn't want me to wake my Darling...'

'You threatening me, verm?' The tank commander evidently didn't want to let it go.

'Just a bit of friendly advice,' he said, and patted the pistol's grip, 'she's a cranky old thing.'

'Know your place, abhuman,' growled the tanker.

Locke took a step forwards, so he was just in front of Pugal. 'Oh, I know it well enough,' Locke assured him. 'It's just above that shrivelled appendage between your legs,' he said, and punched the tank commander hard in the groin. The man doubled over sharply, squeaked in a manner unbefitting of his rank and collapsed to the ground clutching at his bruised privates. The other tankers made to mob the ratlings, who had closed ranks and balled fists, ready to brave the onslaught, when a strident voice interceded.

'Is this just boisterous camp camaraderie I'm witnessing or something else?'

An officer in a long dark coat approached. He had a livid scar down his face that pulled up his mouth into a perpetual snarl. The other tankers' protests died on their lips when they noticed his peaked commissar's cap and realised what he was. The cap bearing the badge of his office shadowed his eyes but there was no hiding the menace he evoked.

'A little early in the campaign for a summary execution,' he suggested, a finger resting on the crimson leather grip of his bolt pistol. 'But I've made exceptions before.' The gun was an artificer piece, master-wrought and doubtless worth an absolute fortune. Raus could practically feel the envy and larcenous desire bleeding off his brother, and threw him a sharp look that said *don't be a bloody berk*.

'Save your ire for Heldum,' the commissar advised, pointing to the horizon where the city ruins burned, a jagged silhouette obscured by smoke. 'You will need it.'

Little was known about their objective. An Imperial city called Heldum occupied by seditionist forces. It was a stronghold and the Militarum had been tasked with cracking it. But Raus thought it was more than that – why else would there be Mechanicus ships slowly descending into camp? No answers would be forthcoming, especially not from the commissar.

He was heading off again when he stooped to retrieve the vellum-pict lying on the ground and give it back to Locke, who acknowledged the deed with a wary nod.

'To your duties then,' said the commissar sternly, 'and don't be so quick to dismiss what's seemingly beneath your notice,' he added for the benefit of the tank commander, who was being helped to his feet by two of his crew. He marched away then, back to his regiment, his authority lingering long after he was gone like the smell of gunmetal in an armoury.

Happig lowered his voice. 'Honest...' he whispered, 'I fathomed them bastards who wore the black were all...'

'Bastards?' Raus supplied.

'Well, aye.'

As they began to circle around, Strigg signed to the others.

'What did he say?' asked Locke, brushing the dust and a little carelessly dropped ash from the pict.

'He said,' offered Raus, as the ratlings converged on their sergeant, 'this place is a real shithole.'

Locke's laugh was as filthy as his fingernails, 'Isn't it just.' He held the pict up to the light. 'What do you reckon, lads?' A rabble of dirty-faced, mildly dishevelled ratlings rendered in sepia looked back at them. 'Turned out all right, didn't it.'

Raus gasped a breath he didn't realise he'd been holding and the air knifed through his body like he had swallowed a mouthful of ground glass. A power fist hammered the inside of his skull and he clenched and unclenched his bound hands to try and restore the feeling to numb fingers.

The furnace heat returned with anvil-like solidity, raising beads of sweat and prickling his suddenly cold skin, and he remembered where he was. The blurred vision eased and resolved into the gruesome face of the psyker. It appeared withered, its eyes more shrunken and long fingers trembling, but it had a hungry look about it that Raus didn't like one bit.

He tried to speak, breathing still not coming easily, his heart a heavy stubber on full-auto as it tried to vibrate its way out of his mouth. He swallowed to lubricate his throat, which was as dry as Locke's wit, but only tasted warm metal against his tongue. The memory of them was almost visceral. All their faces and voices rendered in perfect, aching clarity.

'His mind is strong…' murmured the witch, though its lips didn't move when it made those reedy, echoing sounds.

'Again…' ordered the voice from the shadows, the troopers looking on, adding 'hold on,' as Raus made to speak. 'Perhaps the runt is ready to talk after all.'

The thug trooper with the knife leaned in. 'He's trying to say something...'

'I haven't...' Raus rasped, as parched as an irradiated corpse.

The thug leaned closer.

'I haven't felt...'

'Say it,' uttered the thug, his voice eager, 'say it and this can end.'

Raus coughed. 'I haven't felt this violated since I got cavity searched by the Precipice border guards.'

He braced for the punch he knew was coming but the impact drifted away beneath ice water as the world around him faded...

The cultist's head snapped back, yanked by an invisible tether. A plume of red fountained from the back of his skull, painting the icon bearer next to him. The survivors panicked as the demagogue went down in a heap, brains spattered this way and that. They shouted and looked into the darkness, trying and failing to find their leader's killer.

A second muffled shot took out a tank commander, speared him right through the left eye, shattering his goggles and leaving him slumped like a tired mannequin across his vehicle.

Raus gave his brother a mental pat on the back and chose another target. An officer, this time, trying to get a battery of heavy stubbers into position. He collapsed with a hole in his chest, coughing blood through the gauzy filters of his rebreather. An ammo-hauler with a hefty looking sickle-mag slung over his shoulder spun on his heel, a headshot passing through ear to ear and taking the contents of his skull with it. A third shot killed a gunner, blew out his neck and nearly decapitated him. *Pft, pft, pft.* Three rapid exhalations, lost in the cacophony of small-arms fire. Raus chalked three more marks for his tally and turned away from the window to reload.

Robbed of leadership and under heavy fire, the ragged horde abandoned their assault, turned about and scurried back into the shadows. The enemy were a mix of robed, lightly armed cultists and better equipped Traitor Guard. They had some armoured elements, mainly Chimeras, daubed in ugly sigils and strung with bleached bone skulls, but couldn't breach the Imperial position.

Silence fell for a few minutes, the traitors returning to their lines, before a chain of explosions marched down the shattered plaza, the big blooms of fire and smoke throwing up slabs of rockcrete and dirt. They were distant enough that Raus couldn't see the mortar battery doing the shelling, but close enough that he went back over their plan for egress. He voxed his brother on the lower floor of the burnt-out hab block for a quick sit-rep.

'Thought they only had light armour...' he muttered to himself, then louder to his brother, 'You seeing this, Rein?'

'What's that, Raus?'

'Well those aren't Regimental Founding Day fireworks, Rein. That's heavy mortar.'

'Oh aye, Raus. Founding Day is much prettier.'

As ever, Rein sounded untroubled, which left Raus to do the worrying for them both. The bombardment, while close, was unfocused. The enemy might be trying to sneak something in behind the explosions.

'Eyes on the road, Rein.'

'What am I looking for, Raus?'

'Don't know yet.' He relayed the same warning across the squad and shuffled his rifle stock against the sill, taking care not to catch the light. Evening had crept across the sky with dusky fingers, and had long since fallen behind the northward vista of shelled ruins leaving a grey-black pall, but it paid to be careful. He checked down the scope for the third time.

'Nothing here...'

'Nope.'

'Hold on...' A flash, he thought. Metal catching the light. Maybe it was something in the ruins, innocuous, ordinary – or maybe it wasn't...

'Raus?' The voice was Pugal's from lower in the hab.

'Something up ahead...' Raus adjusted the focus on his scope, trying to find out exactly what, sighting down the barrel and bringing the silenced muzzle in line with his target. Nothing. He swung his scope over the defences to see if anyone else had seen anything.

He panned the crosshairs over a deep gorge of trench-works that zigzagged two hundred feet from the ratlings' elevated positions. Cadians and Vorpese were dug-in, holding as the bombardment thundered in the street just ahead of them. Raus reckoned on over five hundred men in that trench. A Cadian captain had a pair of magnoculars held up to his eyes, scanning the dark ahead. He was relaying coordinates to a vox-operator who had his head down, one hand over his ear against the din of the shelling.

Razor wire strung the upper north edge of the trench, little crowns of jagged teeth eager to rend. Raus and his half of the squad only had a vantage to the east side of the gorge; the west was hidden by a sharp bend, though he knew another five hundred men waited there too.

Still nothing. Whatever he had seen either hadn't been spotted by the Militarum or it simply wasn't there. He swept the road ahead in case something was lying in wait, but between the drifting smoke and steadily encroaching darkness it was tough to make anything out. He switched to night-sight but the heat signatures were all friendlies. He reverted back and looked over at a second partially broken hab sat across from the one he, Rein, Pugal and Munk were in. It occupied a refused position a hundred and fifty feet from the battle-line, and harboured the rest of the Longhorns. It also had a vantage to the eastern side of the trench and the other half of the dug-in Militarum forces.

Raus opened up his vox.

'I thought I saw movement to the north, sarge. Could be infiltrators. Anything your end?'

After a few seconds' pause, Locke answered. *'Sneaky funters. Hang on… Nothing I can see. Sound off.'*

'Fud… nothing, sarge.'

'Happig. Nowt at this end.'

Three sharp clicks told the same story for Strigg.

'All quiet on the eastern front… What have you got, Raus?'

'Not sure.' He adjusted his scope again, running another sweep, but much slower this time.

Above, a duo of distant Marauders made a swift pass, their payloads plummeting like dead weights. The aircraft made a deeper black against the inky sky as they peeled away on flares of engine thrust. Seconds later, a pair of concussive explosions tore up the dark, turning it stark as day, only colder. The hab shook, dust motes spiralling downwards like dead will-o'-the-wisps. Raus gritted his teeth.

'Red-arsed Magnus,' he cursed under his breath, but went back to his scope.

After a few more seconds it became clear that the shelling had abated. A cohort of Mechanicus skitarii was swift to capitalise and had just emerged from a second trench line just outside of Raus' peripheral vision. The cyborgs marched in fearless lockstep, carbines and calivers shoulder-clamped in firing positions, red cloaks flapping in the evening breeze. A small phalanx of walkers tracked their left flank, the riders sat crouched behind the armoured blast shields of their twin-linked autocannons. One of the skitarii turned towards the hab block and Raus had the uneasy feeling it was looking right at him as the focusing rings on its bionic eye cycled in and out. It didn't linger, but raised a hand and brought it down in a swift chopping motion to signal the advance.

'Vanguard is done waiting,' he murmured. 'Always thought cog-heads had the patience of a machine.'

'Militarum is on the move too,' said Locke from the other building. *'Wait…'* he added, as more than a thousand Imperial infantry began to surge into the street and march on the distant enemy positions. *'Something going on down here…'*

Raus looked up from his scope. Something in Locke's voice didn't sound right.

'Sarge?'

'Throne above…' breathed Locke, *'it's–'*

A flash of light roared into being, overloading scopes and pushing out white noise, loud and aggressive enough to knock out the vox. Raus recoiled, pressing his hands to his ears and clamping his eyes shut before the flare blinded him.

It only lasted a few seconds.

'Rein…' He tried the vox at first, but it was as dead as an Ecclesiarchy priest in a Commorrite brothel. 'Rein!' He shouted this time and got a response from the floor below.

'Vox is out, Raus!' Rein shouted back.

'I know, Rein. Why do you think I'm shouting, you berk?'

'What, by the Emperor's holy balls, was that?' bellowed Pugal.

'Pugal,' Raus hollered back, 'have you got Munk?'

'Affirmative. I heard the sarge, he was–'

A shriek cut through the night, sharp as a chainsword,

and when the shells fell this time they struck the second hab. It crumpled like a paper house suddenly lit on fire, the lintels and archways burning and collapsing. With a terrible wrenching of earth and stone, it broke apart, dust and smoke spilling outwards in successive waves.

'Shitting saints!' That was Rein, bellowing from below.

Raus stared in disbelief, vox static rasping in his ears. 'Not possible…' he breathed, fighting back tears.

The sound of footsteps coming up the stairs made Raus turn and pull out his stub-pistol.

Rein crashed through the doorway. 'Off your arse, Raus,' he said. 'We can't hang about.'

'They shouldn't have known we were here, Rein.'

'No, they ruddy well shouldn't,' he said, getting Raus to his feet, 'but someone knew to turn that hab into rubble, Raus. We need to move.'

They met Pugal on the way down, his face as pale as chalk. He had Munk with him; the poor dumb oaf had been bawling his eyes out.

'Something happening outside.' Pugal pointed through a ragged gap in the north-facing wall. Raus saw the trenches overrun. It was hard to tell what was happening but a lot of the Cadians were dead and cult troops were swarming the razor wire, cutting through it and then the men beyond with ritual knives. A last stand of skitarii dwindled farther up the road, taken apart by Traitor Guard heavies and the return of their light armoured tanks. A Hellhound painted in swathes of black with red slashes let off a burst of smoky flame that engulfed the tightly packed Mechanicus soldiers and devastated their ranks. A handful of the cyborgs staggered from the conflagration, machine parts sparking or half-melted, but were cut down with enfilades of las-beams.

Vox-horns sounded from somewhere in the darkness, droning and urgent. Flares lit up the smoke-choked sky like languid arrows of light. A throaty chorus of deep engine sounds rumbled from the south, and the refused Imperial position where command had been stationed.

'Armour's coming...' said Pugal, unable to keep the fear out of his eyes.

'Come on,' urged Raus. They had got as far as the basement and he darted from the hab, rifle slung over his shoulder. Rein followed without hesitation. He heard Pugal chivvying along Munk and then the Longhorns were moving, along the trench line, ignoring the close-quarter battle between Imperials and Traitors, and heading for the rubble of the second hab.

The push for the north gate of the city had penetrated deep but ultimately failed, and as the engine sounds grew louder and their threat more imminent, that meant the Demolishers were coming in to level it. A mass retreat had already begun, sounded on Vorpese bugles and jostled along by Cadian colour sergeants shouting at the tops of their lungs.

Raus ignored them, weaving through the bodies of troopers just as he had done when they first made camp, only now the fervour came out of a desire to survive and fight another day rather than a restive need to feel the earth underfoot.

The second hab, or what was left of it, stood across the road. It still burned. The devastation was almost total as barely a shell remained, with chunks of fire-black masonry jutting into the air like cadavers' teeth. A small band of Cadians, mainly corpsmen with a single medic bearing the white caduceus, heaved at the rubble which had spilled out onto the street, burying fighting men under its avalanche. Several bodies lay prone under blood-stained olive-drab sheets.

As he closed on the disaster zone, Raus caught sight of a diminutive form lying in the street. The stretcher dwarfed the ratling, his feet barely halfway down its length.

'Strigg!'

Raus ran harder, rifle banging against his back as he scurried to Strigg's side. He slung the weapon aside when it got in his way.

'Raus?' Rein called, a few strides behind, huffing with the weight of his pack.

'Still breathing,' Raus shouted back. 'Still chuffing breathing…'

Pugal had got ahead of Rein, his slightly longer legs giving him the advantage in a foot race, and slid down by Raus' side. 'We need to get him out. Tanks are coming.'

Raus glanced behind them to the horizon where the bulky silhouettes of the Demolishers crept into view.

'Anyone else make it out?' he asked of the nearest corpsman. He had his hands full; the Cadian medicae were falling back too, as keenly aware of the approaching armour as the ratlings. He shook his head, grim-faced and flecked with blood that was not his own.

Strigg's lips were moving, but too fast to understand. And he was badly burned, one side of his face and both hands. Signing would be near impossible, but he lifted his scorched hand anyway and Raus blinked back smoky tears to try and discern what Strigg wanted to say.

'I don't… I don't know what that means. What about Locke, Happig and Fud?'

Strigg drew a shaking, red-raw finger across his neck. The tears on his face washed furrows through the layers of ash and dust.

Raus' head sank. He felt Rein's firm grip upon his shoulder. No jokes now. No banter.

'Come on, brother,' Rein said. Search lamps had begun to strafe the city as the Demolishers zeroed in. 'We have to go.'

'They're dead, Rein. They're all dead.'

'And so will we be if we don't move.'

So they ran, hefting the stretcher between them, one at each handle.

The battle in and around the trench had broken down to a few desperate skirmishes. Men lay face down in the mud, bayonets in their backs, or their skulls flash-burned by a close up las-beam. Else they were blown apart, limbs hither and yon like a butcher's leavings. Bodies quivered at the trench edge, ripped apart by razor wire, strung up on its teeth like dead puppets. Death hung over the Imperial lines like a heavy shroud and Raus felt its terminal weight as they barrelled towards safety. They went west, back towards the hab, rather than straight south. The guns roared just as they reached the threshold of the hab, as the Demolishers sang their song of fire and fury.

Scurrying inside, they got Strigg and his stretcher under the stairs and hunkered down, murmuring prayers to the Emperor that they would be spared.

It was only then, as Raus met the gaze of his brother, that he realised he had left his rifle behind.

'Can't go back, Raus,' said his brother, as if reading his thoughts, but then he wondered if Rein actually meant something else. 'Can't go back.'

'The enemy shouldn't have known,' Munk murmured between his tears. 'It was a safe place.'

'Nowhere is safe now,' said Raus.

Pugal's face wavered between anger and stoicism. 'Imperium in our blood,' he said.

'Imperium in our bones,' replied the others.

Raus looked down at the blood and dirt on his hands. His fingers shook and his voice was a croak of strangled grief. 'Long live the Longhorns.'

Raus squirmed against the psyker's mental touch. It was like hot knives and cold needles all at once, invasive and nauseating. His hands spasmed, fingers splaying in sudden, unexpected pain until he felt his brother's firm grip and found a reserve of strength he didn't know he had.

'He's buried it deep...' murmured the witch in its eerie, sibilant voice, *'layers of truth and memory and falsehood, masked behind trauma and pain...'* It gasped, and Raus took no small measure of satisfaction from its discomfort.

'Leave off him!' snapped Rein. 'He doesn't know where it is.' He wriggled in his bonds, trying to turn and face their captors. 'I'm the one who hid it,' he said, as his voice began to crack. 'It was me, you berks, you ruddy groxshit bastards.'

'He lies...' hissed the witch. *'This one knows... he can tell us.'*

'Open him up, then,' said the voice from the shadows, 'every secret, every truth, every lie. Let it spill out and we'll sift through what's left. Delve deeper, as deep as you have to.'

'Leave off,' cried Rein, and gripped his brother's hand but Raus was shaking now and could barely hear or feel him any more. 'Raus!'

Raus slipped back beneath the cold water again and the memories flowed back...

They were sitting in the lee of a battered Chimera when Pugal returned. He had a sergeant's chevrons on the shoulder of his uniform, a rapid field promotion for the ratling sniper squad. He also had a dour look on his face.

Munk stood up from the box crate he was sitting on, his look expectant. Pugal gestured for him to sit back down.

'They're pulling us off the front line.'

Rein scowled, pausing in the cleaning of his rifle. 'Eh? Nah, that can't be right. There's a reckoning to be had, for our lost.'

'The squad is no longer needed. Different tactics, they said. We're to await reassignment in the barracks.'

Raus had started to pace, mind awash with questions. After they had made it back across the lines with Strigg, it became clear how large a blow the defeat in the plaza had been to the Imperial war effort. The ratlings had been part of an infiltration force, intended to breach the Traitor position where it was thinnest, to establish a beachhead for the armour and then push deeper into Heldum. The failure of that plan – in part due to the enemy being much better dug-in and equipped than Imperial intelligence had suggested, and because they had the precise coordinates of their hidden assets and military strength – meant the Militarum were effectively stymied and facing a long and drawn-out besiegement.

'Something is off...' muttered Raus, and stopped pacing.

'It's perfect,' Rein replied, slapping his rifle stock.

'Not the rifle. *This.* How could they have had our position?'

'Not possible,' said Rein, prompting vigorous nodding from Munk.

'Maybe it was a fluke? Locke and the others just ended up in the way?' suggested Pugal.

'That was a pinpoint strike on the hab. It hit dead middle. They were taken out.'

'But why though, brother?'

Raus rubbed at his whiskery chin. He paused to let a band of battle weary tankers tromp past. They gave the ratlings a dirty look but were wise enough not to linger or say anything.

'I can think of one reason,' said Raus, 'but I don't like it.'

Pugal's eyes narrowed. 'A turncoat?'

Munk frowned. 'Who's a turd goat?'

Pugal clipped him around the ear, eliciting a squeak. 'No, you berk. A *turncoat*,' he whispered, 'a traitor in the ranks.'

Munk looked around sharply.

'Not right now, you numbskull.'

'Perhaps they saw something.' Rein had set down his rifle across his legs and lit up one of Locke's cigars.

Raus gave him a flinty stare, at which Rein shrugged.

'I stole it before...' He puffed out a cloud of purplish smoke.

'Sarge's not going to be smoking 'em,' said Pugal solemnly and, as if suddenly remembering something, he fished around in one of his packs. 'Here,' he said, and pulled out Locke's old stub-pistol. He proffered it to Raus in both hands like a venerable relic or a sacred offering.

'Darling...'

'Sweetheart...' Pugal answered with a wink, but there was sincerity in his eyes too. 'You should have it.'

'I've got a pistol,' said Raus, but took the weapon, his rough fingers tracing the barrel and ironwork frame.

'Not like this one. Kicks like an angry grox on heat.'

Raus swapped out his old stubber with Darling. It sat snugly but felt heavier on the hip. Then he turned to Rein, picking up where they'd left off. 'What do you mean, they saw something, Rein?'

'Think about the position, Raus,' said Rein. 'Everything east of the trench line. Whole section of the field that we couldn't draw a bead on.'

'Those cog-heads came out of the east side of the trench,' said Pugal.

'Before being turned into offal and scrap metal,' Raus replied. 'I can still smell the blood and oil.'

Rein inhaled deeply. 'Ah, smells like victory...'

'Smells like a damn ugly mullering, you mean,' said Pugal. 'Cog-heads are after something. I heard one of the Cadians mention it. Something buried in the city. Don't know what exactly, but have you ever known a tech-priest not to have an agenda?'

Munk looked dumbfounded. 'I don't know any tech-priests.'

Pugal snarled. 'It's a figure of speech, dingus.'

'It really isn't,' said Rein.

Pugal growled, face reddening.

'Not helping, Rein...' said Raus.

'But it isn't...' he whispered, offering a facial shrug.

'Whatever's going on, we can't trust anyone,' said Raus. 'Only we four.'

'Five,' replied Pugal, nodding towards the medicae tent that was a short distance from the Chimera.

'We need to speak to Strigg. Find out what he saw.'

Pugal nodded, as if weighing up the risk. 'Orders didn't say anything about not talking to one of our own.'

'No, they did not,' said Raus.

The medicae tent had fallen silent but for the groans of the soon to be dead and the dulcet chiming of the machines keeping some of them alive. The place had been louder earlier, before the morphia. Back then there had been much screaming. A metallic stench lay heavy on the air, mixed with the acerbity of counterseptic. It was clean, considering how unimpressive the Militarum camp was on the whole, and more than two hundred souls lay supine on rough beds awaiting their fate. The injured were ranked in long rows, divided by three aisles. Low lighting from overhead sodium lamps threw grainy shadows. Both Cadians and Vorpese had taken a severe beating. Both regiments were well represented. No Mechanicus, which was to be expected from warriors that were more metal than flesh and fought with oil as well as blood in their veins. Orderlies were supposed to patrol the tents, especially during the night hours, but none were present.

'Does that seem odd to you?' asked Raus as the ratlings fanned out to find their wounded comrade.

'No corpsmen or medics, either,' noted Pugal.

There had been a guard stationed at the entrance but he'd waved the ratlings through with barely a glance.

'Here!' said Rein, prompting the others to converge on him.

Raus made it first but slowed as he came to Strigg's bedside. 'He's...'

'Dead,' murmured Pugal, hands loose by his sides and curling into fists.

'The turd goat...' whispered Munk, fighting back the tears and earning a barbed glance from his new sergeant.

Strigg stared at the canvas ceiling, whatever or whoever he had been looking at lost to the past. Only the gloom and the glow from the faulty lamps remained.

Pugal leaned over the body, about to close Strigg's eyes, when Raus stopped him.

'You see that?'

A thin film of foam layered Strigg's upper lip.

'A seizure or something?' asked Pugal.

Raus caught sight of a few stray, gauzy fibres snagged on Strigg's teeth.

'Or something,' said Raus.

The hand closest to them had been tightly bandaged. Strigg's burns had been severe. The one farthest away, the one that Raus now circled around the bed to inspect, looked much more ragged. The bandages had been chewed off, quickly and urgently. Rigor mortis contorted Strigg's fire-blackened fingers into a claw.

'Poor bugger...' uttered Pugal, softly. 'Must have been itching.'

'Not an itch,' said Rein, ever the observant one, 'a message.'

'Same one he tried to give us on the road outside the destroyed hab,' Raus concurred.

Pugal frowned. 'Meaning what?'

Gently, Raus took Strigg's hand and lifted it up away from the bed. Meanwhile, Rein had hooked a sodium lamp with his rifle and dangled it behind Strigg's hand. Instantly, a shape flickered into being on the tent's dark canvas.

Pugal squinted as he tried to discern what the image was meant to be. 'Looks like...'

'A bird?' queried Munk, scratching at his bald scalp.

'A raptor,' said Rein, sharing a knowing glance with his brother.

Before the start of the campaign, any relevant intelligence that had been garnered about the field of operations had been trickled down to the Militarum. This included what was known about the city, the bottlenecks, choke points, potential staging grounds and so on. In order to make coordination of troops easier, the city had been codified into specific sectors.

'He wants us to go back into Heldum,' said Raus, pulling out a map from his kit and laying it out across the bottom half of Strigg's bed. He jabbed a finger into a maglev station designated *Raptora*.

'That's pretty far north of where we were...' said Pugal.

'Deep into enemy-held territory,' said Rein.

Pugal looked at Raus. 'You're the pathfinder, can you get us in without us being seen?'

Raus smiled. 'No one ever notices us, sarge. I can get us in and steal their spiky chuffing helmets while I'm at it.'

'But what about orders?' asked Munk.

Pugal hawked and spat onto the ground. His gaze lingered on Strigg, cold and lifeless, betrayed by his own side. 'Balls to orders.'

Raus smiled, revealing bloody teeth.

'Balls to orders...' he murmured, caught between past and present.

He felt the cold waters lapping at the edge of consciousness.

'Not... long... now...' rasped the sibilant voice in his head. It sounded like it was in pain...

Raus crouched behind a tumbledown chunk of masonry and squinted at the darkness of the maglev tunnel. The line had fallen into disrepair, hindered in places by rockfalls where sections of the vaulted ceiling had collapsed in. Mild tremors radiated the floor and curved walls as the Imperial forces maintained a heavy, constant bombardment against another part of the city.

'You hear something?' asked Raus.

He felt Rein shake his head just behind him and crouched at his right shoulder. The ratling had his sniper rifle trained on the gaping tunnel mouth ahead.

'Not unless you mean Munk's bowels, Raus,' his brother hissed back.

From across the opposite side of the tunnel came a whispered apology and then a louder curse from Pugal.

'I swear, if we get killed because of your flatulence, Munk...'

'Shhh!' Raus urged them to be quiet.

They waited silently in the darkness, trusting to their naturally strong night-vision to alert them to any threats. Since taking the maglev line, they had encountered no resistance or enemy presence of any kind. An attack was happening elsewhere, hence the bombardment, and it was drawing the traitors to it. Getting into the tunnel had not been easy, though. The entrance was mostly buried and the rubble too thick to breach with charges, but Raus had found a narrow cleft in the rock that had allowed the ratlings to slip through.

'Anything, Rein?'

'Cleaner than a Munitorum priest on sabbatical to the Covent Prioris, Raus.'

Raus leaned behind him to pat Rein on the shoulder, and his twin moved up slowly with one eye pressed to his rifle sight. Raus then gestured to the others.

'Station coming up,' he hissed. The place looked abandoned, little more than a raised platform and broken plascrete overhang, but after what they had already seen on the road, Raus was taking no chances.

Deep into the northern wards of the city, the depravity of the enemy had become apparent. Strange sigils were daubed across walls or cluttered plazas. *Evil marks* was how Pugal described them, and the ratlings had steered well away. They saw captured Guardsmen hung from scaffolds or else crucified against the crossbars of tank traps and left to rot. Strange bonfires exuded a greasy black smoke, choking the air and filling it with the smell of burning pig's fat. Several armed patrols had passed the ratlings by, ignorant of the interlopers, and at several points they had witnessed gatherings of men and woman wearing carven wooden masks and crimson robes. Here they had deviated again, leaving the chanting of the demagogues and the inhuman bleating of their sacrifices behind.

The ratlings had moved swiftly and silently through these places, cloaking themselves in shadows, their faces fully camouflaged for infiltration.

Even via the disused maglev tunnel, it had taken almost three hours to reach the Raptora station. Standing at its threshold, the ratlings encountered a much wider part of the tunnel, but now that they were here Raus could find nothing unusually untoward about it.

He gently touched his brother's shoulder. 'Close enough…'

A watch house sat next to the expansive station platform. It had a tower like a crow's nest that rose above the station and into the vaulted ceiling of the tunnel. A crack in the tunnel roof let in papery light, but as it was still night above, it did little to leaven the gloom. Raus pointed to the watch house. They needed a vantage, a lookout.

Rein nodded, and moved towards it.

The others fanned out, slowly reconnoitring, but found nothing. The station appeared to be truly abandoned. Whatever cataclysm had overtaken it had left this place empty and in severe disrepair. Judging by the dank and stale air, it had been this way for some time. Underground, out of sight, it had simply become forgotten. Until now.

Raus opened up a channel on his vox. 'Rein?'

'In position…'

'See anything?'

'Yep, you could say that, Raus,' Rein replied. *'Head east about fifty or sixty paces… and be sure to watch your step.'*

The others followed Rein's instructions and gaped collectively at what they saw.

Partly disguised by the position of the station, a long furrow had been ploughed into the earth and bedrock beneath Hel-dum. A path of rubble and scattered wreckage led down into a huge crater where the ground had been torn open. A ship lay in this pit, or at least part of a ship. Evidently it had crashed landed and several pieces had broken off. The main hull appeared to be intact, though there were no signs of life. Painted by dust and the accumulated dirt of what could be decades or even centuries, it was of Mechanicus origin, Raus realised, but that was as far as his knowledge extended.

'Is it a warship?' asked Pugal, gingerly leaning into the edge of the ship's re-entry furrow for a better look.

'I don't think so,' Raus replied. 'Can't see any obvious weapons.'

It was a large vessel, bulky like a lander. Though there were no obvious troop compartments, a hatch on the port side had been torn open… from the inside.

'Something got out…' whispered Munk, clutching his bandolier of ammunition and grenades as if it could somehow protect him.

'Could've been years ago,' Raus replied, but heard the slight tremor in his own voice as he said it.

'Except this place has been sealed,' said Pugal, unhelpfully.

Raus glanced at the ratling sergeant. 'We don't know that for sure.'

The vox squawked sharply, prompting a bout of terrified swearing. Munk let out a tiny squeak of nervous flatulence.

Pugal scowled and sniffed. 'If you've followed through…' he warned, just as Rein's voice fuzzed into focus.

'Careful where you're standing, chaps,' he said. *'According to my scope, some of that subsidence is recent.'*

'Must've opened up for some reason. A tectonic shift or something,' muttered Pugal.

Raus stared at him.

After a few seconds, Pugal became aware of the fact. 'What?' he said, frowning.

'Didn't even think you knew *tectonic* was a word, let alone how to use it competently in a sentence.'

Pugal pointed to his newly minted rank markings. 'This means I can have you shot, no questions asked,' he grumbled.

Raus put up his hands plaintively. 'Are we going to take a closer look or not?'

Pugal got on the vox. 'You see anything else? Anything at all?'

'Not even a grot's nutsack...'

'Charming,' Pugal grumbled to himself, gesturing to the wreck. 'Let's get a better look, shall we...'

Pugal led the others down the ramp of earth and rubble. They had almost reached the stern of the broken Mechanicus ship when the vox crackled again.

'Incoming! Keep your heads down!'

Raus scrambled back up to the edge of the ramp to see stab-lights from the tunnel up ahead, parting the shadows with strafing magnesium cuts. And moving fast.

Munk was scampering on all fours as he made to leapfrog Raus. They hadn't got that far but footing was treacherous and he slipped. Raus lunged and grabbed the scruff of his collar.

'No time,' hissed Raus, and dragged Munk back.

As the ratlings hunkered down amidst the churned earth and the debris, Raus stole a peek into the shadows. A clamour of booted feet preceded a host of warriors – a platoon of Vorpese and a cohort of Mechanicus skitarii.

'They're coming this way,' hissed Munk. He sounded scared. 'What do we do?'

'Stay put,' said Pugal.

'It's the ship they're after,' answered Raus. He caught the

faintest glint of his brother's scope in the watch tower that overlooked the station. He had yet to move. *Shoot then relocate*, this was the sniper's mantra, and Rein followed it like a religion.

'Then they'll reach this ridge and see the crater,' said Pugal, 'and us in it.'

'I think that would go badly for us if they do,' admitted Raus. He dared not open the vox. The Mechanicus might detect it, and the ratlings would have to trust to fellow soldiers. The memory of Strigg resurfaced like a corpse in water. 'We should hide. Now.'

The allied Imperial contingent advanced into the station itself, almost forty Guardsmen and twenty or so Mechanicus led by a tech-priest. It was impossible to see what manner of creature the magos was beneath its robes, but Raus detected the undulations of what appeared to be tentacles moving beneath the red fabric. It moved with a scuttling motion, like an arachnid, and compound red retinal lenses flared with amber light beneath its hood. A staff ending in a cog-toothed blade and clutched in the tech-priest's cybernetic claw paced out its steps in a clicking, metallic refrain.

Raus shuddered at the sight of it, but the allied contingent came close enough that he could recognise the officer leading the Vorpese. It was the commissar they had met earlier. He saw something else too, something that made his heart leap, and he cursed himself for his own stupidity.

Munk saw the commissar too and brightened instantly.

'They're allies!' he said, and scurried up the ramp of earth before Raus could stop him.

Munk vaulted the summit of the ramp, arms waving as he declared his allegiance to the Throne and the Imperium, and fifty guns turned in his direction. The air crackled with the heat of volkites and the crack-hum of lasguns.

'Imperium…' he said, the hope dying in his eyes, usurped by fear.

Raus saw what had put the fear of the Emperor in Munk and felt it like the cold touch of a winter wind.

Unbeknownst to the Mechanicus, the Vorpese had shifted their aim. The retinal lenses of the tech-priest went from amber to red and as he turned, he emitted a blurt of machine code that hurt Raus' ears.

'Down, Munk!' cried Pugal as a firestorm erupted from the guns.

Outgunned and betrayed, the skitarii were torn apart. A few got shots off from their calivers, but did little to change the outcome of the slaughter.

Only the tech-priest survived, protected by a barrier of force projected from some piece of arcana attached to its robes. He scrambled away from the Guardsmen, who advanced menacingly, executing the critically injured. Munk had thrown himself prone, but was rising again and turning on his heel back towards the ramp and the relative safety of the crater.

Everything moved quickly now, a pict projector pushed to maximum frame rate, but Munk appeared to run in slow motion – so too the tech-priest, who also fled for the crater.

Or was it the ship?

Raus had no time to consider which as one of the Guardsmen took aim… Raus tried to shout but his warning was smothered by the Guardsman's sudden cry as the side of the would-be shooter's head exploded in a puff of crimson. He crumpled, prompting a bellow from the commissar.

'Sniper!'

Rein could not relocate. He had to stay put. So he did. Three more Guardsmen died before the commissar zeroed in on his position.

And as the commissar stepped fully into the glow of the stab-lights, the truth of who he was and what Strigg's warning had really been about came into sharp relief. It was the scar on his face, easy to miss at first glance, but impossible *not* to see now. It was shaped like a claw, or a beak. A raptor. Dumb luck had brought the ratlings to the right place, even when they were looking for the wrong thing. None of that mattered now. An Imperial traitor had been revealed, and he would certainly want every one of them dead to protect his secret.

'The tower!' he cried, stabbing in its direction with his chainsword, 'take it down!'

A squad of Guardsmen lit up the side of the tower like it was Founding Day, azure light stabbing in a host of hot knives.

The tech-priest reached the edge of the ramp just as its shield overloaded. It sparked once then blew out, taking a chunk of the adept's hip with it. Raus was showered with fabric, hot oil and blood. A piece of shrapnel struck his left eye and he screamed as white heat blazed through his retina. He had never felt such pain and would have passed out had Pugal not grabbed him.

'Shit!' Pugal cried. 'Hang on, Raus!'

Raus clutched his eye, but knew it was gone.

The skitarii were all dead but the tech-priest kept crawling into the pit, seemingly oblivious of its other occupants. The ship lay fifty feet or so farther into the crater. Through his blood-soaked vision, Raus saw the tech-priest's head arch back. Its hood fell, revealing a mechanised cranium, the neck canted at a ninety-degree angle. The jaw levered open as the tech-priest emitted a death-blurt of lingua-technis before it collapsed and did not move again.

'Is it dead? What the hell was that?' asked Pugal, head down as the Guardsmen switched aim and hammered the edge of the ramp with a fusillade of las-beams. 'Is it dead?'

'Yes, definitely dead,' said Raus, his hurts burning through his skull. 'And we're next.'

The Traitor Guardsmen had them pinned. Through splashes of hot light and the edge blur around his good eye, Raus saw the commissar advancing with his pack of traitor dogs. They wanted the ship, or perhaps whatever had been in it.

'We ain't getting out of this one,' said Pugal. He hugged his rifle to his chest, slotting in the high-calibre rounds. 'I'm sorry, Raus,' he clutched the other ratling's arm, 'first day as sergeant and I get the squad killed. Locke will be pissing in his pants somewhere.' He smiled grimly. 'Not going down without a fight though.'

Raus gripped Pugal's rough hand. 'Imperium in our blood...' he said, and pulled Darling from its holster.

It was then that Munk suddenly found his courage.

A grenade looped over the edge of the ramp, its parabola high and long, the perfect blind throw that evaded the Traitor Guardsmen's beams and landed right in their midst. The explosion went off like a thunder crack, kicking up dirt and flinging bodies. Limp Guardsmen fell like rain.

'Imperium in our blood!' Munk roared, as he vaulted over the edge of the ramp, tossing a second grenade. Las-beams searched for him, cutting little razor slashes of light in the shadows, but Munk was fast and nimble. The second detonation shook the tunnel. Part of the wall blew out in a cascade of scything brick splinters and choking dust. More traitors fell, ripped apart by the blast.

'Imperium in our bones!'

Munk was almost screaming now, and Pugal took this as his cue to get Raus to his feet.

'Up you get,' he said, hauling them both back out of the furrow. Moving was evidently a bad idea for Raus, whose head swam, and he staggered before Pugal caught him and looped his arm over his shoulders. 'With me...' he grunted, hoofing towards the watch tower.

A third grenade went off, though the Traitor Guardsmen had gone to ground now and were taking cover so the impact of the explosion lessened dramatically.

'Long live the–'

The words died on Munk's lips, a las-beam through the throat silencing them and silencing him for good. He lay in a crumpled heap, forlorn, forgotten.

Raus held back tears as he and Pugal hurried like all the hells of the warp were chasing them.

Three shots rang out. Three Traitor Guardsmen fell in quick succession, as Rein's voice came over the vox.

'Haul arse!'

Munk's sacrifice had bought them the slightest chance, and as Pugal shoved him onto the watch tower's ladder, Raus realised how. Dawn light was breaking through the crack in the roof. Faint but clear enough, even through his red-rimed vision.

'You go up,' said Pugal.

Raus reached for the rifle slung across the sergeant's chest but Pugal smacked his gnarled fingers away.

'*You* go up,' he repeated. 'You can't shoot for shit with that eye anyway.' He slapped the grapnel gun strapped to Raus' belt. 'Up, and away.'

Raus gripped the other ratling's wrist. 'Pugal...' Las-beams were thundering in like hot hail now. A low wall delineated the edge of the watch house and it served well enough as a barricade, but it wouldn't last. Nor would Rein's ammunition, though he was making good use of it. 'I won't forget you, Pugal.'

Pugal gave a quick nod before solemnity gave way to scorn. 'Bugger that,' he said. 'Just get the ruddy hell out of here.'

Then he turned and braced his rifle against the lip of the barricade.

Raus climbed, las-beams searing the paintwork near his face or snatching at his feet as he took two rungs at a time. As he reached the summit, he practically threw himself into the crow's nest, which had more holes in it than an ogryn's undergarments.

'Rein...' he said as he collapsed into a heap.

Rein snapped off a shot, and glanced over his shoulder. 'Raus, you look a right mess.' Another bullet cracked out and a distant but loud grunt of pain signalled its success. 'Pugal?'

Raus shook his head and he eyed the crack in the roof, wondering if, given his flawed depth perception, he could pull off what he was planning on doing next. 'It's just you and me, Rein. Pugal's not coming.'

He could hear the discharge of the sergeant's rifle from below.

'Ruddy berk...' muttered Rein, but Raus caught him wiping his eye with his sleeve.

They were holding the Guardsmen for now, but the lasstorm was intensifying as the traitors closed in.

'How far you reckon to the roof, brother?'

'Fifty-three feet,' answered Rein without hesitation.

'Hope this line is long enough.'

'Me too, Raus,' said Rein. For the first time since Raus had gained the crow's nest, he turned from the firing lip to crouch against what was left of their cover. 'Down to my last one,' he said, brandishing the high-calibre round between thumb and forefinger.

Raus scowled. 'Then, Rein, you should kill that shit-eating grox-rutter.'

'As you wish, Raus,' answered Rein cheerily, slapping the bullet into the breech. He steadied his rifle stock against the lip. 'Never trust the bastards who wear black...' he said, and the shot rang out.

The commissar spun, though through the dark and the mayhem and his pretty seriously impaired vision, Raus couldn't tell where he'd been hit.

'Is he dead?'

'He's as dead as he's going to get right now, Raus,' said Rein, packing up his rifle in double time and pulling at his brother's jacket. 'Up we go, eh?'

Raus took aim with the grapnel, hoping it had a generous degree of accuracy, and fired...

'Did you check the range of the line?' asked Rein as a plume of pneumatic propulsion sent the cable unfurling in successive ascending coils towards the cleft in the roof.

'Bugger...' Raus crossed his fingers and hoped.

Below, the sound of Pugal's defiance abruptly ended and the brothers shared a mournful glance before the *clang* of the grapnel finding its purchase had them both looking skywards.

'Hold on,' said Raus, flinging his arms around Rein, who did the same.

'Now we find out how many grox-shanks is too many,' Rein replied, patting his paunch as Raus set the grapnel recoiling. In seconds, the line went taut and they were rising, slowly at first but then picking up speed, arrowing into the vaults with las-fire cracking around them. Raus felt the breeze against his face and the gentle heat of a dawning sun as it touched his skin and then there was just light...

* * *

'Nearly there now...' hissed a voice, but not the one inside Raus' head. *That* voice had ceased to make any sense a while ago, reduced as it was to gibbering non-sequitur.

'I want to know everything...' said the shadow voice. Even in his half-dream state, Raus recognised it.

The ice waters returned, though not as deep as before, presaging a final plunge...

In the time it took for Raus and Rein to get back, the camp was in bedlam. Whatever had happened below in the tunnel had happened above too, only magnified tenfold. Skirmishes had broken out everywhere and order was collapsing at an alarming rate.

Mechanicus ships were soaring skywards, small cohorts of skitarii and other defenders attacking anyone who came close. Whatever they had come here for, their tech-priests either had it or knew they could not obtain it. They were leaving, their pact with the Militarum violated and none could have convinced them otherwise.

Cadians and Vorpese fought openly, the latter having declared their allegiance to the enemy. It was as if some signal had been triggered and all coats turned in that single, bloody moment. Cultists and other ragged chaff were storming from the ruins too, the Militarum armoured brigades unable to keep them stymied as they had to look to defend themselves against their own ranks.

Hit square in the left flank by a missile, a Griffon tank exploded, the heavy chassis flipping over completely as Raus and Rein hoofed past the burning wreck. Several of the ferrocrete structures comprising the camp burned too, the flames spreading eagerly and filling the air with thick black smoke. The ratlings used it to conceal their desperate flight through the madness, choking and running. Trying to stay alive.

'What the fragg do we do, Raus?' Rein huffed as he ran, his heavy rifle held tight across his chest and his legs pumping. 'Everyone's killing everyone!'

Raus could barely see a thing, relying on his brother to navigate. He was vaguely aware of the blood on his hands, his uniform, from the wound to his eye. It had stopped bleeding at least, but the sight in that eye had gone. He gestured to a Mechanicus ship, a cargo lander by the look of it, battered around the edges and held together more by prayer than actual rivets or welding.

'That piece of shit?'

'It's tough and no one is trying to shoot at it currently, Rein.'

'Fair enough.'

They hurried towards the lander, nimbly avoiding the servitor guards that emerged from its hold. The pallid-fleshed cyborgs had been fitted with heavy cannons, and the shuddering report of their guns spooling up thudded like an angry drumbeat as high-calibre shells began chewing up the camp and everyone in it.

Raus went to ground just before the shooting started, dragging his brother with him into a latrine ditch.

'Oh, Throne...' said Rein mournfully when he realised where they were, 'I do hope we don't meet one of Fud's turds in here, Raus. Because that would cap off a very stressful day.'

Holding his nose against the stink, Raus saw the blurred shape of the servitors move away from their post to engage some distant force with their guns. Raus patted his brother on the back.

'Rein!'

Scurrying from the ditch, heads down, the ratlings barrelled across the lander's ramp and into the cold, anonymous dark of the hold. They were barely ten feet inside when a thunderous explosion rocked the side of the lander and they saw flame spill across the open ramp. A few seconds later, one of the servitors staggered into their eyeline. Burning from head to foot, it was an effigy of a man turned into an inhuman candle. A loud *whoosh* indicated that whatever was fuelling the creature other than blood had been ignited.

Raus shouted, 'Down!' a moment before its ammunition case cooked off and the servitor was blown apart by a series of rampant detonations. The ramp began to rise and the hull shook as the lander's engines fired. Evidently, whoever was in charge of the vessel had decided it was time to leave and abandon the rest of its servitors for dead. A rattling cacophony struck up, small-arms fire battering at the side of the ship, as the ratlings hung on to whatever they could to avoid being dashed against the walls of the hold.

As the daylight faded, shut off by the closing ramp, the ship attained some small measure of equilibrium and the rattling eased. Raus sagged against a munitions crate and let out a long, shuddering breath.

'Are we dead yet, Rein?'

'Not yet, Raus,' his brother replied, pressing his nose up to the hermetically sealed armourglass of a view slit as the cargo lander breached the atmosphere and engaged forward propulsion.

'See anything, Rein?'

'At least twice as much as you, Raus.'

Raus scowled. 'Piss off.'

'We're headed towards another ship... A big one.'

'What?' Raus hurried to his feet, elbowing his brother aside so he could stare, one-eyed, through the frost-rimed view slit.

A large junk freighter loomed in the void ahead, the cargo lander burning fuel to reach it. A docking bay opened up in the freighter's flank, the massive doors parting slowly like cog-teeth as it made ready to accept the lander. It put Raus in mind of a minnow being consumed by a leviathan.

Rein had turned away to inspect the rest of the cramped and cluttered hold, when Raus heard him remark, 'Raus... I'm not sure we're alone in here.'

Raus turned sharply just as the lander entered the junker's docking bay and the internal lights of the cargo hold went out. Then he felt heat, the fiery heat of pain...

It took Raus a few seconds to return to cognisance, but as he did he saw his interrogator now lay jackknifed on the floor, shuddering with psychic discharge. Worms of corposant rippled across the psyker's withered frame as the creature gibbered and foamed. Clenched teeth broke, spewing outwards in pink, blood-soaked chips. It screamed as its eyes turned black and then dissolved in their sockets, until only slits remained and these lengthened into crimson slashes of cracked bone and torn meat.

The Traitor Guardsmen recoiled, fumbling for lasguns and bayonets before the figure stepped out of the shadows and put a bolt in the psyker's distending skull.

A ragged, dark uniform clung to his body, which had been muscular once but now carried the atrophying effects of exposure to the fortress. A breastplate layered his otherwise naked torso, and it was replete with knife-carved images of Ruin. An eight-pointed star stood prominently, declaring his allegiance to the Dark Gods. The same mark had been cut into his face, a red-raw wheel of pain, but it could not quite obscure the existing scar. A claw, like a raptor's.

'There was no such place as Raptora Station in Heldum,' he said. 'Clever, though, trying to mask your memories like that to mislead us. I often thought your kind had a low sort of cunning, but this is almost impressive. Not that it really matters now.' The commissar raised the bolt pistol he had just used to execute the psyker and put it in Raus' face. The crimson leather had cracked a little and patches of rust and other, less savoury materials had colonised its artificered frame and barrel.

'You should take better care of your weapons,' rasped Raus. He felt Rein clench his hand, and Raus clenched his back to let him know he was all right.

The commissar chuckled, turning the bolt pistol in the light as if examining it properly for the first time in a long time. 'You're probably right. Not many artificers here in the stygian dark, though.'

'Did you all turn?' asked Raus. 'All the Vorpese?'

The commissar nodded solemnly. 'We did. It doesn't matter why...' he said, his eyes seeming to glaze over for a few seconds. 'I can barely remember the reason. I serve the gods of Ruin now. That is all that really matters.'

'Throne preserve us, Rein,' Raus hissed, as if speaking conspiratorially, 'I didn't ask for his entire military history.'

'Some people are just "me, me, me", Raus.'

'No more games,' said the commissar, calmly returning his pistol to its holster. He turned to his lackeys, who had yet to recover from their brief encounter with the warp-possessed psyker. 'Get them up. We're moving out.'

'To where, lord commissar?' asked the sergeant, as he warily eyed the slowly dissolving body of the psyker.

'The Raptora,' he uttered simply.

* * *

A map of sorts had been produced by the commissar's henchman and on it was scrawled a crudely rendered schematic that represented a section of the fortress. Several chambers had been listed, as well as a series of runic calculations pertaining to their approximate positions at any given time. The fortress was as unknowable as the depths of the void itself, and some believed it had an *anima*, a will of its own. Foolish superstition, isolation madness or perhaps some sentient remnant of an era long lost to the benighted veil of history – whatever was the cause, the fortress *moved*, and its transience was the root of not insignificant consternation to those who dwelled within its myriad halls.

'Nothing ever stays the same in here…' murmured the commissar, as he pored over the map. He paused to look up at the corridor section they had ventured into before laying a gloved finger against his desired destination.

'Is that why you need to get to the vault?' asked Raus. He had to push his weary body through the tight confines of the fortress, his haggard face reflected back at him in the black obsidian every time he sagged on his feet. Rein trailed behind him, a Traitor Guardsman placed between them in the order of march. Anyone would think the ratlings could not be trusted if they were together…

'It's what's *inside* the vault that interests me,' the commissar replied, sending two of his thugs to scout ahead. Despite the fall from grace and the abandonment of the Throne and everything he once must have stood for, the military instincts remained, and Raus saw them echoed in the commissar's every order and stratagem.

'Same here,' Rein piped up from somewhere in the back.

The commissar's mirthless laugh sent a chill through Raus.

'Oh, you'll never see it. Once I have the other half of the talisman...'

'I assume that ominous pause means you'll let us go,' said Raus.

The commissar didn't answer, which in itself was an answer.

Raus suppressed a small gulp.

'A geomantic sceptre.' The commissar turned, his cold gaze falling on Raus. 'I assume you know what that is.'

'You want to fix it in place, the fortress. Or at least, part of it.'

'Yes. A foothold would be beyond price. I am tired of being a nomad. I want it to end.'

'I can end it for you easy enough,' Rein muttered from the back.

His words elicited a smile from the commissar. 'Oh, I bet you could.' He turned away, gesturing to his men. 'It's close.'

And so it proved.

An open path led the expeditionaries to the Raptora, a chamber mercifully empty of any of the more bestial and less discerning denizens of the fortress.

'Almost as if it wants us to breach the vault...' murmured the commissar as they stood at the threshold. It was a graveyard, a vast chamber festooned with technological detritus like some junker dragon's hoard. Old heat coils wound like ivy around machine parts, bionics and spent fuel canisters. Wheels, engines and pieces of fuselage agglomerated into a mass of metal that undulated like hills. It stank of petrochem and fyceline, a machine-shop aroma with a scrapyard aesthetic.

'Needle...' said Raus, beaming, 'meet haystack.'

The commissar did his best to hide his annoyance, silently ordering three of his men to begin searching.

'You expected a locker or something, didn't you,' said Raus. 'Far safer to hide it here in plain sight, eh, Rein.'

'Up top for thinking, down below for scarpering, Raus.'

'Gag them both.'

Raus felt the rough hands of one of his captors as a dirty piece of rag was yanked across his mouth.

The Traitor Guardsmen took to the junk pile like flies to dung, but achieved little more than buzzing around with nothing to show for it.

Losing patience, the commissar sent in the rest, but the junk pile was immense.

Raus mumbled against his gag, trying to be heard. The commissar glared but relented, slashing the rag with a serrated knife that nicked the ratling's cheek.

'Do you ever wonder how we came to cross paths again?' asked Raus, stretching his mouth to massage out the stiffness of wearing the gag. He expected a backlash from the commissar but the man paused instead, as if he also wanted to know the answer to that question. 'I mean, after all this time, across the gulf of the void, all the way to Precipice and beyond… The chances are pretty slim, I'd say.'

'There had better be a point to all of this,' the commissar warned.

'You went your way, spikes and ritual sacrifice, and we went ours, surviving, thieving, doing what we do. That we came back together, in this time, in this place… makes you wonder, doesn't it? If there is a purpose or if perhaps we're fated in some way.'

'Mine is the Eightfold path, a servant of the Dark Gods. I deny the Corpse-Emperor, as should you.'

'Recruitment, is that it? Is that why you did it? Turned coat and all that,' Raus pondered. 'Tempting… but I don't really like tattoos or whatever *that* is.' He pointed to the eight-pointed star cut into the commissar's face. 'Don't want to spoil my handsome disposition now, do I.'

'Enough.' The commissar pulled his sidearm and the dull metal barrel shone in the light, almost eager to be discharged. 'I am no longer amused, *verm*,' he snarled. 'Where did you hide it?'

'Thing is...' said Raus, 'it's *in* here but it's not where we hid it, not really.'

The ratlings were knelt either side of the commissar, on their knees, as if waiting for summary execution. Raus supposed that was probably true. He felt the cold press of the bolt pistol's muzzle against his right temple.

'Start talking.'

'I promise to tell you where it is if you'll answer me one question,' Raus replied brightly.

The commissar scowled like he wanted to pummel Raus' skull. 'Ask it, but this is the last time. No more stalling.'

Raus hoped he had stalled just enough. His expression darkened. 'Why did you have to kill Strigg? Locke, Happig, Fud... killed in battle. I get that. I can understand that. Even Munk and Pugal. Casualties of war. They'd have killed you too, given the chance. Seem to recall that they did. Quite a few of you.'

The commissar was scratching at his shoulder, where Rein's bullet had struck but not killed him, Raus now realised.

'But not Strigg,' said Raus. 'He wasn't a threat. You murdered him in his bed. I reckon we could've let it go if not for Strigg. So here we are.'

The commissar had stopped listening. He was focused on what was happening in front of him instead. 'What the hell is that–'

'That's where our piece of the talisman is...'

A red glow lit up one part of the chamber. It looked innocuous enough, just a lumen slit half buried amidst a heap of old servitor parts... until it rose to its feet, a metal-plated battle-automaton with a crackling power claw and a long-barrelled assault cannon.

'How can I be of assistance?' it asked, the traitors dumbfounded as its weapon arm spooled up.

Raus flung himself to the floor, trusting his brother to do the same, as a hail of high-powered munitions tore through the chamber and the Traitor Guardsmen who occupied it. A tongue of muzzle flare lapped the air as the cannon panned left to right, leaving nothing but dismembered body parts in its wake.

To his credit, the commissar managed to get off a shot, screaming, 'You little bast–' before being obliterated. Raus was still picking pieces of him out of his hair and clothes, having already slipped his bonds a while back, when Rein crawled over to him.

'Don't even think about it,' Raus snapped as Rein was poised mid-filch, his larcenous fingers inches from the commissar's fallen pistol.

'What?' he protested. 'He's not in a fit state to use it again, is he, Raus?'

'You really want that corrupt thing in your possession, Rein?'

The robot settled it, crushing the fallen bolt pistol under its heavy tread as it lumbered up to the ratlings.

'Bugger...' sighed Rein.

Raus, meanwhile, looked up at their saviour, tossing his sovereign ring, which had just abruptly stopped flashing, into the air. 'Handy little homing beacon.'

Rein patted his brother on his back, a broad grin on his scruffy face. 'UR-025... I could kiss you.'

The glow behind the vision slit in the robot's dome-like head flashed gently as if it were trying to process the request, but then gave up. Instead, it held out its claw, and within was a sickle-shaped object.

'Have you retrieved the other half?' it said.

Raus was already rifling through the commissar's pockets and emerged with the talisman he had taunted them with earlier. 'Present and correct,' he announced.

The battle-automaton designated UR-025 handed Raus the other half of the talisman for the ratling to fit together. As the two pieces snapped into place, a dull light lit a small gemstone in the middle. Raus pressed it with his dirty thumb and a great rumbling shook the chamber. Islands of scrap tottered and collapsed, or else rippled aside as a pair of blast doors opened outwards in the chamber floor. Pale, shimmering light flooded from this revealed alcove like an undersea cavern. All parties moved to the edge so they could peer inside, the two diminutive ratlings and a hulking but dutiful robot. Raus reflected that the image they presented might appear faintly ridiculous to the casual observer, but his attention quickly turned to the mirrored vault and the artefact within.

'Doesn't look like much,' said Rein, turning the sceptre over in his hands. 'Shiny, though.'

The gems encrusting the slender wand of gilded metal glinted in the light of the scrap chamber as he handed it to Raus, who in turn gave it to UR-025.

The robot made no comment, except to issue a short blurt of lingua-technis as he alerted his Mechanicus overseers that he had acquired the object of his mission. Raus had never seen these supposed *masters*; all of his dealings, including this one, had always been conducted by UR-025 in person, but as the automaton deftly unscrewed the base of the sceptre, in which was secreted a unique data-coin, he reflected that he had never been given cause to distrust it.

'Nice doing business with you,' declared Rein, and sketched a little bow as UR-025 returned the rest of the sceptre to him.

'You are welcome,' it replied in a clipped, mechanical monotone. After a moment's pause, it added, 'Interrogative...'

Rein recoiled sharply. 'You want to *inter* what? Nope, no probing for me!'

Raus sighed. 'That's not what that means, Rein. It wants to ask us a question.'

'Oh...'

UR-025 took this as its cue. 'Why risk your continued biological function and endure physical harm for what is, in fact, an item with little commercial or scientific value?'

Rein shrugged, and tossed the sceptre over his shoulder. It *plinked* as it struck a jutting obsidian bulkhead before slipping through a crack in the floor and falling into whatever stygian darkness lay below their feet. 'Sometimes, it's not about treasure.'

They parted ways after that, UR-025 delving deeper into the fortress as Raus and Rein headed for the Stygian Aperture and a return to Precipice.

About halfway back, Raus fished inside his pocket and pulled out a crumpled pict. It had faded with age and was foxed around the edges but the memory was as fresh as yesterday. He wiped away a fresh tear for his fallen comrades, the first he'd shed in a while.

'Sometimes, it's about vengeance, Rein.'

Rein put his arm around Raus' shoulder. 'Long live the Longhorns, Raus...'

'Long live the Longhorns, Rein.'

'Right,' said Rein, hiking up his belt and tightening the rifle strap around his chest, 'let's go and find where I chucked that sceptre, shall we.' He had turned on his heel and was already marching back the way they had come. 'I reckon I can still find it, Raus. Should be worth a pretty penny, all those jewels. Quite a bit, I'd say.'

'Quite a bit, Rein,' said Raus as he gave chase and smiled, stuffing the pict back into his pocket. 'Quite a bit.'

ABOUT THE AUTHORS

Darius Hinks is the author of the Warhammer 40,000 novels *Blackstone Fortress, Blackstone Fortress: Ascension* and three novels in the Mephiston series, *Mephiston: Blood of Sanguinius, Mephiston: Revenant Crusade* and *Mephiston: City of Light*. He also wrote the audio drama *The Beast Inside* and the novella *Sanctus*. For Warhammer, he wrote *Warrior Priest*, which won the David Gemmell Morningstar Award for best newcomer, as well as the Orion trilogy, Sigvald and several novellas. His work for Age of Sigmar includes *Hammers of Sigmar, Warqueen* and the Gotrek Gurnisson novel *Ghoulslayer*.

Josh Reynolds' extensive Black Library back catalogue includes the Horus Heresy Primarchs novel *Fulgrim: The Palatine Phoenix,* and three Horus Heresy audio dramas featuring the Blackshields. His Warhammer 40,000 work includes the Space Marine Conquests novel *Apocalypse, Lukas the Trickster* and the Fabius Bile novels. He has written many stories set in the Age of Sigmar, including the novels *Shadespire: The Mirrored City, Soul Wars, Eight Lamentations: Spear of Shadows,* the Hallowed Knights novels *Plague Garden* and *Black Pyramid,* and *Nagash: The Undying King*. His Warhammer Horror story, *The Beast in the Trenches,* is featured in the portmanteau novel *The Wicked and the Damned,* and he has recently penned the Necromunda novel *Kal Jerico: Sinner's Bounty*. He lives and works in Sheffield.

Thomas Parrott is the kind of person who reads RPG rule books for fun. He fell in love with Warhammer 40,000 when he was fifteen and read the short story 'Apothecary's Honour' in the *Dark Imperium* anthology, and has never looked back. 'Spiritus In Machina' was his first story for Black Library, and he has since written 'Salvage Rites', 'Fates and Fortunes' and the novella *Isha's Lament*.

J C Stearns is a writer who lives in a swamp in Illinois with his wife and son, as well as more animals than is reasonable. He started writing for Black Library in 2016 and is the author of the short stories 'Turn of the Adder' and 'Blackout' which have featured in various volumes of the anthology *Inferno!*, 'Wraithbound', and 'The Marauder Lives' in the Horror anthology *Maledictions*. He plays Salamanders, Dark Eldar, Sylvaneth, and as soon as he figures out how to paint lightning bolts, Night Lords.

Denny Flowers is the author of the Necromunda short story 'The Hand of Harrow' and novella *Low Lives,* featuring the characters of Caleb and Iktomi. He lives in Kent with his wife and son.

Nick Kyme is the author of the Horus Heresy novels *Old Earth, Deathfire, Vulkan Lives* and *Sons of the Forge*, the novellas *Promethean Sun* and *Scorched Earth*, and the audio dramas *Red-Marked, Censure* and *Nightfane*. His novella *Feat of Iron* was a *New York Times* bestseller in the Horus Heresy collection *The Primarchs*. Nick is well known for his popular Salamanders novels, including *Rebirth*, the Sicarius novels *Damnos* and *Knights of Macragge*, and numerous short stories. He has also written fiction set in the world of Warhammer, most notably the Warhammer Chronicles novel *The Great Betrayal* and the Age of Sigmar story 'Borne by the Storm', included in the novel *War Storm*. More recently he has scripted the Age of Sigmar audio drama *The Imprecations of Daemons*. He lives and works in Nottingham.

Gav Thorpe is the author of the Horus Heresy novels *The First Wall*, *Deliverance Lost*, *Angels of Caliban* and *Corax*, as well as the novella *The Lion*, which formed part of the *New York Times* bestselling collection *The Primarchs*, and several audio dramas. He has written many novels for Warhammer 40,000, including *Ashes of Prospero*, *Imperator: Wrath of the Omnissiah* and the Rise of the Ynnari novels *Ghost Warrior* and *Wild Rider*. He also wrote the Path of the Eldar and Legacy of Caliban trilogies, and two volumes in The Beast Arises series. For Warhammer, Gav has penned the End Times novel *The Curse of Khaine*, the Warhammer Chronicles omnibus *The Sundering*, and recently penned the Age of Sigmar novel *The Red Feast*. In 2017, Gav won the David Gemmell Legend Award for his Age of Sigmar novel *Warbeast*. He lives and works in Nottingham.

David Annandale is the author of the Warhammer Horror novel *The House of Night and Chain* and the novella *The Faith and the Flesh,* which features in the portmanteau *The Wicked and the Damned.* His work for the Horus Heresy series includes the novels *Ruinstorm* and *The Damnation of Pythos,* and the Primarchs novels *Roboute Guilliman: Lord of Ultramar* and *Vulkan: Lord of Drakes.* For Warhammer 40,000 he has written *Warlord: Fury of the God-Machine,* the Yarrick series, and several stories involving the Grey Knights, as well as titles for The Beast Arises and the Space Marine Battles series. For Warhammer Age of Sigmar he has written *Neferata: Mortarch of Blood* and *Neferata: The Dominion of Bones.* David lectures at a Canadian university, on subjects ranging from English literature to horror films and video games.

Guy Haley is the author of the Siege of Terra novel *The Lost and the Damned,* as well as the Horus Heresy novels *Titandeath, Wolfsbane* and *Pharos,* and the Primarchs novels *Konrad Curze: The Night Haunter, Corax: Lord of Shadows* and *Perturabo: The Hammer of Olympia*. He has also written many Warhammer 40,000 novels, including *Belisarius Cawl: The Great Work, Dark Imperium, Dark Imperium: Plague War, The Devastation of Baal, Dante, Darkness in the Blood, Astorath: Angel of Mercy, Baneblade* and *Shadowsword*. His enthusiasm for all things greenskin has also led him to pen the eponymous Warhammer novel *Skarsnik,* as well as the End Times novel *The Rise of the Horned Rat*. He has also written stories set in the Age of Sigmar, included in *War Storm, Ghal Maraz* and *Call of Archaon*. He lives in Yorkshire with his wife and son.

Nicholas Wolf is an author, artist and occasional musician. He's written science fiction for several publications, and his work includes the Warhammer 40,000 short stories 'Reborn' and 'Negavolt' for Black Library. He lives and works in Arizona, with his family.

YOUR NEXT READ

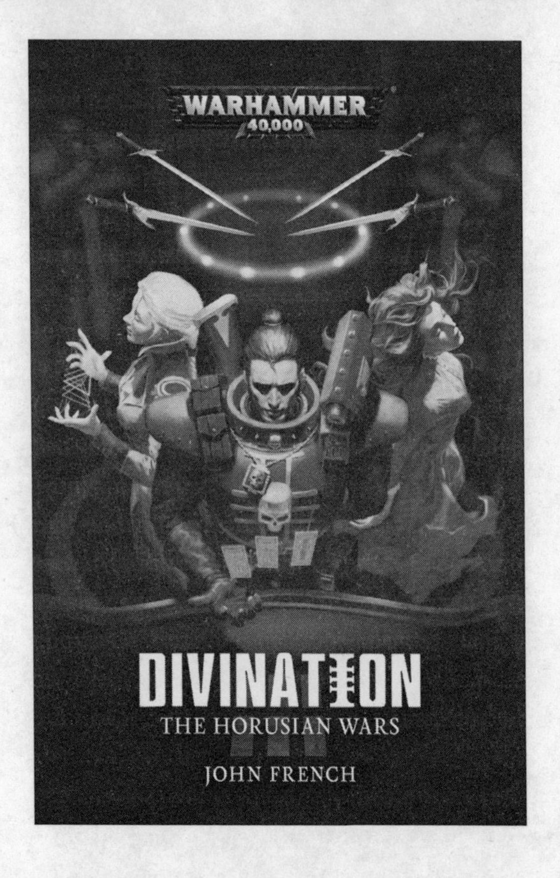

THE HORUSIAN WARS: DIVINATION
by John French

Inquisitor Covenant stands against the plans of the sinister 'Triumvirate'… but he does not stand alone. In this anthology are tales of the allies – rogues, agents, psykers and killers – who aid him in his battle against the darkness.

For these stories and more, go to blacklibrary.com, games-workshop.com, Games Workshop and Warhammer stores, all good book stores or visit one of the thousands of independent retailers worldwide, which can be found at games-workshop.com/storefinder

An extract from
'The Purity of Ignorance'
taken from *The Horusian Wars: Divination*
by John French

'Do you know why we do what we do?'

'No, sir. That is not my... I do not need to know.'

'We do it for the survival of humanity.'

'Yes, sir.'

Lieutenant Ianthe, Second Squadron, Agathian Sky Sharks, sat at attention, hands on her knees, eyes straight ahead. The man sitting across from her was a priest, his bulk covered by an off-white robe. Crude tattoos spidered the knuckles of his hands, and hard, knowing eyes glittered in the wrinkled lump of his face. He was called Josef, or that was the name he had introduced himself with. Now after half an hour talking with him, Ianthe thought he seemed more senior sergeant-at-arms than a priest in the service of an inquisitor. But what did she know of the Inquisition?

'Do you understand what that means?' said Josef, as though hearing her thoughts in her silence.

'If we fail, so does the Imperium,' she said.

'True, but not the whole truth. We fail and there will be

no humanity to be called an Imperium. Not here, not on distant Terra, nowhere. There will just be a thing that was once call mankind, weeping as it eats itself and the darkness laughs. You understand me, Ianthe?'

'Sir,' she said.

He cocked his head, and scratched his stubble-covered jaw. She did not move her own gaze but she could feel his eyes moving across her face, searching for something, watching for something.

'Tell me about your service before this,' he said at last.

'Sir?' she began, and fought to keep the frown from her face. 'My apologies, sir, but I thought we had covered that.'

He shrugged, muscle and fat rippling under the folds of his robe.

'Humour me,' he said.

She listed her record, passing through the last twelve years of her life in clipped bites of information: Karadieve, command of platoon in the assault on the pirate holds; Anac, command forward reconnaissance units, wounded; Grey Klave, command primary assault squadron; and on until her record ran out, and the silence formed again between them.

'And now you are here, with us,' he said.

'Yes, sir,' she nodded, and then felt her expression twitch before she could stop it.

'You have something to say – say it, lieutenant,' said Josef.

Ianthe nodded, licked her lips and then spoke. 'Is this interview related to the mission, sir? I have been over my record several times, and my appraisal of the soldiers under my command.'

'It is related to the mission in every way, lieutenant. In every way.' He paused, watching her. 'Is there something else you wish to say?'

'No,' she said. 'It's just that I have never had the honour of serving the Inquisition, sir. It is...'

'Irregular?' he finished for her, and nodded. For a second she thought she saw a glimmer of something like sorrow in his eyes. 'That it is,' he said, and there was an edge of weariness in his voice. Then he stood, shaking out his creased robe, and rolling his shoulders like a pugilist before turning and moving towards the door. 'Ready your squad. It is time.'

Spire Mistress Sul Nereid woke with a scream between her teeth. For an instant the nightmare smudged her sight with bloated flesh and blood-covered chrome, and she felt the acid kiss of vomit rise to her mouth. Then it was gone, draining away with her panic as the dawn light filled her eyes. She shifted, feeling the silk padding of the throne at her back, and the smooth silver of its arms beneath her hands. She stretched, smiling. She had fallen asleep in her chair, just as she had when she was a child and used to sneak into the throne room at night. She laughed, and the sound slid out to meet the sun rising behind the crystal walls of her room.

The throne room sat at the tip of the hive spire. Crystal walls set in frames of polished adamantine encircled a single open space within. A flight of shallow steps led from the foot of the throne, each one carved from a single piece of dark wood. The pelts of a thousand white felids had been seamlessly stitched to create a rug that flowed down from her throne to spill onto the open space beneath. Slender columns of ivory rose from the black glass floor, each holding a frozen explosion of gemstones and light, which glittered in rainbow hues as they spun in suspensor fields. Beyond the clear walls the cloud layer ran to the arc of the sun slipping above the horizon; the crowns of cumuli rose above a soft sea of white and folded purple and orange. At the apex of the sky's dome stars winked against the last darkness of the night. In the far distance the pinnacles of Tularlen's other hive spires rose from the plateau of clouds like shards of diamond set on cushions of spun sugar. Nereid sighed at the sight.

This moment, this perfect moment, had been hers ever since she had inherited the spire throne from her father. He had treasured both the view and the position it represented, clutching both close to him even as he had fought the doom that claimed him at last. It had been a sad end, but it did mean that the pleasure of waking to this world was Nereid's now.

'Are you hungry, mistress?'

Saliktris' voice came from just behind and beside her throne. She half turned her head, enough to catch the impression of the major-domo standing just on the edge of sight, clad in plum and crimson velvet, his smile an echo of her own. He was always there, just where he needed to be.

'I am...' she replied, and shifted on her seat, tilting her head to one side as she thought. 'But...'

'Some music...' said Saliktris, smoothly.

Nereid's smile widened.

'Yes,' she said. 'That is it. The arrangement from last night would be...'

'Perfection,' he said, and her smile widened. Others might object to a servant talking so freely with their betters, but Saliktris always knew what to say, and what she wanted. She did not know what she would do without him.

The spire throne was no doubt something that many coveted. The House of Tears, the Extrabati and their Mechanicus backers, the Sons of Lupolis, and all the other lesser power blocs regarded this seat, and the power it represented, with a hungry eye. That jealousy had been one of the poisons that had marred her ascension, that and the riots burning in the factory core of the hive, and the Administratum's suddenly inflated tithes of manpower and materiel. Apparently there was a war, and Tularlen had to feed every scrap of flesh and wealth into its gullet.

No matter that it was draining the wealth of the hive houses, no matter that discontent was curdling to violence in the drone masses, no matter that it could not be done, the Imperium demanded and would not be denied. Nereid shuddered as the memory rose in her mind, and her mouth twisted as though she had just bitten into a rotten fruit.

The expression and memories faded, and she smiled again.

'Mistress...' whispered Saliktris, and she looked up.

The ensemble players appeared as her smile bloomed. They filed out into the space beneath the throne, thirty-six men and women robed in white, their instruments gleaming in the brightening day.

'Do you wish for dancing?' asked Saliktris, and all she had to do was nod.

Two of the thirty-six players stepped forwards, their limbs trailing tapers of silk that shimmered like the inside of a seashell. They halted, and stretched their limbs, becoming statues poised on the edge of movement. The first notes rose from the instruments, blending as layers of melody harmonised from tuned strings, silver flutes and taut drumheads. They began to sing, voices rising to meet the swelling chords of the instruments.

Nereid closed her eyes and tilted her face back as the sound pulled her senses up through the greyness and into a world of unfolding glory. This was what the dull words of preachers never could convey; this was what it was to touch the divine.

She opened her eyes just as the dancers started to move.

'Wait,' she said. The dancers froze, bodies suspended in mid-movement as though they hung on strings in defiance of gravity. The music from the ensemble did not cease, but circled through harmonies, holding just beneath the peak of its ascent.

Nereid turned her head slightly to the right, and a mirrored platter appeared, heaped with glistening fruit, each one a jewel taken fresh from its tree. A chalice sat beside it, the wine within almost black in the daylight brilliance. She reached out, took the chalice and raised it to her lips. Warm liquid kissed her mouth, filling her nose with sweet scents and the promise of endless days of laughter. She plucked a fruit from the platter and popped it into her mouth. It burst, and the flavours of the wine and the juice briefly warred before fusing into a taste that slid through a thousand shades of sweetness.

Nereid swallowed, and breathed out.

'Now,' she said, and raised the chalice to her lips again, 'dance.'